Our Seas of Fear and Love

by

Richard Shain Cohen

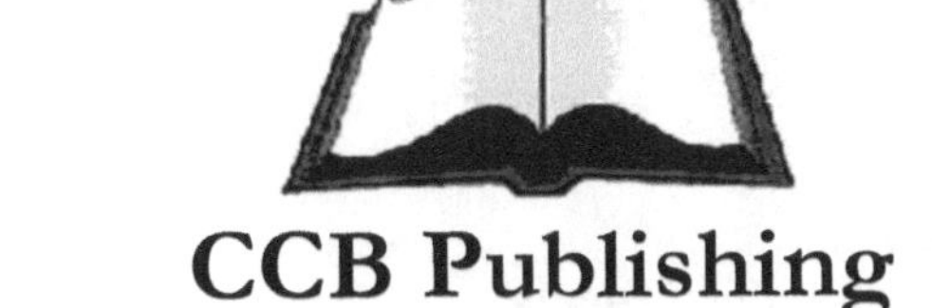

CCB Publishing
British Columbia, Canada

Our Seas of Fear and Love

ISBN-13 978-1-77143-079-1
First Edition

Library and Archives Canada Cataloguing in Publication
Cohen, Richard Shain, 1928-, author
Our seas of fear and love / by Richard Shain Cohen – First edition.
Issued in print and electronic formats.
ISBN 978-1-77143-078-4 (hbk.).--ISBN 978-1-77143-079-1 (pbk.).--
ISBN 978-1-77143-080-7 (pdf)
Additional cataloguing data available from Library and Archives Canada

United States Copyright Office Registration # TXu 1-846-843

Richard Shain Cohen may be contacted through: **www.richardshaincohen.com**

Cover artwork by Rose Kennealy.

Publisher: CCB Publishing
British Columbia, Canada
www.ccbpublishing.com

DEDICATION

I dedicate this book to my World War II brothers with my love and very fond remembrances of their continuous support through my growing up trials and adult life:

Manley Benjamin Cohen, M.D., thoracic surgeon (U.S. Army Medical Corps - Bronze Star, two Purple Hearts);

Alfred - Bob-Robert Cohen (U.S. Army Air Corps, England), poet, artist, advertising director and designer of movie advertisements such as "Space Odyssey: 2001";

George Matthew Cohen, O.D., (U.S. Navy, North Africa, Sicily, Italy, achieved rank of Commander)

They not only served their country in war but also in their given professions in which they excelled during peace time.

Books by Richard Shain Cohen

Be Still, My Soul

Monday: End of the Week

Petal on a Black Bough

Only God Can Make a Tree
(Poetry co-authored with Alfred R. Cohen)

The Forgotten Longfellow: Man in the Shadows

Healing After Dark:
Pioneering Compassionate Medicine
at the Boston Evening Clinic
(Co-authored with Morris A. Cohen, M.D.)

Our Seas of Fear and Love

CONTENTS

ACKNOWLEDGMENTS

I wish to thank for reading this book when in manuscript form:

Rosemary Coleman, artist and Professor Emerita of Literature, Illinois Benedictine University who has always been supportive of my work and whose criticisms and proof reading have been so helpful.

J. Arthur Faber, writer and Professor Emeritus of Literature, Wittenburg University, who also supported my work and whose reading of and comments regarding the manuscript was also so helpful.

Carol Felberbaum, an avid supporter who has continuously and willingly given her time for my writing and commentary.

I thank Bonnie Kaye for her utmost interest in this novel and her important suggestions.

The following two nurses gave me information regarding the RN when this story takes place. I thank them for their unhesitant help and guidance:

Janet Geanoulis, R.N., Lowell (Mass.) General Hospital and her sister Karen Martell, R.N., M.S.N., University of Southern Maine School of Nursing who referred me to her sister Janet.

The following are source materials or places that I consulted:

Digital Journal with special thanks to David Silverberg

Dixon-Kennedy, Mike, *Celtic Myth & Legend: An A-Z of People and Places*

Green, Miranda, *Celtic Godesses: Warriors, Virgins and Mothers*

Lawrence, Frieda and Kiowa Ranch: This imagined

conversation of a female character is only in part an actual one I had in a lengthy meeting with Frieda Lawrence in Taos, New Mexico. I also did meet Ravalgi, and also had a long talk with Lady Brett who drew a map for me to Kiowa Ranch that now hangs in my office. She met me with a large ancient phonograph sounder held to her ear for hearing better. The talk at the ranch and visit are actual, These meetings were the result of research for my Master's thesis: *The Rananim of D.H. Lawrence: His Pursuit of Utopia in the New World.*

Life Magazine from 1950s - use of fashion ads and some information considering the McCarthy Hearings and the Korean and Viet Nam Wars.

McIntosh, Elizabeth P., *Women of the OSS: Sisterhood of Spies*

Mayo (The) Clinic gave me permission to use from their website the article by Mayo staff on the Placenta previa birth problem. I sincerely thank them for granting use for the idea in a scene in this book.

Portland (The) Press Herald, Portland, Maine for information from the 1950s and 1960s.

Portland (Maine) Public Library where I had help from very cooperative librarians when it came to newspaper readings.

I would be remiss if I did not thank my wife, Arla who has constantly supported and encouraged me and who also read, commented upon, and recommended changes.

Chapter I

Italy, Chelsea Naval Hospital
Gregory and Brigit

I used to be somewhat adventurous. When you live in Maine and along the coast, the ocean does that to you. You walk the beach or sit on the rocks or ledges and watch the ocean in its varying moods, its magnificent but dangerous anger when the waves roll in white caps and crash against the rocks, or in its days of peace when in a tide pool you may see sea gulls floating or gliding above you and the calm blue sea. There are times when you want to see the anger, for it is beauty that hides the dangers, something like in my life when I grew older. There had been a wreck of a schooner that beached in the frosty wind of a winter storm. It enchanted me.

This day I remember was sunny. The wreck of the *Nancy* - I called her the *Yancy* - perhaps too young to pronounce it correctly no matter how many times my mother or aunt or a brother told me N - *Nancy* - not Y - *Yancy*. Well, still not old enough to be left alone, I managed to wander away from my mother, Jocelyn, and an aunt. I was determined I was going to see that hulk I'd seen before and that bewitched me. What did I think it would tell me? I left them sitting on their blanket and finally came to her. The wood was gray and rough and splintery. At first, I looked back and couldn't see my mother. That scared me, but the magnetism of the *Nancy* swept fright away. Waves wound about the listing hulk. I touched the side, the rough wood, looked up, somewhat apprehensively, then smiled, because she was there for me. But what was she telling me? There were secrets to uncover. That's why I had to see her, talk to her.

I looked back. I didn't see the family. I was scared and ran along the shore, yelling for my mother. I had lost my direction. I cried, walked, called. The *Nancy* was no longer there. I yelled at her, blamed her. "I'll never come see you again." Because of the secrets, though, I knew I was lying. Then a Park Ranger found me, then my mother. But I was still afraid and crying. You see, the *Nancy* did that to me. She churned my life. Looming, invulnerable, she withheld the secrets - the future to come - the ships - the women.

She kept them until I found the answers, or thought I did. For some years later it was another ship. Why is it that ships and women are thought to be in communion? Because they are both female, according to Roman prayers to a sea goddess?

But I have never told you about my town. My mind wanders. You see, you do not know the state of my mind or of my body. It's a lovely town, three traffic lights that you can never pass through without a stop. There's no such thing as synchronization. Perhaps it's because Main Street is somewhat long with its grocery, jewelry, clothing stores, and a bank. Oh, and there's an Indian shop that sells woven baskets and blankets. We call them American Indians; perhaps we don't want to confuse them with India Indians. They like to be called Indians, so they told me. Well, this is the town of Cape Astraea, Maine. Mostly everyone knows one another or about them, at least so people think. We lived in a Victorian house, two blocks off of the main street. A stream flows between the main part of town and where we, my family and I, lived. Later I inherited the house. For a few years it was vacant, oh, occasionally rented with trepidation. Here's why the worry. There is a portico in front held by two Doric columns. The front doors have the original engraved glass. The entrance hall separates the dining room and the living room, and beyond that is a pantry through which you cross to the large kitchen. A curving banister rises along the rather high stairway, and there along the upper hall are the bedrooms, and beyond these is a sitting room that looks out on the street. Well, at least you may get the idea. We loved that house, my family and I. My mother, the singer, my father, Aaron, a doctor, my brothers and sister, Mary, who would go to medical school. She's a lesbian. Yes. We've come to accept it. Intelligent people must. That's what we call ourselves. But, you see, they knew nothing about my secret with ships and the sea and wouldn't for years.

~

Oh, the other ships. That was supposed to be a holiday. My mother took Mary and me, thinking it would be fine for us to see other places. We were just out to sea. Our Captain did not see in the fog the large freighter headed toward us. There was a sudden shudder. The lights went out, the door fell; I could hear water loudly flowing in not far from us. I heard screaming. It was so fearful. My mother had fallen to the deck but pushed herself up quickly, grabbed my arm, pulling Mary and me along the passageway. I heard the music but was too scared to look. People rushed along, pushing one another. My mother stopped for a moment, seeing a closet with life jackets, grabbed two to put on us. I protested. "You don't have one." She just pulled us along. Suddenly a ship's officer was there directing people to a long gangplank down along the ship's side. As we went down, I looked up. The hull of the huge freighter seemed as though it would fall and bury us. It was gigantic, fearsome. We stepped in water while I kept looking at the looming hull of that freighter that made me shake. I felt my mother pulling at me as she gripped Mary. She swam, pulling us somehow toward a tug boat that had turned back when the crew heard the cries and perhaps the crash. A crewman dragged us aboard and took us to a cabin. We lay on a bare mattress with one bare pillow. I listened to my mother breathing so hard trying to catch her breath while sobbing, "Why no life boat, why no life boat?" as I listened to my heart pounding against my chest. I don't even remember how they got us to the hospital.

When we returned home, I was the hero to my schoolmates. And I bragged, hiding from everyone the fear that would embed itself, only I didn't know it then. And my mother. There was this large photo of her on the front page of the paper. The phone kept ringing at home until finally my mother wished she could tear the phone lines out of the house. There being more than one, I would imagine her going from one room to room, ripping out phone cords. "But, mama, we're heroes." "Gregory. We aren't heroes. We're three fortunate people who lived to come home. You remember that. Sometimes everything works out well and other times not so well." That was one of the rare instances I remember my mother going to church, taking me with her. I still see her lighting a candle, kneeling, crossing herself. She was brought up Catholic, but my father was Jewish. Religion in our house was barely ever mentioned. But when I think back, I see how brave my mother was. She was a woman who often kept things to herself, unless my father and she argued or tried to talk alone without one of the children hearing. Sometimes she would go to her room and ask not to be bothered, that she needed time to think. She was beautiful, such an ordinary word. But she was. Her hair was light brown and her eyes blue, her nose small and straight, her small lips, full and red, though I liked her without her lipstick. The redness faded but only to a degree. She was tall and later I realized how sexually appealing she was with her shapely legs and a fairly thin waist broadening to her hips, her breasts that seemed so slightly low but straight out. I admit there were times I wondered what she looked like naked. But what went on in her mind? Did she think about love, my father, of other men? When she put on her cosmetics, was she thinking of a seductive look, of her lithe body's appearance, of the men and women who fawned about her after a performance? Well, she could be seductive with her smile, her soft voice, and soothing hands. I used to think that probably most of the time she was concentrating on her music. But growing up, what I do know is that she spent as much time as she could with her children, kissing us, smiling, and she could make us laugh. Other times she would sing to us, a lone personal performance. Sometimes when she sang to us like that, so intimately, I thought that the shipwreck bound her to Mary and me more than to my brothers. The mind of a young boy - he dreams of glory on a battlefield or as fast-draw sheriff in the Old West. But how that fancy changes when the sea is cold and about to drag you down into its unknown world.

Years later, 1942, there was another ship, a frightening sight taking me back to the *Nancy*. It was the burned hulk of the *Normandie* lying on her side, some frantically, incorrectly, crying it was sabotage, the former majestic liner that fled the German invasion, a symbol of fallen France. "Why," I asked myself, "always wrecks?" How ironic. It was just before I entered, of all the services, the Navy.

~

Now I lie here. The doctors allowed me to come home,

because the town is near a large hospital. And I can always get to Portland, perhaps Boston, rather fast. Sometimes I walk around town with Pamela, one of my daughters. My wife wanted her to leave Wellesley in her last year and attend a college near us, then wait for graduate school so she could look after me when my wife was away on one of her mysterious trips to look with some older guy - what the hell is his name - oh, Étienne, a very important guy she always reminded me, she just has to work with - searching for art or archeological items for that antiquities museum. Sometimes I wonder. But there's still Melinda, my oldest daughter, a M.D., not so far away. So it's obvious the war and the oceans I sailed couldn't kill me. But . . .

We had swept the minefields at Anzio, and now our wooden YMS - yard minesweeper - lay at anchor. On board, we could hear the shellfire and small arms weapons. Part of the horror was watching as men fell near the shore. Soon German bombers were coming over every hour on the hour while German Messerschmitts flew low across the water machine-gunning ships and men.

A lieutenant junior grade, I was standing on the bridge. Suddenly another German fighter came at us and at a destroyer anchored nearby. I dived for cover, listening to bullets strike the boat. As I dived I felt a sharp pain. A bullet had grazed my arm that I had raised in an effort to protect my head. I grabbed the arm, yelled at the plane, "You fucking son of a bitch." Grimacing, I called a corpsman who gave me a shot of morphine. I began to relax, even smiled despite the havoc around us. "Now the bombers," I thought. "Typical German bastards, everything by the clock." I looked at my watch.

Soon I heard the engines. My heart pounded. My head felt

warm. The bombs always fell too close. So far we had been lucky. One hit on us and there would just be splinters. Others in my squadron just disappeared, had been sunk either by mines or blown apart, shredded, by the bombs. Our sweeper was one of the last of the squadron left, eventually the only one. How kind the waters that protected us. Perhaps Neptune was weary of the shattered hulks cluttering his sea bottom.

Six bombers. There were vapor trails and a swirling of fighter planes. Anti-aircraft fire threw up shrapnel. One bomber, hit by an American fighter, exploded. I watched the pieces and flames falling, cheered, shaking my fists in temporary glory at the planes, as did others on deck.

Another bomber flew below its fighter cover and the American planes sweeping toward the anchored ships. Bombs fell, one between the destroyer and our minesweeper, grazing the destroyer, exploding, throwing shrapnel in so many directions. Men ducked. Then I felt the shock. Something hit my leg. I screamed, grabbed, looked down, watching the blood flow. I tried to stand, fell to the deck. "Christ. Fuck."

I pulled off my belt with my uninjured hand and arm, but could not use it, finally realizing the wound was at or above my thigh, not at my lower leg. I couldn't move. Finally, the corpsman crawled to me, looked at the wound, shaking his head, grabbing a gauze pad, holding it tightly where the blood flowed. He administered another shot. I tried to move. "Relax, Lieutenant."

The bombing continued. I could barely hear the corpsman. "Jesus. Why don't those fuckers stop," I kept yelling. "STOP." I tried to raise my head but fell back wearily.

Not too long after, I was transferred to a Hospital ship. A doctor came to me. "Does it hurt?" The first thing I thought was, "You stupid bastard, of course it does." Instead, I answered softly, "Yes, Sir." "Don't worry." It was obvious my hip was damaged. And probably I may have seen the last of action. At that I smiled despite worrying about my body, how I would be affected, what would happen in the future.

In the operating room, they pinned my hip, arthroscoped my knee, played around with the nerve, I found out later.

The hospital plane left Italy, landing in Boston. From there, we were transferred to the Chelsea Naval Hospital. The navy tried to place us as close to home as possible.

Once settled, however, near other officers, nurses took me to the OR where doctors unpinned my hip, did several more arthroscopies. The entire time I lay in bed, either talking on the phone to family or friends or to nurses and doctors. One medical officer finally told me my leg was permanently damaged because of nerve destruction, that my navy days were over. On that day, depression hit me, thinking of future plans, how family and those I had known would see me. I would not be able to keep up with my friends who made it home after the war. For the rest of my life I saw myself walking with a limp, supported by a cane - a cripple. In fact, when I got back to Maine walking with crutches, a neighbor who saw me asked my mother what happened, exclaiming how sad the wound but how *marvelous* I survived.

Later, I pushed myself from the bed and managed to shove a chair by a window. The Boston skyline, that always brightened my thoughts, seemed dull in sunlight. It made little difference to me now, almost disappearing from view as I imagined a crippled future. My leg hurt, kept reminding me of a dim future, no matter how much I tried to ignore it. I don't know how long I sat by the window. The voices of the other officers disappeared as I sank more deeply into self-pity.

Four of us were in a room, the door open so we could see into the hall to the nurses' station. Usually officers get privacy or perhaps a roommate. I was partly asleep when one of the guys raised his voice. "Hey, Greg," one of the men called. "Look what's comin' in this time. We got it made. Christ, the nurses, all this female stuff around us. We can make out. Look at that one over there standing by the desk. What a beautiful ass. What's wrong with you? Wake up." I finally heard. "Shut up, Frank. You're goddamn lucky we have them to take care of us and in the States too. Just shut up." I turned toward the window. Perhaps I was something of a rarity. I could not stand hearing lewd remarks about the nurses or just generally about women. I loved them as much as any of the other men, would gladly have one to lay. It had been a long time since Sicily where a woman seemed so easy to get. Yet, I looked at them as human beings who wanted attention as much as did the men, who had sexual or any needs like men.

A while later I listened to one of the other officers talking to a nurse, asking for a date when he got discharged, one telling at another time how beautiful she was, my roommates at one time or another making lewd remarks. One day a nurse they had never seen before entered the three-bed room. The man nearest the door whistled softly when she entered. Some one near the door said, "Hi, Lieutenant." She glanced at me. "Hello," she spoke softly, kindly. I took her smile as an invitation or hoped it was. "How about a date, Lieutenant, when I get out of here?" Ignoring me, she walked further along. Another man, watching her, spoke loudly to another patient as she passed, "What a piece of ass she would make." I lay there upset by his remark while watching her.

The nurse grimaced, commanded the wounded officer to hold his mouth. Obviously, if she could, she would never take care of him. I wanted to say something and turned my head toward the voice. I have a habit of looking at a woman's face, her eyes, and then at her breasts. But it was her hair, her face and eyes that struck me. I watched her walking toward me. She was fairly tall, perhaps five foot seven, her hair light reddish brown, her eyes green. About her small, straight nose there was a hint of freckles. "Irish," I told myself.

"How are you, Lieutenant?" as she leaned slightly toward me. Her voice was soft, with almost a musical lilt. She had a slight southern accent that she seemed to be losing, perhaps from having been in Boston for so long. I don't know. I don't know where she came from, how long she had been here. I just liked hearing her voice and the way she pronounced her words.

"I'm O.K." I tried not to stare, but our eyes met just momentarily in the attraction and instant recognition that occurs occasionally between people. In following days, she came by aware of my depression and lingering pain. Eventually, I asked her name.

"Brigit."

I smiled.

"Do you know who I am?"

"What? No. I don't. We just really met," like I was crazy.

"I mean my name. Brigit was a Celtic goddess of doctors, for one thing and could foresee events. I even worry about impending births to look over and protect." She laughed. "Oh, I'm all that."

I knew she was kidding, or I thought she was.

She interrupted. "But don't try to hit on me, Lieutenant. You'd disappoint me," she continued softly as she began to raise my blanket to look at the wounded area.

There was a kindness and gentleness that enlivened her, so it seemed, each time she came to my bed. One time she came in and said, "Hello, you," took my hand and just held it, comforting me. Every day, I watched for her, and began forgetting myself as I anticipated her shift, talking to her, feeling her hand on my shoulder. Then, during one of her shifts, I rang for her. I couldn't urinate and I hurt.

"What's wrong, Gregory?" She had never used my first name before. I felt a chill in my spine, gazed at her, as she put out her hand toward my shoulder. "What's wrong?"

"My bladder, Brigit. I haven't been able to go."

She threw back the white blanket and sheet, raised my Johnny. I watched as her hand moved toward me, fascinated by her fingers yet afraid but wanting to feel her touch. She opened the string of my bottoms, pushed them down slightly. I felt her fingers against me gently moving about my lower abdomen.

"It's distended. You need to get an x-ray, fast." She hurried from the room, returned, and without waiting, wheeled me herself. A wet plate indicated my bladder was filled with urine. Brigit took me back.

She left, returned with a catheter and other materials she needed. "I'm going to put this in. It will relieve you. She gently pulled down my pajama pants. I watched, felt, as she placed her gloved hand about my penis. How long had it been since a woman had her hand on my cock? She smiled, as she pushed, withdrew the catheter some, then pushed again. "You know, it's easier with a woman. It just goes directly in." She said it with a slight smile. I laughed quietly. How I liked the way she held me there despite the momentary discomfort. It felt so warm, despite her glove. I wished she'd leave her hand wrapped about it. I imagined her playing with it.

"There." She made certain the catheter was working well. "You'll feel better now. Remember. Don't let anyone give you morphine." I don't think she could help herself as she pulled off her glove and put out her hand and lightly touched my face.

~

When they transferred me to a private room, I was aware I'd be in the hospital for a long time. It depressed me more, thinking of home and how distant it seemed, yet by train one could travel there in short hours. There were visitors. My mother came, my father when he could, and also my sister, often accompanying my mother. Then there was that one time my sister came by herself, peeking in the door to see if I was awake. I heard about most of that visit later from Brigit, because my sister barely mentioned what happened.

I was in pain and had been for some time but didn't want any more medication. Looking up as the door opened, "I don't want any visitors. Get out!" I didn't even know who it was, whether a nurse or another visitor. A nurse would have been upon me with one of those commanding looks.

My sister came to the foot of the bed, smiling. "Get the hell out of here." Her face flushed, she started to speak. "What's . . ." "Get OUT." Hurt, shaking, she quickly turned and left, waiting hesitantly in the hall. I know she was crying and I didn't care. When she looked up, she saw Brigit at the station, unknown to her, just a nurse lieutenant jg.

"Please," Mary interrupted her.

Brigit answered, "Yes." Instantly, she saw the redness, the distress on Mary's face. "What is it?"

"He's never like that - my brother."

"Who?"

"Lieutenant Hurwitz. He's my brother. He was just terrible, shouted at me to get out of the room." Her eyes teared. "There's something wrong."

Brigit left her chair, went to Mary, placed an arm about her. "Don't worry. I'll go see what's wrong. You wait. Sit here. She gently touched my sister's hand. Brigit left her, hearing her softly crying, perhaps both for herself and for me.

Opening the door, not knowing who it was, I shouted again. "GET THE HELL OUT OF HERE." The pain was almost unbearable. It had never been this bad. When I saw Brigit, I began to apologize.

"What's going on?" Her voice was cold, acerbic. "What's the reason for that disgusting display, especially for nothing, Lieutenant?" It annoyed me that she didn't use my first name. "I'm in pain, goddamn it. It's terrible."

"Don't you swear at me." I started to interrupt, to tell her I wasn't swearing at her, but she didn't give me a chance. "Then why didn't you call? What's that button by your bedside? How many times have you been told to use it? You also left your sister in tears." She started to walk away, glanced back at me, "I'll be right back." She returned with a pill. "Take this," she commanded, her cheeks flushed with anger.

Her attitude both annoyed and hurt me.

"You ought to feel better soon," Brigit icily told me. "You also ought to see your sister and apologize. She drove from Maine by herself on those narrow roads and down that horrible Newburyport Turnpike." Brigit started to say, "And she's so . . . ." "Young," I finished. "She knows how to take care of herself."

Now Brigit was really angry. "Yes. She's young. She loves you. And that young woman driving by herself to see YOU. Anything could have happened to her. And to be thrown out of your room, because of your vile temper." Brigit turned away but not until she said, "I never thought of you with such a temper."

"I just didn't WANT to see anyone. I just want this pain to stop. I want to get out of here," my voice softened. "Please, Brigit."

She stared at me. The stare faded though as she continued looking at me. What was she thinking? What did she see?

~

His black hair and hazel eyes, the semi-round face, yes, I like those.

But his chin. I love it, fairly sharpened with the cleft. Below the sheet and white navy blanket – I'd like to raise them and look at that trim, tall body, 5 foot 11. His thing, oh, I can feel my face getting warm. I wondered what it would look like when I put in that catheter. He is handsome. And his face is always smooth shaven. His nose? Well, it's a bit large but straight. Admit it, Brigit, you like everything about him and enjoy looking at his body when the blanket is thrown back. Good heavens. That was an unguarded moment when I told Kaye when we were on duty that night I liked that he was not one of those muscle bound officers like some of the others, and their dirty remarks. I hate it. I could slam them; I also told her how I liked his voice. That knowing smile on her face. But I couldn't help myself and went on and on about his usually kind, often soft but strong voice. I love art and music and imagined he could sing beautifully in a tenor voice. Funny, his sister told me he had done so professionally on the radio before he went to war. He'll wonder why I'm silent. Stop dreaming. I'd enjoy his arms around me, feeling his fingers wandering up my arms and about me. Stop it. My face is really hot. He sees me blushing. Before he says anything . . .

~

"Let me tell your sister to come back. And you apologize." She smiled. Each time I saw her, there was that tremor I felt, the gladness throughout my body. Only right now, I wondered how much of it was the medication she had given me.

"O.K. Lieutenant. You win." I felt a sting in my leg, forced a smile beyond the grimace that she noticed. "Brigit." She stopped. "Are you mad at me?"

"Yes. I think your treatment of your sister was abominable. Do you know how fortunate you are to be near enough for your family to visit as often as they do? And your sister is lovely, a lady."

"You're right." I answered contritely. I did not like my

temper either, disliked treating people poorly, and got angry when I thought of others being maligned improperly or being needlessly hurt. "You see that sea gull on the sill," I tried to joke. "It was pecking at my leg, thinking it had found a new fish flesh."

"See your sister, Gregory."

The medication made me somewhat sleepy. There was a silly smile on my face. "I like you, Brigit."

She ignored me, opened the door, but I know there was a smile on her face that she tried to hide from me, as she went for my sister.

~

I turned my head toward the window, opening my eyes, rousing myself from the drowsiness and the crappy thoughts that had been bothering me. "Fish, flesh," I whispered. My pillow was a little damp. I rubbed my neck, then ruffled my hair, grimaced, smiled as I thought of my sister and Brigit. Long ago, I kept telling myself, the naval hospital. Now it was almost no different. I felt as though I were still a cripple, that I had never recovered. In effect, perhaps I never had. I've been ill for so long, taken care of by my daughter, occasionally by my wife, Deirdre, also a nurse she hired. Brigit, too, the healer. I let her go. Wonderful daughters. Perhaps they have some of Brigit in them, because we were so close. I want to believe it, Brigit. The goddess in you gave them some of your healing and protective force. And you'll watch over them when they give birth - if I live to see that. They've always been loyal, the way they always seem to be standing between my wife and me. I can feel their admiration and love. They know I feel the same way about them. My wife, always busy, selling her archeological artifacts or always off at some socially important function that will help her business or give her notice. The girls, Melinda and Pamela and then Kaitlin - now gone. They were no longer girls but young women. My God, Kaitlin - dead. Why?

Kaitlin. My God. She wandered away like I used to do. When I heard, I sat there, my heart pounding. The whole family sat, no one saying anything. Suddenly, everyone was crying. Either Pamela or Melinda screamed. My wife had her hand over her mouth, mumbling, weeping, "Why did we do it? Why did we let her go?" And I sat there repeating, "My Kaitlin - five years old."

I never recovered from the emptiness left by her death. I often thought of her, expected to see her in some part of the house, even thought of talking to her about her music. Occasionally Melinda and Pamela with tears talked about her, once in awhile my wife. I could not forget. How could any of us?

I've got to stop thinking about her. I forced myself to think of other things. Then I smiled. I'm a doctor, and I can't even take care of myself.

When I was in high school, somebody asked me what I wanted to do when I went to college. "College? That's not the end for me. I'm going to medical school." The guy smiled. "How do you know that?" "I just know." "Nuts. You're just doing it or saying it because of your father." "I am not." I stopped. "Well, I guess he does influence me, my oldest brother too."

Then there was the girl who has a summer place by the water in our town. We liked each other, became good friends, dated. As we went along in school, I talked more of what I wanted to become. Then, one night, when we were in our senior year, when I dared to kiss and fondle her, when she seemed glad, she pushed me away, but as I moved toward her again, she relented when I felt her breasts. We kissed, I lay on top of her and rubbed against her – we were on the beach – but then she said, "That's enough. I mean it." She suddenly said, "You'll get married and be a rich doctor."

"I don't care whether I'm rich. But I do want a good wife. Don't you want a good husband?"

"Silly, you know I do."

"Would you ever think of marrying me?"

She did not answer.

"O.K.," I continued. "Suppose I told you I love you." I hesitated. She had always left me with an ache "I do, you know." I hurried on, unaware of the surprise on her face and the smile. "Would you wait for me until I finish med school?"

"Greg. We may be carrying this too far, don't you think?" This time she hesitated. "Greg. I would wait." She moved closer to me. Pressed her breast against my arm. I put my arms about her, drew her nearer, ran my fingers through her hair, along her neck and went to her breasts again. She was so relaxed, more than she had ever been before with me. When I went lower on her body, she grabbed my hand. "Cut it out." She sounded angry, and I said "I do love you. I wish . . . ." "No. I know what you're going to say or ask. I won't do it, Greg."

I was perspiring again. I thought of changing my pajamas. How I wished I could get back to the laboratory, to the work that had given me my standing, my place.

And then Pamela came in. "Dad, are you all right?" She could see the perspiration on my forehead, looked at my pillow. "Do you want a clean pillow case?" She didn't wait for an answer but left for the bathroom and returned with a wet face cloth, put it to my head and held it there. "Oh. You hold it. I have to get the pillow case." She ran from the room, as though she were about to cry and wanted to hide her face from me.

~

Deirdre was lying in the bed, holding Pamela who had been born a short time before. The baby was an accident, just a night of sex, we thought. When Deirdre knew she was pregnant, she asked me if there was someone who could give her an abortion.

"What the hell are you asking me? Are you nuts? So you're having another baby. I want it. And if you ever ask me something like that again, so help me God, I'll throw you out."

Abortions were forbidden then. I believed in them, thought of the women who died because they couldn't have them or who went to the back alleys. But I would never have given up everything for that, illegal, disgraced and banned from the profession. Deirdre scoffed. "You brave man, war hero. You'd throw me out. Bull shit you will. You have more prestige in this community because of me. I made you what you are. Bull shit, Gregory. Piss off."

I watched her in the bed, thinking perhaps now she would love the child, would be happy she had it. I sat there watching her.

She grimaced. She hurt and still bled. Another pad was becoming wet. She wanted to scream at the indignity she had to suffer for this. She seemed to force her fingers back from squeezing the baby's tiny arm.

When I entered, I knew she forced that smile when she lied, "Look at her. Isn't she adorable? Another girl. You don't stand a chance, Gregory."

I smiled. "I don't care." She wrinkled her nose. "Look at her. What have you got there?"

"You're terrible. She's beautiful," as she wrapped two fingers about Pamela's tiny hand. I believe she may have meant it. But then she immediately said, "Gregory" - she never called me Greg - "I'm bleeding some. Get the nurse. I need more pads," and grimaced.

~

I wasn't listening any longer or looking at her face that once mesmerized me so. Rather, lying against the clean pillowcase, I saw Kaitlin standing near me, "Daddy, I love you," as she put her arms around my neck.

"Dad, you're smiling. Do you feel better? Is there something funny?" Pamela interrupted.

"I was thinking of something."

"What?"

"Your sister, Kaitlin."

"What was so funny?"

"It wasn't funny, just a thought." I looked at Pamela and the quizzical expression. "Oh, Pamela, maybe when you're a mother. . . . No. I was thinking of one time when she . . . ." I tried to hide my tears.

I thought of Pamela delaying grad school to be with me, and the sadness hit me. How I still missed Kaitlin as I did Melinda, Melinda the doctor, alive. The rent within my heart overwhelmed me as I thought of my beautiful, young daughter forever the same as on that day but lost, yet still there for the remainder of my life.

I had gained so much, lost so much, so much of love.

~

Brigit. Whatever possessed me?

I see her clearly now, that first time she stood before me -

after the hospital - when our arms were about each other, kissing, tongues heatedly seeking one another. She drew back then, gently moving away from me, standing, reaching for her blouse, slowly, ever so slowly, it seemed, her straight slender fingers moving to the buttons, loosening each, the blouse flaring open. I reached for her. "No." She smiled. "Wait," her voice so soft. In a swift movement she unclasped her bra.

Chapter II

Brigit

Brigit Donavan, born in the Southwest, raised, like Gregory's mother in the Catholic Church, took her religion very seriously from the time she went to parochial school where nuns taught her the meaning of life, what it was to be a woman in the eyes of God. She was a reflective student - that may have caused her problems. Though she took her studies seriously, she wasn't so sure she was just meant to grow up and be a wife and have lots of children for God and the Church. The older she became, the more she thought of what was beyond her teachings. She would joke, play tricks, in fact, and occasionally, she would get into fights with other girls. Those fights could be nasty, pulling one another's hair, even scratching or punching. Well, one time she pulled a schoolmate's hair, then scratched her arm. Horrified, not only by the nuns who came running to them but by the blood leaking at the wound, Brigit pulled away from one of the nuns. "Leave me alone, Sister. I have to fix her," as Brigit wrenched away. Through her tears, Brigit, horrified and frightened by her nastiness toward the nun, begged the nun to let her fix the girl's arm. "I can do it; I know how," she told herself. She may not have known it then, but it was the beginning of what she had been destined to do – to heal.

The nun, Sister Antonia, pulled Brigit away and sternly told her to apologize to the girl while forcing Brigit toward the schoolhouse. "You're a disgrace, Brigit." "I didn't mean it, Sister, not the blood," but she laughed at me when I said I could cure people and would some day.

Sister Antonia took Brigit to her office, "You were wrong, Brigit. We don't teach you to fight. You're here to learn and to help. You must learn also to take the teachings of the Lord seriously."

"All I wanted to do was to stop her bleeding, to fix her, even if she is always a pain in the neck and trying to get me into trouble."

"You think you know about those things? You're too young. That's God's work. That's what good women do. I always thought you would be a good nun because you're intelligent and gentle. But where is that gentleness? You have fooled me. And, you remember," she emphasized, "this is the Lord's school and His words and work you're learning besides your other studies."

The Lord. Who was the Lord that Brigit admired and was told she must love so? But there was an emptiness in her when she thought about the Lord. It was more than that, if only she could fill that void. *There's something telling me who I am and what to do, and it isn't the Church. It's strange. I think it has something to do with being Irish. Oh well, I'll find out someday.* She barely heard Sister Antonia and the stern admonition as these thoughts troubled her.

Then when she was older, she tried to find out more of who she was, what she wanted. She found a medical book with some of the other girls. A man lies on top of a woman. How can a woman allow that? It must crush her to death. And he does something to you to have a baby. "I don't like that." The girls looked at her. "Well, some of them may be so good looking, you may want to kiss him." "Well, maybe" "Maybe that's when he lies on top of you."

Brigit suddenly blurted, "The nuns told us we weren't to let boys do things to us."

Brigit discovered one time what the nuns meant. She was by herself and felt strange below. She was thinking of a boy kissing her. She felt like jelly in her stomach, as she described it to a friend much later. She put her hand to her pubic area. It felt good when she rubbed it. She rubbed more, feeling wetness in the opening between her legs. Soon she couldn't stop. The more she rubbed, the better it felt. Suddenly she felt a shock, a wave of heat rushing through her body and to her head, her back arching, her thighs pressing against her finger, and she cried out as she let her fingers slide between the wet and widened opening between her legs. The nuns had told them it was a sin to do this, but how could such a feeling be a sin? Sin would exasperate her when she was older, but she loved and admired her growing female body and the changes occurring.

With time, and as she continued her studies, she found herself more interested in helping with cures. When her friends hurt themselves, she would hurry to help them and try to heal what wounds they suffered. One time in a particularly bad sand storm, one of the girls went outside the building. The wind was so strong, it wrapped her in the dust of the playground and the desert surrounding them. Sand clung to the girl's hair and got in her eyes. She hurried back to the building, crying. Brigit heard and was there before the nuns and the other girls. She placed her arms around the crying girl. "The sand. It's in my eyes." "Keep crying," Brigit told her. "It will wash out the sand." "But it's still there." Brigit hurried to her bed and ran back with a cotton swab. "Here, Alicia, let me see." Brigit gently raised Alicia's head. By then the nuns were there. One started to move Brigit away. "Leave her alone," Sister Antonia told her, watching in fascination Brigit's gentleness and her knowledge of what to do. The girl quieted. She gratefully placed her head against Brigit's arm.

Soon everyone was calling her Doctor or Nurse Brigit. She

was already reading stories about scientific discoveries, about Florence Nightingale, or Dr. Elizabeth Blackwell, the first female physician in the United States. Her past nemesis, Sister Antonia, encouraged her to become a nurse. A friendship had developed between the two as Sister Antonia helped Brigit find more reading and began to look up information to give Brigit about schools. It was then in 1940, a senior in high school, that Brigit decided to travel to the northeast to study. She not only wanted to travel, but she wanted especially a hospital in the northeast, because she believed they were the best.

When she finished high school, the family was happy expecting her to come home to the cotton and alfalfa farm, a huge tract of land. Her parents never thought of college for their second daughter. Her mother took care of the house with her daughters, if they weren't at school. One had already decided she was going to be a nun. That thrilled the parents. She had already been accepted at the convent from which Brigit had just graduated.

Brigit was sitting on her bed looking at school catalogues she had hidden from her parents. The thought of being deceptive annoyed her. Yet, the more she thought about nursing, that defiant and independent part of her personality almost yearned, despite some fear, for the coming confrontation. She moved about her bed nervously. The catalogues lay spread across her bedspread. Aggravated, she shoved them aside so she could lie down. She clenched her fists. *I'm going to do it, and no one's going to stop me.* She knew her father would be angry. *That's his problem.* She felt the skin on her face tighten. *You can't be afraid to confront him. Remember how it was when you were at school and even Sister Antonia finally gave into you.*

Undoubtedly, some thought of her as spoiled, always seeming to want her way. What any number of people or acquaintances didn't recognize was that she had a given insight for knowing what was right.

She rose from the bed and went to the kitchen, found her mother scrubbing at some pots, mumbling to herself. Her mother heard Brigit. "This is wonderful woman's work, dear. I guess your time may not ever come if you are going to be a nurse."

"That's what I want to talk to you about. I'm going to apply in the northeast."

"Northeast? You mean up in New York or something?" Her mother had turned then, surprised. "There are plenty of good hospitals here. Are you out of your mind?"

"The big and the best hospitals are there. I want to go to Boston." Brigit blushed, "I already applied. I know I didn't ask, but I've been in my room looking at all those catalogues. I know I'm right. That's what was meant for me, not only to be a nurse but also to be where I'm needed. I just feel that."

"You feel it? Or is this just another one of your, 'I've made up my mind?' Who do you think is paying? You talk to your father. Well, you have to anyhow. He makes the money decisions." In fact, Brigit's mother had more influence about money and other things than she wanted to admit right now. A woman just knows those things, the men being so damned stubbornly sure of themselves. For a moment there was a slight smile on her face. Brigit and she looked so much alike. Brigit saw the change on her face. "You're smiling." "Not because of you right now." "What?" "Your father - men. And by the way, if you do get your way, and I'm not saying I'm going to help, you stay away from those fast easterner men. I mean it. You're old enough. In fact, that's one of the reasons I don't want you to go there." "Oh you sound like a nun. I never told you, mom, one of the girls got pregnant. How she ever sneaked out of the convent and made such a shame of herself. Anyhow, you're way off." "Am I? Have you looked at yourself in the mirror lately, that face, your hair and eyes, and that chest." "Motherrrrr. I know what I've got." Her mother laughed. "I should say you do. The men around this ranch and the way they look at you. I know what they're thinking. They look at your other three sisters almost the same way. But at least one of you will be a nun. Imagine, Brigit, four daughters, one to be a nun and one a nurse. But, I DON'T like you thinking of the east. And don't think you're just going to get your way."

"Mother, I was meant to be a nurse. I know that, have known it for years, just something in my heart and mind. It's so strange."

Again her mother smiled. "We'll discuss it tonight. But you wait 'til after supper." Her mother looked at her. "I know. You were always trying to cure or fix something on the animals before the vet got here. Once, when you were little, you even tried to fix a cotton ball that you said was sick looking. As I recall, it was drooping - something like you right now, because you're waiting for me to side with your father. Hmmm. For all I know, he may agree with you. Uh,uh. Not him. It's one of the things I love about him. He's got a mind that works fast and firm."

During supper, no one said much except that her father talked about what happened around the ranch, farm, whatever they decided to call it at any particular time. But living in the Southwest, it was a ranch. Brigit, who usually had a good appetite, picked at her food, ate slowly.

"Why are you so quiet tonight, Brigit? All of you? What's going on? I never saw such a bunch of females keeping so quiet. Usually I can't even get in a word," a lie on his part. All he had to do was raise his voice. He was a tall man, husky, handsome, with blue eyes, a face always shaven to please his wife, even the girls, who would sometimes rub their hands against his face to feel his morning beard. There was much love in the Donovan family. But when he was angry, the girls would get out of the way and leave it to their mother to calm him down. Sometimes they would hear her yelling back at him, "You stop hollerin' at me. I won't stand for it. Keep it up and I'll just leave the house. I mean it. I'll take the girls and you can get your own damn meals." Suddenly there would be quiet while they were both apologizing to one another. It made Mrs. Donovan nervous when he lost his temper but not enough to cow her. She had a temper of her own, rarely shown.

"O.K." Luke Donovan began, as he put down his fork, not even waiting for coffee or desert. "What's goin' on around here. Like I said before. It's just too quiet."

The girls appeared scared. Maureen Donovan looked at Brigit.

"It's me, dad," she spoke up, her voice slightly trembling. She was never afraid of her father, always stood up to him, something he admired about her.

"Well . . . ."

"I've made up my mind where I want to study nursing."

"El Paso? I hear they've got a couple of good programs there, especially the Catholic hospital, Hotel Santé."

"No, dad."

"Where then? What could be better than a good Catholic hospital? I'm payin' the bills don't forget."

She was reticent, something that surprised him.

"What's better? You'd be close to home and . . . ."

"No, dad," she interrupted, regaining her natural firmness, yet still hiding her apprehension of his reaction. "I've applied to school at three of the hospitals in Boston. I hope I get into Boston City General."

"BOSTON." Brigit's sisters cowered. "What in the good Lord's name do you think you're doing? And without asking. I'm payin' the bills around here, Brigit. I don't give a damn how smart you are."

"Before you get goin' crazy," Maureen interrupted.

"Crazy? Our family's been here for generations, and she tells me she's goin' to Boston with those," he started to swear, hesitated, "with those GD Yankees. Girl, you're goin' to school somewhere you know the area, not among all those free-thinking rats."

"I'm not, dad, even if I have to pay my own way." Brigit's voice rose with the last words. Suddenly she was no longer afraid. But before she could say more, Maureen interrupted.

"I'm not going to have my supper ruined by all this yellin'. Stop right now, both of you. Either discuss this quietly, reasonably, or . . . ."

"Or what?" Luke interrupted.

"Listen to me, Luke. You calm down. Yes. You know my usual answer. I just won't have my house in a volcano because my daughter tells you what she wants and thinks. You think she's some dummy who can't think for herself ? She's a young woman now, and don't you forget it."

Maureen hadn't intended to defend Brigit, because of her own doubts, but she was willing to listen but not with her husband shouting, scaring the other girls and trying to force himself on everyone with his temper. "Maybe we can talk about this later when everyone's calmed down."

Sometimes what the family failed to recognize was Maureen's sensitivity. There was a time she had thought of leaving Luke because of his temper, but she also knew that after he lost it, everything was forgotten and the usual calm prevailed in the house with the exception of the usual girl-fighting, screaming at one another, crying, but always the love among them.

Maureen and the girls cleared the table, while Luke sat motionless, hardly watching, calming himself. Unthinkingly, he looked at Brigit and Maureen, marveling at the resemblance of his beautiful wife and daughter. Brigit. She had both of them in her. The eldest, Anne, who was to be the nun, all of them were females to be proud of, not just because of their looks, but because of their intelligence and willingness to learn and to speak up. He started to smile. *I should know better about Brigit. She has always thought she can cure people, that she was born to that, but who in heaven's name ever thought she'd have to go east, the NORTHEAST. Ah, it's all the Irish up there. Well, if she falls in with them. It just gets me. Whoever thought a daughter of mine would want to leave and go so far. Yup, I expect them to marry, Ellen and Marie, and leave, but marry good Southwesterners. And maybe they'll be Irish. What difference does that make? Brigit, you make sure you're among the Irish. Those are your roots.* Suddenly it occurred to him. *The Irish goddess, Brigit. She was known for doctoring and especially looking after women having babies. You win, Brigit. I've helped bring into this world a goddess – or back to it. You look like one sure enough. And when you play the piano, you're so good. You'll get to those eastern concerts, probably go to poetry readings. But the men. What does she know? I don't know what she's aware of. Her mother has to have talked to her. I will. Oh hell, Let her go, Luke. Otherwise, you'll regret being mean to her and you'll avoid that sad look and a few tears, and then a hug and a loud, 'Daddy. I love you but' – All the women in my life. Maureen, couldn't you at least have had one boy?* With that thought, he whispered, 'Maureen – how lovely you are, how soft and warm to hold, so reassuring. I'm lucky.' *God, I'll miss you, Brigit.*

So, in 1940, age eighteen, they put her on the train in El Paso. She sat by a window so she could see and wave to them, hoping not to cry. But that was useless. All of them were crying. Even Luke had tears. When he admitted it, he loved her most, and if she ever married, and he knew she would, the guy better be good.

It was a long trip. She had to change in Chicago for a train to

Boston. She knew there would be more people than she had ever seen, but the confusion of the station overwhelmed her until she found a porter wheeling some luggage and had help from him, where the track was, the waiting area for her train. She read, slept restlessly when it was possible. She was nervous, missed her family, her talks with her sisters. She was alone, and this scared her some. Everywhere she looked, there was strangeness that unsettled her. Yet, being a strong person, she talked to herself, settling herself by pretending she was with her father for protection, especially when there was a man who got on with her in Chicago. She noticed he was following her after she had seen him in the waiting room gazing at her. She clenched her fist. Her father had told her how to take care of a man who became a nuisance and who tried to touch her. The man watched her walk, looking at her legs and up to the slight sway of her hips and buttocks and then to her red hair showing below her hat. When she took her seat, he sat beside her. Her discomfort grew. She tried to ignore him by looking out the window. Waiting, he finally asked where she lived. She didn't answer. "Well I live in Boston. You know Beacon Street?" She knew only what she had studied on the map of the city she had bought, where the hospital was, where she'd be living. "I don't know much about the city."

"You mean you've never been there?"

"No."

"Well, where I live is one of the best. You'll have to see some of the houses on the Hill. What's your name? We may as well get acquainted. We've got a long way to go."

She hesitated. "Is that important?" Brigit wanted to tell him to get another seat or to just leave her alone with her thoughts. She moved closer to the window and closed her eyes to keep him from bothering her. She was also concerned about being alone for the first time and being so far from everyone and everything she knew, wondering if she had made a mistake. Perhaps it would not be so bad to talk to this unknown male. She opened her eyes, looked at him, analyzing his face. It wasn't very appealing to her. He had a large nose and round face and chin, a bit of bulge to his cheeks, not fat, but a face she did not particularly like. She wanted to see his eyes. "My name's Brigit."

He looked at her and smiled. "I like that," he lied, but she had given him more of an opening.

"What are you going to do in Boston, Brigit?" She didn't answer but asked his name. "Frederick. People just call me Fred. So why are you going to Boston?"

"Curiosity about the city." She had no intention of giving away her age by telling him why she was actually going or where she'd be. She turned away again, thinking again about the large hospital by the river and the nursing quarters. Who would she meet? What would the people be like? She had always heard that people there were cold, hardly ever talked to a stranger. Yet here was this man, Fred, trying to get to know her. Perhaps it was just as well. They did have a long way to go. Why not get to know someone? Only she wished a woman had sat beside her. Then it occurred to her again how she had noticed him looking at her. Well, she was safe on the train. She was going to enjoy herself and her freedom. If she had to lead him on that she was a tourist, she would. If he became too annoying, she'd get the conductor or move her seat. Suddenly she actually was sleepy and closed her eyes again. A little while passed. She felt his hand just above her knee. Swiftly, she bent her arm and as hard as she could pushed it into his ribs. He started to say something. Instead he turned his face from her, appearing to look about the car.

"I didn't mean anything."

"I'll swan, liar. Either get out of here or I'm calling the

conductor. Beacon Street. Yeah, I heard of Beacon Street, saw it on a map, know some people who live there. They're not like you. Now get out of here," raising her voice, noticing a woman across the aisle looking.

"Is something wrong, dear?"

"I want this man to get away from me."

"I'll call the conductor."

He interrupted. "No need." There was perspiration on his forehead. He rose, grabbed for his luggage and tried disappearing in another car. The woman moved next to her. "There's always terrible men like that. What happened?"

Brigit hesitated, "He asked annoying questions." She thought for a moment, wondering if she should tell what happened. It embarrassed her. Perhaps the woman would think she encouraged him. A memory came to her of one of her dates in high school and the boy she liked. They had gone to a movie, had a soda, and then he drove out on the desert and down a short road and stopped. It was one of those magnificent desert nights, the very dark sky, stars so clear. In the distance she could see the black outline of the mountains. She sat against the door. He reached for her, placed his arm about her shoulder and pulled her toward him. She moved so easily, waiting for him to kiss her, urging him with a whisper, "What are you doing?" She could see his smile, and there they were, kissing, kissing, until he put his hand on her breast. Her first reaction was to pull back, but she let him keep it there. But that would be all, until his hand moved lower. She grabbed him, told him to stop.

"Keep your hands away. I don't even know why I let you touch me where you did."

"Oh yes you do."

"And you know I'm not one of those girls, and don't ever forget it. Let's go home."

"Not until you kiss me once more." She leaned toward him,

liking the feel of his lips and keeping to herself that she would like to do more, that she did want him to caress her breasts, but afraid of what could happen, if she allowed him to go beneath her blouse.

Thinking of that and sitting next to the woman, she knew she would say no more. They stayed together the rest of the way to Boston, the woman giving Brigit her phone number and address, if she ever needed anything.

~

The cab took her to a drive that rose to the entrance. The building seemed so huge. Her heart raced some. Behind her were three-story red brick buildings, looking like the picture she received in the mail, and the letter telling her she would be assigned living quarters in one of those. She went in. People passed on their way in and out, some appearing quite sad, others laughing, pleased a patient was doing well or recovering. At the reception desk, she asked for the nursing school where she would have her first meeting with the head. In the office, she looked at a woman behind a desk. She wore glasses, was a stout woman who even behind her desk appeared a bit fat and round. Her eyes were kind, her voice soft, hiding the sternness necessary for her work. Brigit felt comfortable, perhaps for the first time since she left home.

"Brigit Donovan. I'm Nurse Andrews," as she put out her hand in welcome. On her left hand, resting on the desktop was a wedding ring. "You've come a long way. We chose you because of your grades, particularly in science. We also like a mixed class, girls from various parts of the country. But most are from Massachusetts. You'll be one of the few foreigners. Does that bother you? I know you've never been away from home."

Brigit felt she liked the woman but was somewhat

apprehensive, unaware of what emotions the head of the nursing school could display, what she might expect from Mrs. Andrews and the other teaching nurses and doctors. "Here is the information you need to get your books, uniforms, where you'll live, etc. If you need anything, you let me know. And trust the nurse instructors. You can talk to them We've all been through what you're about to experience."

Brigit relaxed. Andrews watched her and smiled, "You'll want to settle in your quarters. I'll get one of the women to show you the way and where you'll be staying." And so was the introduction of Brigit Donovan into the profession she chose.

What she didn't learn from her classes and books was about nurses and doctors, orderlies, technicians, the many people who worked in the hospital that she would sometimes never know but to whom she was always kind, like the cleaning staff. Some of the orderlies she would come to like, others she would despise for their behavior. If she could have heard them talk in their dressing room, perhaps she would never talk to any of them. The conversations were filled with 'ass', 'good fuck' (often just the word itself), 'those knockers,' an entire dictionary of words for nurses or any other female who occasionally appeared on the floor. Or there was the time she finally got to work in the OR, aiding the scrub nurses. They were wheeling a female patient from the OR, but hadn't covered her completely. Her bare breasts lay partially full and still pointing upward. Brigit noticed an orderly standing nearby, heard a quiet whistle as she tried quickly to cover the woman. Glaring at the orderly, he merely smiled, and ran his hand across his chest. Or there was the time in the recovery room and a scrub assigned to the room taught her how to bring patients about. One day, a burly man, who had been in surgery for about two hours, started to awaken. The nurse, a short, shapely woman, leaned over him. "You fucking bitch. Get the fuck away from me."

Brigit, astounded, afraid for the small woman, placed her hand on the nurse's shoulder, trying to bring her toward herself. "No, Brigit. Get used to it. It wasn't meant for you and me."

"How do you know? He could be terribly belligerent, hurt you."

"Well it's never happened yet and won't. If we needed help, we could easily get it. Remember. These men and women are asleep, and what's coming out of them is their subconscious. The women can be just as bad, believe me. Watch their fingernails and teeth."

It was then that the past of her inheritance emerged, but it would not help her with some of the experiences she had with surgeons in the OR to whom all nurses, everyone who helped during surgery, were inferior beings to some of those outstanding men. She never saw any female surgeons.

There was the day she watched in fascination a neurosurgeon who operated equally as well with right and left hand, who was always kind to everyone who worked with him. There was one who insisted that she be with his private scrub, because he noticed something exceptional in her. One day he demanded her presence when by that time she was no longer in surgery. Or there was the gynecologist performing a D&C and disliked anyone looking over his shoulder, and even though Brigit was female, he demanded she stop looking. Brigit started to reply about learning, but the scrub nurse put her finger to her lips and motioned her to the nurse's side. The nurse whispered, "He's a fool. He knows you're here to learn. And as if you don't have the identical female equipment that woman lying on the table has. Yeah, but I bet you want to see inside all the way to really know what you are like in there. It's natural. We all do it, look outside, and in." Brigit blushed beneath her mask. The nurse started to laugh and whispered to her, "You're red above the mask. Don't you know better than to wear rouge in the OR?"

~

So the passage of time, and she was in her second year. December 7. Horrified as were all Americans, many of the women openly cried or moaned because they had brothers, boy friends, fiancés, husbands. Some eventually left the hospital to enlist. Brigit several days later as the shock and reality of war deeply affected her and all others in the hospital, decided she would enlist in the navy when she finished school. A number of the doctors left or were called asking them if they would accept commissions. Numbers of interns and residents left as soon as 1941's year of duty was finished.

1942 seemed to pass too slowly for Brigit, as did 1943, but in between there were the OB and the psychiatric wards, the depression of looking after the cancer patients, so many diseases, seeing so much dying, torn bodies from accidents, or knife or gun shot wounds from burglaries, the police who brought in prisoners and stood outside the ER rooms to assure no one would escape.

It was in the OB unit that Brigit seemed to have arrived as doctor and nurse. The head nurse was a lovely woman, hefty with a large bosom and handsome face and kind eyes that gave one a sense of the goodness and caring within the woman. Yet, she could also be rough, on the students, on the patients too, if she thought an expectant mother was overdoing the wretchedness she felt. One night when Brigit was on duty and getting instructions from the nurse, a woman in her early twenties lay in one of the small rooms. Suddenly she started screeching, yelling above her pain, perhaps thinking she could make that pain disappear. Nurse Albright went to her, told her to quiet down, that she knew it hurt. Brigit heard "I've had them too. I know what it's like. Settle down."

Albright felt Brigit touch her back as she was bending over the woman who quieted but then started to scream again. "May I sit with her?" Albright turned toward her. "Yes, nurse. Stay here until I need you." Albright rose, smiled at Brigit, lightly caressed her face, "Nurse, she called me nurse. Are you with me goddess Brigit? We're going to help the poor, suffering mother to be."

Brigit pulled a chair alongside the woman who was now moaning. She watched the woman breathe in about to scream again. "God help me! What did I do to deserve all this pain? I wanted a baby. What for? For this? A night of love. This isn't love," she screamed.

Brigit placed her hand on the woman's arm, rubbed it up to her shoulder and down to her wrist, placed her hand on the woman's swollen belly. "Take a deep breath." The woman looked wretchedly at her and took the breath. "Good. Do it again." The woman breathed deeply, let out her breath and murmured, "Is it always like this? Have you had one?"

"No. I never have, but I want one some day."

"You want one watching and listening to me? Nurse, it hurts. It's coming again."

"That's all right," Brigit softly told her. "You scream, but remember what I told you. Take deep breaths. Tell you what. I'll breath with you."

The woman seemed calmer, and soon they took her to the delivery room. As Brigit walked beside her, Albright looked up from her desk, smiling. "You're all right, Brigit. Think about becoming an OB nurse."

Between serving and learning in different areas of the hospital, there was always time for recreation and going places she had always wanted to see or visiting one of her favorites, the Museum of Fine Arts. In the summer there were the Esplanade concerts with Arthur Fiedler that she'd go to with friends from among the student nurses.

One night, an intern who was obviously taken with Brigit's beauty flirted with her and she with him, touching her face and hair, looking away and then, after blinking, straight at him. Her eyes mesmerized him.

"I'm off Saturday night. Are you?"

"I am. Why?" She was learning from her girl friends, magazines, and knew innately how to be female. She liked herself. What men who now approached her didn't realize, however, was that she was an honest person who usually said what she thought.

The intern asked, "Would you like to go dancing? There's a nice night club not too far away."

She had never been to a nightclub, knew about them only from what she heard from her friends in the dormitory, particularly her closest friend, Lynne, who came from Boston but whose family went to Maine a lot. They often talked about the doctors, about men generally, the many college students that roamed the Boston area. Lynne said her family would take Brigit to Maine some time when they had vacation.

"Brigit. Would you like to go?" the intern interrupted her wandering.

She tried to hide her excitement. "Yes. That would be wonderful."

"I'll pick you up about eight, O.K.?"

Hiding her anticipation, "Yes. That's fine," she calmly told him. "You don't know what dorm I'm in. It's the one at the corner of the street before you get to the hospital."

"See you then," he smiled. He was as excited as was she. To be seen out with perhaps the most beautiful female the interns knew. The interns had even had a contest in which they put in a hat the names of the best-looking student nurses. Brigit was always closest to if not on the top. Perhaps she would not have been too happy about that. She wouldn't. She never considered herself a beauty queen and disliked beauty contests and girls showing off themselves. It was disgusting and indiscreet. However, she learned in Boston where to buy fashionable clothes and how to appear not only as the naturally beautiful woman that she was but also how to appear still more noticeable, hips, bosom, with knit dresses, for example, and when she could afford it, dresses that emphasized her bosom and showed her legs. Not only was Brigit learning style, but she was revealing her personal charm.

"See you then," appearing unconcerned, she smiled back; but to encourage him, she added, "Thanks, Henry. I look forward to it."

On Saturday night, with the help of Lynne fussing about her, Brigit started to brush her shoulder-length hair. Lynne took the brush from her and combed and combed until her hair was the brightening red Lynne wanted to see. Brigit put on a red lipstick, but not too dark, enough to say, "Try it." Brigit smiled. Lynne shaped her eyebrows that she thinned and made certain they came to just above the corner of her eyes. "Ah, you beauty; alluring vamp." Brigit then put on her dress that fell just below her knees, that emphasized her bosom and her hips, but wide enough at the skirt to allow comfortable dancing.

She moved about in various positions, hands to her hips, swaying in front of the mirror to see what she would look like were she so inclined - which she wasn't. She started smiling, and then both of them were laughing, as Lynne pushed her on the shoulder.

"You're stunning," Lynne exclaimed. "I'm almost jealous."

"You are *not*. Look at yourself. If I were a guy, I'd be after you in no time."

Suddenly, Brigit thought of her father. He would disapprove. All he can think of is a woman wearing kitchen-maid clothes. If you go out, then the woman can wear a simple dress that shows she's a female. Not what Brigit was wearing tonight, the latest fashions in Boston, in fact throughout the country. Luke not only realized there's no denying the breasts, he loved looking at Maureen's, would gaze at her when she undressed at night, and often, despite the years of marriage and four daughters, obviously he would want to enter her and she would allow him. He would never force her into sex, however. If she were not in the mood, sometimes she would hold his penis, play with it, put her mouth about it until he had an orgasm. She enjoyed this play. Yet, despite having a beautiful wife, he seemed never to notice that Maureen, even in the house, would wear light rouge and a dull red lipstick, enough to make her lips desirable and to help emphasize her face, and enough to keep him interested. But if he saw Brigit tonight and Lynne encouraging her, he would be angry. Brigit started to laugh.

"Lynne, you know what. My dad would be furious if he saw me. I'm supposed to be that simple girl in the convent school, wearing my uniform and never even being pubescent, never growing up."

"You're joking or exaggerating."

"I'm exaggerating some. But he would not approve," as Brigit stood before the mirror, turning, twirling, admiring herself. "Here's to a great night, daddy. Oh. Don't you worry. I'm still a virgin and will be until I decide I don't care to be anymore. Hmm. Maybe I guess that will be when I marry. Well, daddy, don't worry. I won't even allow his hands to wander. But perhaps a little kiss goodnight won't be so bad. That O.K., *daddy*?"

"Listen, if your father saw you now, he'd be wowed."

"I wonder," she answered sadly. "I really wonder. He's just such a prude. But, don't think I don't love him. It took him a long time to accept me being at Boston City General, let alone Boston, the city of sin and Yankees. You know, people like you, Lynne."

Lynne pretended to laugh. "Listen, I've got a great book you should send him, *The Late George Appley*. Then he'll think you've really been ruined. Does he read much?'

"You think he's ignorant? Yes he reads," she laughed, "Oh well, mostly westerns. But if I tell him to read it, he will. What's it about?"

"Oh, it's great. About Boston highbrows. Talk about corruption. He'll wonder if the Protestants have converted you and if you've met any of these people. Just don't tell him about me and where I live. He'll be ordering you to stay away from me and my bad influence."

"Cut it out," Brigit laughed. "Keep it up and I'll get you to go to mass with me." She looked at the small clock on the dressing table. "Henry ought to be here soon. You sure you like the way I look?"

"You're kidding. He's going to want," and she stopped. "You know what I mean."

And that was the first night club date of the many to follow. Yet, no male was ever able to get close to her, although they kept trying. They admired her defenses. She did over time come to pet, but mostly kisses, if the man appealed to her, either those in the hospital or those she got to know among college students. Many, however, were drafted or enlisted and became fewer and fewer. The rationing, the news, the collections of rubber and metals to help the war effort. No matter how happy they could be, the girls were never far from the war either in the newspapers, *Life Magazine*, or in the loss of nurses who had taught them and who had joined or the doctors who had left.

Yet, in Boston, no matter how much she enjoyed it, it was a world so foreign from home that never left her. She still dreamed of nights and the skies so clear and filled with stars and moon. She missed the desert in all of its seasons, the warmth, especially in winter when she knew it would be more comfortable than Boston. Yet, she would never forget her excitement with the first snow or the Fall and the lovely trees that reminded her of a painter's palette, how she marveled at Spring and watched for the buds and the sudden full leafing of the trees. She especially enjoyed walking through the Public Garden and smelling the flowers, watching the children playing, laughed at herself when like a child she rode on a swan boat. Unreal as that was, it was the Charles River that truly fascinated her, the sculls from the different universities, watching the small sailboats. On one day, she told Lynne she would like to learn how to sail.

"They give lessons. I'll go with you. I never bothered." So when they had time, they would go where the river flowed nearby the Boston Esplanade and take lessons. Once, in a playful mood, they took separate boats, sailed out to the middle of the river, took their oars and started a war, splashing one another, screeching in joy. Back on shore, Brigit told her, "We're supposed to be serious nurses," still partially laughing.

"Oh bull. You think my father would be able to continue taking care of patients if he didn't have fun. He even gets to take out a scull now and then. He was on the Harvard team, you know."

"I wish I could ride in one of those. Oh well."

Meanwhile, the world was at war. The student nurses knew they were preparing to help the country in some way, either by joining a service or volunteering to take care of the homecoming wounded when they received their RNs; that is if they were allowed to volunteer.

And then there were the Esplanade concerts with Arthur Fiedler when she and Lynne and some of the other girls would go and sit in the grass to listen, to feel the beauty, be fascinated by music that took them separately to their own secret lands and dreams.

Aside from the music at the Esplanade, she had enough money from her father so she could go to Symphony Hall, where she could concentrate on Serge Koussevitzky and the music he would evoke. To save money but to get a good seat, she would sit in the corner of the first balcony overlooking the stage, to watch the movement of the conductor and look among the musicians and their expressions as they played. One night she was fortunate to watch the young Leonard Bernstein.

~

During her nurse training, the time came when Brigit and her class went to a mental hospital. Her time as a student was coming to a close. Through most of this time, as they endured the war, read the news, shuddered, Brigit wrote her family for news of the effects upon the town and heard of boys she had known who had gone off to war, some of whom had been killed, others wounded. The boy she liked best who had given her her first kiss had been killed. When Brigit read the letter, she teared and thinking more about him and their youth together, she began to cry. It was then she told herself she was going into the service as soon as she became a RN. In a letter from Maureen, her mother wrote that her sisters, Ellen and Marie, becoming of age, joined the WACS. *It's so lonely. Brigit, it's hard to explain how your father and I feel. How we miss you and your sisters. But we know it's something we must endure. Your father has lost to the service some of the men who worked for him. Now he's hiring more Mexican workers. He has expanded their quarters. I don't know what we'd do without them. And remember Maria Marcipal, the very pretty girl, daughter of one of the doctors, well she's going to become a nun. She was going with a Jewish boy – imagine - who left for the army. I guess the family allowed it, because his father is well known in El Paso. At first she thought she'd join one of the women's services. I'll miss her too. She became like another daughter to us. But nothing can make up for the girls we love so and miss. I give you a kiss and* strong *hug. Do take care of yourself and be safe and come back to us one day. I know you. You haven't told us, but I know you'll go in the service when you finish school. True, huh? Have you met more nice boys like that Henry you went with for a short time? What happened to him? Did he get fresh or you just tired of him? I know how that is, dear. We never forget those things, how our old boy friends treated us or who we liked but then came your father. You know the rest. It will happen to the three of you. You know I want the gossip. God bless you, dear one. – Mother. Dad sends his love and wants you to know he misses you. You could heal his wounds he gets around the ranch. You know how careless he sometimes can be. Love again, Mother.*

The mental hospital was startling. A nurse took the students to the different floors. She started on the worst, a floor with rooms having heavy closed doors and small windows so the patients could be watched. In one a woman sat naked in a corner, curled with a hand to her mouth, appearing to hide herself, feces on the floor against a wall opposite her. On another floor, in wards there were catatonics or in another, women or men in baths. The students stayed in a separate building. For meals they would go to a dining room in a nearby patient building. At every meal, patients would be at the windows, clawing at the bars, screaming. On one particular day as Brigit walked through a room of tubs in which women lay with canvas just to the top of their breasts, one yelled at her, "Hey, dearie. You're a good looker. We could make out. I can show you tricks you never thought of; make you feel great so you'd scream with delight. C'mon, dearie. Let me feel your clit, rub it for you and kiss you down there, kiss and lick, and my fingers inside. How about it?"

Horrified, Brigit, hurried past the woman and from the room while another patient loudly laughed. But she would have to return to take care of these people and realized she would have to become accustomed to what she heard.

Another, sadder time, she was in a men's ward. A man, sitting in a tall-backed wooden chair, a blanket wrapped around him, stared, she thought at first at her, but it was at nothing, or nothing she would ever know. A nurse came up behind her. "He's catatonic."

"Yes. I know. I feel terrible seeing him this way. How horrible not to be able to talk to someone or for us even to know if they are aware of us."

"He came back from the Pacific that way, dear. Imagine the hell he endures now and did then. They sent him to us when the naval hospital could no longer do anything. This goddamn rotten war, shitty goddamn Japs and Germans. I'd crush all their balls."

Brigit listened without answering; and for one of the first times, she wished she had said that. Crush a man's balls and he loses his manhood. One of the nurses at Boston City General took it upon herself to teach the new students how to kick a man there if he tried to attack her; but Brigit rarely thought of it except when she worked the late shift and had to walk in dark to the dormitory. Startled, Brigit hushed herself, made a quick cross at her chest and promised God she would be more careful. She was a healer, after all, and she realized and accepted that the experiences here were to prepare her for taking care of such patients, as it would help her to soothe battle scarred minds.

Thus the year 1943 arrived, and that June day her parents left their secure desert home and traveled to the land of the devil - and they did enjoy it, especially after watching Brigit pinned as a RN, meeting Lynne and her parents, and others of the class along with their parents, if a father wasn't off to war. Many had brothers, uncles, cousins, friends serving, fighting.

After the ceremony Lynne's parents, Dr. and Mrs. Brock, had the Donovans to their home and invited them to Maine where they had a house nearby the ocean. In between, there was much hugging and kissing. It was then Brigit told her parents. "Mother, dad, I'm enlisting in the navy. They'll make me a Lt. junior grade. They just say j.g. I've been to the recruiting office and will be inducted after you leave."

"Well, that's a welcoming," Luke kidded. "May we stay long enough to see Maine?" he added, then quickly, "Do you know where you'll be?"

"I think so, daddy, probably the Chelsea Naval Hospital not too far from here." She couldn't help herself, moved quickly to her father and placed her arms about him and kissed him hard at the side of his lips. Father, mother, and daughter each had his or her own tears. "I love you both so dearly, and don't you ever forget it." And they were softly crying and tenderly touching one another.

At the Brocks, on Beacon Street, across from the Public Gardens, they entered the hall. Maureen and Luke were astounded. They looked and floors above, the walls appeared to curve inward until they formed a funnel atop of which was a large rounded stained glass window. Brigit had been there before and knew how her friend lived at home. The Brocks took the Donovans to the second floor, not to be showy - that was not part of their character, the home being something they merely accepted. On this floor there was a large reception room. To one side there was a paneled library. There was also another library facing the street front. Directly on the opposite it was the large dining room looking out on the river. One floor higher was a dance hall mirrored on two sides that extended the width of the house. All the bedrooms were on the fourth floor with the fifth for the servants. Dr. Brock not only had a successful neurology practice but both he and his wife had inherited large sums. Lynne's mother and father, who met after her father returned from France following World War I, married in June, 1921. It was the social event of the season.

Without waiting any longer, Lynne hit Brigit on the shoulder. "C'mon. Let's show them the river."

"Excuse us, mother and father. I want the Donovans to see the river at its best." They went to the third floor where there was a hidden room off the ballroom. They looked on the Charles which slightly rippled from the soft breeze. "You see," Lynne said, "how lovely it is. Look there! The sailboats. Aren't they almost magical the way they glide?" Suddenly, Lynne became thoughtful. "It's so peaceful as it flows toward our beautiful Atlantic. But the Atlantic takes all those men to war. It's so horrible, I hate thinking about it." She had one younger brother who, if the war lasted long enough, would end up in the service. He was now 17. "I can't stand the thought of Andrew IV going off to war. I just can't." Her face became both despondently thin and angry, as she tried to keep herself from crying. She shook her head. "Brigit and I have spent a long time by the river. But I guess she told you."

The answer was a simple, "Yes" from Maureen, closely watching the two girls, happy they were such good friends but sad for Lynne's terrible thoughts and the wretched images she imagined fleeting through Lynne's mind. The peaceful river that the girls loved, perhaps dreamed by of the men they would one day marry but carrying them to fear and perhaps hatred.

The dinner went well. At first the talk was a little stilted, but then Luke started talking about the ranch and the Southwest desert. Dr. Brock told a little about his practice. It was the women who spoke the most. The stars, though, were Lynne and

Brigit, the parents of the girls telling them how proud they were, and Brock jesting with Lynne about coming to work in his office eventually and what a terribly difficult boss he would be. Luke interrupted that there would be nothing at his place for Brigit like that, except that she could come home and look after injured workers. At one point he rather criticized his daughter, telling the group, but especially her, that she could come home after the war and work at the Catholic Hospital and help at the ranch. Naturally, the parents knew their daughters would be exceptional, so Luke had no expectation of what he said.

The Brocks became more comfortable about the Donovans coming to Maine with them. Dr. Brock somewhat looked down on Luke, perhaps as a laborer, yet admired the strength of the man and the success he had made of his work.

Maureen, at first, felt uncomfortable about Nancy Brock, her aristocratic face, the kind one sees in the newspapers, say of the king and queen of England, except that Nancy was not as, well, as frumpy, Maureen was thinking, as Elizabeth. But it was the manner, the sophistication, the accent when she spoke with her long a's and cutting of the r's, an accent even beyond Boston but what she had learned from her parents and in school, an accent far above the crowd. Maureen was uncomfortable at first, felt herself dowdy. But both women were tall and fair, their aging bodies not having accumulated much fat beyond what they had when married and before the children. In their dinner clothes they wore the proper cosmetics that emphasized their best features, dresses that still allowed a man to turn to see their busts and slightly protruding hips. Yes, in physical ways, there was a resemblance. Nancy tried hard not, however, to show the superiority of her Boston upbringing. She had that way of making people feel comfortable, though she may have thought them inferior, whether it was a store clerk or dinner guests such as they had tonight. In fact, she liked Maureen. Both women were somewhat like their daughters in this way. They just naturally admired the strengths they saw in one another. Nancy felt, that despite the difference in their upbringing, that had they lived closer, they could be friends, perhaps like Lynne and Brigit. Lynne did not have her mother's aire about her, never had, something Nancy sometimes regretted. But when Nancy came to know Brigit and having been struck by her beauty, and knowing Lynne was a rebel like Brigit, she not only accepted Lynne's personality but that of her close friend. She also knew that her husband reveled in Lynne's difference, not only from his wife, but from most of the girls with whom she played, grew up, was close to through the high school years. Somehow, she seemed always to choose the outspoken, the less self-conscious of their position in society. Lynne, in fact, almost had a fight with her parents about her coming out. She did not believe in it. From where her ideas came about equality and social nonsense was beyond her parents, except they knew they had a very intelligent daughter who read many books, as well as the newspapers and grew older discussing the world events, the differences that they saw among people in newspaper articles. It was because of this that Lynne's father came to accept his daughter's independence much sooner than did her mother.

In this short time, having tested and learned about one another, the parents and the new nurses knew that they could tolerate a weekend together in Maine. Because Brock was a doctor and had a C gasoline sticker, they could get enough gasoline for the trip to Cape Astraea. Andrew had two cars, a Packard sedan and station wagon. They took the station wagon that was still crowded, seven people with their luggage. It could be Andrew's last summer in Maine. He had a cancer. This thought, despite the merriness of the trip, traveling up the narrow two-lane Newburyport Turnpike, the same kinds of roads in Maine, only these more tree-lined and magnificent, particularly riding alongside rivers with trees bending over them, watching small waterfalls, or crossing small bridges over the quietly floating water caused the Brocks and Lynne occasionally to become silent until someone in the car spoke.

When they arrived at Cape Astraea, driving toward their house, they passed a large Victorian home. Lynne said, "They're friends of ours. I used to think I was in love with their youngest son Gregory. Oh, Brigit, talk about looks. What a guy. Sometimes at night, thinking about him, I'd just swoon like he was Sinatra. We used to go swimming at Crawfish Cove. I'm planning to take you there so we can swim." Lynne saddened. "Now he and his brothers are off to war, one in Europe, one in England, and Greg somewhere in the Mediterranean. He's in the navy like you'll be. Sorry. I'll take the army." Lynne added, "He's Jewish." She knew that bothered her mother. "But I don't care. Would you?"

"Uh, uh, I think."

To tease her mother, Lynne continued, "I'll snag him when he gets back. A good catch. His father's a doctor like mine, and I think he wants to be one. So what more could a woman want?" Then she glanced at her father, watching him wrinkle his nose. The Donovans said nothing, tried to appear uninterested. Then Maureen glanced at Nancy Brock who raised an eyebrow and shrugged slightly, hoping the girls didn't notice. "Girls," she said to herself. "Not girls, desirable women." She imagined her daughter entangled in bed with a man, but it had to be the right man. Yet, she knew, no mother or father could control that despite any advice or talk and that eventually parents could either accept or not the man a daughter chose. "But," she told herself, "being too pushy about the right man could drive a woman faster to the perceived undesirable mate." Anyhow, she didn't have to worry about Lynne and Gregory, because she knew it was girlish infatuation.

When Lynne and Brigit got away from their parents, they went alone to Crawfish Cove. They had all been there together, walked about the land jutting out into the ocean, watching the waves roll against the rocky shore and the white caps. Because the Donovans didn't swim, the Brocks sat with them in the grass or on the large, time-eroded, tantalizing rock formations while admiring the scenery or watching other families with their children or those with friends sitting in the sun, others down on the beach running along the shore or swimming.

But alone for the girls was best. Lynne grabbed Brigit's hand and ran close to a small sheltered part of the beach. "We used to make out over there," as she pointed toward the area. "Oh, not all the way, though, well, we cammmme sooooo clossse. Terrible, huh? I bet you have too. With Henry. You never would tell me what you two did after you got to know him. Well, anyhow, we didn't do it. I did let him lie on top of me once. It felt good, but whew, its weighty having a guy lie on you. He'd move up and down over me down there" and she pointed just below her mons, "and come. I liked the feeling too. Don't you wonder what it's really like? Sounds like fun. It hurts the first time a friend of mine told me. I was sometimes sorry I didn't let him go all the way."

Brigit nodded, laughing. "I'd like to know too. I let Henry rub against me, feeling his big thing pressing near my, you know, and could tell when he came, you know, that 'uhh' and pushing of his body against you."

"Oh well," Lynne told her, both now laughing, "We have to stay virgins for our one and only. Maybe," she added.

Chapter III

Love's Awareness

Before she stood facing me on the deck, silently but through her eyes telling me there was possibility for us, I had grown so weary of being in the hospital. She lessened the anguish of my recovery period by wheeling me out where we could look over the navy yard, watching ships going off to God knows where, carrying men who had either been in battle or would be for the first time.

"Brigit." How I wanted to reach up and bring her down to me and kiss her. She placed her hand on my shoulder and I my hand atop hers.

"I wish. Oh God, I want to get out of here and be with you. There's so much ahead. How or when this f . . . . . . ," I stopped before finishing the word and heard a slight chuckle. "Naughty Lt." I laughed. "I know you've heard it all before. Admit it. You use it too."

"I do, but I have to be really angry, so don't ever get me mad, Greg."

"Look at the *U.S.S. Constitution* over there. You know, I used to read about the sea and wish I could have been born then so I could sail on a ship like that, climb the yardarms. But what a horrible and dangerous job those men had."

"And just what do you suppose you've been through on that little wooden boat of yours?"

"I'm a very lucky guy," it suddenly hit me as I spoke to her. "We lost every other boat in the squadron. What saved us?"

"G . ." and she stopped. I think she didn't know if I believed in God nor did she know what it was like being Jewish. She had told me she was Catholic. But so what? My mom is.

"Brigit. I'm not sure if I believe. But you know my mother's Catholic like you. My dad wanted us brought up Jewish, and she didn't care. Well, I did later and hated it, all religion." I had no idea how this would haunt me one day.

"Are you religious?"

"I went to a convent school." She smiled. "I didn't like it at times, but there was a nun I liked who kept me from becoming a bad girl," she laughed.

How people's minds work. That deck, the silly talk but still serious. Eventually, when they allowed me to leave the hospital, an Admiral came in when I had just gotten into my dress uniform. He pinned a couple of medals on me. Yes. It was nice. My family would be proud, and the town, I feared and dreaded it, would welcome home the hero or another hero.

The last ceremony was receipt of my discharge from the navy. I was sad. I liked the navy, but there was a life ahead. Some life. Look at me. I'm sweating from this fucking CLL. Chronic lymphatic leukemia. Some joke. Survive the fucking war for this? Think of something better, you damn fool.

Yes. Brigit watched when they put the medals on my chest and smiled at me and put her hands together in a clap. I couldn't let that be the end, and I know she wanted no end to us either.

After the ceremony and when the crowd had disappeared, she lingered. I couldn't help myself and said it, "My golden red-haired goddess." "Be careful what you wish for," she answered with an enigmatic smile. I ignored that as teasing. I looked to see no one was about, placed my arms about her. She didn't stop me. We were looking in each other's eyes with desire and surrender. We kissed, short at first, but then I kissed her longer and she kissed me back. "I believe, Brigit, I love you." She didn't answer, just smiled, her eyes brightening still more. "We're going to see one another. Right?" She shook her head and then whispered, "I'm never going to let you go," and she held and turned to hold herself against me so I could feel the softness of her breasts in my chest and kissed me, placing her tongue in my mouth. "And don't forget that."

"When I get back from home. No. I've got it. You come to Cape Astraea."

"Cape Astraea? I've been there, Gregory. You're the one who went with Lynne. I didn't meet your parents. You think I should?"

"I don't have to think. Lynne?? No kidding. I hope she didn't tell you too much.

"Just get a few day's leave and come. I'll expect you." We kissed again, not wanting to leave one another.

"I've got you now. No Lynne." She smiled. "I know what you did with her. You think you're going to do that to me?"

"That depends." We laughed together, kissed again, separated, sliding our hands along our bodies and slowly withdrawing from one another.

~

I left the hospital, when, February, March - I don't quite remember. Why? What's wrong with my head? - early, anyhow, 1945. I had been in the hospital so long. My leg was worse than they originally thought. The allies were finally, moving slowly at times across France, approaching the Rhine after having been surprised and stalled by the German offensive that became known as the Battle of the Bulge. My brother was in that. In the Pacific we were about to recapture the Philippines. By that time I was safely recovering with the help of Brigit who seemed, though we cared dearly for one another and were getting well acquainted, to have these mysterious healing qualities about her that no matter how close we may have been at the time seemed inexplicable.

She would touch me, lovingly I felt, and my mind would relax, and I would feel safe with her. She encouraged me, not like Deirdre who doesn't care if I live or die, probably wants the latter and my money - as if she hasn't accumulated enough with those peculiar art and archaeological deals of hers. Where does she get it all? How? Oh, the hell with her. I can't trust her. If it weren't for the girls. . . my daughters, I mean.

Brigit. I swear she had a special quality about her that came from far off, a place no one would ever know except Brigit. Oh, my beautiful, loving Brigit. How I loved her. I still do. I wonder if she can sense it. She knows, doesn't have to sense.

But I could get along, even walking with a cane. I applied for med school. Brigit and I had discussed that. Hmmm. It's funny. It's almost like the time with Lynne when she said she'd wait for me. But I thought Brigit would even marry me if I pressed hard enough. Then again, maybe not. The religion thing. Yeah, I know. Catholics, my mother and Brigit. It's peculiar and makes you wonder. But we just agreed to wait until after med school. I also told my father and mother. My father was ecstatic, my mother pleased but I know wondering whether I could take the intensity of the study. Even the admissions office wanted to know whether I was sufficiently recovered, the asses. You either have the desire and the brains or you don't.

~

When I was home in Maine, it was almost as though there had been no war for me. At least, I felt so comfortable, as in the past, my mother in her music room practicing, listening to her thrilling voice. Occasionally she would travel to Boston to be with her maestro. My father was at his practice.

So, alone, there were times I moped around the house, time going slowly. The fellows I had known were in the service. My mother came home one day soon after I returned wearing my uniform and ribbons, hobbling along. "Oh, what happened to Gregory, Jocelyn? Is he all right?" After the usual answers and "Yes, he's going to be fine. He has his father, if anything bothers him." My father was a marvelous diagnostician and let the rule go about doctors never taking care of their families. Yet, he was helpless, sometimes, even my mother's music when I became depressed or lonely for Brigit, for the men I had gotten to know in the hospital, those on my ship. I would wonder what had happened to our last minesweeper. After the invasion of Southern France, I finally heard that my boat was decommissioned and the men sent to the Pacific. It was a terribly difficult time. I looked forward to the Fall and starting med school. What really kept me going was Brigit, thinking about her, dreaming of her. Marvelous dreams in which we made love. Sometimes she would withdraw or hide her face in her shoulder, as if telling me it was never to be, or maybe because she was a virgin in the dream. In fact I don't know whether or not she was, but in that dream she didn't want to arouse me. Those were lousy dreams. The others rejuvenated me. I would wake both pleased and happy, then sorry because she was after all not beside me.

Summer came. June. The gruesome Battle of Okinawa was over. Aside from reading and thinking about the war, Brigit and I we talked on the phone, telling one another how we missed being together. Then she told me she got a seven-day leave and was coming to Cape Astraea. There was such strength in her voice when she said it. "Gregory. Your parents. Can they stand having me for that long? You've told me so much about your mother and your father's being well known for his evening clinic. I've seen articles in the paper about him, your mother too."

"Well, he's semi-retired now since we moved to Maine and takes the train to Boston three days a week in time for clinic hours. The new director, for courtesy's sake, defers to him. When the time comes, and he wants to keep busy, he'll see patients in a Portland practice that said it would welcome him. Anyhow, forget what you've read about them. They're just good parents you'll enjoy and vice versa."

"I'm just a farmer's daughter - well, rancher's. I didn't meet them when I was up there with the Brocks after graduation. But don't forget. I know about you and Lynne. Greg, she writes me. I'm not going to compete with her, if this war is over by then. Do you think it will be?"

She was afraid of meeting my parents and just had to talk without my interruptions. Finally I said it. "Stop. Right now. My parents are going to love you. And you're not competing with anyone or ever will. Just come. I'll take you to Crawfish Cove, we'll swim," She laughed but never said she was thinking of Lynne and me and what she heard. "We'll go into Portland, to the art museum. We'll listen to music. My mother will sing for you. You'll have a private concert. Hurry, Brigit. Good heavens. My heart's pounding."

"Well, mine is too."

"Brigit," I wanted to say it to her looking in her eyes, the brightness of those eyes but couldn't help myself. "I love you."

There was hesitation, a deep breath I heard from her. "Gregory." She stopped, "Gregory. I'm kissing you. I wish I could feel your lips; you're mine though. But it won't be long."

At first my mother wanted Mary to drive to the station, but I insisted everybody wait at home. I had driven some and was beginning to feel more comfortable in the car. Here it was June.

The war in Europe was over and the Pacific would be over soon. My thoughts, however, were on the train and watching that lovely woman coming down the steps.

She appeared in her navy summer uniform. Seeing me she waved, and as she stepped carefully down holding a suitcase, I watched the curve of her hip, and there she stood, tall, her red hair showing below her cap, the litheness of her even in uniform. We were together, our arms about each other, kissing. The marvelous softness of her mouth.

"How's my hero?" She smiled, moving back from me to look. We both did at arms' length, but holding onto one another.

"Oh, Brigit, I never thought this would happen." I started to laugh slightly. "You know what? I'm thinking of all those guys in the hospital and the way they would makes passes at you.

And I'm the lucky one."

"It isn't luck, mister." She hit me lightly on the arm. "No woman is luck. Oh, those nasty comments about all of us. Like all women are for one thing. Oh, I should stop this. Except, you're beautiful, Gregory, well, handsome, and you look so good I could lick all the frosting off you right in front of everyone."

I took her bag, although she tried to stop me. "Listen, nurse, I'm O.K."

"I'm still a little nervous, Greg."

"Listen, they'll take a look at you, and that's all they'll need. And when they hear your voice. C'mon. Wait til you see where I live. Of course, we don't have those huge swaths of land your family does."

We looked at one another, our eyes holding us. From her movement, it seemed Brigit felt a chill. I believe she wanted my arms about her, the warmth of them, the feeling throughout her body when I held her. "Gregory, I want to kiss you right here."

I didn't hesitate and took her to me and kissed her, my

tongue seeking hers.

Though she kissed back, she pulled away, "Not here in public. Coming off the train. O.K." Her face was a bit red. "You feel so good."

At home, I insisted again on taking her bag. She looked at the house. With Lynne she had only glanced at it. Now, she pulled lightly at my arm. "I want to look. I love it. Oh. Those beautiful doors. And the long windows."

"Come into my shelter, dear one, and be safe from the world. I'll carry you back in time," I hesitated, wondering if that were true. We could not escape the war. Could she forget? Inside were often frightened parents, like the time during the European war they saw a photo in *Life Magazine* of a captain, a doctor, killed, only his shoulders and rank showing, the rest of his body buried in mud. Was it James? The fright was unbearable. When after a week or so later a letter arrived from him, my parents relaxed some. I was home. Matthew was writing, but each time they saw a picture of a bomber going down or men in parachutes, they shivered. I felt much the same as they, even experienced a little guilt, before the war ended in Europe in May, that I was home. I'll admit, too, I fantasized looking at the ads in *Life* that showed the women in the stylish two-piece bathing suits, a bra top, short skirt; or the bra ads and light, zippered girdles. I'd wonder what Brigit looked like in her underwear or in one of those suits. I'd find out soon, at least about the bathing suit.

I introduced her to my parents waiting at the door. My mother, who was never overly demonstrative, I could see, was taken by the attractive young woman standing somewhat nervously before her. My father waited for my mother to talk. "Brigit. Welcome to our house. It's time you came. Gregory would unhinge us, talking about you, wondering if you would ever come."

"Some sailor, my son. Brigit, you're welcome," my dad warmly said.

Brigit's smile and eyes, the redness of her hair, her lithe tallness, surely appealed to my parents as one would expect.

Then my mother, uncharacteristically, asked, "Would you mind a hug?" She may have wanted relief from her worries about my brothers. Brigit didn't answer but stepped toward my mother, more relaxed, as both women reached for one another. My father was smiling, and I, I was ecstatic. Mary stood back, waiting her turn, knowing Brigit, and having told me how she liked my choice and how fortunate I was. There was a peace in the house that had left it when we went to war. It made little difference how long it would last, even if for the week Brigit would be here. I looked at two handsome women, both about the same height, hugging lightly, both apparently happy with one another. My mother whispered something to Brigit that Brigit told me later, that my mother was aware how deeply I felt about her and that perhaps the best thing to happen to me was her arrival. It wasn't like my mother to judge quickly. Usually she would wait to analyze and finalize her judgments. But I knew my mother would still watch and judge us. My father? He'd get me aside, and even knowing the months that Brigit and I had been together in the hospital, that she had nursed me, med school was just ahead. "Don't do anything hasty. Don't propose or marry while in school. Your mother and I went through that."

~

I'm sweating and starting to cough. Thoughts. Dreams. Nightmares.

~

Brigit and my parents got along so well. My mother told me later how much she liked her and how good my mother knew she was, how lovely she looked in her uniform but how feminine in her night clothes and some new fashionable, knee-length dresses she had bought in Boston to wear while at home. My mother felt sorry for her, because it had been so long since she had seen her parents, away for about two years. I felt that Brigit would have a home here, that she could come whenever she chose; for as the week passed, my parents and Brigit found the beginning of a parent-child love, perhaps another daughter.

Dinner was usually around 7. So there we were seated at the table. There was talk about Cape Astraea, a little gossip thrown in, but mostly about the war, wondering whether James and Matthew would be coming home or sent to the Pacific, wondering when the war would end. It seemed as though it could not last much longer. Yet, the Japs would never surrender until the entire country was wiped out, obliterated. The fire bombings did not seem to have had any effect on the Emperor – I could picture that ugly man riding on the horse, hear the Banzais. "You'd think they'd know when they're beaten," I said angrily. "What they did on Bataan, the bastards all ought to die." I was getting excited, thinking about the German bombers and our men dying as they waded ashore. Everyone was silent as I ranted until Brigit placed her hand on my arm to calm me.

Here I am struggling to stay alive, like we all did during the war. I can still feel that touch and the caring and the love in it. I suppose she didn't want to say anything with my family there. But everyone noticed the effect on me.

I turned to Brigit, fighting to calm myself. "I'm all right, Brigit."

She seemed embarrassed in front of my folks and weakly smiled as though she were apologizing for interfering. But my mother would have noticed and not cared, seen the love in that touch, as well as the dismay in her eyes. I think that is probably the time that Mary really felt close to Brigit, perhaps remembering the incident in the hospital. Perhaps, too, the three women communicated with one another, sensing the warmth.

"Let's try to forget the war," my mother said, though that was impossible. I doubt she had ever had a good night's sleep ever since we had all gone away. Sometimes I would see her standing alone, placing the back of her hand to her eyes. And my dad. His false stoicism. All of us frightened, if the doorbell rang and we weren't expecting anything.

Although Brigit was supposed to wear her uniform when she went out, she didn't in Cape Astraea, except when we went out to eat. We drove to the different beaches, would walk along the shore or just sit, she in her two-piece bathing suit, a bra that just covered her uplifted breasts, the short skirt of the suit with the cloth that covered her pubic area. Oh, I looked there and, obviously, my imagination overwhelmed me, seeing in my mind those breasts and nipples and her genitalia. We would sit, watching the water, the waves, when the wind increased, the rolling and spraying white caps against the rocky shore. Here it was so peaceful. I would look at the horizon and think of what was beyond, of ships sinking and men dying. As I managed to make those thoughts recede, I would feel Brigit against me. We would sit, sometimes never saying anything, perhaps thinking the same thing about peace and war, our arms about each others' shoulders or back, our skin touching, both aroused. I would look around to make sure there was no one in sight, bring her to me, or she would do that to me, and we would kiss, fondle one another, kiss on the lips, behind ears or on the neck. I would get hard and wondered whether she were feeling a sensation below. It was then, a couple of days later when we were sitting that she nuzzled against my neck, raised her head a bit, blew in my ear, and whispered, "When are you taking me to the Cove?" She placed her hand on my hardness. "Oooh. You're big." I started to place my hand on her breast, but she stopped me. "It's too open here. I want you to take me where you and Lynne made out." I laughed. "You're jealous."

"I am not, but I have this feeling," and she stopped. Blushing, she whispered, "Well, you know where."

We drove to the cove. I was glad we had bathrobes with us. Coming around a curve, she sighed loudly. "You took all this time to show me this. It's beautiful." The land jutted out into the water. Far off was a lighthouse. In the distance you could watch waves striking against rocks.

We walked along a path to the part of the beach surrounded mostly by bushes, yet with just enough sand to be comfortable.

I took her hand trying but unable to walk fast. "Come on."

"What's your hurry, Mister? Don't you know we women don't like to be hurried. Slow and easy," and she turned my head toward her, her alluring green eyes gazing in mine, "Lovingly." She laughed. "You're funny. Don't you know I've been waiting?"

I placed the soft blanket on the sand, held her arms as she sat. "Ah, so this is the spot. Wait 'til I write Lynne."

"Oh. Would you please stop talking about her? That was high school." She laughed again. "I know that." She lay back and gently pulled me down beside her, not wanting to hurt my leg. "Now what did you do?" "Stop that, Brigit." "You're annoyed. I'll stop."

We kissed more. She rolled over on me. "I feel you," and she moved up enough to be sure my hard penis would be touching her clitoris and a little below. I started to move up and back. Pushing against her faster until I came. She lay there a few moments, then rolled back to the ground. I turned on my side and asked her to loosen her bra. She untied it at the top but would not take it off. I placed my hand over one and then the other, then started to move lower. After a while, I asked her to rub me. "It feels like a brick bat," as she placed her hand inside my bathing suit, took hold of me and gently rubbed up and down until she felt me jerk and took her hand away as I came again.

I reached to the edge of her bathing skirt, went inside, feeling her hair. She took my hand and moved it outside but allowed me to rub. "Gently," she said. Suddenly, as she became more aroused, she took my hand and placed it inside directing me how to rub along her clitoris. I placed my fingers inside her where she opened after spreading her legs. She pushed against me, moaned softly, arched her back as she orgasmed. We lay quietly, breathing, resting. "You think I'm a hussy," she whispered as she laid her head on my thigh. "No." For a long while we lay there saying nothing, just feeling ourselves against one another, satisfied, yet wanting more but knowing not for now.

On the Saturday evening before she left, she and my mother went to mass, my mother knowing she believed in prayer and her religion. Perhaps my mother thought she could pray for both of them, though the few times I went with my mother, the few times she went, I would watch her kneel and cross herself. She would also light a candle. There could be no doubt she was thinking of her sons, praying they would come home safely. I don't know. Maybe her prayers brought me home even with the fucking Germans having crapped up my leg. Anyhow, I didn't go with them. I wanted them to be alone, to have time together.

On Sunday we all went to the station. My mother and dad told Brigit to remember them to her parents, that they wanted her to come again. Mary hugged her tightly. Later, Mary told me what she said. "Don't let him go. I hope you'll marry him. Aside from his temper, he's a terrific brother." My mother actually used the word love that she rarely did unless it was for her family. While she was hugging Brigit, she whispered to her, "You're a love, and you have mine. Now you take care of yourself." I saw Brigit's eyes tear. My dad kissed her on the cheek and told her to return. Then the three of them left us alone.

"Brigit. Oh God, I wish you weren't leaving. I love you, dearest. Remember that. Oh, how I love you."

Not taking her eyes away from me, "I love you too."

~

At home I went to my room just wanting to be alone, to dream, to be in my imagination with Brigit as we had been at the Cove or as when we walked around the town, went into some of the shops for people to meet her or to look at some clothes. She's so beautiful, intelligent. We belong together.

Mary was with my mother at the time. I heard this later, again from my sister. She told our mother, "She's the one for him, mom."

"I think you're right. I hope you are."

~

In September the war was over. We had dropped the A-Bomb on Hiroshima and Nagasaki. The Jap warlords had been eliminated or would be, and the Emperor issued the surrender, trying to save what was left of his Banzai country.

That September I started medical school in Boston. James and Matthew would come home on the *Queen Mary*, Matthew in that stormy sea at that time. The family was whole again, James picking from where he left off with his surgical training, Matthew going off to New York, eventually becoming known for his art work.

My schooling meant seeing Brigit again who would not be

discharged until 1946.

So we were both busy, she taking care of wounded sailors, I with my first-year science studies. We did, however, when there was time, visit the art museum or on an occasional night attend a concert at Symphony Hall. The most exciting of these was when my mother appeared. We sat in the balcony overlooking the stage, our favorite seats. My mother appeared in a dark gold-fringed evening dress that clung to her upper body and swirled at the bottom, especially as she kept in time with her notes and the music's urging. Her solo was Strauss's "Klänger der Heimat." As I listened to the soulfulness of being far from home, it reminded me of my longing to be in Cape Astraea when I was away at war.

Brigit sat motionless, mesmerized by the music and my mother's voice - her beauty. How, I wondered, could there be three such women as my mother, Jocelyn, Mary, and Brigit who I was determined would eventually be my wife.

Now I was in my mid-twenties and finally in med school that I had for years dreamed about, influenced, no doubt, by my father and brother James. The first year was study of the sciences. The second year seemed much more interesting, because it was the beginning of our clinical studies. I suppose I was somewhat surprised when male and female students had to examine one another. Oh, I had had a couple of women in Europe, but looking at a female classmate, thinking whether Brigit looked the same, tantalized and annoyed me. No two people are alike no matter where, from mind to genitals. And then I wondered what it must have been for the female students handling us, poking their fingers inside to the prostate. Finally, I realized the foolishness of my teenage thoughts, and we went about our clinical rotations ignoring that phase. So, from then on, actual clinical work became more complicated with more to think about and being asked questions by the doctor professors, pushed to answer, some disgusted if one of us made a mistake. There we were, as our learning passed into pediatrics, psychiatry, oncology, epidemiology, ob-gyn. As we advanced I believe most of us became more confident. We saddened when one of the class failed.

One day, walking into the hospital, it hit me. I would enter research. Medicine was on the edge of isotope research, and I wanted to be part of this.

~

Oh. I remember when it happened. The night Brigit stayed late at my apartment, and we decided she'd sleep over and get off to work early enough. I had studied. She had made dinner. We barely made love. Then how I sat as she stood before me and unbuttoned her blouse and dropped her bra. Glancing sideways at me as she turned and pulled down her panties, she then faced me; but again standing sideways she ran her hands along the sides of her body and to her oval straight, enticing breasts, caressing them, raising them. No, We didn't do it. She just walked slowly to my bedroom, I hard but satisfied by how I had never seen her before but had always wondered and wanted. Her body was so glorious. She knew I would like it and not be angry. She knew I wanted to see her, perhaps thinking, *This is what you'll get someday, Gregory.*

~

When would someday be?

On a week during the summer of 1947, we took the train to Cape Astraea. The house was large enough for Brigit to have her own room down a step at the end of a short hallway. It was now known as hers and was always ready. I'm sure other guests used it; but when she came, it seemed to me either Mary or my mother would spray a faint perfume to feminize the bed covers and the rest of the room.

Mary, by the way, had been engaged to a medical resident. She broke with the fellow when she decided against hiding her sexuality. I love her for that. She would, after her fellowship, come back to practice near Cape Astraea. Anyhow, it seems my family had a difficult time staying away from medicine. I told Brigit about Mary. She was at first shocked but then must have decided if they were to be sisters-in-law, she had to accept it. I know they cared for one another. I did wonder, though, how much Brigit appealed sexually to Mary. I'd never know. They would go off by themselves, shop, go to other towns where there was still more shopping and one they liked in particular because of the sandwich-coffee shop, Dugans, in Mansfield. Oh yes, another wealthy town. Other times, when Mary could get her away from me, they went swimming alone and tell me I could catch up later. However, Brigit and I managed to get away by ourselves. We would swim and then go to that part of the cove where we could sexually satisfy ourselves, make promises. Promises. I despise making promises anymore. Who promises me? They are a façade for lies. Lies. Isn't life a lie? That isn't so when I think about Melinda and Pamela. They and the thought of Brigit keep me alive. Brigit just walked by my door and looked in, sneaking that look, she thought, to make certain I am all right. I'll call her back. But Pamela appeared before I could call Brigit, so I asked, "Pamela, have you finished your writing?"

"For now."

"Satisfied?"

"I guess."

"Come here, dear." She came to the bed. "I know you're upset with being home."

"Dad. I got over that some time back. It was mom's fault

anyhow. You fought her over Wellesley, now grad school. I heard your arguments. It was my decision to wait, for now, anyway, so I could be with you. And mom - now where is she? Overseas? The house is full of that art crap of hers."

"Listen, I didn't ask you to come in here to complain," I smiled at her. "I just want you to know I love you very much."

She smiled. "I love you, dad," and she came to me and hugged and kissed me on the cheek. "Do you need anything?

"Nope. I'm going to get up in a bit. I'm sick of lying here. I'll make myself a complete invalid if I keep it up. Maybe it's to keep you and every so often to get Brigit here. You know what, I'd like to drive over to Crawfish later. O.K.? We can watch the ocean. The breeze will be causing some magnificent waves. But just leave me here for a bit. O.K.?" I wanted to dream a little more. "Do you mind going?"

That was a silly question. Unless some boy friend was after her. She was now twenty-two. But before she left the room, she said, "Dad, we have a letter from Melinda, one for you and one for me. How could I forget that?" She continued, "Dad, she's an intern. Don't we have enough of that in the family?"

I just laughed and said, "What's a few generations?"

What are a few? For Brigit, for me, for all of us? Deirdre didn't need any generations. She made her own, What the hell is she up to? Crap on it.

Oh that week with Brigit. My mom would sing and play for us. My dad would have Brigit come to his office. She even helped one day. I was angry, because it was a waste of our vacation. Anyhow, there was that night. Brigit and I stayed up later than everyone and went softly to her bedroom. She pushed me lightly to sit on the bed and stood before me the way she had that night at my apartment. She seemed shy at first and went to her large closet and started to undress. I pulled off my clothes to my underwear and threw them on the floor. She walked out in her underwear and slowly took off her bra and panties, came to me, kissed me, fondled below, kissed me harder and pulled off my underwear. "Get up," she commanded and threw back the covers. We climbed in the bed at about the same time, looking at one another, fondling. I lay her on her back. She spread her legs. I entered with her pulling at my sides and raising her legs to place about me. As I continued, she moved to meet me. Then she was on top, rubbing and sitting. She tightened. It was exquisite. Later, when we lay side by side, she said softly, "Simultaneous expression."

"Not just once I answered."

"I'm all wet, my own and yours."

I turned and took a box of tissues from the night table. She stood, wiping, asking me not to look. I was actually wishing I had made her pregnant, but I knew she wouldn't have done it if she thought her body would respond to that. She had faith in her monthly cycle.

~

The summer of 1947 Brigit had a call from home. The Southwest summoned her once again. Her father was sick. They needed her. Despite her father's illness that bothered her terribly, she looked forward to seeing everyone. Ellen and Marie were now married. Maureen was often alone with Luke. Brigit left Boston immediately. Though her sisters were not far off, they weren't nurses. Brigit also looked forward to seeing the desert and the ranch again. She told herself she would heal her father.

I had not been to the Southwest yet. At school I would read about it, look intently at the pictures, imagine her sitting beside her father, doing whatever she thought was necessary to make him comfortable while also consoling her mother and sisters.

Brigit was a strong woman who many times tried to hide her tears from the others. She would look at her father, soothe him running her soft hand across his face. Once he looked up at her and said, "You're such a loving and lovely daughter. That boy friend of yours. Does he know what you think, what you feel, how good you are?"

"Daddy, what woman tells a man, especially a special one, what she's always thinking. They're supposed to guess. Right?"

He smiled. "Brigit, your mother still confounds me at times. I was watching her one night making dinner. A smile appeared on her face. When I asked her what she was thinking about, she said, "Oh, the usual, and then something about you and me, about the girls, remembering when you-all would scream at one another in an argument. Can you imagine Anne, oh, Sister Angelina, screaming in the convent?' She laughed, 'Remember how we wondered how we would last through all that running and screaming, and then the love among them, whispering about boys.' Then she looked right at me, you know, Brigit, the way a woman looks at a man, telling him without words how she loves him."

Brigit turned away momentarily from her father. Rubbed the corner of an eye. She was thinking about her family but also about Gregory and that night at his home, felt a slight thrill along her spine. She heard also the rush of the waves, their crash on the rocks, thought of the peace they could now bring the world when before they had helped destroy, almost killed Gregory. She loved the water now as much as the desert. She thought of how they sat on the beach, their arms lightly about one another looking out to the horizon, feeling part of that vast Atlantic, spreading themselves along the rounding horizon, they and the sea one. There were times when she thought *I may never have known Gregory, never have received the love I have from him. God saw to it, and no matter what happens, he'll always be mine. You're mine, Greg, and don't you forget it. I have that power in me. I was born with it. That's how I know I'll cure my father. I don't care what the doctors think. How can I be so fortunate as to have so much love in my life? I'm smiling. The way I look at myself in the mirror and put on all those come-hither looks, make sure I'm fetching. No other man is going to come near me, Gregory. I promise you that. But I'm stumbling in my head. What if something happened to you, or even me?* She felt her heart beat a little faster, and she said aloud, "I'll destroy any woman who goes near you." She stretched her fingers, her nails noticeable, allowed to grow while at home, as she involuntarily raised her hand and her eyes narrowed. She was now jealous and angry about an unknown rival, her eyes showing her fury. No one could be more alluring than Brigit, although reasonably she knew it was possible. She sat by herself continuing to think of Gregory, a handsome man for her, thinking of how other women might see him, how he could be lured by a perfume, by a dress revealing those female's attributes, a touch, a flirtatious look, and flip of the hair. Only in those few moments did she feel unsure of herself. So far away. So necessary. She perked up. *He loves me every bit as much as I love him.* That a war, that barbaric war, should have brought him through a sea of fear to her. Nothing could change that. The war would forever be a part of them, as would the suffering. No matter. Love exists despite atomic weapons, death, whatever attempts to subdue it. It is the ultimate victor. *Oh, Greg, how I wish I could hold you, want to right now so we could be as we were in Astraea – in my bedroom. I did think of my virginity, how I was taught, and how I overcame it, not caring because of our love.* She laughed. *Oh, how I wanted to take a shower – with you. We were too afraid we would wake the family. Did they ever guess what we were doing? Greg, that morning shower after you sneaked to your room, was a cleansing of doubt, of hesitation. I committed myself to you and NO ONE. NO ONE – will ever take you from me.*

After her musings she went with her mother to the hospital to see Luke, lying fretfully waiting for them. Occasionally when he looked at Maureen and Brigit he thought he was seeing twins. No one could take Maureen or his daughters from him. He did not want to believe his doctors, for he did not want to leave them behind. He would not. Brigit would see to that. And then there was Anne, Sister Angelina, who sent whatever she thought he might be able to digest, though many time the nurses took her small gifts from him. She wrote him notes of how she prayed for him; and occasionally, accompanied by another nun, she would receive permission from Mother Superior to visit her father.

Luke, thinking of the past, appreciated the wealth of his life, especially when they walked in the room, Maureen kissing him on the lips, Brigit on the cheek, and soothingly running her hand across his chest and face. "I'll make you well, daddy. Believe me I will." He smiled at her certainty and his wish.

That night Brigit sat alone again on their front porch swing, above a valley where from a distance lights were seen but rising above them the dark peaked shadows of mountains, a Southwest night of a dark sky adorned by the myriad of stars, the entire universe laid out for her. She lay back on the swing, smiling, causing the glide to move gently. She placed her hand on one breast, then the other, passed it over herself, imagining it was Gregory. She was with him. She reached for the button nearest her neck, unbuttoned until she reached above her bra, stopped, realizing it was fantasy, smiled and whispered, "I love you."

It was then she decided that no matter how long it would take her to cure her father, she would go back east to see Gregory who had been asking her in letters to come to Boston and Maine just for short stays.

~

Brigit decided she wanted to spend right after Christmas through New Year's 1948, in Cape Astraea with Gregory. It was the last of many vacation times, the end of his class studies and start of clinical introduction. After that there would be little time, but they had written and promised one another they would manage.

Luke was at home now, and Brigit felt she could leave him for a week, though she worried about his nursing. She decided, however, that Maureen had become fairly well accustomed to looking after his needs for that short time. She seemed to forget her mother's strength even in her sadness that Brigit saw each day, the fear. It burned in Brigit, but there were times the two women would sit together, holding one another, softly crying, their hands caressing through each other's hair, kissing cheeks. Brigit prepared Maureen, giving instructions, Maureen occasionally smiling and telling her, "I know, dear. You go to your boy. If I need help, I'll call the doctor and even your sisters. You need your love. I see it, feel it in you every day, that desire to be with him, that loneliness. You deserve the time with him. Go and don't worry. Besides, isn't this probably Gregory's last whole week's vacation before his clinical work? You seem to forget how much you have told me and how much you talk about him. Don't you think I know how lonely it can get, what it was like for me before your father and I were married? I would lie in my room at night and imagine him holding me, talking to me." Her eyes teared. "And now, my darling, I'm going to lose him. It is going to happen. But it still makes no difference, does it? C'mon, let's not be morbid. You are going, and you are going to be happy."

Brigit flew to Boston. When she took the train to Portland, she purposely sat by a window so she would see the countryside and the snow that, despite the cold, she missed. She enjoyed New England and the changing seasons. More, she longed to watch the winter sea, believing because of some unknown spirit she would gather more strength, more curative power from across that windy cold ocean. She would never tell anyone what she believed or why she felt this, for she could not explain it to herself. It was a feeling, a knowledge and sensitivity that had been born with her from ancient times. She did not realize this yet. Was she real? Her feelings, though, were real, how she sensed others, her agile mind that understood not only her emotions but those in other women and men. In this way, perhaps she was no different from other women. But she was aware of something others weren't. Perhaps this would protect her in later years, even protect a loved one like Gregory.

When Gregory met her at the train, he watched her as she held the car's exit handle, how, in a short passage of time, she stepped down carefully, her hip pointed outward, her long, slim leg stretched attractively, sensually, her skirt pulled up above her knee. She stepped on to the platform, quickly straightened her skirt, all the while smiling, looking for Gregory. Some men, as was usual and what she expected, passed her, turning to look, perhaps wishing they knew her. They reminded her of the naval hospital, unpleasant remarks, disgusting voices, and scenes that would never be forgotten.

While she was temporarily lost in those thoughts, Gregory rushed to her, and they were hugging, kissing, unwilling to let go except that they became self-conscious as people passed, looked, smiled. It was as though the war was still in the minds of all.

The three-quarter hour ride to Cape Astraea was talk of both homes, their parents, brothers, sisters and then just about the two of them and how they would use the vacation.

Brigit concentrated on his profile, thinking how endearing it was. Intuitively she placed her hand on his neck, moved closer, putting her hand on his thigh and kissing him on the neck and below his ear. He hunched his shoulders. Watching him, she laughed and whispered, "Will you come to my room?"

"Don't do that to me when I'm driving."

"Poor baby." She enjoyed the sound of his voice, his accent so different from hers. Suddenly she asked, "Do you still sing? You used to sing to me."

"I'm too busy at school. Fool. Sure I do, but not as I do to you."

She stopped teasing him, thinking of the few inches difference in height between them, how easy it was to raise her head and mouth for their lips to meet. "I want to kiss you right now."

"We'll crash."

"No good. But I still want to, and I want your hands caressing me. Are you getting excited?"

Gregory smiled, looked at her, brushed his hand over her face, "How was I ever so lucky? And if you aren't more careful, I know where there's a wooded path where I could take you."

"You mean you never took me there? Why not? Oh. It was special for you and Lynne. I know men like you. Do you ever hear from her? I do. She's in the med school hospital in San Francisco, loves it there."

"Truthfully, yes, I took her there. Do I hear from her? Never. Do I hear about her? Yes. From her folks." He forced a short laugh. "She's terribly attractive. What a woman. Her mother showed me her latest photo. Jealous?"

"A little. Is she really as lovely as when she and I went to school?"

"Brigit. Don't take me seriously. Yes, She's just as attractive, more so. But beautiful. No. I fell in love with a beauty."

"Then it's just my looks you're interested in."

"Well, no. Dearest, if it ever comes to that, you should leave me." Gregory slowed the car before coming into town, pulled under a tree that he hoped hid them, turned and gently moved her face toward his, and kissed her. "I'll never leave you, give you up."

As she kissed him, an unpleasantness occurred to her. *I wonder*, and her jealousy rose as she thought back when she threatened that imagined unknown woman. "Love me, Gregory. Be faithful. I'll always be to you."

"Silly. What's wrong? Look at your face. It's almost drawn. Why?"

"I was thinking of my father," she lied. She bent his head toward her and kissed him hard, long, he responding, placed her tongue in his mouth, in his ear, wanting to see him shudder. He did. "Yes. You do love me. I have it. When you become a doctor, I can be your office nurse. O.K.?"

"It's a deal. But when you have kids, what then?"

"We'll think about that a bit later," she smiled. Then she laughed. "I can be my own midwife." She grimaced a bit thinking of the delivery room and some of the women who had suffered so. She would not be like that.

"We've got to get home."

Why am I thinking of fate? What does it hold or portend? "Look. There's your folks and Mary. You're a fortunate fellow, and don't you ever hurt them." *Am I thinking of myself?*

"I never will. That too's a promise."

Chapter IV

Toward Tomorrow

On New Year's Eve, Gregory and Brigit went to a Portland Hotel with the Hurwitzes. Brigit wore a strapless black gown, lacy at the slightly emphasized breast line and cut just above her ankles. She danced with Aaron Hurwitz and Greg, drank only ginger ale. She, Mary, and Jocelyn chatted throughout the night, occasionally seriously, mostly lightly, laughing with one another and about Aaron and Gregory, teasing them, cautioning them not to drink too much. Only at one point was politics mentioned when Aaron brought up the coming November election. The Republicans controlled the Congress, and certainly that would give an advantage to Dewey. There was immediate disagreement, Aaron laughing because he had started a brief debate. Suddenly Jocelyn, to change the conversation, raised her glass to the family while looking at Gregory, Mary, and Brigit with bright and loving eyes. Hers was a feeling of comfort and satisfaction not only with herself but with her family. She included Brigit as a member for she felt so warmly toward her. The two loved one another. Often Brigit would talk to her in confidence about her feelings, what she was thinking, pleased that Jocelyn had become a second mother, despite the wait for marriage. Jocelyn looked about the table, raised her hand to her lips as a kiss to Aaron, and spoke, "To my children. May nothing ever again interfere with their happiness, disrupt their plans, and may they be happy together." She paused. "And my Mary, may you find what you seek and if there is that only one in your future" - she paused - "I know there is. May you be happy, ignoring the criticisms and often hatred, in your growing SUCCESSFUL career in medicine. I love you all." Having learned self-control in public, she suddenly lost a bit as her family watched tears forming. Aaron got up and kissed her cheek.

How long does happiness last? Gregory was thinking.

And Brigit, despite her enjoyment, felt a chill, and unknowingly repeated Gregory. *How long does happiness last? Perhaps we should marry now. His folks may object, I suppose, but they wouldn't be angry at us. Should I talk to Greg? What a foolish woman you are.* Yet, her mind appeared to close at the thought of losing Greg, and her heart beat a little faster with some unknown fear grasping at her. She decided she was allowing her emotions too much sway. Looking at Jocelyn, she told herself *I am going to be like her, firm and always sure of myself. I learned that certainly while in nursing school. Nurse yourself, Brigit. You're too sensitive to what might happen, not to what is happening and what you know you can control.*

She felt a hand sliding gently on her bare arm. "So deep in thought, sweet. Come'n, let's dance some more. I love the way you glide and you fit so well in my arms. I want them around that slim, beautiful waist. You see, what school has done to me. I'm being anatomical."

She smiled at him and rose from the table. As they danced to the middle of the floor, she rested her head on his shoulder. "Greg, we'll always be this way, won't we?" She laughed quietly. "Well, within the bounds of whatever happens to married people with time."

"Are you proposing to me? I haven't asked yet, you know."

"You will," and she secretly kicked his shoe.

"Ouch," he whispered.

"Well, that's a sample. Otherwise you'll leave me a ruined woman."

When they came home, they waited for everyone to go to bed. When it was quiet, they crept down the hall to her room, watching one another undress. She took him in her mouth, slipped her fingers about his testicles, stroked to the tip of his hard penis, lay back as he slipped into her, her eyes tightly closing to the streaking sensations of arousal throughout her.

After, laughing quietly with satisfaction, lying on their sides, she kissed his face, then raised herself to kiss his mouth. "You see, I'm right. You'll leave me a ruined woman. Don't you ever dare. There's a power in me you should be aware of," she smiled down at him, kissed him again.

"Oh, yes, you are powerful. I'm worn out. I'll be careful." Then he told her, "I don't want to go to my room. I want to stay here and sleep with you." He turned toward her, placing his arm across her, holding her breast.

~

They took the same train from Portland. Brigit would have to wait several hours at Logan Airport. "Are you looking forward to school?"

"You bet. I'm going to get into clinical studies." He thought for a moment. "You're worried about how you'll find your dad, aren't you?"

"Yes," and she answered more quickly, "But I'm going to cure him." She paused. "Oh, I wish I could. You have to meet my parents and sisters, you know. The next vacation, you come to the ranch. Promise me."

"Yes. We'll cure him together."

The countryside went by rapidly. It was about a two-hour ride.

"I used to build snow forts. My brothers would help me. And we had snowball fights while trying to duck behind the walls. Other times we would take my sled and coast. I miss that, the closeness. Now, I'm more fortunate. I have you."

His words enveloped her, and she wanted to hug him. She thought of Jocelyn and her apparent almost severe control, and said to herself, *If I can grow to be like her. She has that warmth in her that I feel right now, and she protects.*

At North Station in Boston, they kissed long, hugged, reluctant to leave one another. Outside, as Gregory watched their cold breath puffed in clouds toward the sky, he looked sadly at her, telling her there goes your plane above our clouds. He glanced at the grey sky, then back to her. She was trying not to cry but could not stop, sniffled, looked up at him, blinking, "No it's not a cold, is it? I need a handkerchief," as she searched through her pocket book. "Oh fiddle," and she could no longer help herself. "I'm going to cry, and that's all there is to it." She licked her lips, rubbed her nose as dry as possible. "Kiss me and hold me, damn you." She rarely even used that word. He held her, and she tried hard to settle, felt her body tremble, and whispered, "I love you, and don't you ever forget it"

"I promise I won't." He was crying now. "See the proof." And they both stood together, crying softly, knowing it would be a long while before they saw one another again, but this time in the Southwest.

Gregory took a cab to his rooms and Brigit one to Logan, he anxious to start his clinical clerkship come next semester.

In the taxi she took out her compact, lightly brushed her face with rouge and put her light red lipstick on her slightly full lips, brushed lightly with her finger at the corners of her eyes, smiled at herself in her small mirror, thinking *that's better. Now you look the way he likes you and you too. He also likes me without makeup, and why not? You're admiring yourself,* looking at herself again.

~

As much as he looked forward to clerkship, he rode back to his rooms somewhat morose. The thought of Brigit so far away was as though he would never see her again. He already missed her face, her enfolding voice, the sound that thrilled him as no other could, not even his mother's music, or, for that matter, his own. He thought of the nights they rode out into the countryside and he sang to her while she leaned on his shoulder. He shook his head. He had to think of the beginning of the week. He would be starting on the medicine floor. He would be able to talk and to write to her about his experiences, knowing she would understand what he was telling her, how the sick people affected him. He had already seen patients, and it came soon to him how he would have to become inured to the illnesses, the ulcerated skins, the stabbed or the shot, the cancers that ate away a body, the psychotics, those on the verge of psychosis. What bothered him most at the moment was the idea of being with birthing mothers. Again he thought of Brigit and making love to her, how they never thought of pregnancy but of their enjoyment. Well, occasionally she would say something afterwards when she felt the aftermath of his orgasms, hers, too, when her body had relaxed and she began to close and she realized what could happen despite their precautions. But this was not for now. He did not want to think about her or their love making, only the beauty of what she had given him, knowing she felt the same.

On Monday morning, there was a meeting of his classmates with the doctor who was taking over their introduction to medicine. He knew, from stories his father or brother told him, what it was like that first day, the nurses smiling, some trying to hide their amusement. But after several days came the general acceptance between both groups. However, the head nurse, a short, heavy-set woman with a pleasant face could be quite severe, almost as bad as the doctor who would grimace when one of them made an error or seemed not to be paying attention. It was to be from that nurse, particularly, that he would first learn how to soothe a patient.

One day he was standing at the nurse's station talking to a pretty one who had attracted him. Her powder-blue eyes seemed to have so many expressions. When they talked, they would look straight at each other, warming to and understanding through their eyes how each felt and what their good or bad days were like. And then she appeared.

"Hurwitz! Stop trying to make out with my nurses. You're here to learn. Are you becoming a doctor, hopefully" she growled derisively, "or a lover? My nurses work on this floor, and they don't need your distraction." In fact, Nurse Mayfield liked Gregory but could not help teasing him or keeping after him when he was on the floor and talking to that blue-eyed, shapely nurse so unlike Mayfield. She wore her uniforms as tightly as professionally possible. Then, he would ask himself if he were leading her on, despite being drawn to her, something of which she was quite aware. In fact she drew him on with her eyes, her movements, knowing her body and voice had trapped him. He did not count on Mayfield knowing about Brigit when Jocelyn came one day to find him in the hospital before she had a performance that night.

Jocelyn had sought out Mayfield, wanting to know how her son was doing. It was close to the end on the medical floor. Mayfield told her that Nurse Littleton had made a conquest, perhaps Gregory had. Jocelyn looked at her quizzically.

"Has he been going out with her?"

"I'm not sure. They certainly spend a little time together on my floor and irritate me."

Jocelyn did not want to believe her. She loved Brigit. She was Jocelyn's second daughter, hoped she would be legally, even if it was a way in the future. Jocelyn hesitated.

"Break them up," she firmly told Mayfield. "I'll talk to him too," she said even though it was against her belief that she should interfere in such ways with her children; worse, talk to a stranger so. After all, he was no longer a boy, not her responsibility, only another of her children she cherished and wanted to protect. Although Brigit saw severity in her, and it was there, there was softness that enfolded all she loved. She would protect Brigit as she would her own children.

Mayfield was astonished by Jocelyn's firmness. "That's not up to me, Mrs. Hurwitz." In fact, Mayfield felt Jocelyn was taking advantage of her. Jocelyn sensed her reaction and was further appalled at herself.

"I know it's not your responsibility. You see, he has an outstanding girl friend." Again she hesitated. "I don't want him going astray and hurting her." As she said that, Jocelyn knew there was something unusual about Brigit which she could not quite define at the moment. She continued, however. "But men, what they see, what they can get, and, yes, he's my son, but he's a man." Jocelyn surprised herself still more that she spoke so openly to a stranger. She sought her self-control.

"I can't do anything," Mayfield repeated. "My responsibility is the nurses on the floor and to be certain they take care of their patients properly. I can't help you."

Jocelyn's face colored. She could not believe she had spoken as she had, had not been as restrained and firm with herself as she was accustomed. Perhaps it was nervousness about tonight's performance; because she was thinking of retiring and that this could be her last public appearance. What she was thinking about she very well knew, the hurt she had experienced when Aaron had strayed, how it nearly destroyed her. It was one of the reasons they moved to Maine, despite the inconvenience for Aaron and her. Perhaps distance would make it easier for him, but she hoped the state he loved and where he was calmer and enjoyed the fishing would help him regain his obligation to the woman he loved more than one who had briefly taken him away. She did not want to see that in her sons or to have it happen to Mary with perhaps a chosen woman, or for that matter, her sons with an unfaithful wife. This was more important to Jocelyn than the rest of the world.

She looked away from Mayfield and down a long corridor to a window overlooking the Charles.

In that world out there, outside her family, the medical school and the hospital, there was continuing turmoil. The election of 1948 was coming. The Russians were as bad as they had been when they drove into Europe. They had enslaved Czechoslovakia. Later in the year the UN would declare the Israeli State and the Arabs and Jews with their hatreds killing one another. Later, in 1961 they would erect the Berlin Wall with people being shot for trying to escape from East Germany. So how much had the world truly changed from the end of the war?

In the meantime, after the performance, she would, as usual, be staying at The Condon Hotel. If she missed Gregory because of his schedule, he could, if possible, meet her there. She would also leave a ticket for him at Symphony Hall should he be able to attend the concert.

She thought of apologizing to Mayfield for her personal release but did not. It had been an unrecallable error on Jocelyn's part, and she would not apologize to anyone. Love nor cherishing need no apologies.

Gregory had no idea his mother had been in the hospital. He and other students had been with one of his professor doctors on another medical floor where more severely ill patients had rooms. They were in the room where lay a veteran of the war who had suffered shell shock. When he returned to the United States he had begun drinking more than anything he could get in Europe. His war had been long, having been a paratrooper dropped behind the lines just before the D-Day landings. He then fought his way across France and collapsed just before the crossing of the Rhine and the push into Aachen. Having been hospitalized in England and then sent back to a VA hospital near Boston, he was finally medically and honorably discharged. His family did all it could to make him feel safe, but could not stop his drinking. He tried Alcoholics Anonymous once or twice but failed at that, despite the help the members tried to give him. Now he lay in the hospital with a bleeding liver. Blood dripped constantly from an IV. Gregory listened to the man's history, looked at the paleness and shrunken cheeks, picking up the blanket when told to do so and saw the bony legs and wasted body. He started to choke, imagining himself in the bed, feeling the obscenity of what had happened to him and to so many of them. The doctor watched Gregory, started to ask him a medical question, then went to him and quietly told him to leave the room, seeing Gregory's tears and the slight trembling. The others looked at him. There were one or two veterans among the group but only one had been overseas. All looked away and pretended to be examining the patient. Gregory went into the hall, looked about and allowed his tears to flow, cursing the war, what had happened to him and to the man lying there dying. About two days later the man was dead. Gregory could not forget him, never would; and occasionally in his own illness, a vision of the man appeared to him. He began to wonder whether he cared to be in primary care for a specialty. He decided to call Brigit.

He told her of his experience on the wards.

"Greg, you aren't even started. You still have a long way to go, and there will be many more such experiences. Are you going to quit medical school? I remember what it was like for me, and I didn't go through what you must. For someone who has gone through what you have, who has seen what you have, a man dying in a hospital is sad and often terrible to watch. C'mon."

Gregory felt his face redden and was glad she couldn't see him. He was not only embarrassed that he told her but that he reacted as he did. Yet, it was going to be that continuing nightmare. It may have been because it was the first time in a hospital that he felt helpless, that he was a student who created his own unpreparedness for the sights he would witness.

"Brigit, I'm sorry. I shouldn't have told you. You're right. I'm behaving like an innocent."

As he lay in his bed thinking back to that time and the call, he imagined himself wasting away. He lifted the sheet covering him on the warm summer day to look at his body. He had lost weight, but it was still much the same body that thrilled Brigit, that aroused her.

He saw her now, felt her running her fingers through his hair, down about his body. That short call and the desire to visit her in the Southwest were as vivid as on that day years ago.

"When I have time, I'm coming to see you, even if it's only for a few days. I want to lie beside you. I dream about you too. They are some dreams but so frustrating."

She laughed. "You see the power I have over you from such a distance? You can never escape me. Was it a real sexy one?"

"You know it, you idiot. I was . . ." He stopped.

"You were what?"

"Deep inside."

"As long as it wasn't another nurse or one of the medical students, you may keep dreaming."

"I promise. I've got to go, but remember I love you, that you're mine. You don't need one of those cowboys that you live near.

"Brigit, your dad. How is he?"

"Well, you know that cancer they thought was spreading. It isn't. One of the radiologists reading the plates made an error. I told you I would cure him." And she laughed. "Well, it's not gone, but it isn't spreading. I want my mother and dad to think about having his pancreas out now. Imagine that guy telling us it was spreading to his - to his intestines and lymph nodes. I could kill the guy. There we were, my sisters, Ellen and Marie, my mother, and I, crying. It was like a wake. Greg, I despise that radiologist. Sure, anyone can make a mistake, but if you had seen the four of us so distraught. I think there was a pool of tears at our feet. They'll operate on him pretty soon."

And in his next round, Gregory was in surgery. There were myriads of operations. Some of the doctors brought their own scrub nurses. Most used those who worked for the hospital. Gregory had earned praise for his work on the medical floors and the same was expected of him in surgery. His first assignment was with a thoracic surgeon.

The surgeon told him to come closer for better observation. There was hardly any conversation except for the surgeon explaining to Gregory throughout the procedure what he was doing, occasionally asking what part of the lung they were looking at, what did Gregory anticipate would be the next move for excision of the tumor. "Well, what do you think? He's breathing O.K. His heart rate's consistent; the anesthesiologist believes I can go on."

"I'd say go ahead and cut it out."

"You're right," and the scrub and the doctor both laughed. "I start with the fairly easy questions first. You know, if this is all that grows and I have it all, she's going to be all right. It may be that in some of the procedures you watch, some one other than the surgeon will close. I always do my own."

When they finished and an orderly was cleaning up the room and the nurses cleaning their instruments, the surgeon took Gregory to the dressing room, and in a soft, gentle voice, explained the entire case, going beyond what they had discussed together in the OR. "You're not a thoracic surgeon yet, but you asked the right questions. Good fellow. I hope the rest of your time here will be just as good."

Gregory was proud of himself because of the compliment. As time progressed, he saw D&Cs, vein excisions, breast lumpectomies, breast or testicular cancer, removal of the breast that hurt him, thinking of what the woman would experience with that loss and the attempt to keep her alive, hopefully for years. There were also epididymis repairs, appendix cases, limb removals. It went on. He aided in the operations, holding instruments, cutting sutures. With the progression of his rotation, the surgeons would allow him to suture. He returned in his mind to the naval hospital and the wounded who did or did not recover, thought of the men with whom he became close and the manner in which they kidded one another but hiding their fear of the future as cripples. There were times during his schooling when students would ask Gregory what happened to him during the war that he limped. It was natural curiosity; but there were times he believed they felt sorry for him. He hated that.

When the year came to an end, it was still closer to the election, the Truman, Dewey tangle. Gregory enjoyed watching the conventions but could not stand the spite that came through in speeches. He was to have a short time off after the voting that would allow him to see Brigit.

Gregory voted absentee for Truman who had also been his commander-in-chief and whose honesty he appreciated. Then there was the foolishness of the *Chicago Tribune* announcing Dewey's victory and Harry Truman never believing he would lose. He didn't.

There had been the beginning of the Berlin Airlift of which most Americans were proud. It would take a man like Truman to see that through, World War II planes remodeled and flyable, daring the Russians and making the Russians look like the barbarians Gregory thought they were. His brother James had met up with the Russians and despised them. He often spoke of their gruffness and lack of manners, their officiousness.

Then there was Truman's courage going against Marshall and recognizing Israel. Why not a vote for this courageous, clear-sighted man, despite his lack of Hyde Park manners?

"Yes, we were fortunate to have had Commander in Chiefs FDR and Truman," Gregory throughout the election time repeated to himself and in arguments with those who wanted Dewey. It was then he learned there would come a day when as a doctor he would have to be cautious when it came to discussions of politics.

Thank goodness Brigit and her family supported Truman. I can't wait to get there. Will we get along? Why not? What is her world like? How will I take to it?

~

Gregory took a plane to El Paso from where Brigit had told him they would drive to her home. He landed late in the afternoon. Brigit watching the plane land became more excited. She had fussed in the morning with her hair and what she would wear, bothered Maureen with what Maureen liked. Finally, in the afternoon, after sitting and putting on her makeup and spraying her perfume lightly and placing some on her wrist, she chose a reddish-green dress that came just below her knees and that matched her hair and eyes as well as possible. She brushed at her hair that came just above her shoulders thinking how he liked her hair, looked first at her eyes, to her breasts that were emphasized by her cinched waist and then, as always looked at her hips and legs. She was proud of her looks and her figure. She wore an expensive perfume that he had always liked.

As she stood at the gate waiting, she imagined him already with his arms about her, placing his face in her hair and smelling the scent of her. She also had a surprise for him.

The plane came over desert that Gregory had never seen, dropped below mountains that surrounded the city, noticing a road that curved down into the valley. The plane landed smoothly. Impatiently he waited for the passengers in front of him, finally walked down the stairs. When he saw her waving, his heart beat faster.

They were kissing unashamedly, hugging. He moved back for a moment to look at her. "My Brigit. You're beautiful. I thought coming from Chicago the plane was taking too long." He moved closer to her again, kissed her below her ear, wanting to inhale her scent as though he had forgotten it and forever wanted to remember. After he got his baggage, she told him she was going to take him to eat. "You are somewhat hungry, aren't you?"

"Somewhat."

"Well, by the time we get to Las Cruces you'll be more so."

They drove northward through the desert and into the small town. She laughed. "People think of this as Billy the Kid country. All I can think of is home. They drove by the jail in Old

Mesilla. "That's where he's supposed to have been kept and then broke out of. Exciting, huh?"

"Well, I've always liked Westerns but never had any sympathy for him. Forget all that. I can't realize I'm sitting beside you. I want to grab you to make sure you're real." He placed his hand on her arm. She felt the enjoyable pleasure of his touch, the flowing of desire. She drove into a side street, looked to see if there was anyone, and stopped the car, moved toward him, placed her hand on his face, turned it toward her and kissed him, placing her tongue in his mouth, holding him tightly." She let go. "We can't do this where people will see us and who probably know me." She smiled. "Are you excited?" She placed her hand at his zipper, smiled at what she felt, moved back to the steering wheel. "I've teased you enough. C'mon. I'm taking you to a Mexican restaurant. You have to experience the Southwest."

While she had been talking he was looking upward toward the mountains. What's up there?"

"The Organ Mountains is what you've been looking at. And up within them is Cloudcroft. I intend to take you up there. It's lovely. You'll think you're back in New England. The woods are filled with aspen trees, ponderosa pine, oak. I know you'll think of birch when you see the aspen. People build cottages there or houses. I won't say more.

"Oops. Here's the restaurant."

She ordered beef fajitas with black beans. To comfort him, she ordered tea. Before the food arrived, the tan-skinned waitress brought them salsa and tortilla chips.

"Now, my dear, take a chip and dip it in the salsa. Careful, don't put too much on."

He did as she told him, bit, and screwed up his face. "My God, what are you trying to do to me?" His mouth burned.

She smiled. "I'm getting you accustomed to the great

Southwest. After all, I may want to lure you here to practice."

"This is a lure? A fish would spit it out. What's the meal like?"

"Listen, child. Eat slowly and enjoy the meat, beans and guacamole. I swear you'll like it."

When the meal came, she gave him instructions, watched as he cautiously picked through the beans and the meat. "Brigit. I swear you're trying to kill me."

"And I swear, just eat the meal, and you'll become a lover of Mexican food and miss it when you go back home. Besides, you'll remember the meal and me. Oh, maybe not with love, but love will take over."

As they left the restaurant, and he was looking about at the town and the people, he listened to the Spanish, and looked at the women, many very attractive, many with bodies or faces quite ordinary, people like any others of the great white race. In fact, the mixture of Mexican (for that is what they were called even though so many were born here, were here so long before the land became part of the United States) and whites fascinated him.

"Stop looking at all the women. I'm here." She pulled on his arm that she was holding as they walked to the car.

"I won't ever forget you're with me. I'm tantalized by the difference,"

She smiled. "I expected you to be. There's so much to see. The Indian culture, their art work, the Mexican, our own. I love it here, and actually wish sometimes that when we marry we'd come to live here. But I know where you're headed. It's not just that you want to be in Boston and Maine. It's the work you told me in a letter you think you may want to do. You won't be able to do that here. When my dad is better or close, I'll return to be with you. It's horrible."

When they got in the car, she told him. "Kiss me. I don't care who sees us." He did and they held their lips together. When they parted, she continued, "I can't stay here when you are there. I have to be with you. I'm shameless."

"No you aren't. You're honest and know I want you with me."

When they came to the ranch, she drove along a short road leading to the adobe house. It was two stories and spread widely along the land. Beyond it lay land, mostly with alfalfa. Beyond that would be the cotton. But his attention was on the house. He imagined Brigit growing up here and playing with her sisters. Inside, was an entrance hall where Maureen met them. The ceiling was beamed, as were other rooms. The furniture was as one would find in many eastern homes. There were drapes and curtains in the rooms he could see.

Maureen smiled, pleased that he looked as Brigit had described him. Yet, she was the wary mother. She was attracted to him, as was he to her. The resemblance between Brigit and Maureen amazed and pleased him. She held out her hand, not as neatly manicured as was Brigit's. But then, Brigit kept her nails as she usually had since nursing school.

"We're happy to have you, Gregory. Obviously, we keep hearing about you. I hope you won't mind but I invited my daughters and their families for supper. I suppose I could have waited, but I thought, let's have you meet the whole family except for Anne, Sister Angelina, and then we can be alone for the few days you're here. Now come. I'll take you to meet Brigit's father. Manuel will take care of your luggage."

They went to the next floor and her parents' room. In the bed, the former well-built man lay weak and pale, his body thinner. It was something to which Maureen and the daughters had had to become accustomed. He was still recovering from the surgery of a month ago when they removed the pancreas and, for safety, a few lymph nodes. He had expected to be dead by now. With Brigit's care, he had become more comfortable, less scared of his future of wondering what the family would be without him, in what ways they would miss him. He felt good they would be left well off. The ranch was a successful venture. He knew Maureen was strong and could run the business and get the help she needed. Then there were also his sons-in-law.

Now here he was facing a new stranger who would take his daughter to a Christian-Jewish home. Jewish. He was raised Jewish. How different was he?

Brigit and Gregory followed Maureen into the room.

"Luke. Here's Brigit's Gregory." She forced a smile when she looked at her husband whose face scared her. She still wondered whether he would recover, what she would do without him. She continually imagined herself alone in that bed. If anything happened to him, she would have it thrown out of the house. She shook her head, brought herself to reality and her daughter and probable new son-in-law. She had set chairs near the bed so they could talk.

"Father. This is Gregory."

Luke raised his arm to give his hand, his eyes still able to analyze a person. He watched Gregory as he took Luke's weak shake. He liked the certainty he saw in Gregory, his lack of hesitance in taking his hand. Then Luke thought, *But he's a medical student and should be used to seeing dead, dying, recovering sick.* Yet, he was aware that this was a man who had seen war, whom his daughter had helped recover and who now was going to join her in a profession he had finally come to admire while in the hospital, except for that one radiological mistake.

"I'm pleased to meet you, Mr. Donovan," Gregory said before Luke could speak. "I've waited a long time for this."

"Me too. What do you think of our part of the country?"

"Well, I already know the food can kill me."

Luke laughed weakly. "She said she was going to do that to

you." Then he looked more closely at Gregory, then at Brigit. *Is he good enough for my elegant daughter? They are both handsome. But it's not just looks, Luke. Yeah, I know all about his family. He'll look at us like what we are, just a bunch of farmers.* He knew, though, that Brigit had already met his family and that they liked her. She had told him they were good people, no fuss about them, no pretenses. They were just who they were and that they accepted her. She had told him how Jocelyn treated her like her own daughter, how good Mary and Aaron had been to her.

"Tell me something, Gregory. Do you adhere to your religion?" It was typical Luke.

Brigit's and Maureen's faces colored, Brigit's heart beating harder than it had been anticipating the introductions. Brigit pulled on her mother's arm. Maureen looked at her, shook her head negatively and started to put her finger to her lip and stopped herself. He would have said it at some point anyhow. Might as well be now.

His remark made no visible impression on Gregory. Luke was facing a future son-in-law who was certain of himself. "I was raised Jewish. I'm sure you've heard of Bar Mitzvah. Well, I was. If you want to know or are uncertain of what your Brigit and I will do with children, I don't know. That's up to us. My Catholic mother brought up five children in the Jewish religion because she loved it. I don't know what the future will be any more than you." Gregory's voice was soft and firm. It seemed to Brigit that he had thought about this happening anyhow. In fact, she started to smile and tried to hide it, thinking of his reaction to the Mexican food. It may have burned, but he could accept and smile and joke.

"I see," Luke answered. "And what if my wife and I object?"

"I don't think you will. I know you questioned Brigit going with me, but you accepted that. I know you are a man of strong opinions. I know you want to find out more about me. You should. But I won't back down from Brigit or what you may not like. I want your acceptance, yours and Mrs. Donovan's." Gregory stopped, looking more intensely at the sick man, wondering whether he had said too much, whether he had upset him. Gregory thought, *What a terrible start.*

Luke showed no emotion, then spoke. "You love my daughter. You make a good- looking couple. That's not all there is to it, as you know." He smiled. "You know, Gregory, we Southwesterners always have to take the measure of a man."

"Isn't that true for everyone anywhere."

" Are you upset?"

Firmly, "No." He paused. "In fact, I expected it but not just so soon; Brigit told me how important your religion is to you. You have a daughter who's a nun. Do you think that bothers me? Don't forget what you know about my family. One day we'll all meet, I hope. When you are better and strong enough, I hope you'll come visit us and see how and where I live."

"What are you all going to do here?"

Brigit interrupted. "Dad. He's only here a few days. If we can, we'll go up to Albuquerque. And tomorrow afternoon, I'm taking him to Cloudcroft. We'll camp over night - or maybe the other way around."

Luke and Maureen looked at one another. Maureen knew they had already been sleeping together, could see it in her daughter. Maureen tried to keep her husband quiet by looking sternly at him.

" Alone? The two of you?"

"Yes, dad,"

He shook his head. "You've already forgotten what the nuns taught you."

Again Brigit's face colored, this time with anger. "I'm a woman, dad. I think I know how to take care of myself." She calmed a little and almost said, "I'm not the virgin Mary." She looked at her mother, pleading for her to stop him.

Maureen saw her. "Luke, stop now. She's a grown woman, and she can do what she wants. You think they're going to take the family with them wherever they go? Be pleasant."

"I am. I just have to ask questions. Nope. She's a grown woman. Any man can see that, even her father." He started to say something about pregnancy but stopped. *Even if that happened, she would always be my daughter. Besides, she's a good person and she wouldn't be loose. Calm down and be a good host. I never knew a Jew, don't know a damn thing about them except what I've heard, and that's not comforting. But I like that guy. I like his calm sureness. Probably would be good on the ranch.*

That last thought was one of resignation and acceptance. He looked at Maureen. *Women know about women, but why the hell should I know what she does? It's none of my business or is it?*

~

The dinner went well. Ellen and Marie came in excitedly and didn't hesitate hugging Gregory. Their husbands smiled, held back until the women finished their opening chatter, and welcomed Greg with smiles.

Maureen as always, despite company, first served what food Luke could eat to make certain he ate and drank water. After that evening ritual, she went to her family.

It was a large dining room with beamed ceilings and large furniture. Celestina, the maid, served the meal during which questions went back and forth across around the table. What did Gregory think so far of this country so new to him, what medical school was like, what his parents were like, even though they had heard it from Brigit? Then came the usual, "Where are you going? What are you going to do?"

There was a silence when Ellen's husband asked, "What do

Jews do when they pray?"

Daniel stunned Maureen who looked at him thinking of what she would like to say but held back. *Why don't you find out for yourself? You fool. Insulting Brigit and Gregory.*

Brigit started to answer but Gregory stopped her. "We pray like anyone else with our own ancient customs, depending what we consider ourselves, Orthodox, Conservative, Reform. Do you believe in God?" Before Daniel could answer, Gregory told him, "I sometimes do and sometimes don't believe in God. My mother who's Catholic, by the way, believes in God. My father and sister - they're Jews, you know, believe in God. In fact, as I recall, Jesus was a Jew. Do you know much about his life? I should think so. Do you go to church? I assume so. Do I care? No. You worship as you please, and I'll do the same. You know, we fought a war for religious freedom and just plain freedom. You recall that?" Gregory was getting truly angry. He felt Brigit grasp his thigh under the table.

"Let's stop this," Maureen interrupted. "I won't have this at my table, have a meal ruined, a guest insulted - especially if he's a future son-in-law. We are a family. Have you forgotten, Daniel?"

"I'm sorry, mother. I wasn't trying to start an argument. I was just curious." He looked at Gregory and Brigit. "I apologize if I insulted anyone."

"Forget it, Daniel. I admit I was getting a little hot under the collar. Let's just accept one another as we are. We may or may not like each other, but we'll find out soon enough. But for Brigit and her parents and all of you, I'll always be there for you." He chuckled. "At least that's what I intend."

Everyone settled and the chatter resumed. Yet, Brigit and Gregory, before they went to their rooms, sat and talked some about it. "Greg, they're not anti-Semitic. They're perhaps ignorant, but wasn't I until you taught me and took me to

Maine?"

"I'm not worried about it, dear. I just want you, and I want your parents to accept me. The entire family would be good. I'll work at it, if it's necessary. Promise."

Maureen had already soothed him. She wanted him to know she cared for him because of Brigit, though they both knew it would take time to know one another.

They were standing in the hall in front of her bedroom door that was next to his. Before she entered, he moved toward her, placed a hand on her breast, then about her waist. "I love you. I want you." He hesitated, "I wish . . . ."

"I do too," as she placed her arms about his neck, kissed him, and told him quietly, "Wait until we go away. Wait a minute. Is that the only reason to see more of the state?" She paused, breathing a bit more heavily from desire, moving back from him, whispering, "Suddenly I'm thinking of when you were in the hospital and knew I was falling in love with you."

"Well, that's one answer, but what I was going to say is that I wish we could be together tonight."

He could not see the pleased flush and brightening of her eyes. She placed her arms about his neck. In a whisper, she told him, "Agreed."

They stood for a while, kissing, hugging, moving against one another, whispering adoring words. She then moved away from him, aroused, feeling heat throughout her body, that jelly feeling in her abdomen, as she described it, and the flow within her. "I think we should go to bed. We're getting up early so we can get to Albuquerque."

~

They drove across the desert. She took him off the road to go toward Alamogordo and White Sands for a sight unlike any in the United States. He asked her to stop. They left the car and stood admiring the dunes, she still amazed by the whiteness and he captivated by the contrasting land and sky. In fact, he felt that way about the desert, the longer they drove northward. He was now driving, and he enjoyed the freedom of speeding at 70 and 80 miles an hour, thinking to himself, *Were we to go off the road, we would hit nothing but sand.* He slowed. The sand could wreck them.

"Are you getting tired, Greg?"

"No. I want to drive fast. Have you ever seen any wrecks along this road?"

"Yes. Reckless head-ons, rarely one on the side of the road. Well, you are driving faster than I would, but that's what the desert does to you. Sometimes people drive faster just to get over it and get where they're going. We're almost there anyhow. Why don't you let me drive again so you can see as we enter the city?"

Mountains also surrounded Albuquerque. He saw dots of houses on the mountainside. There was a train station where Indian women sold the cheaper jewelry to exiting passengers. There was the Indian Museum that she wanted him to see, as well as that at the University of New Mexico. But how much time would they have? She'd make sure they went to the Indian first. She not only enjoyed it but also occasionally bought something there, whether pottery or jewelry that she liked. She would also take him to Old Town where she liked the artistry.

They drove to the motel she had chosen. She thought perhaps they would have dinner there. Lunch would be in Old Town. Now settled in her plans, they registered, went to their room and lay down to rest for a while. She glanced at him. "Are you tired?"

"Nope. It's nice to rest, though, after the drive. I like it here." He lay on his side, looking at her admiringly. "I'm a lucky fellow, Brigit. Do you think your parents like me?"

"Well, I know my mom does. She told me. My dad? He's got to get used to you. They're both a little wary of the religion thing. I hate that. You know what though? I was thinking I'd take you to church, just for a few minutes, so I can light a candle for you and me. Would you mind? We could do that in Old Town."

"No. I don't mind. I've done that with my mother. There was one time during the war, just before I went that she took my dad, Mary, and me. James and Matthew were already gone. It was so terrible for my parents. Yours were lucky having all girls."

She laughed. "You think so? Well I wonder how they felt listening to us as we grew older, jealous of what one or the other had, and the screeching. It was a mad house of females. They had to have been terribly relieved when they knew the nuns controlled us and they could have some peace." She paused. "I didn't like the convent." She looked at him. "Funny, isn't it? I liked Father Emanuel who came for mass, and when he would talk to us I was always sorry to see him go. But then, I don't know. I thought the nuns were too strict. One would hit us with a ruler when we misbehaved. And from the time when we had our first periods. Warning, warning, warning. And now you, Greg." She made a fist and brought it lightly down on his side. "You've taken my chastity. I've sinned." She sounded almost repentant. She lay back, thinking. *Am I really damned to Hell? God wouldn't do that to me, to any woman who truly loved.* She turned to him again. "You and I have sinned, I guess; but I can't accept that. Not when we love the way we do."

There was silence. Gregory reached and turned her face toward him. "Just think of one thing. I love you, and whatever we do is good." He stopped. "Listen, we're well in our twenties. We're human beings. And if you want to believe in your Bible, well that's fine. But don't cover us with regret and sin. I don't believe all that. You know that. And you. You could never sin, whatever sin is."

She smiled at him. "Sometimes I think we're such worlds apart that I wonder what we're doing together. Oh. This is getting too serious. I'll ruin the trip." She thought a moment. "But I have to tell you. My mother wondered, and I know she wanted to ask me. Then the way she looked at me. She knows, and I don't think she cares as long as I don't get pregnant. My dad would be furious and hate you, blame you. Greg, why can't I stop thinking about this?"

"I said it already. We're a man and woman in love, pledged to one another. Don't try to make me believe in sin." He was obviously getting angry.

"I just wanted to talk about the way I feel, what I think about. Maybe it's because since I came back here and have been working at Hotel Santé. That was a mistake. I should have gone to Southwestern. I'm sorry. Forgive me." She turned on her side again and pulled him toward her. "I'm going to kiss you and make you a promise. I'll never mention it again. But you've got to let me tell you what I think. You should do that to me too. Now come here." She kissed him and wouldn't let go as though there were some force, a fierce sand storm, which would separate them.

"Hold me, Gregory. I'm so glad you're here. Hold me tight."

He kissed as hard as she, and they held one another firmly. When they separated, they lay looking at one another, their eyes holding them. Suddenly she laughed. "You took my cherry. Funny, I never knew there was a cherry there. Who in heaven's name ever thought up that one? Did it taste good?"

"Stop it. Now. Don't even joke." He kissed her again. "It tasted like it had been dipped in a martini. But it was seedless. What could be better?"

They lay back laughing.

"Do you want to go?"

"Yes. I also want you to take me to church and the candles. I'll have a talk with your God and tell Him to give you back your hymen - I'm a med student don't forget - but with a condition. That place is still mine and yours to share, like mine is yours too. O.K.?"

She got up. "That's enough of that. Let's go. You've got to see what we came for."

They did go to the church and then walked about Old Town, went into one of her favorite stores. He had already made up his mind he would buy her turquoise jewelry. They walked about, went into one store he liked.

"You wait here," he told her. After a while he came back with a package. "You may have this when we get back to the motel. There she opened the gift, a turquoise ring and matching necklace with the artist's name visible on the larger part of the silver chain. He placed the ring on her left hand ring finger and kissed her. She then went to the mirror and placed the necklace about her neck. It hung to the top of her bosom. He could see her delighted reflection. At first she said nothing, just feeling the charm and the love engraved within the gift, that no one would ever see or feel but she. "I'll show it off tonight. Put your arms around me. I feel a tingle. Hmm." She turned toward him. "You came to me from across the sea like a boy on the dolphin and fell at my feet where I picked you up and felt each sea drop that portended you and me."

After love and exhaustion, they fell asleep, awakening early next morning, she first, watching his face, feeling his arm, running her hands along his spine until he mumbled and woke, turned to her, smiled, "Good morning you," as he kissed her lightly.

"We have a long way to go so I'm blowing the bugle."

~

As they rode along the narrow road cut through the mountain that climbed toward Cloudcroft, the railway trestle surprised Gregory. It was, in a sense, a memorial to the trains that once had taken people to the town. They had passed mesquite, the tumbling tumbleweed of song, that one would see rolling along in wind blown sand. The higher they climbed, they drove by ponderosa pine, oak trees, and the aspens that did, as Brigit told him, remind him of Maine. When they came to the camping area she had chosen, it was cooler and why she had told him to bring along a jacket. He looked about at what could pass for either parts of Cape Astraea or northern Maine. He immediately felt comfortable and pleased. When they left the car and unloaded a double sleeping bag and the tent, she had an idea she would have to show him how to help. He had never spoken of camping in the woods. But he seemed quite at ease and happy. She watched him as he looked about, walked away to look at the trees, the bushes, the sky. It was clear and cool, and, in a sense, caused a little homesickness. He was happy to be here with her, breathing the air, relieved of the desert heaviness, despite having embraced what to him was this foreign part of the country where people spoke both English and Spanish, some intermingling, others keeping a separation. He found a land where the whites - Anglos - looked down on the Hispanics - Mexicans to them. The Hispanics labeled themselves Mexicans, some even sardonically joking about the word. It would be a number of years before these people would band together and begin electing their own to various political offices. The women often served as maids, as in Brigit's house; the men, many as laborers in the fields. Yet the men had already started separating themselves from that bondage, as did a number of the women, by attending college and earning degrees both undergraduate and graduate, including medical. But this mixture of the races intrigued Gregory who liked it and wanted to know the descendents of the Spanish Conquistadores.

"I presume you have none of that Mexican blood in you."

"We are all Irish. You like what you see here. Maybe someday you'll consider coming here to live. Also, my dear, there's a secret life hidden in me that you don't know about that my Celtic ancestors bequeathed me."

"C'mon."

"I'm serious." She had never spoken to anyone about this and wondered whether she had seemed foolish telling him this myth or history she imagined and often believed.

"If you're that serious, what is it? You don't want to sound crazy."

"My parents were guided to my name by a spirit left from the past." Now she was certain she had made a mistake. "You look at me so curiously. I shouldn't have said anything. Now you will think I'm crazy and leave me."

"Well, not just yet. But it's a good story. Is this my camping ghost story for tonight?" He looked to the sky. The heavens in the Southwest were so clear, the stars so bright, constellations so readily distinguishable. Astronomy had always fascinated him. Now here was the woman he loved telling him a tale. Here they were sitting at the entrance to the tent, and she was telling him something about herself of which no one else was aware, including her parents.

"Tell me more about yourself," he jested.

"Why do you think I became a nurse? I was led to it. I'm naturally known for doctoring, curing, and helping mothers in delivery, calming them, assuring that the child is born. Don't you think you were led to what you are doing?"

"Well, sometimes I think about that. I've pretty well known

it since high school. But it's not quite the way you tell it."

She laughed. "Don't you know anything about Celtic women? How powerful many of them were, goddesses, queen-goddesses, just queens, that women were highly regarded, not like we are today, playthings, our place in the home, no power. Yes, women see differently, feel differently, sense things that men can't." She paused, something frightening her. She would discover what it was later or in the future. "Oh forget it. I'm leading you on."

He thought about what she said and almost took her seriously.

She interrupted, "We didn't think or worry about virginity. We mated and when it was over we went to another man, or the man went to another woman. How glorious. No sin, like you and I are supposed to be living in. Ooo. I'm feeling warm and desirous. Come and get me," Again she laughed and to herself it came again, *Who is it lurking in the future? What frightened me. Another woman? Something happening to Gregory, or somebody in my family? No. I think it has something to do with me. Oh. Never. He already came to me in the hospital. I helped put him together again. He's my love and lover. No one else.* She wanted him to touch her, to assure her. She glanced upward, at the trees, phantoms against the moon and black sky, casting their shadows across them, trees she so loved, the smell, their look, their shapes. They were the women of the earth, surrounded by their maiden flowers and multiplicity of plants.

Gregory had already placed his arm about her, but she hadn't felt it until she looked at the trees. She turned toward him. "I'll make supper for us. O.K.? You must be hungry. I am." He built the fire while she prepared the food. While watching the fire and the food cooking, she looked at him. "Forget what I told you. It was a tale I heard a long time ago, probably when I went to convent school. Sometimes it was nice there, but I didn't like it the way my classmates did. I was a pain for the sisters.

Am I a pain for you - sometimes maybe?"

"Will you keep quiet? I won't listen to that. I suppose we're both pains to one another occasionally. That food smells good and tells me you're a good cook. When we get back to Boston or Maine, we have to get an apartment. O.K.? I don't give a damn what people may think."

She felt warm, needed. "We will. I want that. And as soon as you finish your training, we'll get married. O.K?"

"You didn't wait for me to ask," he laughed. "Will you marry me, Brigit? I need and love you, can't live without you. That's corny"

"I do love you. Let's stop. The dinner's ready."

They ate somewhat silently, glancing at one another, kissing lightly between bites. When they finished, they lay back on the softness of the pine needles, their heads on the unrolled sleeping bag, listening to the whispers of night. They turned toward one another. "Thank you for bringing me here, Brigit. I love it. I feel like this is our first home - maybe a little primitive, but we just evolved from the cavemen. And here we are, I lying beside an alluring woman. You have such a seductive body. You know that?"

"You want to see me?"

"You question?"

"It's sort of cold. Oh well." She pulled at her heavy shoes, took off her jacket, then slowly began to undress. She unclipped her stockings from her panty corset that she pulled slowly off and then, as he watched, having hardened seeing her pubis, she unclipped her bra and slowly let it fall. "I'm here," her voice low, seductive. "Your turn." She watched him quickly unbutton his shirt, unzip and pull off his pants, his shoes already gone. He pulled at his T-Shirt and then his underwear shorts. She watched his hardening penis as she grew more desirous, feeling the wetness inside her. She turned for him to lie on top, then she on him. The evening was that way until they could do no more but lay completely weary, satisfied, pleased, happy in one another, their binding yielding confidence in herself and her beliefs.

This was what she imagined life with him would be, not just sex, but the satisfaction and pleasure of being with one another, each helping each even when the day came and they would have their children.

He had mentioned an apartment. She would spend the remainder of her time at home, thinking of that, helping him with his studies, working at his hospital, and being home before him, keeping their home.

The tent was the beginning.

As he fell asleep, she shivered, her heart beating faster at the frightening sound of a barn or ghost owl crying from a cavern, while the trees began blowing in a stronger breeze. She moved closer to Gregory to know he was hers and to hold his warmth.

Chapter V

Tomorrow is Now

They returned to the ranch where he would spend this day with her parents, telling himself he would pay most attention to her father, hoping to gain his acceptance. Gregory perhaps should have guessed that Maureen had already preceded him in the assault upon Luke's bigoted and fearful shell. For he was afraid of losing Brigit, despite knowing that a time would have to come, if he lived through this cancer, to see her wedded and leaving the family for the East. That is where her heart lay. He had to accept that, despite her love of the Southwest. He should have known that he would never actually lose her.

While they were away, Maureen thought of them sleeping together, assuring herself Brigit knew how to prevent a pregnancy, that she would never bring disgrace on the family. She liked Gregory. What she did not know was that the first time Gregory and Brigit lay together and he was on top of her, she suddenly and softly asked, "What if I get pregnant?" He looked down at her and told her, "Then you'd have to marry me." She still hesitated, thought of her cycle, wondered if he had protection, though she felt it was safe when she surrendered. Later she sat on the floor, her face on his thigh, "Do you think I'm a hussy?"

"Don't be foolish. We love each other. We've talked about this enough." She looked up at him and said, "I told you you would fall asleep before I would and you objected with a firm 'No.' You were funny. You know men always fall asleep first.

That's the way they're made." While he was running his fingers through her hair, she raised herself to sit beside him, to kiss and hug him. "We're bound."

What would Maureen have thought? Brigit worried more about her mother than her father. She was thinking of her mother before and after. She found it difficult not to think about them. However, with time, she knew that her love, no matter what she did, was her own, no one else's.

God? Well, God had given her freedom of thought and action. The nuns were wrong. Women have minds and will do what they think is right for them. And if Brigit never found a man she loved, then she should become a nun or do something that would not arouse her sexuality, not bring her in contact with men. And could she ignore the urgings of her body when thoughts occurred? Did the nuns? She would not dress her body in black and mourn her birth as a female. In fact, she would celebrate her femaleness in any way she decided. She was assuredly bound to Gregory.

I have grown weaker. Or is it my imagination? I'll call Pamela and have her sit with me so I can think of something other than myself. Brigit! What have I done? Deirdre. You bitch. You leave our daughter to take care of me. Did you ever care? Or was it always that Étienne fellow? Is there anyone else? And despite what I did to her, Brigit comes over. A love that never dies.

~

Gregory had now been ill for almost twenty years, had lived and worked to see the United States go to war again, first in Korea and now in Viet Nam, a useless war that killed men for what? A war that that gave no honor to those men as the country did to his generation. Disgusting.

"Pamela!"

"What is it, dad? Are you all right?"

"Are you writing?"

"Not quite. I feel sort of lazy. What's wrong? Please tell me."

"Oh, I wish I were in the lab."

"You'll be back there. I know it," she answered, wanting to be encouraging.

"Did I ever tell you about my last two years of med school? I was thinking about that too."

"Sort of."

"It's just that there are things you talk about and others you think will bother people - sort of like not talking about war. Anyhow, I just wanted your company for a little while. Give me a hug, dear. Mmm. That's good."

The girls obviously wanted to protect him. Melinda often called home from school. She swore to herself she would never be like her mother and hoped the same for Pamela who had little affection for Deirdre. It was Brigit who upheld his morale through school and more when he needed that support. The girls knew that. Had he told them?

"Tell me, Pamela, are you angry about waiting for grad school?"

"Oh, dad, stop that. I'll get there and when I decide. Let's stop talking about it. Repeating, repeating."

Hesitant, thinking she was harsh, she decided to return to his thoughts about medical school. "What was it like in medical school?"

"Forget it."

Wanting levity, she added, "Yeah. But I bet you loved the nurses." Immediately she was sorry she said it, thinking of Brigit.

"Nurses are dedicated people. Well, there were some who

were mean, especially to us students. Oh, not so much mean as stern."

"Is mom coming home tonight?"

"I don't know." He tried to speak calmly. "She's got lots to do."

"Yeah." *My mother is a bitch adulteress. I've heard her talking. Why doesn't he divorce her?* "O.K. I'm going back to my room. Call me if you need me."

Oh, how I remember. The emergency room seems to stick out, though there was that night in Ob/Gyn with the woman we thought we would lose when she had a miscarriage and bled so profusely. In the past, she would have died. I actually thought after that perhaps I wanted to change my mind and specialize in Ob. There are too many women's needs that are ignored. Then again, it came back to research. There had to be more of it dedicated to women's health care. It sickens me, the cancers that can erupt *in those magnificent bodies of theirs and destroy them, breast (God the thought of what they must go through losing one or both), cervical, ovarian, vaginal. And men thinking 'oh that body was made for me to enter.' It reminds me of Chelsea and the guys looking at the nurses as just pieces of ass. It also reminds me of the nineteenth-century medicine and the primitive treatments women received. At least there was Lister and then chloroform. My dad told me a story about New York in his training when he used chloroform at a tenement and the husband thought his wife was dead and tried to kill my dad with a kitchen knife. Thank goodness relatives restrained the guy. Today, no one gets into the OR or delivery room unless they're supposed to be there.*

And that emergency room, the stabbings, gunshot wounds, and killings, the fellow who came in shot through the heart muscle. I got to watch that operation because James was the surgeon before he moved away. The way the bullet creased the heart and missed anything worse. The tenseness in the OR. He recovered because of James' superb surgery. I was so proud.

The worst was the psychotic woman who came in after drinking methyl alcohol. When she wasn't being watched for a time for some reason, she somehow loosened a long strap, wrapped it around her neck at the end of the bed, hanging herself. I still see her, her head drooped to one side and too late for anyone to do anything. Melinda will see it all studying medicine.

And how exciting the isotope research. Brigit. Oh God, beautiful, enchanting Brigit.

And then those were the days when the country was mesmerized by the Berlin Airlift, cheering for the Air Force and the United States, the hatred of the Russians. I still despise them. James had more experience with those barbarians, meeting up with them in the southern part of Germany

The airlift, though, the pride we felt, and the Russians defenseless against Truman's determination. It all started in 1948 after the Russians blockaded. We refurbished the World War II planes so we had sufficient aircraft. That continued up through my last year of school, 1949. *Also a year of decision for me. My internship. I keep thinking of the emergency room. It's amazing how we learn to steel ourselves against illness's ravaged bodies. Sometimes I thought I was back in the war. Well, in effect, it is a war. I wonder how many people think of it that way, doctors perennially at war against disease? That's what in residency changed me. The epidemiologist who tutored me. We went over to the laboratories at the med school one day. They were doing research with isotopes. Maybe that was one thing the atom bomb did that was good for humanity, turning our focus away from the horrendous destruction of life to saving lives – eventually. My fellowship.*

Gregory called Brigit at the ranch. He was so involved in his work, but he missed Brigit. They had only seen one another occasionally. Most of the time she returned east to Gregory's apartment, because he could not get enough time to go to her. "I miss you terribly. It's like a nightmare without you." He laughed. "But I have dreams about you"

"I'm probably one of your nightmares." She imagined him waking, changing his pajamas. She felt a thrill, just the word dream, almost like the caress of a silk dress.

"No nightmare, just annoyance at those dreams, you know, as if you're here. At least in sleep you're often with me. When are you leaving for good?"

"Next month. The leaves will just about be turning in Maine. But Boston. We can go to the Public Garden. On a week-end we can go to Maine.

"Greg, we thought my dad was having a relapse. He suddenly got weak. He'd been strong enough to work around the ranch. The end of last week I wrote you about it. Did you get the letter?"

"I did."

"Well, they thought perhaps the cancer returned and was in his lymph nodes. We were so frightened. It turned out the pain in his abdomen was from his bowel. He'll be O.K. I think I can leave. I am going to leave unless he wants me to stay. You wouldn't want me to leave."

"No." He wondered if her father wanted to keep her close by. He would never truly reconcile himself to Gregory, despite her mother. It was so unlike the way Gregory was brought up. Not in his house would that have happened. But in Brigit's house, how different. Maybe her father might reconcile himself to their marriage. Gregory hoped, because Brigit told him, how Maureen worked on Luke, telling him how Gregory would look after her, how her mother could see and feel it. But he doubted whether her mother could ever completely change Luke.

"It turned out to be diverticulitis, Greg. Maybe I have been the one to bring him back to himself. You think?"

"I know it. I'm not going to doubt your magic. You've used

it on me."

"Greg, I'm lonely, miss you beside me. I'm thinking about, well you know. Sometimes when I'm alone in bed, I have a hard time falling asleep and then start imagining you beside me, I can feel your chest and the slight hair on it. I imagine running my fingers along your arms, watching the way you hunch yourself when I kiss you behind the ear. Do you feel me?"

"And what do you imagine I think about?"

"I'm not going to say it on the phone."

"You know what? When you get back, we've got to go to the symphony and museum. I'll see if there's a good play in town."

"I'm coming soon. I love you, dearest and have my arms around you. Feel them?"

"Just get here. I'm going to look for an apartment near the hospital. I'll also send you what's available for nursing staff. Apply as soon as you get it or do it now. O.K.?"

"Oh yes. Make sure there are two bedrooms, maybe three. You need a study. Maybe we'll have guests, Mary, Lynne. Maybe even my sisters will come. O.K.?"

"It sounds good. Love you."

~

He found an apartment on Beacon Street not far from his maternal grandparents' home that Jocelyn, after moving with Aaron to Maine, gave over to her brother Joseph who had remarried several years after the war. His first wife, Elena, had been executed when caught spying against her home country Germany. So there was family close by. Gregory considered Joseph and Elena the real heroes of the family, both having been spies for the British and eventually only the Americans.

From the back of the apartment they would be able to look out on the Charles River, a scene they always enjoyed. So, they would be located between his ancestral home and Lynne's family, the Brocks. Lynne was now working in California. Perhaps she returned at times so Brigit would be able to see her. It was farther away from the hospital and labs, but he preferred it that way. There was comfort in thinking that his mother's home was nearby. Perhaps it would make Brigit feel as though she were becoming part of the family.

He gave little thought to family right now, however. Most of what was on his mind was how to use I 131 to help diagnose liver disease. In the laboratory where they had collected blood samples from animals, medical students who were paid $25 for allowing an injection and then giving blood samples, and also patients in one of the nearby hospitals who may or may not have volunteered. The samples were then placed in planchettes, dried in a high-degree oven, then submitted to tests and mathematical analysis. There were no computers then, but there was that marvel, the slide rule. Often Gregory would sit with one of the lead doctors and outdo with his mind the solution to a problem while the doctor was still sliding the glass along the plastic, numbered surface. They would laugh, look at the figures, chart by graph the results, and add them to a pile that would eventually become a paper published in a medical journal. Gregory did much of the writing until eventually he became a lead author.

By this time, he was gaining notice in the daily seminars that the labs held at the medical school. This was one of his most relaxing times, when they would drink tea or coffee while one of the researchers would talk, answer questions, and sometimes end up defending his work. Yet, there was never the nastiness that one would expect.

In the lab next to his, they were already studying the effects of smoking on the lungs. Pieces of lung were taken and subjected to the isotope being used. What was fascinating to

Gregory was the grayness of the tissue, proving even in the early part of the 1950s that smoking was hazardous. Yet, there were the many years that passed before recognition of the effect of smoking and the rush to stop people from using tobacco.

Meanwhile, in his early introduction to research, Gregory awaited Brigit's return. She already had a position in the hospital near the labs.

~

"Greg. I got a position without even having to come for an interview. I'm going to be on the OR floor. They offered me OB, which I guess I should have taken, but after the ordeal with my father, I decided on OR. I know I was meant for OB. I don't know. Maybe I'll change, if they let me. How's that? Oh, I'm excited. We'll be together soon, darling." While she talked, *I can feel him, his hands on my body, the arousal from his touch and leaning against me.* She touched one her breasts while they talked.

"I'll pick you up at Logan. Hurry. You're going to love the apartment."

"You never told me where it is. That's mean."

"That's your surprise."

A few days later, her mother and father reluctant to let her go, and her sisters, all at the El Paso airport, watched her board a Continental plane, Maureen and her daughters with tears, Maureen drying her cheeks, listening to Luke roughly talking to himself. "She'll be back."

Maureen heard. "Yes. She'll come home once in a while."

He turned angrily to his wife. "I mean, she'll be back."

"You're terrible. I won't listen to or have that. Grow up, man." She almost said, "She's not only an older woman, but she's not your virgin child any longer."

But she did add aloud, "You get over it, Luke. She's going to marry Gregory, and I won't listen any longer to your religious nonsense." She wanted to shock and tell him she'd no longer go to church. She knew she would, though, believing in her religion as she did. Then there was Sister Angelina, *Anne, my oldest. She was the hardest birth, the contractions lasting for, what, two? three? days and breach. I was so weak for so long. But now. There she is. A nun. I'm proudest of her and Brigit. Shouldn't be. Oh well.*

"I won't listen to your grumbling any longer. Grow up." She was still a lovely woman to look at, despite the years, and hadn't broadened too much, her hips still curving outward to reveal the woman from which her present body grew.

Luke started to answer, looked at his wife, an elegance she would always hold for him, stopped. "Maureen, do you realize what an eye-full you still are for me, always will be?" He leaned closer to her to smell her perfume. She smiled, listening to, "You win. I'll try. I really will."

The plane took off and all stood there with more tears, waving, knowing she could not see them, but that she would feel them. Despite the excitement of the trip, she, too, was tearful, holding a handkerchief to her eyes, trying to hide her face from hostesses or other passengers. It seemed that ever since the war everything was departure, arrival, sadness, even if they did not know the men or women flying planes or being nurses, and the glorious happiness when it ended. Brigit was fortunate she stayed in the United States, though she had wanted to be on a hospital ship. And now, in Korea, having started in September, 1950, was another war, more sadness and hatred of an enemy. Along with another war, the country was subjected to a battle within started by self-seeking Joseph McCarthy culling out the Communist menaces in our country and government, a libel of people stopped for the most part by Senator Margaret Chase Smith of Maine who in a fifteen minute speech to the Senate brought McCarthy down with the words that berated McCarthy as being on a political "vilification's ride the equivalent of 'The Four Horsemen of Calumny, Fear, Bigotry, and Smear'." At about the same time, there was the egomaniacal General Douglas MacArthur who refused to follow the orders of President Truman, his Commander-in-Chief and was therefore fired. Thus the country was in turmoil once more. The people often did not know what to think or what to do or whom to support. Yet, we cannot know the future, people would often say, but they could be stunned by it. They could, however, admit to one another or to themselves that one should expect distress aside from the delight of apparent harmony and love.

It was in this family discomfort and national turmoil that Brigit and Gregory moved into their new apartment kept rather bare by Gregory until Brigit could decorate it. As she had asked, one room was for Gregory's office with some space for her, if she needed it. The rest was distinctly family comfort. He had, alone but by consultation with her, bought a bed. When she saw it, to herself, *He bought what I hoped he would. I can see the two of us now lying there, making love, sleeping, waking in the morning and rushing to get ready. Perhaps we can shower together to make it faster, oh, but that would be too exciting. We'd be. Yup. We wouldn't be able to resist. O.K. Separate showers except, perhaps, after lovemaking.*

She walked about the apartment with him, looked out from the back on the Charles and toward MIT where she always watched for the large sail boat that would return in late spring and anchor until summer's end, her barometer of changing seasons; her feeling of self-mystery that lay within her world and being. Allure that she could create or recall.

"You like it, sweetheart?" he asked

"I love it. I knew you'd choose a place like this." She took his arm and turned him toward her, hugged him tightly, "I do love it," as she kissed him and he fell in with her, both smiling, laughing as they hugged and fell to the floor, rolling back and forth. "It's ours," he shouted. "It's ours," she shouted back.

They kissed, their tongues in one another's mouths against one another's tongue, his hands reaching to her breasts and hers between his legs. They stopped. He looked into her eyes and she the same, "I love you," he said softly, forcefully. She smiled, kissed him. "I love you just as much." They lay side by side on the floor, gazing at the ceiling, then at one another. "It's ours. The world is ours," Gregory spoke as in chant, repeating the words several times, turning back to her, pulling her toward him so he could slip his arm beneath her and hold her tightly, she feeling her breasts pressed by his chest. "I can hold you better on the sofa," he said, "and save my arm from gangrene." They rose; she lay back between the arm and back of the sofa and pulled him toward her, the two pleased, satisfied they were again together – in their refuge.

~

So they lived as a married couple, happy about their work and almost always looking forward to coming home. Occasionally there were the arguments - why didn't you go to the grocery store; why don't you clean the bathroom better; just like a man; do you have to leave the sink wet and dirty?

Or there were those times when Gregory stayed much later at the lab. His work was becoming known. He had published several papers, twice as lead author. Yet no one knew where the work would lead, whether it would help in diagnosing liver disease. Then in the laboratory he became careless. A planchette with a blood sample, that for some reason a lab technician did not completely dry, spilled on to Gregory's hand. Gregory did not tell Brigit or any of his colleagues. The following week, when he had his usual blood test, his white cell count had decreased. Still later he felt ill and had nausea and diarrhea. Brigit hurried from her day duty to be with him, taking his temperature, washing him, not allowing him to shower alone, because he was becoming somewhat weak.

"Greg, I'm worried. I'm going to call Simpson," the internist who took care of their needs, except that she insisted that her ob/gyn exams be with a female specialist. Simpson was too good a friend, and she would not submit to exposing herself to him.

Simpson insisted that Greg be admitted to the hospital for further examinations. He was there for a week. Brigit never felt so lonely. When she came to the apartment, there was no laughter, no almost teen-age rambunctiousness. In the quiet, she prepared less elaborate meals. To amuse herself, she would pretend he was home and try on dresses and turn about or flirt with herself in the mirror, pretending Gregory was watching and becoming excited. Or she would perform a strip tease imagining his penis growing hard, seeing it as he approached her. Finally she would become disgusted with herself. But one late night, lonely and longing, she moved her hands sensuously about her body, her arms, breasts and nipples, vagina, started rubbing herself and increasing the pressure, rubbing more quickly, inserting her fingers, then tasting the wetness, pulling a pillow between her legs until she felt the orgasm approaching and then returning to her fingers, inserting, rubbing, until fulfilling her desire as she shuddered and moaned. She lay still, frustrated and sad thinking of Gregory in the hospital. She wanted to dress and go to be with him as she did every afternoon and night.

At the end of a week, Gregory came home, confined to bed for about a month. Brigit was a nurse in her own home and enjoyed taking care of him, pleased he did not need anyone else, except when Simpson came for professional visits that lasted longer because of their friendship. One night he looked closely at Brigit, watching her face that could not conceal her concern.

"Brigit."

She looked at him. "You're going to tell me that I'm not his doctor."

"I've been watching you."

"I know, Ed. I'm O.K."

"No. Your face. You're weary. You can't make yourself sick. He'll recover and be like always. I promise, or promise as much as I can. I really do believe he'll recover and get back to work. Of course, he'll need more blood work. I also think we ought to check his thyroid."

"You're dear to me, Ed. I trust you to do whatever you must. I hate that isotope research he's in." She forced a laugh. "But you will have nothing female to do with me."

He smiled. "I wouldn't dare. You know, when you come in here, you feel the love."

"That's nice." She thought of her own home, the love infused throughout it that they always felt when being brought up, how Maureen struggled and worried about the girls when they were ill, and the terrible tension and strength taken from her during Luke's illness. They would never be so sure of themselves as they had been before his cancer that they all knew might or could recur.

Now she had the same worry about Gregory. Perhaps they should marry right away, stop putting off the inevitable. She was beginning to feel weary of not wearing a wedding ring, of the emotions that embroiled her, making love in sin, despite the mutual enjoyment of living together, making love when they desired. She was becoming jealous of the nurses who mentioned their husbands or children. She cared little for what she would inherit from Gregory as a married woman, but she did want publicly to state he was hers, worried that something terrible could happen to him because of his work. Despite her pride in his accomplishments, she did regret the field he had chosen and decided she would talk to him about it.

However, she did not have to have that conversation. Some time within the month that he was home, one of the research directors came to the apartment while Brigit was at work.

"Gregory. We have decided it's time you became a director. You will have your own office suite for seeing patients and for overseeing others under you. We want to keep you out of the laboratory. This experience has frightened us, and your welfare and our success is dependent on people like you. Besides, your wife," Gregory was going to interrupt then but did not want to expose Brigit or even himself. "will feel better." He then revealed that she had called. When Gregory heard what Brigit had done, he became angry, feeling as though she were interfering in his work. She had no right. However, he did accept the new position and the honor.

That afternoon, Brigit came in, and in a loud voice called out to him. "I'm home. I've got news for you."

He was in his office playing with some figures, his slide rule in his hand. He turned, his face grim and was about to speak when he saw her wondrous smile that always subdued him, seeing that she was in a happier mood than she had been for a long while since his illness.

"Greg." She kissed him firmly. "I've been named a supervisor." *Shall I bring it up now. The head nurse said how pleased she thought my husband would be. The other nurses, including the head, I know have noticed, I never wear a ring. One even asked when I would have a child. They know, no doubt, we're just living together, probably think, oh who cares what they think? But I do. I'll tell him now.*

Before she could speak, he rose and went to her, smiling, hugging her, congratulating her.

"I knew you'd be glad."

"I want to talk to you about something, Brigit."

She would wait.

"You called the laboratory at sometime and told them you were worried about me. Don't you think that's interfering in my life?"

"Your life? Your life is what's important to me. To hell with you." She rarely swore and surprised him. "Yes, I called. I'm worried sick, and you resent that I called someone for your good, for mine too?" She turned and started to walk out of the room.

"Wait. Calm down, will you? I haven't finished."

"What?", with anger rarely exhibited.

"Come here. Dr. Thayer was here today. He's the big cheese. Yes. I was angry with you."

"Sure. And I told him I was your wife." She paused. "Do you think I was going to tell him I'm your mistress?"

"Stop that, NOW. Fuck. Let me finish. He offered me a director's position, an office at the hospital. I'll oversee others who will work in my labs. And I'll be able to write papers, review what the others are writing or intend to, check their figures, etc."

"Don't you use that word around me. You know I hate it. Is that what you tell people you do to me?"

The argument was almost uncontrollable now. She left the room in tears. *I've ruined everything. We've ruined everything. All that joy we should have had in one another ruined.* She cried uncontrollably.

She didn't hear him come in the room. He walked softly to her and put an arm about her, running his fingers through her hair. "Please."

She pulled away from him. "Leave me alone." She started to say she was leaving, unable to think logically.

He moved toward her again but did not touch her. "Listen to me, Brigit," he spoke quietly. "We should be happy for one another. And another thing. This is important. I love you so dearly. You're my life. I would never use that word about you. I never, ever talk about you and love making. I've never told you this. But when I was in the navy, I'd often overhear some of the men talking about their wives, what they were like in bed. It disgusted me. I swore I would never be like that, would never talk about my wife that way."

She looked up, and in a trembling voice, her tears still falling, "But I'm not your wife." She tried to stop herself. "Will I ever be? Am I going to go on being a kept woman?" She hesitated, almost smiled, "Well, not kept. I make my own living."

"Don't talk like that. Please. Let's start over. I'm so pleased for you. You are too good to just be looking after patients, but the patients will be losing such a marvelous nurse. Well, not necessarily. You'll look in on them.

"And I swear, Brigit. I would never talk about you and what we do, unless it's something most married people talk about, like plays, concerts etc."

"And what women talk about. That's what I'm like, no different. I am happy for you. And even if you're angry with me for having called, I couldn't help it. I have been so worried."

"I know. And I'm pleased. It's truly an honor they bestowed on me. Wait until my dad and mom hear, and your folks too - about both of us."

There were wet tissues scattered on the bed. She glanced at them, tears still in her eyes. "Give me your handkerchief." She tried to dry her eyes better. "But I still am beginning to feel, not always," she interrupted, "like I'm nothing but a sex object even if I know I'm not."

Shall I say it now? Why not? It's time. "I know we're going to marry as we planned. Greg. Let's get married. Please. Soon." She held out her hand. "I want a ring on that finger."

There was silence, she embarrassed because she asked him,

and he because he felt miserable. He thought of the women in Sicily, the few he had bedded without feeling, for the satisfaction. He looked at Brigit. *This beautiful, unbelievable woman on the edge of the bed who has given herself to me and those whores.* "Brigit. We've achieved what we said we waited for. Marry me, dearest one. You set the date. Tell your folks. We'll both tell mine. I guess my parents and Mary will have to come to the Southwest. We have to be married where you grew up. Marry me, Brigit." Gently he pulled her to her feet. "I love you." Looking in each other's eyes, she answered, "I love you."

Chapter VI

Deirdre and Shadows

In fall 1924, a baby girl was born to a chicken farmer and his wife, the Cunninghams of Warrington, Maine. The birth occurred in a typical Maine farm house of the time, a white building with wraparound porch, a barn for the chickens. The midwife had a difficult time with the delivery, Christine, the mother, screaming loudly, praying to God, screeching for her husband, breathing, pushing when the midwife told her. Finally, hours after the wretched pain, the tear that occurred, Christine held a cleaned child and placed it to her breast, smiling through her pain and weariness. Later, the doctor would tell her this was the only child she would be able to have because of what the birth had done to her body. Edward and Christine were happy to have had one child, after Christine reconciled herself to the doctor's news. They baptized the girl Deirdre, a name associated with dominance and disharmony in Celtic mythology, something of which they were ignorant.

The farm was actually owned by Edward Cunningham's brother, himself quite successful. Edward had tried to make a living as a salesman in the northern part of the state. His brother told him it was a poor location, the population spread, and towns difficult to access. Edward, however, being the older, thought he saw opportunity among the Aroostook people who would want the latest kitchen appliances at lower than catalog prices. After all, it was after Coolidge's presidency, a period of calm and restored integrity, a man who believed in business.

Though the country was in the 1930s depression, Edward believed he could not fail in that part of the state that many ignored for the south. After all, it was farming country, and he was from a farming family and could talk their language.

That language brought him back to Warrington where in embarrassment he accepted his brother's offer of part ownership in the farm his brother had bought after the death of the farmer who had owned it and whose widow wanted to move back home to Kansas to be near family. So by default a chicken farm became partly Edward's.

Edward accepted his failure in business and finally realized he was, after all, a farmer. So it was that Deirdre, a lovely looking but often annoyingly devilish child grew along with the chicks she adored and carefully held when old enough. They were in her power. One time she thought she might squeeze one to see if it would die. Quickly she dropped it, looking at her hands in terror, then smiling. Perhaps she could decide at any time what or who she might hurt or help. Her parents, however, were trying to teach her loving, loved her almost unstintingly to assure she believed she was special. After all, her parents adored her and gave her whatever they could afford. She had heard them say their daughter would have the best.

They would never punish her unless she did something too terrible for them to ignore. Every day when old enough, she went with her father to the chicken coops, helping him take eggs, throwing food to them, watching them change from chicks to hens or roosters.

One day, when in one of the coops without her father, she pushed at a rooster because it ignored her. Quickly, before she could take away her hand, the rooster pecked, and before she could withdraw her hand, it pecked again. Deirdre yelled, "Ouch, oh, you hurt me." She had begun to bleed a little. "You rotten rooster. I'll kill you." She grabbed at it, but it pecked once more and fled with a flap of wing in its short flight away from her. She tried to reach inside the coop to get it but her arm was too short. "I know. I'll get even. I'll get one of your children. You will never do that to me again."

Deirdre saw a yellow chick. "I let you go once, not this time," she shouted. She grabbed at the chick, picked it up. "You're his child. Not anymore." She squeezed, squeezed harder. The chick peeped, went soft into her hand. Deirdre looked at the unmoving yellow fluff in her hand, gasped, and dropped it, running toward the house. "Mommy, daddy, look what the rooster did to me. Kill it daddy." She didn't mention what she had just done.

Her father saw her hand and the blood drying. "What happened?"

"It bit me. I didn't do anything. I was only trying to play with it."

"Well, roosters will do that. They aren't playthings, deary. They're to make other chickens, the kind we sell and eat."

"What do you mean make other chickens."

"Oh, forget it."

They came to the dead chick. Edward looked down. "What . . . ."

Deirdre watched his face, smiling at his surprise. *Should I tell him I did it? That it deserved it as punishment for what the rooster did to me. Next time I'll kill the rooster. But then we'd have no more chickens, daddy said. Should I tell him? No.*

Just then Edward looked at his daughter. The mischievous smile on her face told him.

"You did this. Don't you ever come near these chicks again." He raised his hand, dropped it. He thought, grabbed her hand, sat on a stoop of cut-down tree, pulled her toward him, and threw her over his lap. Just then, Christine came into sight. Deirdre had looked up, screaming, "Don't, daddy. I won't do it again. Don't," she shouted more loudly, having seen her mother coming closer. Christine saw Edward's hand come down on Deirdre's bottom. "Ouch. Daddy, don't do it again. I'll be good."

"Edward, what are you doing to her. Stop."

Deirdre slightly smiled.

Edward pointed toward the dead chick. Christine was horrified.

"You did that, Deirdre? How could you be so mean? I should let your father punish you more, but I've got a better way." For a week Deirdre went without candy, except when her parents weren't looking. She knew where her mother kept everything sweet. She was now old enough to pull a chair and get into the cupboard and sneak. She would also get even. She'd do it again, but this time she'd bury the chick. No one would know what she did. They didn't even know their punishment could be overcome if you knew how to sneak.

When old enough to attend school, Deirdre was wary of the strangeness, of having a teacher as her authority. She knew several of the girls in her class and some of the boys. They made her more comfortable.

There was kindergarten when they marched as Knights of the Red Cross on their crusade against the heathens. Deirdre was chosen to lead. The year went that way, playing, learning something about the alphabet and other things they would have to be prepared for to be in first grade.

But the first grade teacher was different. The woman, Miss Curtis, bothered her. She demanded strict behavior and looked, well, sort of funny, because she wore glasses, had a round face and dark eyes, and hair that was streaked with grey. She was also short and thin. Her body and face gave Deirdre the impression of a bat, if she could spread her arms and had flaps of skin stretching from her body to her arms. Deirdre decided that most teachers were just old bats anyhow.

On the first day, when they were assigned seats, Miss Curtis separated Deirdre from her friends. That was enough to anger Deirdre. But she soon got to know one of the girls and a boy that had a handsome face she liked. He was very quiet and caused little trouble in the room, was not always whispering or acting foolishly like the other boys. Miss Curtis rarely had to discipline him. Deirdre would like some wildness. She found that in another boy and a few of the girls. The girls would always gather at recess by themselves, talk about what home was like, what they wanted to do. Deirdre once ventured even at her age to tell the girls what she wanted to look like when she grew up. The others thought that was silly and were horrified but laughed when she talked about breasts. Most of them had seen their mothers' breasts either by sneaking a look when their mothers dressed or being allowed in their mother's room when she prepared for the day. But that didn't happen often and none of the other girls talked about it. That would come later. But Deirdre. She was brave, and they made her their leader. Anyhow, what difference did it make what they talked about? It would be a long time before growing up would happen.

Naturally, the boys chased them. One even grabbed at Deirdre's hair and pulled her to the ground. She shrieked, scratched the boy, managed to get hold of his arm and pulled him to the ground. Without thinking she rolled him over, she was so angry, spit at him, and got on top of him and started hitting him in his chest, once on his face. He could not get out from under her spread legs that she dug into the ground with her knees. The playground teacher, seeing the fight, grabbed Deirdre.

"What's the meaning of this?" the obvious question.

"Leave me alone." She tried to pull away.

"Girls don't fight. You are supposed to grow up to be a lady."

"He started it," as the boy got up and rubbed at the dirt on his clothes.

"I was just joking with her, and she hit and spit at me," he told the teacher in a whiny soft, hurt voice.

"Young lady, you come with me."

"It wasn't my fault." She tried to pull back from the teacher.

"It was," he mocked and smiled slyly, because she was being blamed.

If this is the way boys are, I'll get them before they ever get me. I'll teach them even better when I grow up. I'll show them. Are all boys like him? There's that good-looking one. He seems nice. Maybe they aren't all alike. But I'll find out.

"Come with me. Deirdre, isn't it?" the teacher told her. "I'm taking you to Miss Curtis," leaving the other playground supervisor to watch the children.

"I'm surprised at you, Deirdre. You're such a good learner. Well, here's another lesson for you to learn. When your mother comes for you, I'll tell her what happened and will let her punish you. Don't you ever let this happen again. You hear!" Her voice had risen, surprising Deirdre, scaring her. In class Miss Curtis's voice was always so soft and pleasant, even when she was telling the children to behave.

"I don't like fighting, Deirdre, and I won't allow it. You hear? And a girl. That's the worst."

Deirdre unwittingly smirked.

"Get that look off your face. You're a disappointment to me."

Her tone and what she said hurt Deirdre.

"I'll be good from now on. I promise."

"Well, I'll accept your promise, but I think tomorrow I won't let you go out for recess. Between your mother and me," her voice soft again, "I hope you'll truly learn your lesson."

I'll be good when you're looking. I promise me that. Grownups are so bossy.

It was during these primary school years during the Depression that arguments raged over what should be done. After Coolidge's years and the 1929 Crash, came another well-meaning man, Herbert Hoover, who had gained recognition for his humanity during the Boxer Rebellion and for his help with World War I victims of that destructive apocalypse. However, in these times he displayed some apathy despite his willingness to stimulate the economy, primarily through the use of businesses he thought should contribute some of their assets for the benefit of the people. Businesses, however, still looked after themselves while prices, for example, for farm goods, fell. Still he denied farmers, such as Edward, help. Nor did his desire for a tariff and his belief in a balanced budget during these terrible times help. The country turned to Franklin Roosevelt, the patrician President who cared and knew what to do and how to calm the country as well as possible.

Deirdre was ignorant of what was happening to the country, although she often heard her parents whispering about how much they could spend and how fortunate they were not to have to abandon the farm like those farmers in the dry middle west where the land had turned to dust. Maine people were more independent anyhow. They did not vote for Roosevelt or want to take any of his government handouts. So people like Edward and Christine depended on neighbors, neighbors on one another.

It was during these years that grade school seemed to pass by slowly, because Deirdre was still under the influence of those demanding teachers, and sometimes she thought, even her parents. Her mother tried to soothe her when she was unhappy, as did her father but not as warmly. As she grew older, the years appeared to move a bit more quickly while she strained to become more like a woman. It was then her father seemed to be so weak when she listened to his complaining about business and lack of money. She thought of him as a chick, when he should, she believed, have reminded her of a rooster. Yet, she loved him, especially when he brought her sweets or an affordable toy or doll. Sometimes he would bring home a new board game that, as she grew older and could learn how to play, they would all enjoy together. These games would make the time pass and momentarily take her mother's and father's minds off the strain of their Depression finances.

Her mother, well, there were times Deirdre thought perhaps she could get along without her too. Yet, she loved her mother, the nice smell about her, the softness of her skin when she rubbed her fingers or hand along Deirdre's face or arms. She was anxious to look and be more like her mother with the secret menstrual pads she kept and her ample breasts. One time she asked when she would have a period, like some of the older girls talked about, and grow up top like her mother. Too, her mother also protected her against her father's anger, an anger that came slowly and only occasionally.

There was one day when her mother was in another part of the house and her father at the chicken coops, she decided to go into her parents' bedroom. She looked about to be certain she was alone. She started opening dresser drawers. Inside one was a package unfamiliar to her. Each item was separately wrapped and round. She tore at the wrapping and unwound the long, soft, wrinkly object, laughed, and wondered what her parents did with it. It was like a balloon when she blew on it. She thought that was a treasure find and would take it with her when she left the room. Then she started for the closet and found coins in her father's pocket that he had perhaps forgotten. She decided he knew nothing about them so she took those too and held them with the balloon. She thought her father would never remember them. Her error in leaving the room was the untidiness of the drawers she had gone through. Hearing her father's steps, she sped out of the room and bumped into him at the top of the stairs.

"What's you're hurry, Deirdre? You have an appointment?"

"I have to get the bus to get my doll out of the hospital. She fell and hurt her head. I just got a call."

Edward laughed. "You do have an imagination."

As she ran down the stairs, he went to the bedroom, saw a bit of clothing stuck when the drawer had been closed. He also noticed the door to the closet slightly ajar. He went to the drawer that held the old, leftover condoms used when Christine could have become pregnant, saw the open package, then walked to the closet. He did remember the money, about fifty cents. That meant a lot to him in these terrible times. Obviously Deirdre had been rummaging, and that she took the money angered him.

Rather than a slow anger, the idea of his daughter sneaking and "stealing" the money infuriated him.

A loud yell came from upstairs. "Deirdre! Where are you? Come up here!"

Deirdre heard but instead of going to her father she ran to the kitchen. Her mother wasn't there. *Oh, where is she? Mommy, save me. Oh rats. I don't care. I'll tell that mean father.* Innocently – "Did you want me daddy? I'm coming," her voice trembling. In her hand she still grasped the coins and the condom, squeezing harder. Suddenly it occurred to her to drop the coins on the floor, and she placed the "balloon" in the waist strap of her panties.

"Deirdrah. Come up here. Now!"

"I'm coming, daddy." *I'll show him I'm not afraid.* She forced a weak smile on her face. "Yes, daddy," she spoke softly.

"What were you doing in this room and going through your mother's and my things?"

"I didn't do anything."

"Don't lie to me. You were in here. You even took my money. Do you know how important even a little money is today? What do they teach you in school? Arithmetic, no?"

"I didn't take any money. Oh. I did see some coins on the floor downstairs, near the telephone. You must have dropped them."

"You're lying and deceitful. You were also in the drawers."

"I am not. You and mommy taught me to be honest, and I'm being honest."

"You're lying. I won't stand for it. Come here," he shouted.

Now she was scared. "I didn't lie." She began to cry.

"You not only lied, but you're a sneak. Come here." He moved menacingly close to her and grabbed her arm.

"Don't you touch me," and she kicked at his leg but missed as he backed away and grabbed her skirt. Turning toward the dresser, he saw Christine's hairbrush. "You will not do this anymore," sat on the edge of the bed, dragging Deirdre with him and pulling her over his lap.

He hit her twice on her bottom, raised the brush again, watching her legs quickly moving up, down, listening while she wailed loudly. "Stop. Please stop. I won't do it again." By that time Christine had heard and was at the door. "Edward. Stop. What's happened?"

"She's your daughter. You teach her not to be a sneak and a thief." He quickly told her what happened, his voice trembling with anger.

"Ed, just let her go. I'll take care of the rest."

While she listened, Deirdre smiled and cried at the same time. *I'll teach you, both of you when I'm older. I'll teach everyone.*

What she did not know was that her father's anger came partly from his never having liked being a chicken farmer, with the mistake he had made in Aroostook County as a salesman, until he had come to wish he could be in the city where he could work in a business. Only now, with the Depression and businesses and banks failing and laying off more and more people, even that was beyond his reach. He and Christine had talked privately about his desire, but Christine begged him not to regret his choice of the farm, that at least they were not in a food line. Moreover, the country was the best place to raise Deirdre. She did very well in school, despite her complaints, and if her grades continued through high school she would hopefully get a full scholarship at a good college.

"I know I'm looking far ahead, Ed, but we have to think about her even more than ourselves."

"I suppose you're right, but she can't rule our lives."

"Don't say that. She does not."

"Well, there are times she's such a sneak. How many times have I caught her? And her nastiness every so often."

"Stop that. I won't listen to it. So she's bad once in awhile. Aren't all children?"

"Yes," he mumbled, subdued, thinking when Deirdre was older, though he did love her, she and her mother would be allies in household matters.

The years did pass, and in the seventh grade, Deirdre had her first period. The slight flow amazed her at first. She ran to her mother. "Mom, look what's happening, my leg, I felt it getting wet."

Christine smiled. "You're becoming a grown up girl. Remember I told you it would happen every month when it came." Deirdre was already showing her loveliness, her black hair that came to her shoulders and penetrating dark eyes, the long lashes. She was also tall for her age. Christine believed Deirdre would be a sought woman, that she might even be famous like the woman who appeared in the *Portland Press Herald* newspaper in 1929. The headline read: "Girl Wins U.S. Air Degree" followed by: "Elizabeth Kelly, 20 year old Los

Angeles girl first graduated from . . . approved United States government flying school in California and probably the first of her sex in the entire nation." Now that was something, considering that women were getting some recognition. Of course, they were still, for the most part, held to the home, kitchen, and children. But what Christine did not want for Deirdre was recognition such as the Japanese man studying here she read about in the same paper two days later who told reporters how he admired girls who sat on desks with their short skirts baring their knees. Besides that, they smoked. He liked that. "Not my Deirdre. She'd be a sought-after good girl. And if she wanted to fly or do anything that would bring her notice, as long as it was good, that was fine, along with being admired," she spoke softly to herself.

By the time Deirdre was in ninth grade, she had learned coquettishness. In dance class, she had picked as her partner the shy boy about whom she wondered in the earlier grades, because he would rarely approach her but seemed always to be looking at her mostly in one of the classrooms where they sat opposite each other. In those earlier years, she would shake her long, dark hair, smile to herself, knowing he looked at her, she back and then turning away from him. In the school yard when the boys chased the girls, he would pretend to run after them, come close to her, smell her soap-scented hair, start to reach out to pull her, stop, and run away, causing her to laugh.

But in the ninth grade, the girls and boys sat separately at long tables. She would turn her head, shake her long, dark hair to attract him, and then they would look straight at one another. The dance class was the miracle. His voice was deepening; he was several inches taller than she. When they were told to choose a partner, both walked toward one another.

"Will you be my partner, Deirdre?"

"Oh yes, Kevin," She hesitated. "I was hoping you'd ask

me." With that she smiled, listened for the music, placed her arm about his neck, feeling the somewhat smooth and muscular skin. She had wondered all this time what it would be like feeling a boy. She moved closer to him as he placed his arm about her waist. Her softness excited him. As good for both was being attuned to the rhythm of the music; they danced quietly, swayed, she daring to place her head close to his shoulder. Now she wore a faint perfume, or was it the soap she used? He did not want to take his head from her. Yet, when the music ended, she turned slightly before he took away his hand that inadvertently touched her breast. Stunned, not knowing she liked it, quickly he told her, "Excuse me. I didn't mean that," while still feeling in his memory its yielding softness. She looked intently at him, trying not to smile, "I know, but I like my partner," she whispered.

After school, when she was with her mother, she excitedly told Christine about dancing. "And. mom, remember the boy I told you about before who was always so quiet - his name is Kevin - he's my partner. Oh, he dances so good. We talked a little, but mostly it was just the dancing. I like him, mom."

"Well you can like him, but remember what I've told you."

"Oh, you didn't have to say that. I know."

She did know. That night, in her room, before she undressed, she watched herself in the mirror, smiled, shook her hair, raised her hand to her face ever so slightly, twirled and laughed. She also undressed in front of the mirror, watching her breasts that were becoming larger and shapely, touched them, remembering Kevin's flush and the quickness with which he withdrew his hand. She pressed again, fondling her nipples to harden them, feeling the sensation radiating to her groin. She watched, talking to her image, encouraging it to increase its height. She was now almost five foot four. "You're some girl, Deirdre Cunningham," fluttering her eyelashes. "I'll get him -

or anyone. Kevin, watch it." She then glanced down to the growing dark hair, lowered her hand gently, moved her fingers through the hair and what lay below, rubbed a little, feeling the tingle through her spine, wanted to continue but quickly withdrew her hand. *That felt good. Not now.* She hesitated, looked at herself again. *I'm going to be beautiful.* She started to lower her hand again but stopped. *Coward. What am I afraid of? My mother coming in and seeing me? What if she did? I'd catch it good. I'll find out.*

~

By the middle of December of her sophomore year Japan bombed Pearl Harbor. The students talked excitedly about what might happen, heard that the Japs would invade the West Coast. They worried about bombings and later heard, as the school year ended, stories of German submarines off the coast of Maine. Near Portland they also heard that there were spies being landed. In fact, by her junior year, they read about cargo ships being torpedoed off their coast. In South Portland liberty ships were being built. There were wartime jobs now available. Edward thought of moving the family to South Portland where he would work at good pay in the shipyard. Even Christine would be able to work. They'd make more money, live better, and perhaps Christine's dream of Deirdre going to college would come true. They would be able to pay for it on money they would save. But living in the city after all these years, how would that be? Exciting. Yet, he wondered, wouldn't farming be just as important? The fighting men would need food, as would the people. Perhaps he could buy some cows for milk and meat. He and Christine had decisions to make.

While he pondered what he might do, Deirdre came home one afternoon after school. She was in her senior year. As soon as she got inside, she yelled, "Ma, ma, where are you?"

"I'm in the kitchen. What's all the excitement?" Christine watched Deirdre's joyful face, looked at her beautiful daughter, her bosom having reached the size it would be in womanhood, her long, slender legs, thin ankles below her skirt, her full height of five foot seven. By now Deirdre had experimented with her body, knew how to please herself, often did when she knew her parents would not be in the house or would think she was just studying in her silent room.

"Ma, Kevin sure did break out of his shell last year. He invited me out again to a movie Saturday night. It's O.K. isn't it? But," and she smiled, "you know, I helped him along," she laughed. "Oh, ma, being a woman, well almost, it's such fun. You know, swishing your hair, glancing, walking with a sway or standing with a hip out."

"Deirdre!"

"Well it's true, isn't it? You probably did it with dad." Suddenly both mother and daughter's faces flushed. Seeing her mother's expression, Deirdre wanted to laugh and somehow hide her expression.

Christine decided she did not have to lecture her daughter. With a face and body like hers, she was right, and when the time came, she'd have whomever she wanted. But she had to say something. "You watch yourself. I shouldn't have to remind you. Boys are aggressive in their own way, and if you match them, they'll think . . . ."

Deirdre interrupted. "I know what you're going to say. Don't you worry about me. But, mom, he's handsome, taller than I am, and when he looks a little down at me, I just love it. How he ever broke out of his shell is beyond me. You like him, don't you?"

"Yes. When he's come here, he's been such a gentleman. It's obvious he likes you. Has he thought of what he wants to be?"

"He talks about a journalist, lawyer, doctor. You know he

works on the school newspaper and writes stories for the magazine. But he told me he'll go in the army after next year ends. He'll probably be drafted. He'd be so handsome in a uniform."

"Don't talk that lightly about the war - all those young men being killed, maimed."

"Well, I wasn't going to tell you this, but I'm thinking I'll become a WAAC or WAVE." At this time, neither knew she had to be twenty-five, an age that would change to twenty when WAAC become WAC in 1943.

It had never occurred to Christine that Deirdre might consider going in the service. She was to go to college. She was the top of her class. That mind couldn't be wasted.

Christine wanted to protest, her face growing red. She decided not to fuss about that now, despite the stories she had heard of the looseness of the women and that many were prostitutes that joined. There was time yet.

Not long after the conversation, Kevin drove to the Cunningham farmhouse in his father's 1941 Packard, the last of that model made after the war started. His father, being a doctor, had a C sticker for gasoline. So it was, Kevin's father would allow his son to drive at night, as long as he replaced the gasoline with money from Kevin's part-time job. His father had insisted on Kevin finding out what it was like to work and earn and save. Moreover, his father had an older car that he could use if there were a night call. If Kevin wanted to make an impression on a girl by using the family car, his father was nice enough to let him take it. His father laughed to himself, while telling his son he should have a pleasant time. Too, the family had met Deirdre who appeared to be a nice girl. Like everyone else, his mother and father admired the girl's beauty and her intelligence. Perhaps it was just a high school crush, and they would probably go to separate schools. Kevin was bound for

Harvard, like his father before him - if the war did not take him away before. Dr. and Mrs. Harrelson deeply worried about that. Already they had another son fighting in the Pacific who had had to leave college when drafted near the start of the war. So Kevin could make his impressions and enjoy himself as much as possible in the uncertain world.

Kevin liked the Cunninghams who always treated him almost as a family member. Christine had always wanted a son, but with Deirdre's birth, that became impossible. She remembered the hemorrhaging, the unbearable pain, the tear. Often, not long after, she felt as though her body had deserted her. There would be no other children.

When Kevin entered, both Edward and Christine were in the living room.

"Well, Kevin," asked Edward, "where are you off to tonight?"

"There's a great movie in Rockland, 'Shadow of a Doubt,' with Joseph Cotton and Teresa Wright, an Alfred Hitchcock show. I've read some great things about it. It may," he hesitated, "scare Deirdre a little. I don't know. She's something. Brave, you know, Mr. Cunningham."

Edward smiled. "You mean Deirdre's a girl and things frighten them more."

"Well, not that. Oh, I know she'll like it. We talked about it when I asked her out. She likes Joseph Cotton, told me how handsome he is."

"Well, here she is now, Kevin."

Deirdre walked slowly down the stairs, her black hair curling just above her shoulders, a little lipstick Christine allowed her to use. She purposely moved to show her legs, enjoying the feeling of her satin-lined skirt against them as she stepped down, watching the expression on Kevin's face, his eyes staring at her legs and up to her breasts pointed visibly in her sweater. He seemed unaware it was the bra style. He tried not to stare, remembering he was with her father and mother.

"Hi," was the little she said.

"Hi back. You look wonderful, Deirdre." Kevin's face colored.

"Thank you."

"Well, don't get home too late," Christine said, raising her eyebrows, signaling a warning Deirdre understood.

"We won't," they answered in unison.

The first time they went out, he had driven to a parking spot overlooking the water and where most of the students went. He had tried to kiss her and move his hands to her body, but she stopped him. When he took her home, however, he decided he was going to kiss her goodnight. She did expect it and let him. They held on to one another for a bit until she felt she should stop. It seemed sudden, but they both liked it. She thought of what she would do when he took her there tonight. She had never allowed anything except kissing.

In the movie, they held hands. They always held hands when they walked outside. They talked about school, people they knew, the war. The girls would gather about her, asking what he was like. They told each other stories about the boys they went with, what they did. What it was like kissing and being felt. No one ever admitted going further. Protecting virginity was ingrained. If any one of them did lose hers, she would not tell the others, afraid of being ostracized as loose, or worse, a whore and unmarriageable. It did happen to one girl, because the boy who impregnated her bragged to his friends how they did *it*. Her life became misery. She shied away from everyone and always sat by herself, except for Deirdre who felt sorry for her, befriended and even admired her for allowing her body its freedom to enjoy itself, to satisfy her perhaps. Deirdre did not care what the other girls or boys thought about their friendship. Deirdre had an inherent independence. No one dared confront such a formidable girl.

As the movie became more intense, when Theresa Wright begins to question Cotton's appearance at her parents' home, Deirdre tightened her hand in his, her nails digging into his palm. Kevin placed an arm over her shoulder. They glanced at one another. "Good, isn't it?" he said.

"Yup, but somewhat scary."

"Oh, nothing scares you," he whispered.

She smiled and started to place her hand on his cheek but stopped herself.

When the movie was over they went for a soda.

"What a horrible ending," Deirdre told him.

"Yup. But he deserved it."

"He did," and she stopped. *What would it be like to think you were going to be killed? Ugh. Ugly. Don't think about it.*

"Want to go for a ride after we finish our drinks?"

"Sure," she mumbled from the side of her mouth as the frappe filled her straw. She perked up. "Yes. Let's go for a ride, keep the windows down and feel the fresh air. We need it after that."

They enjoyed riding around. Without asking he drove to the parking spot. "Want to stop?"

Deirdre did not answer. She wanted to but would not admit it to him, just accepted it as natural. Besides, she was anxious for his kiss, to kiss him back, to feel its warmth and the closeness of their bodies. She did like him, liked the car for its spaciousness, the feel of the seat and the smell that was partly from his father's pipe. There was that maleness about the car that appealed to her, even excited her, a car into which she could settle comfortably, imagining what it would be like if they ever married and had one like this, even a large house, Kevin a famous doctor.

They kissed several times, Deirdre growing warmer with each touch of lips, the feel of his tongue and her reciprocation, the slipping of tongues' tips against one another. She began to feel an excitement flowing through her body. "It makes me sizzle," she whispered. Kevin laughed, then placed a hand on her breast that she started to take away but relented as he pressed one, then the other. He then pressed against her body. She felt his hardness against her thigh. She breathed deeply, felt still warmer from the scintillating touches, felt her belly tighten and the wetness begin as his hand moved slowly upward under her skirt as he reached for her opening. In spite of enjoyment, she grabbed his wrist, shouting, "NO! Cut it out." Kevin quickly withdrew, softening some. "I think I love you, Deirdre." She smiled and leaned back, lying across the seat. "We can't do it."

"Can I rub against you?" She didn't answer, pulled him toward her thigh, again felt him harden. He started an up and down sliding as she turned on her side to allow and feel the movement against her thigh, her own wetness, feeling her nipples harden as he placed a hand on her breast, gently massaging its softness, the arousing stimulation throughout her body increasing. He breathed more deeply, made a slight moaning sound as she felt him tighten against her and then relax, still holding her. She kissed him, sat up in the angle between the door and the seat.

They talked some. She did ask him what it felt like. Without answering he pulled at her dress skirt and started to run his hand upward toward her breasts. "I'd like to see them." She laughed. "You would? And what kind of girl would I be to let you do that?" Then, however, she reached to loosen her bra, allowing his hand to feel along the supple nakedness, she experiencing a tingle that darted between her thighs. She led his hand toward the nipples. "Easy." He followed her instruction, feeling them harden as he himself did again.

"Would you like to feel mine?" he asked.

"Yes," she murmured and reached down. "Oh. It feels so hard, like a branch."

"Rub it."

She hesitated but did as he said, slowly moving her hand up and down, feeling him tighten against her.

Suddenly she thought seriously of what they had done. "Do you think I'm loose?"

"No. We care for each other."

Deirdre was uncomfortable, wanting to relieve herself but couldn't because he would see her.

When they came to her house, she tightened her bra, looked in the rear view mirror and brushed at her hair, put on lipstick. She was scared and excited. She pulled him away from the porch light into a dark area where she leaned against the railing. Spreading her legs, she placed her arms about him, pulling him toward her and started her movement until he heard her stifle a low moan. After a pause to recover, she led him to the door where he kissed her, keeping away from as much light as possible. "I do love you, Deirdre."

She hunched her shoulders at the sound of "love," kissed him again. "You're dear, Kevin." It occurred to her before she opened the front door, the light being on in the hall, *What would have happened if I let him do it. I wanted to. What would happen if he had made me pregnant? I did like it and wanted more. I've got to find out what it's like. Should I tell him to get rubbers? No. He may talk about us. In the meantime. Oh, I don't know. He would never tell his friends about us. But if my parents ever found out even what we did tonight. My face feels so hot. I hope they're in bed.*

She reached out to Kevin. "Come here. Do you really love me."

"You know I do," and she felt the warmth throughout her body and brought his head to hers and kissed him hard.

"Don't talk about us. You won't ever, will you?"

"No. I will never. It's our business. When we're done with school, go to college, we'll never be apart, being at Harvard and Radcliffe. I promise. And promise me you'll be mine," he hesitated, "even if I go in the army. I guess I'll have to. All the guys are being drafted. Well. At least I won't have to go to Africa. We won there, despite the rotten Nazi Rommel." He stopped, thought. "What if I were wounded? Would you still be here for me?"

" Stop. I don't want to talk about that. It's horrible. Kiss me again and then I have to go in. I," she wasn't sure she should tell him. "I liked tonight. I feel so close to you."

"Me too." He turned and slowly walked down the steps, looked back at her as she watched him get in the car. Then she went inside, listening to the driving off, smoothing her skirt, again making sure everything was in place.

~

Toward the end of the 1942 school year, the principal, after a perfunctory meeting with faculty heads, announced that Deirdre Cunningham would be the class valedictorian. It was the first time in the school's history that a female would have that honor. Women in the community were excited while the men, for the most part grumbled, "A girl. They got the vote and now they're taking over everything." They were ignorant that other girls in different parts of the country were gaining the similar honor. Too, they seemed to forget that a number of the marriageable single women or sweethearts of servicemen from the area had gone to work in factories and the shipyard in South Portland. They also occasionally forgot that President Roosevelt had appointed Frances Perkins from Maine to be his Secretary of Commerce. Oh, they were proud a Mainer had been chosen for the administration. Still, it was that Roosevelt in office.

Despite the war, many in Maine still did not care for him, neglectful of his having helped them financially.

In Deirdre's home, there was no negativism. Edward and Christine were as excited as Deirdre. They welcomed Kevin to the house with more enthusiasm and decided to have a party to which they would invite the Harrelsons. They were sad, as though he were their son, when they thought of him being drafted, that he could not go on to college as Deirdre would. They were proud. She had received a scholarship to Radcliffe. If the war only ended soon. But that was nonsense. There was too much happening in the Pacific and Europe for that to occur.

Edward had already decided that he would take funds from his meager savings so Christine and Deirdre could buy new dresses for the graduation. He was making more money because of the war and the vast need for food. He would deny his daughter nothing, being honored as she was. He had watched her a little as she sat at her desk writing her speech. It seemed he loved his daughter more because of the admiration she was bringing to the family.

"Deirdre," he called.

"A minute, dad. I want to rewrite these few sentences." She finished. "Yes, dad." She went to the kitchen where her mother and father sat, watching the smile on their faces.

"Deirdre. I have part of your graduation present for you," her father quietly told her. "I don't suppose you can guess."

It was unnecessary to say that. Deirdre had already decided she wanted a new gown that she would be able to show after taking off her white graduation robe. She had even decided that it should be lavender, were she lucky enough to get one. Already something was taking place in Deirdre's mind. She was no ordinary girl. She was becoming a woman at eighteen and by the time she became twenty, she decided she would be studying and working toward social acknowledgement. How that would happen, she was not as yet sure. Too, she had not told her parents, though she and Christine had talked about it, she was going to enlist in the WAAC or the Women's Flying Corps before the war was over, even if she had not been graduated from college yet. She would ask Radcliffe to delay her scholarship. Surreptitiously, she had already written to the college, asking what it would do if she were to leave Radcliffe to serve or work in a factory until the war was over. She watched the mail that came to the rural roadside mailbox to get anything before her parents. In fact, the letter came sooner than she thought. The Admissions Office praised her for her patriotism and told her when that time occurred, they would make a future decision that would depend on space and funds available. If she were a good student they would perhaps. It wasn't the most satisfactory answer, but she would see what happened, regardless. There were many schools in the country that would be happy to admit her. With that inconclusive news, she would wait until Kevin was called up and then perhaps tell her parents. After all, she reasoned, women had their secret selves that other women might see through but not men. She had that self and the power that came with it, she was certain.

Such thoughts came to her as she drove to Rockland with her mother imagining what kind of dress she would find. A new bra would also be important to show off her body and her beauty. Fully grown, she would admire herself in the mirror at home, know she was beautiful, that she was desirable, always noticing how men and the boys at school looked at her, imagining their thoughts.

When they came to the clothing store, Deirdre dashed in, stepped back so her mother could go first. They picked over dresses, feeling them, looking at sizes and colors. 'Here's one, Deirdre," Christine had stopped by a white one. "No, mom, I want lavender. It will show my color better."

"I suppose you're right. But white for this occasion."

Deirdre interrupted. "Mom, I'm not getting married, only being graduated from high school. Besides, I bet most of the girls will wear white. I've got to stand out once we're out of those gowns."

"Don't be so taken with your looks," although both Deirdre's brains and looks made her mother proud. Her daughter looked more like her than her father, though Deirdre had his dark eyes and hair, including that somewhat pointed and dimpled chin. Christine's hair was a brownish blonde and she had blue eyes, was not quite as tall as her daughter. Christine was a handsome woman and older men still followed her with their eyes.

A saleslady asked if she could help. "I want a lavender dressy dress for graduation, ruffles at the hem, but not so long it covers my calves and ankles." And so she found what she wanted, twirled in the dressing room mirror, then remembered the new brassiere, asking for one of the Maiden Form she had seen in *Life Magazine* ads. Trying that on, she was satisfied and comfortable, put on the dress again, laughed, and said aloud, "Kevin will love this." *I know what he'll be thinking. I wonder. No. Forget it. All that soldier stuff.*

"Mom, look. You like it?"

"Absolutely, dear." What Christine worried about was that they had spent more than Edward would like. *But how often does a daughter like ours have an occasion like this?*

That night, Deirdre was too excited to work on her speech, but the next she did.

Graduation day was bright and cheerful. After the diplomas, the principal announced Deirdre.

Concluding the usual introductory words, she looked at the friends and parents, sought out hers and Kevin, tears forming that she blinked back, stood straight:

"We are graduating in a time of war, a destructive, terrifying war engulfing the world. The boys in our class will all be drafted. We cheer and support them and want them to come back to us as men ready to take their places in work, business, or college. We will miss them and assure them we will never forget them. In fact, some of the women - note I'm not calling us girls - will enter the women's services, some work in factories or on the farms to support the war effort. Some may even marry. But what we must remember is that we owe our parents and our teachers our utmost. We who have received our diplomas today are here to support one another and our government. We stand here today, not for ourselves but for all those who have gone before us and who will follow, for all those who are part of us for all our days. We cannot forget we have come into this life to better it, to do what will better our society and ourselves, to work not for glory but for peace for all mankind and be men and women who future generations will thank for our efforts."

The audience rose and cheered. Deirdre smiled, nodded her head, thanked everyone again, and had to blink back her tears that now almost blinded her, everything and everyone appearing as shadows.

Chapter VII

Reality

The Cunninghams and the Harrelsons went to dinner with their children, toasted the children, the Harrelsons hiding their sorrow. Dr. Harrelson insisted he pay the bill. They excused Kevin and Deirdre after dessert, aware the two would want to be alone. Deirdre, as she expected, was remarkable in her new dress.

When they left their parents, he told her. "Deirdre, you look stunning. I love the dress and the girl in it." Deirdre felt a slight chill on her back and in her chest, smiled, *I was right about the dress. I know what I'm doing.* "Thank you, sweet. I knew you'd notice it." 'Me,' she might have added, pleased with herself.

He quickly interrupted. "I received my notice the other day. I'm to report in a week."

"Oh, so soon. I thought your parents seemed, well, sort of sad. I could see it in your mother's face. Your brother's O.K., isn't he? Oh, he has to be. Otherwise you would have told me." The sorrow in her voice was unfeigned. Whatever love was, she was fairly certain it was there for Kevin, although it did not overwhelm her. Her emotions now, however, the unease that she felt, were real, as rapid thoughts of war and reality flickered through her mind. Her hands were suddenly cold. She shivered.

She would not allow this conversation to continue. They were out for a good time. Only now, he was going to leave. She would be somewhat lonely for a while. She had made up her mind too. She was definitely joining the WAAC, even if she had to fake her age. She wouldn't even tell Kevin. "Let's just ride and be happy." She couldn't help herself, however. "Are you glad you're going?"

"I am. I've been wanting to join my brother. Being in the army is exciting but somewhat scary. Being away from the family, you, makes me feel lonely."

"Well, I already feel that way." She started to tell him her plan but held back until later. This was not only their graduation night, but it was also that joy of being with one another, riding, talking, listening to some good swing on the radio, soft love music sung by someone like Frances Langford or Frank Sinatra. They were eighteen, a man and a girl; no, a soon-to-be woman. He would be her soldier. *What if I meet someone else? I didn't promise to be completely loyal. Why would I? Whatever happens. No one is certain about anything in these times. But we promised we'd be together in college. Maybe we will. Maybe we won't. He may not feel the same way about me when he gets out. But he loves me. What do I feel? I don't feel like I'm on a cloud. It doesn't consume me. Well, why should anything consume anybody? You're wrong, Deirdre. You'll be consumed by something, perhaps the WAAC, college, future work. Marriage.*

"Let's go park, Kevin."

"Sure."

She sat next to him so they could feel one another as he drove. He took her to a spot where there would be fewer cars and parked under a tree. "This seems more private." She agreed. It was a warm night. The windows were down. Without hesitation he turned, held her head and began kissing her. She kissed him back, moved her lips to his ear and his neck, licked him on these spots as he hunched a bit and let out a sound of satisfaction. He felt himself growing hard and tried to lean her back. She moved away a bit and toward the corner of her seat, pulling him with her. "Just be careful. I don't want to wrinkle the dress."

"I will." He placed a hand on one of her breasts. "They're beautiful the way they point through your dress." He wished he could see them. "I'll miss all this," he continued, "miss you."

"We'll miss each other." She reached down and held him by his testicles, then opened his pants and moved to his penis. "It's so hard." She began to rub. "Take it out." He did. "Do you have a handkerchief."

"Yes. But I want to put it in you so we'll never forget," as he lightly and reluctantly took away her hand.

"We can't do that." She stopped. *Why not? He's going away.* "Do you have any protection?"

"I got some at the drug store. The guy looked at me peculiarly, probably thought I was too young to be asking for rubbers, but he let me buy them. Want to see one?"

She was becoming excited, felt her body tremble, her vagina becoming wet. "Show it to me." She became more excited, handling it. "Put it on. I have to see that." He did as she asked. He felt his body tighten as she rubbed again with her hand.

"It's my dress, Kevin," she used as an excuse. "And what if even with that rubber I got pregnant?"

"Come on. You won't get pregnant. Not with this."

"My dress," she added again. "No, we can just play with one another." Her hand went up and down on him, squeezed, lightly moved about the tip until he groaned to a finish.

They kissed. She pressed him closely to her, whispered, "Now you can do it to me." She spread her legs as much as the dress allowed, pulled off her panties, took his hand, moved it below her skirt and up to her clitoris. Feel it? Now just do as I tell you," her voice still low and excited; she felt a quiver as her wetness increased. She placed her hand on his and moved it so it satisfied her, then guided him just below to her opening. As she reached her climax, she arched her back, loudly moaned, relaxed, and took away his hand.

"I liked all that, dearest Deirdre. Will you do it to me again and then I'll do you?"

"Yes."

Later they sat, spoke softly, telling each other they would always be together.

~

One week later she went to the bus with him that would take him to Portland and eventually to Fort Devens. The first nights were extremely lonely, but he made friends fairly easily. They talked about females, about their sergeant, what they thought it would be like to fight, how anxious they were to see action. But girls were on their minds most often. Two of the recruits bragged about the women they had had. Kevin didn't believe them. There was a lot of bragging, in fact, what some would do or accomplish, how they would confront the sergeant. Yet, no one dared. And they obeyed, as when he came in and yelled either, "Lights out," or in the morning, "O.K. men," thinking he joked but soon realized he wasn't when he shouted, "Out of bed. Let go your cocks and grab your socks."

Kevin did not like that. Despite his experience with Deirdre, it was offensive to him. There was much that was offensive, the continuous flow of "Fuck you, fuck this or that. Did you fuck your girl before you left? You're a fucking fool if you didn't. And if she didn't let you, you'll find some whore wherever they send us."

After a week at Devens, they were herded to trains. It was raining quite hard at the railroad station. They stood there for at least an hour, sheltering themselves in their ponchos, some fortunate enough to get under an overhanging roof. When they had climbed aboard, thinking they would all have seats, there was another reality to confront. They guarded their duffel bags.

Many sat on the floors, even slept on them, their heads on the duffel bags while a sergeant or corporal pushed through the crowded men, awakening or irritating them. Others did not seem to mind and laughed a lot at dirty jokes, keeping tired recruits from sleep, soldiers rather, for they had been such for a week. The train headed west, though no one knew it until one of the boys saw a sign reading a town in western Massachusetts. Kevin knew they weren't far from the Mohawk Trail that he and his family had driven. It was still raining and late in the night when they boarded another train that took them south. In the morning, Kevin wished he had pen and paper so he could write to his parents, his brother, and Deirdre. He hoped she had changed her mind and gone on to Radcliffe, that the army was no place for her. By the time she received that advice, she had already told her parents what she had done and intended to do.

~

Within the Cunningham family, at the end of Deirdre's second year at Radcliffe, there was furor. Deirdre had told her parents that now being twenty, she had enlisted. In July,1943, the WAAC, by act of Congress, became the WAC, plain Women's Army Corps with some rights similar to male soldiers.

"Who do you think you are, Deirdre?" Her father yelled.

"I'm old enough to make a decision."

"What do you know about the world? Haven't you heard about those women that are in there," he hesitated, "for the men, that they bed with the men?" He reddened. He had never talked about sex with his daughter. "You not only come from a good, decent family; but you have won all those honors. You're good and must stay that way for marriage; and you're probably the head of your class at college with all those A's and you throw that and the WACs in our faces. I WON'T HAVE IT." He was behaving like many men had when the WAAC was formed; some men still thought of the WACs the same way, though accepted by the general staff. They forbade their wives, fiancées, sweethearts from joining, for they would be labeled loose or prostitutes. They had even heard stories of WACs having to carry condoms with them to prevent pregnancy. A woman's place was at home, taking care of the children, shopping, cleaning, preparing meals.

"Dad," she pushed back. "Listen to me." Yet it was a rare time she had shrunk from Edward, he was so angry, yelling at her, approaching her with his fists clenched, then reaching for his belt and about to snatch it off.

Christine was crying and hurt, but noticing Edward's movement, finally recovered to stop his hand. Still crying, hurt, she hoarsely and loudly managed, "Edward. Don't you dare."

"She's always been like this. I never wanted to say it again, but she's a sneak, always has been, and I won't tolerate it anymore."

"EDWARD," Christine screamed. "STOP. I won't let you talk about her that way." She knew, however, that their daughter was not always honest with them. *She'll get over that as she matures. And she does have a right at twenty to start making up her own mind without us. She'll mature. Maybe this will be good for her, the discipline and knowing she's directly helping her country, all of us.*

The tears still flowing down her cheeks, she looked at her daughter, struck by that tall girl with a woman's body, thinking of the agony it might someday endure, that she had in bearing her.

Deirdre, watching her mother, started to cry herself. "Mother, daddy, I'm not a sneak or someone who does things in secret. It's just that," as the crying made her throat catch, "I wanted to surprise you, let you know. Well, they did tell me at Radcliffe, I would probably still have the scholarship waiting, depending on events at school. And I didn't want to upset you." She thought quickly. "I wanted you to be proud of me doing something good and something you would be pleased with. It seemed to me that if I told you what I wanted and you agreed, that I'd be taking something away from Kevin."

This last angered Edward again. He did not believe her. He looked at Christine and started to ask, " Kevin, what has he to do with it? You don't believe all this malarkey, do you?" but stopped himself.

He looked at Deirdre, knowing he loved her, at Christine, knowing, too, these were the two loves of his life. He was proud of his daughter, enjoyed watching people when he walked with her, the way heads turned. Yet, that was not enough. He wanted her to be as outstandingly honest as her mother. Yet her father's anger scared her in a way she had never before experienced. She pictured herself, her bottom black and blue, the pain unbearably searing her body, perhaps her arm colored from his grip. She knew he would never touch her face. She knew he would never hit her, in fact. His wrath now, though, was entirely different. She backed away, thinking him a brute, called out to Christine. Christine stepped between them. "What's wrong with your mind, EDWARD. You're acting insanely. STOP. NOW. I mean it. You hit her, and we'll both leave this house. I MEAN IT."

Edward turned away from them, shaking, trying hard to settle himself, then suddenly crying. He turned to them. "Deirdre," shaking from tears and the calming anger, "I never thought you would be so underhanded. We've loved you so, done all we could for you, and you have honored us and your school." With his back to them, crying harder at her deception, he left the room. Christine followed. Deirdre, alone, started to cry, wondering about this change in her life and the protection she had always known. *It took this to make me realize what kind of person I am. I'll change somehow. But I'm old enough to do what I want. Why am I to blame? I am scared. I'm going to be with many women older than I. I'll learn so much from them. My mom and dad should not be mad at me but proud as they were when I was valedictorian and how my grades were the best in the school and how good they are now. I'll be serving my country. Boys go at eighteen. I suppose it won't be much fun sometimes. Think of the places I'll go, though, what I'll be able to do, at least, I hope.*

~

Fort Devins and Basic Training - About the middle of June, Deirdre was inducted into the WAC. She took the tests and scored quite high, marking her for further attention by her superiors. She liked the uniform, except for the underwear that she managed to manipulate so it would show her upper body. Getting accustomed to the shoes was difficult. Despite these minor irritations, she was proud. She was good in basic training, exercised without complaint, except like most new trainees, complained about the lack of privacy in the shower. It was, though, the tear gas room that unsettled her somewhat. She thought of D-Day, wondering whether Kevin had been in that. He had been in Africa with the tank corps. But D-Day. The dead. She imagined him lying on the beach or in a burned-out tank. This part of the training also further aroused her desire to ship overseas to England. She had heard about the work that some of the women were doing in the OSS and wanted to be with them.

One day she and three others heard their names called while in formation. "Report to the commanding officer." Entering Captain Lewis's office, she smartly saluted, stood at attention. "Cunningham, we decided according to your test scores, we want you in cryptographer school and map reading also. What do you say to that?"

"I'd love it, Captain." She could not help herself. "Will I get to go overseas?"

"I like your enthusiasm, but there's space in this country as well, so I can't say," The captain smiled. "You do well, and I'll see what I can do for you."

She watched the smile on Deirdre's face, admiring the looks of the young woman and her enthusiasm. Perhaps she may have thought she'd make a good agent, or perhaps, despite only two years in college, they should recommend her for officer training. "That's it, private. You show us what you can do. Do it well, and congratulations."

Deirdre wanted to run back to the barracks and tell her friends, the few with whom she had become close, but decided to say nothing for now. Instead, she went through the basic training exercises in her seersucker uniform, marched and never complained, did the foot exercises that were to help them get used to the shoes and the marching. When the men found out about the shoes and the marching, they laughed and had one more reason to make fun of the women who should be at home in the kitchen, waiting for their sweethearts, or having babies if married, unless they worked in factories and the shipyards, or flew as WAFs.

By the end of basic, she had been promoted to sergeant, because of her outstanding ability in mathematics and her proficiency in French. She had also studied some German. She had already been practicing cryptography and map reading. It was not long before she received her orders. She would ship to England.

Sailing on the *Queen Mary*, she arrived in London the middle of August, 1944, already marked by the OSS as a WAC cryptographer. She would be of use either in England or in Europe where the Americans were besieged in the Ardennes and fighting off the Germans at Bastogne.

When she arrived at headquarters, two women met her, a

Captain known as Lynette Boucher and a Lieutenant known as Cheri Dormand. They would not only be her superiors but supervisors, perhaps occasionally her teachers. An enlisted WAC took her to her quarters in the city, a wet and dismal place, as far as Deirdre was concerned. It was also dangerous because of the rockets. She had heard that WACs had been either killed or injured.

The over-all commander was a male colonel. He was a husky man of about 5'10," brown-haired with a small crook in his nose and a round chin, not particularly handsome but who appealed to many of the women because of his usually soft voice and bright brown eyes. When angry, those under him scurried or swore, although the women usually avoided swearing, not caring for it. Most despised his use of fuck and shit when angry, despised it in any of the males. Nor did they care to be seen as sexual objects and proved themselves to the men who came not only to accept them but to admire their abilities. On the streets it was different, "Look at those breasts, mamma mia, those legs. What a piece of ass she would make."

When the colonel met Deirdre, he tried to hide his attraction to this, how could he describe it, "this beauty," "a doll," "a combination Ava Gardner and Rita Hayworth." Deirdre knew what he was thinking but never acknowledged his admiration, stood straight and expressionless.

"Sergeant Deirdre Cunningham reporting, sir."

" At ease, Sergeant."

He watched her momentarily, instantly aware of the intelligence within her eyes as he watched them move about the room, remembering what she saw, analyzing the colonel while they talked.

"Sergeant, we don't know how well you'll do here. We'll find out. From now on, though, you'll be known as Agathe Lefevre." He had already decided upon her fitness, if she had the strength and intelligence he believed was there from reading the reports. If so, she would be sent to France to help the Maquis.

~

By January, after the Battle of the Bulge had been won and the Seventh Army was poised to move for Southern Germany and to take Southern France, Deirdre had already shown her ability with cryptography, had parachuted several times, and complained to others of the WACs about her bruised breasts from the snapping of the straps. Yet, no one knew how long it would take to conquer Germany or undo the damage of the Pétain government completely under control of German troops. The German civilians still did not believe that Hitler would lose the war, despite the mass bombings and the destruction of their cities, including their fear of advancing Russians in the East and the Allies in the West.

Deirdre - Agathe parachuted at night near the Alps, met by Maquis that included one female who would see to Deirdre's female needs and test her reactions to France and the men. They had to be certain the Americans or English had not dropped a double agent. The woman who took her to her quarters was somewhat suspicious. *Perhaps I'm jealous of her looks.* It did not take long to recognize that they had a good agent after the woman talked to Agathe Lefevre. The woman hurried Agathe to meet the chief that night, despite Agathe's weariness. It was then perhaps she could make mistakes they would notice.

The chief was a man named Étienne Moreau. They already had one agent in the German headquarters in Lyon who would prepare for the group's planned attack, hoping to hurry the retreating Germans from Vichy France.

Between Agathe with her messaging and the woman in the

headquarters it would be a good combination, assuring coordination. Étienne needed this new woman, but he would have to make certain she was not an infiltrator from the Germans even though the Americans had dropped her.

"Hello, Agathe," Étienne spoke softly and kindly. She wanted to sleep, but answered strongly about her happiness of being with him and the Maquis. She watched him as closely as he did Deirdre. He was a man of about medium height, broad shouldered, with a hard, handsome face. His curly black hair and blue eyes appealed to her, as did that body which she believed could withstand and give much punishment. She especially watched his eyes as he talked, analyzing her. Agathe-Deirdre started to smile, thinking of the time they were wasting.

"Talk to me some. Tell me about yourself," his voice a bit harsher.

"You know about me. I'm with the American OSS, and I'm here to make sure everything we need gets to us. I'll also be listening for anything in French that comes through from Lyon or elsewhere, transmit it back to England and. . . Oh why go on? You know what I'm doing here," showing her annoyance with these preliminaries.

She wanted to know about him, about the group from his lips, though she already knew much from her information in England. The softness and hardness in Agathe-Deirdre was why the Americans chose her. Though she occasionally showed some fear, most of the time she hid it. She concealed the slight softness in her and was quite capable of showing whatever she wished of herself and veiling whatever she wanted. Deirdre was, in effect, an excellent actress, perhaps could have been a Hollywood star. She smiled at him, turned her body slightly for him to see her figure while watching his face.

"Let me see your papers," he commanded, amused by her turn as though she were a fashion model but fascinated by her face and body. She handed them to him. He closely studied the photo, the wording, the paper to be sure there was nothing that would betray her. If there were to be a betrayal, she would be the one who would reveal it. After a time of just talk and Étienne assuring that members of the group met her, they drank wine as a welcome to the new member. The woman who had taken her to her quarters was there, went and sat beside her. "I'm Juliette, Agathe." She then whispered, "We have another woman in the headquarters he's going to arrange for you to meet." Juliette faced Agathe, placed an arm about her. "I know you're weary. Ah, what a pleasure to have another woman nearby. You'll meet the other who's at the Boche, brutal pigs rather, headquarters. You're a looker. So is she. She fooled them from the first. You could too. They'll fuck any woman, but one like she is or you, hah, that's a real conquering. Frankly, I avoid them whenever possible. They'll want to see what's below that floppy coat you have to wear. You be careful of them. They'll rape and then tell you you wanted it all along."

Agathe, because of the anger in Juliette's voice, wanted to ask about her.

Juliette saw the question. "Why hide it? They raped my mother and me. I hid my younger sister when they came to the house. They killed my father who tried to protect us. I hate the rapist pigs, cried so hard when they gathered up the Jews and sent them to the concentration camps. We're living in swill here, and we'll kill as many of them as we can. They got that bastard Pétain to go along with them. Talk about traitors. He was the hero, some hero, of the first war. Just wait until we can bring De Gaulle to all of France."

"Ah, I'm sorry." "Agathe, I'm a bitter woman and I want my revenge. I try to hide it from the men, joke with them, but they know better than even to touch me. I'm so happy to have you with us, to have another woman I can talk to more often than with others in different places." She looked closely at Agathe. "Don't pity me. Save it. We're here for the same reason."

"I won't talk about it, bring it up. Let's just try and be friends."

"Friends? Maybe that's not so good if one of us gets it."

Deirdre changed from rape to Étienne. "What about him? You like him. It's obvious everyone is loyal and will follow him."

"Hah," Juliette answered. "You like him already."

Agathe tried to ignore her smile.

"He's got some background. He was in Greece and came back to France just in time for the formation of the Petain government. Étienne didn't waste time. He's a natural leader who has headed this group for ages, it seems.

"By the way, has he told you he's going to get you and Diane together?"

"Not yet. I know it's necessary."

"Wait until you see her." Juliette laughed. "Two beauties. Yes, she's got it, what the pigs want. How she puts up with it, being fucked by that Boche pig General. But she gets the information we need. So perhaps besides the pleasure, there's that continual drip of useful information. Hah. I'm wicked. Agathe, I'm truly sorry. I haven't talked so freely to a woman in so long. You can see and feel the hatred in me, no?"

"I do." Agathe started to put her hand on Juliette's face but stopped, not wanting the men to see any sign of affection or understanding.

Étienne had been watching them and interrupted. "Hah, female gossip. Good for the soul. You women."

"Yeah, you women," Juliette barked. Men in the room looked toward them. "We're just chatter boxes, Étienne."

"Stop, Julie. I can imagine what it's like to be with men most of the time. I'm pleased you two seem to be getting along. But it's time for Agathe to get some sleep. It's quite a day tomorrow. I sent for Diane, and there's messages with England needed."

The night ended. Deirdre-Agathe Lefevre went to her small room in a farm house from which she could look out toward the Alps, wondering whether she would ever see her parents again, if they would ever know what happened to their daughter from whom they hadn't heard for so long. She worried just now whether they disowned her. But that hardness that protected her returned - the independent, star student no longer but a member of the Maquis, the OSS, and a killer, if need be. Christine's and Edward's Deirdre had died.

While looking toward the window before she fell asleep, she suddenly thought of an ocean storm, the waves rising, turning a deceitful white spray spearing the coast, spewing their beauty and anger. Had a weary Deirdre died in that surf image? Silence.

~

The following day the group urgently met with Étienne.

"We have little time. We must get to Lyon. Diane has sent a message that Agathe has received." He looked at this new woman, admiring her body and face so perfectly formed it was almost impossible to believe. He turned from her, compared her to Juliette, was angry with himself for doing so. There was no time for women right now. They were also fighters. He would find out; however, Agathe was difficult to ignore - if she were not a German agent.

"The Boche are planning another roundup. Perhaps, if fortunate, we'll save some. Our main plan, however, from the message is that we should attack as soon as possible and force a quicker retreat, get as many papers as we can from their headquarters. Diane will meet a few of us while the rest of you wait my orders on the outskirts. There's two safe houses held by widows, widows because the bastards took their husbands into custody and no one ever heard from them again."

They had an old truck and a car. The truck held bicycles, as well as men; the car Étienne, Agathe, and Étienne's lieutenants.

"We're joining the main group that has been in Lyon. And listen, we're out for revenge against the terror of Klaus Barbie, as well as setting the fear of the French and the Allies in the fucking Germans." Étienne was angry at how long it was taking to drive such a relatively short distance. He wanted to kill Germans for the French and for disrupting his life because of these Maquis with whom he had become so close. He had never imagined being close to anyone, having been on his own so much before the war, having lost his parents to the Nazis who thought the parents knew where he was. He had heard that Barbie had personally tortured them. The Boche would suffer in this hopefully final attack.

They arrived outside Lyon in the evening, having all passed through check points. Once, looking inside the car, one of the Nazis asked Agathe to get out. He questioned her, found her imperturbable. It was her face that drew her to him. He grabbed her shoulder, pulled her into the guardhouse, pushed her, standing with his back to the car. "Open that coat." She started to balk, calmed herself and did as he asked, thought of kicking him in his balls, as he grabbed for her breasts. Grimacing, she stood quite still.

"You like them?" *You fucking son of a bitch.*

"Yah. Soft. They must stand up. Lovely. Leave your friends and stay here. I'll see you rejoin them."

"No. You come to my home, handsome one. We can get together then," she forced a smile. *God help you if I ever see you again.* "My friends are waiting. Please let me go. Here. Look at my papers again, and you'll know where to find me. Meet me?"

she forced another smile, fluttering her eyelashes. "We can have a good time then."

He saw an officer coming and let her go to the car. "I'll see you there," he called just loudly enough for her to hear, as did the others in the car.

When she got in, Étienne started off, looked at her through the rear mirror. "Now you know."

"I know, Étienne. Sometimes it's hard being a woman. But men don't know how we can punish."

"Perhaps. Why do you think you're here?" He laughed. "You're getting tough." Juliette touched her arm, ran her hand along it, telling her she understood.

At the farm house in which they would stay by the Rhone, they unloaded their equipment, took their sleeping quarters. Juliette and Agathe shared a room. The men took another on the floor below.

"Agathe. Come down as soon as you can."

"I'll be right there."

"Tomorrow, very early morning, Diane will be here. I want you two to know one another. You're the new Diane contact. Make sure you get along. With your knowledge, maybe it will be easier." He was making small talk now. It was obvious her skill in cryptography would help them maintain contact with the main Lyon group, as well as Diane, England, and the Allies now in Southern France driving hard against the Germans who in some places were fleeing in panic.

As the sun rose the next morning, Agathe heard a car, jumped from bed fully clothed. She had wanted to sleep in a soft filmy nightgown, to feel desirable. That, she knew quite well, would have to wait. She watched the car approach and stop. A woman about Agathe's height, with reddish blonde hair, a straight short nose, high cheek bones, hazel eyes, wearing a dress that showed the shape of her breasts and hips, her long, slim legs as she walked. *She's a looker. Probably beds any damn Nazi she wants or they want.*

In fact, Diane was the mistress of an aide to the officer in charge of the Lyon headquarters. If she dared sleep with another, she must have kept it secret. Agathe wondered what it would be like to be a spy, to become the sexual partner of an enemy, like Mata Hari, so you could get information. She would not like that. Her lover had to be her choice, or so she still thought despite what she had learned through OSS and here in France.

The two women met outside, greeted each other with a shake of hands, forced smiles, each wondering who was the more desirable, knowing they had to work together, perhaps uneasily.

Diane spoke first. "I am pleased to meet you. Your description was so accurate."

"And that came from Étienne, no?"

"You guessed it. I want to ask him to let you come to headquarters with me, to meet the great high command." She surprised Agathe. What was the purpose? Without answering they went in to have a light breakfast, eating alone with Étienne. Diane looked about, studying the building, deciding how many people Étienne had brought with him.

While she drank coffee, Diane asked, "I would like Agathe to come to headquarters, to see what it's like, to introduce her as a friend. Looking at her, they'll be after her."

You ought to know, Agathe thought.

"I'm not sure it's such a good idea. There's going to be a coordinated attack soon."

"When will it be so I can get free of the pig Boche and help as you get closer?"

Neither Étienne nor Agathe liked the manner of her question.

"Soon. We'll make certain you're safe," Étienne replied slowly. "When do you want her?"

"I thought of taking her with me. I have some clothes, various sizes to make sure there's a fit. Not too fancy, though."

Agathe looked at Étienne. "All right. Go with Diane, but get her back here before evening."

Diane's eyes brightened. She turned her head to hide her expression. Agathe noticed each of her movements. She seemed uncomfortable, but Étienne who worked with her for so long was intent on his own thoughts, the need of Agathe for the radio.

"All right. Get going as soon as she's dressed."

They went upstairs where Juliette was dressing. "Oh. Juliette. You're here too. How nice. I wish we had some time for woman talk, but I'm in a hurry."

Juliette had only met Diane once and did not like her, not only because she didn't trust her but because of the way she flaunted her body. Sometimes she wondered whether she was just jealous. Right now was no time for analysis.

Diane took out the dresses. One, a reddish blue, almost purple with diagonal stripes would fit and not look too rich. "Try this." Agathe wanted to object. "Underwear, Diane?" she asked. She brought out several bras, panties, and slips. When she saw Agathe's body, the straight full breasts, she was somewhat jealous again. She watched as Agathe quickly pulled on what she thought would fit.

"Fine," Diane said. Juliette agreed, wondering if there was anything wrong with this woman. Agathe would notice. She laughed to herself. *Two beautiful women vying with one another for the butcher Nazi's attention.*

As they approached Nazi headquarters, Agathe noticed the concentration of tanks, armored cars cruising about the streets, the many troops in what the Germans considered the strategic quarters of the city. When they came close to the headquarters, there was a guard house and a gate. One of the guards knew Diane but stopped her and asked for both the stranger's papers and Diane's.

They drove up a short street, ending in a circle, buildings on both sides, well protected. It took little imagination to know there were troops on either side. Diane stopped on the right side, took her inside a building with some wood paneling, three short steps to get to the soldier sitting at a desk, his weapon in a half-open drawer. He also knew Diane and was going to waive her on, stopped, seeing Agathe.

"Wait," he curtly ordered. "This one? I've never seen her before. Is she a friend of yours?"

"Yes," Diane answered in a disgruntled voice. "Do you think I'd bring in someone who shouldn't be here? She's a cousin I haven't seen for some time. Can't you see the resemblance?"

More politely, the soldier asked for Agathe's papers. He could not upset a commanding officer.

They took an elevator to the third floor, were shown into a spacious office with floor-to-ceiling windows, partially shuttered, a large desk, where sat a tall, husky man with wide, puffy cheeks, broad arms resting on the desk top.

."Ah, Diane. You brought your cousin. Pleased to meet you, mademoiselle." He rose, went to them, held himself from kissing Diane, and shook Agathe's extended hand. *The perfect gentleman.* Agathe was a bit fearful but also excited. She was in the headquarters they would attack, and, hopefully, capture this bastard. She watched both closely. The general ordered brandy for them. Agathe begged off. She did not like liquor and also needed clearness. She noticed the General look questioningly at Diane. She tried to avoid him and turned to Agathe. "The General has waited a long time to meet you. He's heard much about our friendship since we were children."

After a while, Diane walked to one of the windows while Agathe sat in a corner chair close by a table where they had the drinks. The General stood behind Diane, listening to her whisper, "I think - I don't know – maybe I can turn her. She may look sure of herself, but I wonder." She glanced back to Agathe and smiled. Agathe thought, *Forced.* At that moment Agathe saw her reach back and lightly touch the General's hand.

I've got to get back. This is no act.

"Would you excuse us for a moment, Agathe?" the General asked.

"Of course." Involuntarily, she looked at his crotch. *He's probably so hard he has to get her even though I'm here. Stop being a fool. They want you and all of us. She's a freakin', fucking traitor. I just know, that look and touch at the window, the whispering. I'm, well – not like her, but I am attracted to Étienne. Here I am still a virgin. Hmm? That's war.*

On the way back, Diane's biggest mistake, revealing her a traitor, was asking when the attack would come rather than waiting by her radio for Agathe's short signal.

At the farmhouse, after Diane left, Agathe asked to speak to Étienne.

"What?"

"She's a German agent," Agathe curtly said.

"Now what makes you think that?" he smiled. "She's been with us for some time now."

"And how many members have you lost?"

He thought for a moment. "I know there were some lost in the city. One night we were caught attacking a train and lost a man and woman. But that didn't seem unusual," he lied.

"C'mon, Étienne. You're too smart not to wonder."

That charming smile of his again, damn. I do like him. His eyes. God, I could lie in those arms. Cut it. He has suspected. That's why he sent me.

"She's more than his mistress. I'm sure she's good in bed. That rear of hers and the way she swings it."

"So does yours more than usual sometimes," he laughed. He stopped, immediately serious. "What happened?"

"The way she was with the General, the little signals, the stupidity of asking about the attack instead of waiting for my short signal. Damn. When I think I've been transmitting information to her. They'll be down on us. I know it."

"No they won't." He thought just a moment. "We're moving and will watch and get them, take care of her in Lyon."

Agathe felt sorry for Diane, but only in passing. She wanted the woman dead, hanging like so many of the citizens had been. *Screws her ass off with that General, gets whatever she wants. And now she thinks she'll screw us. Deirdre, you're getting to be a hard bitch.* She smiled. Étienne noticed. "What's going on in that lovely head, Agathe?"

"Revenge," her voice hard. She softened her tone. "Étienne. I just wish this war would end and I could be a woman, a real woman."

"Silly one. You are, well, no I do understand."

They sat looking at one another, her arms bent, her head resting in her hands, gazing at him. *Why did I tell him that? You're trying to seduce him and know you can.*

"Tell me about yourself, Étienne. You know more about me. What was it like in Greece?"

"I was an art dealer, traveled about the Mediterranean, France etc. I hunt for art objects to sell. When the Germans came to Greece, I came back home and quickly got involved with the Resistance. Exciting, no?"

"You joke, but it sounds like fun and good work. I love art objects."

Étienne, watching her, the eyes, hair, face, glancing at her breasts showing just above the table, felt a stirring in his groin. He imagined her naked, wanted to touch her.

Aware of his thoughts, she did not move when she felt his hand on her thigh, slowly moving upward, waiting to see whether she would stop him. Instead, she placed her hand over his and moved it close to her orifice while spreading her thighs but forced herself to stop him, suddenly thinking of Kevin. *I don't know if he's alive or dead nor he I. Now is now. We owe each other nothing. Never did.*

"No. We shouldn't. The quarters are too close," his voice hoarse. She did not want to stop though, feeling her nipples tightening and her increasing wetness.

"No, not here," she loudly whispered.

"We'll get away from the others." They were both breathing harder. "Later, Agathe. All right?"

She let out a loud breath, moving her head slowly up and down once.

And later, they went to the barn and climbed into the back seat of the car. "It should be our only time together in a place like this. I want to see you."

Juliette woke for a moment, noticed she was missing, thought nothing of it until early morning when they had to be ready to leave. "You were late, Agathe," Juliette said with a wide grin. "Tell me. You like him, don't you?"

"We have work to do. Let's get ready." She did smile at Juliette. "I do."

"He's a hard one to resist."

As they dressed, Agathe thought of the car, saw herself taking off her dress, unfastening her bra, feeling Étienne pulling down her panties, his fingers curling her hair, inserting his fingers, his hands then rising to her breasts, murmuring how lovely they were, and the sucking on her nipples. She thought of how in the dim light they had from leaving the door ajar, watching him take off his pants, his underwear, watching his hardened penis as she reached for it and lightly slid her hand along the shaft, as he moved her so he could push inside. She felt the pain - still hurt this morning – yet was happy. She thought of his patience, when soon aware it was her first time. After, she waited, pleased, until he was ready; the next time, he turned her on top of him, parting her legs so her foot of one leg rested on the car floor, guided her, listening to her moaning as she moved back and forth, up, down, listening to her deeper breaths until she shouted, leaning backward. She lay on him, not wanting to leave, wishing they were in a bed.

"Come on, Juliette. We're going to be first ready. Won't we surprise Diane and her General?"

"He was good, I bet," Juliette teased.

"Keep quiet."

"Your face is red, Agathe."

"Oh, stop."

"Agathe, I'm not jealous. I'm not even sure, though I see men that are appealing, that I want one inside me, not after. . . ." She stopped. Agathe went to her, hugged and kissed her mouth.

"Sometimes I wish I could just have a woman," she whispered. "Kiss me again."

Agathe did and eased back, enjoying the feel of Juliette's lips. "If anything happened to me like to you, I don't know what I'd do. I hope I'd be as brave as you." She hesitated, "I'd let you be with me, if I could," She hesitantly mumbled, "I'm not sure. You understand?" Deirdre did then start questioning what it would be like to make love to another woman, that perhaps it would be more pleasurable, softness against softness, each knowing what satisfies a woman.

Juliette shook her head "Yes," and walked toward the stairs, rubbing a few tears from her eyes.

~

Everyone in the car was silent when they started. It was to be a coordinated attack. The Americans and their Free French allies had landed in Southern France and were now driving toward General Patton and Aix-en-Provence, having freed Toulon and Marseilles and much of Vichy France. Soon they would free Lyon with the help of the Resistance in which Étienne and his group were taking part. The main group would attack Fort Montluc, Klaus Barbie's headquarters for the SS, where so many Jews and Resistance had been tortured, murdered, sent to concentration camps.

Étienne reminded them of what was happening, how they must be successful, thus the quiet thinking of what they must accomplish and wondering which of them would perhaps be killed.

Soon, however, one of the men shouted, "We'll demolish the Boche, butcher them. No mercy for the assassins."

Étienne told him not to be so sure, even if it is a surprise attack that comes off. "We'll be the ones going after the headquarters. And if you find Diane, I don't want her killed. Hear me?" shouting this last. "I want that woman myself."

They drove to the outskirts of the city. The men in the truck spread out and walked alone or in twos while keeping track of one another, heading toward the cathedral, Notre Dame de Fouvière. There they met others strolling, despite the German troops and tanks. From there they walked northward to a far end of Place Bellecour moving closer to the German Headquarters where weapons were hidden nearby.

A German staff car conveniently parked nearby in which there were two soldiers. The Maquis quickly came from behind, leaped, grabbed the soldiers' necks, twisting, breaking them, capturing the Germans' vehicle that they drove toward the gate, a German waving them through, quickly stabbed, his hand still raised, two others killed the same way. The attack was on, as Étienne's men crept through, pressing against buildings to avoid notice.

Agathe and Juliette had walked together as two women shopping. Now Agathe's heart began beating harder as they came closer to the headquarters where Diane had introduced her to the General.

The Resistance in Lyon that was already throughout the city, as they had been since the German occupation, had previously taken on the Germans, killing many and losing Maquis men and women. Now, they believed, they would make a difference. The Germans would die and leave them free. Those attacking Fort Montluc also had a staff car, the Resistance men dressed in captured German SS uniforms.

Gun and shellfire burst in the early morning, smoke spreading, obscuring the sunrise, bodies left where they fell, scattered, dismembered. Other dead floated in the Rhone.

The attackers of Fort Montluc broke through, killing Germans in their way, quickly ran throughout the building and to the lower parts, freeing prisoners, helping those who could not walk, taking them to a relatively safe area. Claus Barbie, "The Butcher of Lyon," unfortunately escaped with Jewish prisoners. The Resistance rejoiced, however, having seized the fort.

Étienne's force sat on a corner manning a machine gun, others running into buildings firing. Agathe and Juliette along with men shot their way through the lobby where Diane had previously taken Agathe. Agathe, leading, led them to the third floor, broke through the door, slammed a door open. There in a corner, quivering, was Diane, abandoned by her German protectors.

Agathe, her heart beating furiously, breathed deeply, holding a rifle pointed at Diane. Calming some, she finally spoke. "Get up from that crouch, bitch traitor." Slowly Diane rose, expecting to be shot. "Don't, Agathe. You don't know how helpful I was." She wanted to pee, trembled, put out her arm, her fingers shaking.

"You were helpful. You led us here." Agathe walked slowly toward her, placed the rifle between her legs bringing it up sharply, "Not like your Nazi's prick, huh?" She slowly pointed down the rifle, holding it with one hand, grabbed Diane's long hair, pulled her toward the door, Diane screaming.

Étienne took her from Agathe, gave her to two men who held her arms while Juliette pulled at her hair as she cut it off. When finished the men pushed her to a building wall.

Étienne glared at the trembling, begging woman. "I have no pity, Diane. You have helped send Jews, our compatriots, and others to concentration camps, helped kill them in Fort Montluc. You are guilty." He paused. "Shoot her." Diane fell. All watched, some sorrowfully, some with hatred. "We have finished our work for now. The Allies will soon be here, and we'll help where they direct us."

Agathe stayed with Étienne's group for a while after the fall of Lyon to the Allies. She enjoyed looking at the mountains, seeing their power and feeling their magnetism. She spent time at Étienne's spare quarters, a small apartment. Here they became lovers, thought of marriage, but eventually, she had to follow orders that sent her to Paris and back to London. While in Paris, at headquarters, she received orders to report to her WAC commanding officer. As Deirdre walked into the Colonel's office, the woman smiled, returned Deirdre's salute and walked toward her.

"Because of your meritorious service, Sergeant, you are being given a field promotion to Second Lieutenant." The Colonel held gold bars in her hand, smiled, and told Deirdre to come close so the bars could be pinned on her shoulders. "Congratulations," she said, smiling. "Now you'll have to get a new uniform. In the meantime, I'll just cut off those stripes so you can leave here and be saluted for what we know you did, the bravery you showed working for the OSS in France. You are a credit to the WAC and the OSS. Such a credit. I believe there's a medal awaiting you in London.

Surprised, Deirdre smiled. "I expected nothing. I did what I had to, made friends among the French." She was thinking of Juliette and Étienne. For a moment, Juliette appeared foremost, Deirdre hearing her tell of the rape, feeling Juliette's mouth again on hers later that night, leading to hugs and kisses, searching hands to the following stifled moans in the shudder of orgasms.

"Would you like to tell me what it was like?"

"Not really. The hardest was the attack on the army headquarters, at least for me, and discovering an extremely attractive woman who had become a German double agent, the revengeful feeling, the coldness I felt when they shot her - but now. No. I . . ." Deirdre could not keep back the tears. "Excuse me, Colonel." She choked, her shoulders shaking, trying hard to stop the flow, waited, spoke as the Colonel interrupted to tell her she did not have to say more.

"No. . . . Now . . . ." taking a small handkerchief from her breast pocket and wiping. "Now, I am sorry for her. That gorgeous woman. All that beauty wasted. Still I hate her. Can you understand?"

The Colonel's face was grim. "You deserve every honor you receive, Deirdre. I'm proud to have you in the Corps." She went to Deirdre, touched her hand, "Sit for a bit until you feel you can face that world outside this office."

When she left the Colonel, she walked through the office of smiling faces and soft words of congratulations. She forced her thanks but wanted to get out, breath free air, walk on the Champs-Elysees, suddenly aware she would have to buy a uniform and change her quarters. She would tell only Étienne of the promotion.

They kept in touch through the wireless, reminding one another of their loss, the feel of one another's bodies. At night, she would lie thinking of his hands moving about her, feel the sensations, see herself sitting on him, tightening herself about him while moving slowly, or being below him, or his lips and mouth on her genitals. She heard herself and smiled with joy and then sadden with loneliness. They had decided she would finish school but be partners in his art object searches that they would sell to museums and collectors. He would return to Greece, go to Egypt, and she would return to the United States and set in place what they believed would be a lucrative business. He also promised to visit her after the war ended. Never would she forget the Alps, that small apartment, the killing, the anger, the hatred, the bodies. She buried these within her as deeply as she could. Yet, the outer beauty of Deirdre never forsook her. She had learned from her wartime experience the most effective use of her facial and body expressions. War obviously changed Deirdre. She wondered whether she had become the woman she had dreamed of being when younger.

Chapter VIII

Meeting - Memories - Departing

Deirdre was one of the many who returned during Atlantic Ocean storms. The ocean rolled the ships, the men and women hardly able to stand. Unsecured items flew about until the passengers learned better. During one day, the whistle blew continuously. Two soldiers, who should not have been on deck, and a sailor, trying to save them, were thrown into the roiling sea. It was impossible to rescue them, as some sailors on duty watched as they disappeared under the high, angry waves that buffeted the ship, broke over the decks. Unlike during the war, there were also war brides, many with children, as well as the uniformed men and women when before, in the crossing to war there had only been soldiers and later WACs with them.

The ship landed in New York. Deirdre felt strange when she stepped on the dock. This was her country, but having been with Étienne and the Maquis, and having been through everything she had, she nervously wondered whether she would be able to adjust to the United States and her family. One of the first things she knew she must do was to call her parents. When her mother answered, suddenly Deirdre's eyes began to tear, and she cried with excitement. "Mom, it's me. I'm home. I'm in New York and will be going to the discharge center." Before she finished, Christine shouted, "Deirdre, my dear. Oh, it's been so long." Her mother having shouted Deirdre, now cried along with her daughter, both sobbing. "Ohhh, I don't know what to say. That damn war took you away from us," the words coming with chokes, the swearing something her mother never used. "I just want to see and hug you forever, Deirdre."

"Me too, mom."

By then, Edward was on the other line they had bought during the war. "Deirdre, it's dad. When are you coming home? Will it be long? How we have missed you," he shouted.

All of Edward's bitterness had disappeared, worry taking its place when they had not heard from her for some time. Actually the letters they received were sent at intervals by the OSS with a P.O. address, letters that she had written before leaving for France. They were ignorant of what their daughter did or had done. That was over now, however, and Deirdre would soon be in Maine.

"I have to go to New Jersey, mom and dad, and be discharged. Then I want to look about a little." She thought they would wonder why. "Well, actually, I want to do a little shopping in New York. I promise, though, I'll be fast. I'm so anxious to see you"

"We too. Oh, Deirdre, thank God you're alive after those nasty storms we read about." What would it have been had they known what she had done, where she had been?

"I'm O.K., mom."

Edward shouted. "O.K. You shop but make it fast and come home like our stunning daughter we have missed so."

Deirdre smiled. *Yes, what if they knew.*

After discharge, she went to the best stores, bought perfume, "Evening in Paris", thinking of Étienne kissing her, and of his lips moving to her ears, her neck, aroused by the odor of Paris, slipping inside her, hearing him, herself, waking in the morning beside him. Then there were the lipsticks, color for her face and eyes, the latest dresses. But - she did not wear the clothes. She wanted her parents to see her in her officer's uniform, probably everyone in the town. She had not yet heard about Kevin and was anxious about his news.

About a week later, she went to Grand Central, trains still crowded with troops, then took a cab in Boston to North Station for a train that would take her to Portland, Maine from where a bus would take her to Warrington.

She stood at the door, straightened her uniform, brushed back her hair, and opened the door that was always unlocked, "Mom, Dad." Shrieks, rapid steps, hugs, tears, crying. Deirdre had not realized how pleased she would feel to be home, having been so anxious to leave. Her cap fell to the floor, but then Edward pushed her back a little to see her better. They had received letters that Deirdre, as an officer, had the authority to censor herself. Only now did it occur to Edward that his daughter was a Second Lieutenant.

Deirdre now thought of Kevin, asking if they had heard anything.

"Darling," Christine caught her breath. She thought Kevin and Deirdre would have been writing one another, although that would not have made any difference until the correspondence would have stopped. "Darling," she again drew a deep breath. "He was killed in France."

Deirdre stared at her mother, seeing the dead in Lyon. "When? Where?" she also catching her breath.

"We're not sure. We do know he was in the tanks. Maybe the Germans . . . . Oh, we don't know, Deirdre."

"Dead." Despite her experiences, a chill engulfed her. The death of a friend. Despite the deaths of others that affected individuals, Deirdre having heard it all - how people react, seeing reactions, feeling her own - knew there could be lasting effects. Why had they fought this war to lose Kevins, to have loved the raped like Juliette and been helpless to assuage her recurring terror? Unknowingly, that hatred buried itself in Deirdre. If it came to the surface, she wondered whether it would affect her throughout her life.

As it was, she returned to school and tried to live as she had before. Unfortunately, "before" was lost forever. Often she went to class or social affairs, but lost to her was the self-satisfaction of her youth. Taking its place was a selfishness that would last throughout her life. She would, she told herself, never again allow anyone or anything to prevent the fulfillment of her social or sexual desires.

Chapter IX

Sea's Vicissitudes

Brigit was on late shift. Gregory sat, paced, anxious for her to come home. He had become the youngest chief of research in the short time since finishing his fellowship. He picked up the newspaper, rustled the pages. The news was much the same except that now, in 1952, the Korean War had been a constant reminder of death and hatred. He wondered, looking at the headline, whether the world had forgotten so soon the obscenity of a world war.

MacArthur wanted to use nuclear weapons. The Chinese desired to reveal a new world power.

Gregory smiled. Here he was working in a laboratory to find cures to keep people alive or how to better treat them, and in Korea men worked to undo his work. More dead bodies, more atrocities. Nothing he did in a laboratory could help or stop what was happening. One day, however, he believed he would succeed, that he had not fought in the war for nothing and been permanently wounded uselessly, for his work was one answer. Yet there was the sadness that only Brigit could cure. In her presence, making love to her, the odor of her skin, the pleasure of running his fingers through her red hair, the feel of her response and her calming effect as she lay back looking up at him, seeing their reflections in one another's eyes, was the peace the world sought, that he had found.

He lay down thinking about her, knowing she would be happy when she heard his news.

When she came home, 11:30 p.m., he was asleep on the sofa. She walked softly to him, lightly touched his hair, and went to the kitchen. Although she thought she was quiet, he woke, walked to her and hugged, pulling her against him.

"Oh. I'm sorry I woke you. Here I thought I was being so quiet." She turned and kissed him, looked at him, her whole life seen in him.

"I love you," and he nuzzled his nose in her neck and hair. "What are you making?" He wanted to tell her, but wanted her to relax first, to be comfortable.

"Soup. Coffee. Want some?"

"Hmmm."

She removed her uniform, got a robe, returned. He enjoyed watching the sureness with which she moved, the glow in her face because she was home. "You look so fetching. Come here and kiss me." He put up his arms, and smiling, she went to him. She sat on his lap, kissing and hugging for a while. "O.K. Let's eat," she whispered.

While they ate, he told her, "I have something special to tell you."

"What? You found another woman?" she laughed.

"That's not funny. I couldn't leave you even if dragged by a chain. No one can match that dazzling face and body, that voice. Brigit, do you realize how much I do love you."

She watched his face and eyes as he spoke. "Yes, as much as I love you. Now tell me."

"A friend of mine from Cape Astraea offered me Chief of Isotope Research at the Maine Center for Illness and Research. Coincidentally we were at med school together. He's got an in with the administration and Chief of Staff, and without my knowing or my consent, submitted my name. They told him to get me. Naturally, they'll want to see and interview me. But he thinks there'll be no doubt. What do you think?"

"That's tremendous. See, I told you you were going places." She was somewhat sad to be leaving her position, if they went to Maine. She had become a head nurse in Ob/Gyn and Birthing and would have to start all over again. But she couldn't hold Gregory back, even though his reputation was growing in Boston. *That's why they want him. I can't keep him here. I'm happy for him. Shall I bring up marriage now? It's time. We've lived together long enough. I know they talk behind my back, think I'm a fallen woman. I am. My parents aren't happy. Marriage will satisfy them after all this time even if he is Jewish. Why should I care now? It's Maine, different people. His parents? They've always been nice. Mary and I get along so well. It's no good any longer with him rising.*

"You're so quiet, Brigit."

"Thinking."

"You don't want me to accept?" he questioned quizzically.

She hesitated. Stood.

"What's wrong?"

"I think it's so wonderful for you." Again she hesitated.

"Something's wrong. Leaving your job?"

"Partly." She paused. "Greg, you know I love you."

"I know that. We love each other. But you're unhappy."

Oh, why have I done this? What good is it? The way we're living. I just can't do it anymore. Some of the nurses talk about me. I know they do. I come into a room, and they stop talking. Yeah. They're all virgins - like fun. I know men have gone into their rooms, seen them, heard two of them one night when I had to stay for a delivery. The war destroyed virginity. She smiled, started to laugh. *Virginity. How about the 1920s? The first time, I was scared and excited and wondered whether he had made me pregnant. What's wrong with me? I've never truly cared. I have. I've fooled myself – and Greg. Thomas Erickson's been after me. Asked me out after I helped him with the patient with ovarian cancer. He's a nice guy. No one can take Gregory's place. No one. But it's time.*

Gregory sat watching her, rose and went to her and touched

her shoulder. "Brigit. You're so far away. What's wrong? If you don't want me to go . . ." *I have to go.* "What's wrong, dear?"

She turned, pushed him toward the sofa, fell on him. "Gregory Hurwitz." She looked in his eyes. "Greg. I want you to be good at what you do. You are. You'll be famous." She hesitated, placed her head between his head and shoulder. "Greg. It's . . ." *Why should I be proposing?* "Well, it's time we married. My family, yours, want it, will be happier about us." She stopped, embarrassed.

He pushed up from below her, straightened her so she sat straight. "Brigit Donovan. I love you. Did you know that? Will you marry me?"

"Yes, you idiot." She smiled happily, laughed. "Why have you waited so long? I've done everything I know how to get you to ask. I bat my eyes, do strip teases for you. Say, you never took me to Scollay Square. I buy sexy clothes and underwear. And I bet you . . . ." Her face reddened.

"You don't have to say it," he laughed. "No. Nobody can take your place in bed."

"We'll have to have the ceremony in Las Cruces, you know."

"I know that. Tell your mother to arrange it, but let's wait until I've actually got the position so we can surprise everyone. I won't even tell my parents, until then."

"You can't do that. Someone will tell your father we were there. He probably knows about it already."

"You do want to marry me, Greg?"

"Stop it. We've talked about this. I don't even know why we waited so long."

"I do. Because you've had me." She stopped, sorry she said it, though she had often thought it. *Let a man have you, and he's got you cornered in your own desire. When I think of that nurse, how she was so sure and then dropped. It was horrible watching her.*

"I don't want you to talk like that. Nobody's your equal."

The next afternoon, Gregory went to a jewelry store on Boylston Street, looked at the rings and decided he'd take Brigit with him so she could help choose and get the right fit. "No. She's home today." He called. "Brigit, are you doing anything?"

"Thinking of what to make for dinner tonight. It's something special."

"Well how about if we go out, say the Parker House - or. No. We're going to the Ritz." Before she could answer, he spoke again. "Are you dressed? If not, get into some nice clothes and meet me at the corner of Boylston and Arlington Streets, say in about an hour. That will give you time to fix your face etc. Love you, darling," and hung up.

He waited impatiently, saw her come from the subway stop and walk toward him, watching the movement of her body, watching men look at her, one turning to see her rear and its sway. "Yeah. I know what you're thinking. Sorry, buddy. She's mine." For a moment he thought of the hospital and the men talking about her as a piece of ass. It still infuriated him.

He ran up to her, took her hand. "C'mon." He pulled her gently toward the store.

"Greg. Stop. I'm in high heels."

"Sorry." He slowed, walked beside her. When she saw where he was taking her, she screamed softly. "I was going to do this on my own and present it to you tonight but thought you should have your choice and the right fit." And so the first step, an engagement ring they both liked, that he immediately placed on her finger, and the wedding ring held for later. She wanted to kiss him, hug him tightly. The quivering through her body was almost sexual.

They left slowly. It was twilight. "Let's have a drink. Then we can go to the dining room. I made reservations. O.K.?"

"Yes," she told him quietly. "I want to kiss you right now." She turned to him, neglecting propriety, the crowd of people, placed her arms about him and put her lips to his mouth. They stood together, people separating and passing them, looking, smiling, "I'd rather we go to bed."

"We'll drink and eat first. Can you wait?"

"What an insult. You turned me down." She pulled him harder to herself and kissed him, her tongue licking his. "We can't do it on the street. In fact, we've made a show of ourselves, so we'll do things your way." She doubted she had ever been so happy. She wanted his hands on her breasts, moving over her entire body. "I'm so excited. Are you?"

"I am. Believe me. I am."

They went to the lounge after which they went to the dining room. Seated close by a window looking out on the Public Garden, Gregory happened to turn toward the restaurant entrance. A husky, tall man was taking a wrap from a woman with dark hair and a very attractive face. She moved her shoulders in a provocative manner, enabling the wrap to fall into his hand that he nonchalantly gave to the maître d. She was perhaps as tall as Brigit, wore a bare-shouldered dress, her right ring finger displaying for the public a large diamond ring. About her neck was a single strand of pearls. Exhibiting herself, she walked slowly, self-assuredly to their table. Other dinner guests also watched her. She turned and smiled at her escort as a waiter held the chair for her. She sat slowly, pulling slightly at her long skirt.

Étienne was clearly proud of his younger companion who wore his jewels. Both were known to the staff, they having been here a number of times before. But tonight was special. He had recently returned from Greece and sold two pieces of art to the Walker Museum of Antiquities. Deirdre prepared the way for him, for a number of museums in the United States knew of him and his work. Early on he had introduced her as his colleague to his connections sometime during the past year. Deirdre now had her introduction to the art world and society.

Brigit, talking to Gregory, saw Deirdre. *Now there's a sexy, rich one. The guy she's with has money, knows how to get them like her.* She thought of saying something to Gregory but thought better, only he had also seen her. "Look at that dress and the ring. Wow."

"I don't need one like that. But if you want, I'll get an identical to hear your "Wow."

He laughed. "You're jealous."

"I am not. What's she got that I don't, except for that rich geezer she's with." She was comparing herself to Deirdre but realized the woman was no better looking than was she. Two gorgeous women vying for the diners' recognition. Brigit got the same attention when she walked in, noticing the men and women looking, smiling to herself, trying to appear serious and nonchalant, yet pleased by the attention. When they sat at their table, she displayed her ring in its platinum setting, placing her hand on the table for the waiters and those near them to see.

Gregory smiled. "Well, at least I'm not a geezer."

"No. A famous researcher, Nobel Prize winner to be."

"What faith." It pleased him she regarded him so. "I wouldn't wait for the Nobel."

"I won't, as long as I have you." She glanced at Deirdre, again comparing herself to the unknown woman. *I will get a dress something like that. It'll be part of my trousseau. Gather ye fruits while ye may. How many years can my body last like it is now.* She started to take the mirror from her handbag, wanting to imagine what she'd become. *Stupid. You're desirable.* For the remainder of the dinner there were just two newly engaged people, adoring one another, talking of their future and she interspersing the conversation with wedding plans.

When Gregory was looking at the bill, Brigit did glance at Deirdre. *I need a dress that'll show my bust like hers does. Well, mine does. Maybe we're distant twins.* In fact, their bodies were much alike and a matter of how each would choose to show it.

When they were home and as they closed the door, Brigit brushed against him, hugging him with her coat open, knowing he could feel her breasts. "It was a lovely evening, Greg. I'm so excited." She raised her hand. "It's so beautiful" She went to a lamp, placed her hand in the light. "Look how it shines."

"Look how you shine."

She sat on the sofa. "Come here." And the night of love had begun, their sounds of pleasure ending in the excitement and relaxations of several orgasms. We're one." She rested her head on his chest, moving her fingers over his nipples. "Feel good?" quietly.

Murmured. "Hmm. I love you, always will."

~

Gregory's parents and Mary met them at the station. Mary, in her last year of medical school, asked permission for a weekend off from clinical duties reluctantly granted when she explained. She purposely returned home the night before.

Brigit had already called her parents who had spoken to both of them excitedly, happily. Luke felt the difficult restraint preventing him from saying, "It's about time," but he was as happy as Maureen. "Just tell us when you'll come home, dear, for the arrangements."

"My darling, darling daughter. We're rejoicing for both of you." Maureen looked at Luke, daring him to say anything hurtful. He smiled at her, patted her shoulder, "Don't worry. I'm pleased."

Everyone was happy. Gregory and Brigit went to his home. His parents had arranged an engagement party for people from Cape Astraea and in Portland that included some with whom Gregory could possibly be working. The friend who suggested him for the position was also there. He was an affable family man, knowledgeable, but not as forceful or thoughtful as Gregory. Perhaps because he knew he did not have the insights or administrative skills of Gregory he was aware the Center needed his friend.

It was a gay evening, laughter, music, drinks, dancing in a large room cleared of furniture where the Hurwitz children once played.

Later, when everyone was gone, with the moon shining, Gregory took Brigit for a ride by the sea, calm right now, the moonlight a streak of light across the water, waves gently rolling toward the shore. They stopped, simultaneously turned to one another.

"You're happy, Brigit."

"You know I am. I love your parents, and Mary is such a good friend. I'm glad you have one sister anyway. And we're so close in age. We can have woman talk, no fear of gossip coming from either of us. Oh, how I love you." She put her arms about his neck. He had already moved closer. It was a warm spring night with no need for coats to hinder them. She sat on his lap, first sideways, feeling him moving upward to press against her, turned and faced him, both kissing as they rubbed. She then lay back on the seat for him. She whispered, "I wish we could sleep in the same room."

"I'll come to you when everyone is asleep. And if they're not, I'll just creep softly like I did as a kid."

When they arrived home, Mary was still up. Brigit's face reddened when she looked at Mary.

"Hi. How was the ocean?" She wanted to tease but stopped. "Want some company for a while, Brigit, as if you haven't had enough already?"

"Sure." She could still feel Gregory's hands on her breasts, the tightening of her nipples, his fingers inside, he inside, and remembered she hadn't put back her bra but had pushed it into her pocketbook or that she had not even buttoned her dress completely. *What difference? Mary knows. She knew when she looked at me. As long as she doesn't say something embarrassing. But she wouldn't. When she sees how I'm almost undressed? Maybe I'll tell her I'm tired.*

Mary smiled at her. "Would you rather wait 'til tomorrow and we can have some time to ourselves? You have to be tired."

"Oh no," Brigit quickly interrupted. She kissed Gregory goodnight at her bedroom door, her eyes telling him "later." Mary followed through the door.

"I know you're tired. I said that already." She noticed the dress, knew Brigit was not wearing her bra.

"Let me go freshen up," averting Mary's eyes.

Mary couldn't help herself.

"Brigit. We're friends and always will be, I hope. Don't make up tales for me. You know about me. If I had someone like Greg, only a woman - well, I may; her name is Evelyn - I'd be in his - her bed or on the floor with her, anywhere. As it is. Oh well, I have my times."

"Just be sure for yourself, Mary as I have," Brigit called as she quickly drew a wet facecloth over her thigh, put on her bra, completely buttoned her dress, and returned, not caring about lipstick.

"My brother doesn't realize how fortunate he is."

"He does."

"Well, if he doesn't, he will." She wanted to ask about their intimacy but knew she couldn't, that it would only come out if Brigit said something.

"You'll wait until I finish the year and just before I go to my internship, I hope."

"We've already talked about that. Besides, I want you as one of my bridesmaids. My sisters will also be. But I want you, Mary. Mary, I'm so happy." They both had tears in their eyes and hugged one another. "You know. I think I fell in love with him the day in the hospital when he was so bad to you. That's peculiar. I guess it was after and his remorse for treating you so horribly. I knew he was soft inside. But he was in such pain." She stopped, remembering how sorry she felt for both brother and sister who obviously cared for one another.

"You look tired, Brigit. We both ought to go to sleep."

"Yes."

Mary could not help herself. "Don't let him come to you later. I saw those looks," she teased.

"Oh, c'mon." And they both laughed.

"I love and almost - almost, get it - envy you, Brigit." Mary then hugged her again, kissed her lightly on the mouth, and told her, "I have a sister I always wanted. Thank you." She turned her head, while trying to choke back crying. Once more, however, they were both in tears, trembling, crying happily.

I did go to her room that night. We made love. I think we both fell asleep about the same time. Early morning, she woke me to leave the room. I felt her against me, her arm wanting to hold me back.

Pamela's coming in. It has to be so hard waiting for grad school and looking after me. Except now she has some help. Brigit comes. That amazes me. And there's that home care nurse. Pam's mother is off again, business with the French guy. What the hell are they up to?

No. Brigit and I didn't go to Las Cruces. Her family hates me I'm sure, probably doesn't care, if they know, I'm ill and hope I die. Peculiar how things turn out, and I'm still in love with Brigit, always was. What was I ever thinking? Fucking women with their sexiness, perfumes, and purring, falling all over you and the stupidity of ass-hole men like me. Did I love her? Brigit was with me.

That shadow in the hall. Who was that? Brigit? My mind wanders too much now. I couldn't work even if I could go in. Well, occasionally I do. Everyone at the lab is so nice, but I know they're just feigning, allowing me to look, make suggestions that no one will ever follow. Well, they did one day. I told them to try human cells. I'm certain that has possibilities. It's always bothered me that we have never looked at heart cells. It's so rare they come up cancerous. Oh well. I'm not the man I was. Was I ever a man? The war? Yes. I fucked those Sicilian and Italian women who would let me. No. I never paid, but I did take them gifts of food etc. Remember Brigit asking me about the foreign women during the war? I just smiled. The men on the ship coming back with V.D. But the few I had seemed to come from nice families, like the sisters in that family photo I brought back or sent home to let everyone know I was meeting nice girls.

Oh, God, now I'm coughing again.

"Are you all right, Greg? Want a glass of water? Your water jar's empty." *She places her hand on my sweaty forehead. It feels so right, like it used to, wherever she touched me. Does Pamela resent her? I don't think so. They get along so well together. Better than when Pamela's with her mother.*

"You're here. You are foolish."

"Keep quiet."

"I never stopped loving you."

"Nor I you."

"That night at the Ritz. The celebration all because of what we had achieved in the lab, and the Walker Museum of Ancient Antiquities was celebrating at the same time. And she was there with that Frenchman. It wasn't 'til later I found out she had been a WAC OSS and in France. She and that Frenchman had just sold some art work to the Walker."

"I don't want to talk about it, Gregory. It's over, happened a long time ago. We have our lives now and from that time. I wish you'd try to sleep. I have to make some dinner for Pamela. Your daughter's such a lovely girl. Both of them are." *She and Melinda could have been mine, both ours. I never fought hard enough. I should have become pregnant. Then there wouldn't have been the Ritz, at least the way it turned out. Imagine me going there to celebrate and being pregnant, people looking at my belly. You damn fool, making sure about your cycle and making him wear a condom. Stupid, stupid, stupid. But I loved him inside me, wrapping my legs around him, holding him tightly against me, feeling . . . Stop. You're hurting yourself. Think about him now. I won't leave here, though, without us doing it again. He'll be strong enough.*

I'm standing by the window, gazing at Greg.

"Brigit."

"Oh. Yes."

"You're just standing there, somewhere else. Is it Thomas you're thinking about? Why he let you come here is beyond me."

"No, Greg. I wasn't thinking of him, just thinking."

"That night, dearest. I never . . ."

"Keep quiet."

"I can't help it."

~

We had left the apartment early. Brigit was wearing a long evening dress, blue, somewhat tight. It had just a short slit so she could walk better. She was so lovely, that red hair coming close to her shoulders. She didn't do it up like the other women, knowing I liked it longer. It gave her that allure. Those green eyes. The dress emphasized her breasts and was just tight enough so you would notice her hips and rear when she walked. I was so proud to be able to show her off. Everyone had met her before, but they rarely saw her at something so formal and important. I was to receive a reward for the liver research and how I proved we could diagnose with the isotope. It started with the paper I published. My boss insisted he be first author. But all knew. So we'd both be feted.

And there she was, standing there in that black dress that fell from her left shoulder to just above her breast, holding a drink, laughing, touching – I found out his name later – Étienne's hand every so often reaching to sip at her drink. She turned and we were gazing at one another. Her black hair and brown eyes, tall like Brigit, perhaps a bit shorter, thin and desirable. I couldn't help myself and turned to compare her to Brigit. The museum people then went to another room for their own celebration, but somehow or other she came to our room again, looking at me. She stopped by someone from the hospital. Later she told me she asked about me. It seemed she knew everyone. She did. I found out later how well she knew. Seeing that Brigit was talking to someone else, I asked about her, who she was. No one seemed to know except for the man to whom she had spoken. He told me later she seemed interested in me.

Brigit did notice the interplay but said nothing, just used her female senses. How stupid men are, forgetting the ability women have to notice, to observe, to feel, to hear, to perceive. We neglect their insight and sensitivity.

It was just before we went to Cape Astraea. I kept thinking about her, the way she looked, the gaze as she stood there before she disappeared that evening to go to the museum party. I excused myself, said I had to go to the men's room, looked at Brigit and knew her eyes were following me. I walked into the connecting hall between party rooms, saw her chatting with her male friend and other people, men and women. She saw me and waved. I bent my head and smiled in greeting. She seemed to excuse herself and came toward me.

"Hello." It was soft, shimmering.

"Hello."

"You're one of the doctors being honored tonight. I asked about you."

I did not know what to say except, "Yes." In fact, my heart beat faster. She was extremely attractive. I could not help noticing the way she used her body, shifting, bending her back slightly above the waist, just enough to emphasize her bosom more.

"Well, I have to get back. They'll be calling on me soon."

"Give a good talk. By the way, doctor, what's your name?" She already knew, had asked. I know because she told me later when we were getting to know one another well. I answered her, hoping my voice was normal.

"I'm Deirdre Cunningham, in case you want to know more about art or want to purchase something unusual," she said slyly as she seemingly inadvertently touched me with her hip when she turned to walk away. "I have read about you," her face turned partly toward me. "I hope we can meet again," she said invitingly.

"Well, if you were a researcher. But you have something to do with the art world. I doubt we'll cross paths. But it was nice meeting you."

"It was nice." She started to walk back to her friend, glanced back at me. "We'll meet again." And she looked at me, her eyes bright and directly lingering, flirting. I watched her walk with that sway and have to admit I wondered what she'd be like in bed. "Whew," I softly told myself.

When I got back to the table, Brigit asked if I was nervous. "You were so long." In fact, she had gone into the hall looking for me, fearing I'd be late for my talk. She saw us.

"I was worried they'd call you before you got back." There

was a moment's pause. "Who was she, Greg? Someone you know? We never met." There was subdued anger in the way she talked.

"Oh, her. I don't know. She met me in the hall, stopped to talk and asked me what our party was about. Curiosity I guess." I flushed.

"Oh, come on. You were flirting with her. I'm your woman, and don't you ever forget it, Gregory Hurwitz," and under the table she kicked my ankle.

"Ouch" I almost said aloud.

She smiled. "Remember." I swear there was a sadness in her face as though she felt there could be trouble.

I gave my talk, people stood and clapped. Newspaper and med school or hospital photographers took pictures. I looked toward Brigit. She was smiling, pleased and happy and without care sent me a kiss, rubbing her palm over her lip and toward me.

How much more pleasant could life be? For a brief moment I thought back to the mine sweeper, thinking how my life had been saved for this moment of recognition and the love of a woman such as Brigit.

~

The days in Cape Astraea were so pleasant. The weather had warmed. We woke to sunshine. The sea was calm except when a breeze came up. We would stand on a jut of land feeling the wind against our faces, I watching Brigit brush back her hair. We watched the water and point when in the wind the sea became angry white foam that erupted against the rocks, streaks rising, falling rapidly, warning of the sea's fury and deceptive beauty, until in the calm its other self rose to the surface and lured us forward to walk barefooted, carrying our shoes, along the edge of the soft lapping. Brigit couldn't resist the sea any more than home. "Greg, I so love the desert and often miss Las Cruces. You see the sands, sometimes like rolling waves. Yuk, but the dust storms. I used to laugh when I would take a shower and the floor would become almost a mud pile when the sand washed from my hair and body. I think I belong here, but I shall always love my home."

Suddenly she reminded me of "Heimat," that haunting aria. I saw the wistfulness in her face, tears coming to eyes. "Are you all right?"

"I am. I'm happy," and she pushed against me. She looked straight at me, with the tears of that joy and sadness. I thought then I would never do anything to hurt her.

"I love you so. I promise you we'll go to your home whenever possible. I liked it when you took me there. I'm anxious to see your family again. But you know what I liked, maybe almost most? Cloudcroft. It's so much like New England. It made me think of here. Oh. We are a pair of lost souls."

She looked at me suddenly, questioning, here eyes wider. "Why did you say that? Promise you'll never say that again."

"What's wrong?" Astonished, I asked.

"I just don't ever want to hear you say that again. We are not lost. Only God . . ." and she stopped, except what she was thinking was obvious. Her religion, at least what she still believed, would always be part of her. Perhaps that was part of the almost indescribable beauty. Perhaps her God placed her by me.

But would her God allow to happen what did? I don't even want to think about it.

~

She and Pamela are here together. I can hear them talking.

Pamela, having made an office upstairs for writing, very much likes Brigit, perhaps wishes she were her mother. Don't start that ironic laugh. Yes. Remember the time she thought she was pregnant? She told me she missed her period, something that never happened. She almost seemed ashamed, "Greg, I've got something to tell you. I think I'm pregnant," but instead of looking at me, she looked down as though embarrassed, but when she raised her head, she was smiling. "We'll have to," she hesitated. "We'll have to get married. You don't mind this way?"

"I wouldn't care any way. I should have asked you ages ago."

" Are you happy?"

"I'm happy, pleased. Maybe it'll be a girl like you, two beautiful females in the house." But then she came to me some time later and told me she had her period. She was crying. "I wanted to be pregnant. I want a child, our child." I moved her to the sofa, put my arms about her. "One day it will happen, be true. We are going to get married. You've gone through enough of this being single sex stuff. I feel sometimes as though I'm taking advantage of you."

"You aren't," she said through her tears, sniffling.

But Pamela wasn't her daughter. Goddamn this world and the mess we make of it and ourselves.

There's that Viet Nam war we've just been through. The stupidity. The lives destroyed. The fucking dumb generals. Leaders. Fuck them all. Fuck my life.

Brigit came to the door. She sat on the bed beside me. "Hey. Push over and give me some room. . . . Greg, you're angry. What's wrong?" I told her nothing, but she knew better. "I'd like to crawl in there with you. I can make you happy, cure you. You know my powers." But what powers? She didn't have them to stop what happened. "Do you want me to lie beside you?"

She looked toward the door. "Pamela's upstairs writing." She pushed the blanket aside, neglecting my partly wet pajamas, pulled up her skirt so I could feel her legs against me. "I hate this fucking world, Brigit. What I did to you. I never stopped loving you."

She pulled me closer to her, ignoring the perspiration. "I never. . . ." She didn't finish. Perhaps she was thinking of Thomas. But then she looked at me. "I never stopped loving you either, dearest one." There were tears in her eyes. "I want you to be better. I want you inside me." She placed a leg over my side and pushed into my thigh. "I want to. Do you think you could?"

Somehow we managed, and I was happy though I was so exhausted. She looked so content, the way we used to be with one another.

We heard Pamela coming down the stairs and Brigit slipped quickly from the bed and straightened her clothes and brushed back her hair. I think Pamela knew, from her somewhat surprised look when she came to the door, her quick gaze going from Brigit's hair, reddened face, to her skirt. But if she did, she ignored it. By her eyes, however, it was evident she knew or realized Brigit and I were having sex. She began to retreat, having seen Brigit's hand movements.

"Oh. Pamela. Come in. Done with writing?" forcing a normal voice but obviously embarrassed, also hesitant. Pamela managed "Yes," Pamela's and Brigit's faces both coloring. "Come in, Pamela. Your dad and I," and she stopped. Lying was preposterous. Brigit refused to become lost in subterfuge. Pamela looked at me, hesitated, and came in when I motioned. Pamela walked to Brigit, looking intently in her eyes. "I hope you're making him happy. He needs that," she stopped a moment, "and you." She blushed. She was uncertain about continuing. "Brigit, there's something I've wanted to say."

"Fine. With me just say it."

Brigit could see the questioning in her face.

"I love you, Brigit. I do. I – I wish you were my mother." Her face flushed again. "Oh, that's terrible, but I don't care. I mean it."

As Brigit kissed her, Pamela looked at me in the bed, at the messy covers at which I had quickly pulled.

Her face coloring again, she blurted, "You all belong together," Her voice dropped. "You're both married to others." She had to be thinking of our adultery and tried to shrug it off. She wanted to say something more. Before she could, Brigit placed her hand over Pamela's mouth. "I wish I were too. You're so easy to love, and I do love you. You remember that, regardless of what happens. I'll always be there for you." Brigit looked away, then back to Pamela. "I guess you remind me of my daughter, as if you two were sisters. I wish . . . ." and the words were lost in the seas of fear and love. She had cheated on Thomas, I on her, who I wondered on Deirdre. I know Deirdre was screwing that Frenchman and God knows who else. What did it matter anymore? But I believe there was pain for Brigit.

I knew Pamela would talk to Melinda. "If only," perhaps Pamela was thinking. "But only's don't count." She paused, stammering, "I love you both. I'm going back to my room. O.K.? probably write a little."

Brigit looked back at me, her hand inadvertently going to her inner thigh and lightly, quickly rubbing. "I do love your daughter, Greg, and I intend to take care of you both." Later she told me, "I meant what I said, regardless of cost – except for my son and daughter.

So much has happened and so much before watching and listening to Pam and Brigit. Brigit who could have been her mother. Pam wishing it so.

The first time a Chinese antique - a Ming vase Deirdre told me - appeared in our living room, I wondered why this suddenly became part of the décor. "Deirdre, where did that come from?"

"Oh, Étienne gave it to me for a present, for the work I helped him with. Remember my last trip?"

"Yes. I just was wondering if you were thinking of changing the living room around. It seems out of place."

"Oh, it does not. It's beautiful right where it is. Who knows, maybe I will change as we come across more things."

"What, every time you get something new, everything changes?"

"Stop being foolish. There won't be that much. Most of what we find you know goes to the Walker Museum."

And now that the Korean war was over, it became a bit easier, perhaps, for Étienne to travel to the East. Somewhere he always wanted to go. But he never lost sight of Greece. That country was becoming more protective, but he managed somehow. He knew the right people.

"He's good, Gregory."

"I don't trust him. You're going to get into trouble Deirdre."

"Stop being so damned stupid. Gregory." She always called him Gregory, as though she were talking to a young son. "You know I knew him in France, how we fought together."

"Yeah. You and I. Two war heroes. Only I didn't have a woman on the ship."

"Are you accusing me of fucking him?"

"I said no such thing. I only want you to be careful."

~

Careful. I thought back to Boston, the first time I saw her, and then the second in that gown that expressed every part of her body, left the rest to imagination. How she came forward, sultry and slowly to me, eyes wide, directly on me, her deep brown eyes mesmerizing me when Brigit had gone to the powder room. I and other men, stared as she crossed, showing her face and body to the hushed and admiring men. The women curious to know who she was, some jealous, others fascinated, others wishing. All the women but Brigit could have been outshone if she cared to be seen and known as a voluptuous sex object, perhaps a representation of Heddy Lamar. I continued watching as though she were about to reveal herself, what she had to offer but would hide and take away when the expectant heart and mind of the viewer stopped and she slid behind a curtain then purposely teased by showing a bare leg and thigh. Beckoning.

"Dr. . . . by the way, what is your name?"

Why is she fibbing? She already knows my name.

"Hurwitz. Gregory."

"Do you come from Boston?"

"No." I looked toward the ladies' room.

"Dr. Don't worry. She'll be in there like the rest of us, touching up ourselves to be more tempting.

"Well, where are you from?"

"Maine. Cape Astraea."

"Really. I'm from Maine, not such a fancy place. Warrington." She moved her leg against mine. "Any chance of our meeting again?" as she saw Brigit coming through the door. "It would be nice. I'd like it very much. Your work interests me. Perhaps mine would fascinate you. I travel here and there looking with my friend for art objects for the Walker Museum of Ancient Antiquities."

"Yes, I know from the last time you all were here when the lab had its party."

My mouth was dry. I wanted to see her. Brigit sat beside me, surprising me. She saw Deirdre slyly smile. "I'm Deirdre Cunningham," she told Brigit who was watching her, I imagine Brigit wondering which one of them was the more appealing.

My face is hot, an emptiness in my stomach. That's foolish. There's something sophisticatedly cheap about her. The way she's looking at Greg, though, like she's ready to seduce him. I wonder if he's dumb enough not to notice. I'll fight, but I can't flaunt like that one.

Whatever she may have been thinking, Deirdre interrupted her thoughts. "I came over, because I was here the night he was honored and just wanted to say hello." She looked at Brigit's left ring finger. *Woman. I can take him from you. I just may.*

She rose slowly for Brigit and me to watch her. I looked at her breasts, even thought about the underwear she might be wearing, gazed at her slim waist cinched by the dress and emphasizing her hips.

Brigit, rarely vicious, could not help herself, even though I believe now she thought she might be the loser. "Careful, dear, you almost caught that long skirt in the leg of the chair. You don't want to embarrass yourself with a fall. It's terrible when people see you in an awkward position. And you could twist your ankle terribly. Think of being laid up for a while. I know, being a nurse, and seen some of that." Brigit, Deirdre did not know, was sorry she had said anything, that she had made herself appear bitchy, which she knew I noticed from the disgust on my face.

Deirdre angrily stared back at her. *Neither you nor he is going to escape me, you bitch. I'll show you how to trip.* She walked slowly away, turned back to us and smiled, her eyes partly closed then opening, knowing her long lashes had been visible and swayed her hips a bit more with her back to us. *You're no match for me, bitch Brigit.*

Suddenly she returned to the table and in a soft, seductive voice, told me, "Don't forget, doctor, you said I could see your laboratory. I'll make an appointment." She smiled at Brigit, and as an afterthought, "It was nice meeting you." *But I doubt we'll see each other much again. He's mine.*

I stared after the sultry woman who would remain in my imagination.

"What did she mean by that?" Brigit interrupted.

"What?"

"Why's she coming to the lab? I can't imagine she knows anything about what your work means diagnostically." Unfortunately, Brigit, also rarely jealous, said, "I bet she's ignorant about anything to do with science." Brigit's face was growing hot with anger that she could not hide. "Who the hell is she?"

"Like she said," I answered with annoyance. "She saw us at the honors and was curious. What's wrong with that? Why are you so angry?"

You stupid man. A whore appears and you're lost – in her pants. If you're such a simpleton, she can have you. Brigit's face colored again. *Why am I mad? Calm down. I could tear his and her eyes out. If she means so much to him, he can have her. Then let's see what happens to your grand design for your future.*

She must have decided she would not mention Deirdre again, that we would spend the remainder of the evening dancing and talking as though nothing had happened. With that, when we arrived home, Brigit seemed to be herself, but she was unsettled and was determined I would never know. We kissed goodnight while she turned away from me, staring into the dark bedroom, looking sad she had lost her temper, had shown it; but she knew this woman was a Venus's fly trap for men.

~

Deirdre decided she would wait a week or even two before appearing, surprise him by arriving about lunchtime, so he would be forced to ask her to lunch. From there the remainder of the day would tactically be hers.

"So, Dr. Hurwitz," surprising him, touching him on the shoulder as he heard her voice and started to turn from a microscope.

"Oh. Hello. Come in." He rose somewhat awkwardly and gave her his seat and took another for himself.

"Please just don't touch the microscope." He felt stupid for telling her that.

"It must be something interesting. May I look?" She glanced at him, smiling. "Well, I don't know much about these things, though I did take a science course at Radcliffe. But don't worry. I'll be careful."

"Oh, I didn't mean to . . . ."

She interrupted. "Oh, don't be embarrassed. I should have called before coming and would never touch anything without your permission. But I am interested."

By now, the focused scientist seemed to have lost his calm from seeing her, trying furtively to look at her from her face to her feet. Her dress was short skirted, coming just below her knees but raised when she sat. She made no effort to cover them, knowing he would be distracted.

"It's nice to see you again, Miss . . . . I don't know your last name."

"Well," she smiled, her eyes directly on him, "Let's not be that formal. I'm Deirdre. You're Gregory. O.K.? Now show me what's in the microscope."

He came closer, telling her what to do, though she knew and having taken more than one science course, thinking they might help her with the art she concentrated on, learning scientifically, if possible, what was fake and what was real, learning disciplined thought.

Their shoulders touched. He moved away. "No. Come here,

Gregory," she said in a low, sultry voice. "You need to tell me what's here, like those little things wiggling in there. What does this have to do with, oh with isotopes?"

"Well, something, I believe. If I can diagnose with what we are using, and then we can treat the disease, we'll erase what you see there. It's not really wiggling, you see. They're cancer cells moving about in the solution."

"Oh," she easily made herself sound excited while all the while concentrating on him, his voice, what he would be like as a lover. She had already decided to find out. For Brigit, despite her appeal, was no match for her. *Here we are two models on the runway, but I'll run with him, Brigit dear. I want him. He's known, has money from what I heard. That's for me. If he isn't that great a lover, I'll teach him.*

"Well, that's interesting. She purposely looked at her watch. "Oh, it's lunch time. I'm keeping you."

"No," he replied almost too loudly. "We can go to that small restaurant just across the street. My treat." He paused. "That is, if you have time. I'm pleased you came. Actually, I remember you said you would, but I thought it was just. Oh well." His face colored. "I'm glad you came," he repeated to hide his exasperation with himself and wanting to quiet his faster beating heart.

At the restaurant, a friend noticed them and came for a curious hello, questioning who this woman was. When he left, Deirdre laughed. "Did you see his face?"

He tried to ignore her, thinking of Brigit and whether anyone would say something to her.

She interrupted the silence. "Are you free after lunch. You know, my partner and I do deal in art, but I think I could persuade him to give money for your work. If you're free, why don't you come with me, and we'll talk about it."

"I'd love to," and he criticized himself for answering so quickly. He hesitated, calmed some, "Yes. That would be nice. I can take off. I'll just call in."

Deirdre had almost and so easily completed her plan, laughing to herself, enjoying the thought of her eventual conquest.

She took him to Étienne's and her apartment at the foot of Beacon Hill. She had always wanted to live on the hill, but for now a house was unobtainable. This man with his money and his reputation? Étienne? He was a jealous man, occasionally wondering whether she thought of him as too old for her, despite his ability to satisfy her sexually and with money. He'd either understand how an association with Gregory would help them or she'd persuade him as she usually did. She'd have both men, any she wanted.

Gregory hesitated. "Is something wrong?" as she held his arm and pulled slightly toward the door.

"I, I was just thinking of something."

Thinking of that bitch of his, so sweet, lovely, homebody. Well, in a while I'll be your somebody, everything you think she is and more.

In a sweet voice, "Come on Gregory. If it's something at work that can't wait, well another time," she feigned.

"No. I'll take care of it later." He feared going in with her, knowing she could easily enrapture him, mesmerized as he was now and had been the first time he had seen her.

She started to raise her voice, caught herself. "Well then, come on."

When he heard the door close, he knew, despite what might happen, hoped would, Brigit would never know.

"You sit there on the sofa. Take off your jacket and be comfortable. You can even loosen your tie. Here let me." All the while her voice was soft, tantalizing. She went to him, pushed him toward the corner of the sofa. "We can talk better this way."

There was a painting of a nude on the wall facing them. He

gazed at it as she undid his tie.

"You like that painting? Well, you should see me."

Her comment astounded Gregory who tried to hide his surprise, still thinking of Brigit and that he would not do what was about to happen. But when Deirdre began to unbutton the back of her dress and stood before him in her zippered latex corset and fashionable pointed bra and her panties, Brigit disappeared. Deirdre leaned toward him, started to unbutton his shirt, stopped. She took his hand. "Come," and she continued, whispering, "We belong together. I knew it the first time I saw you."

"Come," and she led him toward her bedroom, the large bed, sat him on the edge, watched him move back to become more comfortable, unbuttoned his shirt, undid his trousers, pulled at them and took off his underwear. "That's nice," she added, watching him grow, leaving him there, his heart beating faster as he became hard. She went to her bathroom. "I'll be right back." She unzipped her girdle, took off her garter belt and stockings, smiled. She put on some perfume, returned, undid her bra, stepped out of her panties and stood before him. "You like what you see?" as she ran her hands from her breasts to her inner thighs.

He swallowed, nodded, his hands reaching for her breasts and moving below in a slow massage as she closed her eyes, purposely loudly moaned, lying softly on top of him, then pulling him with her as she turned on her back, spreading and raising her legs to fold about him.

~

Arriving home late was nothing for Brigit and me. We expected it. When I walked in, she had been waiting and had eaten alone. She was reading the evening news about what was happening in Korea and the horror of MacArthur advocating atom bombs on Manchuria. She hated war, had seen too much of its damage and what it had done to me. She despised MacArthur. I did too. In disgust, she threw the paper on the floor.

"Hi, sweet." I watched nervously as she came toward me, put out her arms, placed them around my neck. Guiltily I hesitated and then put my arms about her and took her to me, happy to see her. But she drew back suddenly. "What's that?"

"That odor in you hair." She was obviously stunned. I had showered at Deirdre's but the perfume lingered slightly. "You have a soapy smell, not ours."

"It's your imagination," I nervously told her.

"Greg. You're lying. You've been with someone." She hesitated, her eyes wide. "You fucked that woman." Then, though she hated the word, rarely used it but could not help herself nor did she care, she repeated, her voice loud, "You fucked her."

I never thought while washing my hair, never would have thought of perfumed soap. It was on my body and what we had done. Did I feel bad? Well - yes. More importantly, sadly, I was still thinking of being inside Deirdre, what it felt like, the smoothness of her skin, her firm, lovely-to-feel breasts, both of us looking at our naked bodies as she watched me shower, that captivating smile, her alluring voice telling me she would be here, in this place, any time. Then, with certainty, "You'll be back as soon as you can so we can be ourselves, no pretending to care, and - she smiled - enjoying ourselves." I don't think, or didn't, there could be any other man for her now. I stood there, wet, looking at that lithe body, not wanting to leave it or her. It was as though she could read my thoughts, for she stepped into the shower and moved against me, tantalizing me, and with those soft, caressing hands gliding over me, telling me I was captured. And truly I was. Brigit had faded from my conscience.

But not here in Brigit's and my apartment that brought me to reality, for with a jolt, Brigit forcefully pushed me away and ran to the bedroom, sobbing.

I stood, unable to move, not knowing whether I should go to her. I did think of the ring I had given her and the plans for Las Cruces and the wedding, asking myself how I could have failed her and given in to my sexual desire. But I did admit to myself that I enjoyed it and Deirdre. There I was, punishing myself, thinking of Deirdre, her softness and the enjoyment, and Brigit, the woman I was to marry or had been going to marry.

Brigit came to the bedroom door, walked slowly into the living room, shaking, crying, rubbing away the tears with the back of her hand, her face red with anger and disbelief.

She raised her left hand, pulled off the ring, and threw it at me. "I could never trust you again," and she sobbed, sadly mumbled, "Never again. That whore is all yours. Marry her and have a good life. That's what she wants. Well, she's got it," she paused for some time, staring at me, her hair disheveled, her face streaked, "Got it all."

She started for the bedroom, turned. "I'm packing and going to the nurses' quarters. You can screw her here from now on, in public for all I care." She thought, spoke again. "You know, Gregory, you have destroyed your life."

I suppose you'd expect her to fight, but I believe she didn't want to be involved in something messy or to lower herself by fighting Deirdre, something of which she was quite capable. Rather, I think she preferred, hopefully, to see either Deirdre or me demolished in our self-desire.

I do know now we never stopped loving each other.

~

Brigit took a vacation and went home to Las Cruces, wanting to hide herself in the desert. As she drove from El Paso to home, occasionally she would stop, look, comparing herself to the desolate and sparse growth. She had loved this land, her home that was green below Alamogordo. Thinking of Cloudcroft, she thought she might go there to be alone even if it would remind her of New England. Yet, she did not want such a vivid memory of Gregory's visit. On one stop, she pulled to the side of the road, looked in the mirror, brushed her hair with her hand, reached in her pocketbook for her lipstick, saying to herself, "Why bother? What good has this body been to me, this face? And I let him have it, soil me. Never, never again." She laughed. *I could find a woman for companionship and, well, yes, sex. That way, we'd understand each other, what we feel, how we feel, none of that pretending. That's what I've been doing. Pretending. Oh shut up, Brigit, you fake. You still love that man and always will.*

Her depression faded as she drove up to her house. Her mother, hearing the car, had come to the door. Here was that solid, certain woman, who in her younger years could have almost been a twin of her daughter. Brigit had always loved looking at her photographs before and after she was married to Brigit's father. As one would expect, Maureen loved all her daughters. Perhaps, though, she also felt God had given her a twin of whom she would always be proud and protective. Now, as she watched Brigit running toward her, her arms outstretched, letting out a little scream of love and happiness, protection was most important to Maureen. As their arms enfolded one another, Brigit felt since leaving Boston the touch of love that would never die. Gregory could not kill love, but he could instill hopelessness, loneliness, and uncertainty of a woman's attractiveness and holding power. At least, that was for now. Would it ever change? Brigit determined it would. No one could defeat this healer and saint from the past. She lived now. That her parents named her after the healer and the saint was all in the distant Celtic past and early Christianity. Brigit had never believed any of this, but now she wondered. *I am strong, and I do have love. It may be a different kind of love, but at least it's lasting and real. Well, I'm no saint. Saint Brigit was a virgin.* She laughed aloud. *I'm sure not the Saint, world. But, I'll never regret. It's almost like I can feel him inside, or there with his mouth, or my arms about him. So good.* She frowned. *Stop thinking about it. I don't want to remember any of it. You always will, Brigit. Believe it, fool. You still love him and just accept him. You willingly gave yourself to him. You'll always be part of him. He'll find out. He'll rue. Don't be a vengeful witch, Brigit. But he will. I know it.*

Her mother interrupted her mind's rambling. "It's so good to have you home." Maureen was sorry she said it that way, as though nothing had happened, that the family had been preparing for a wedding never to be. "We're so glad you're here. Oh, dearest." Maureen started to cry. "I'm so sorry. You must be . . . ." and she stopped, not wanting to inflame a wound so deep that only her daughter could feel, that no one else in the family had been so defiled, insulted, embarrassed. She hated Gregory, never wanted to hear his name again, wondering what she would or could do to help Brigit. Perhaps being with her sisters, perhaps visiting the convent and Anne, spending time in the peace the convent offered. Perhaps. All was "perhaps" now. Except Maureen knew Brigit was the strongest of her daughters. She would ask no question, however, tell Luke not to, but wait until Brigit said something. Maureen had seen deserted married women, listened to their bitterness, their swearing, their desire for vengeance. Once she made the mistake of suggesting a priest and the quiet of the church to a friend, the rejoinder being a damnation of religion, the church that did nothing but demean women as the preying beings responsible for their own downfall - exhibiting and dressing in sexual clothing and colored faces to lure. The women to whom Maureen listened always said it was the other woman who caused the break-up, that it was her flirtations that ensured the hungering men's sense of victory and her own. The deserter was always vile, stupid being trapped and leaving a loving wife and his children. The victims, unsuspecting Brigits. But the church blamed the good woman, if there were such a person.

Maureen, horrified, took many months to forgive the abandoned friend because of her damnation of the church, although she coolly kept in touch with her, Maureen still sorrowful for the woman's pain. *The world was cruel. In Korea our soldiers and the unprotected civilians being killed, maimed while a craven General urges atomic weapons which if allowed would end us all, our torments, tears, pleasures, laughter. How different here at home is the pain and suffering? Here we smother the greatest gift – love – with plundered sexual satisfaction. My daughter. A man treating her the way he did, a woman so beautiful, so good, so loyal, so accomplished. Don't say anything, Maureen. Let it all come out of her. She'll talk to both Luke and me. I know that. And she has her sisters.*

But was there anyone who could end the agony of betrayal and abandonment? The tears, the memories, the unspeakable hurt? A deserted woman thrust aside by a lover deceived by that female predator.

When Brigit entered the house, the familiarity wrapped her in its memories of growing up on the ranch, horseback riding, traveling northward across the desert to Albuquerque and Taos. She would sometimes ski in Taos and learned as much as she could about the Pueblo, remembering the men sitting in the small town square in the early morning, wrapped in their blankets, rarely speaking. Or there was the time she was in the Pueblo, startled by the beauty of the young pueblo woman leaning against her doorway, watching, so silent, so apparently content. Brigit told herself at that moment that she must find her way to such peace, such self-possession. It was a religious experience found only in oneself. From that time, Brigit never forgot the young woman and always felt a kinship to her, a spiritual connection that she never felt in church. She had decided that she would never tell her parents but that it would be part of her secret self never to be revealed.

Now she wondered whether she had destroyed that image and feeling by having given herself to Gregory and having been deserted. The more she thought about it, however, perhaps it would be her triumph, her rediscovery of herself and the love that she had given so freely. Perhaps, she began to think, she didn't despise Gregory, that her love might never fade.

In a conversation with her sisters Ellen and Marie who appeared so satisfied in their marriages, she told them of her sorrow, the pain, the many tears. Hearing what had happened, they were angry, Marie even raising her voice and cursing Gregory and Deirdre.

"Stop," Brigit insisted. "Don't yell. I can't stand it," and she began to cry. "I'm so miserable. I look at you all apparently so content, your children. I suppose I pictured myself living like you, having children running about. Are you both as happy as you seem?" Her conscience suddenly bothered her, for she wanted an answer that told her what she saw in Marie's and Ellen's houses was appearance.

Ellen placed her hand on Brigit's face. "I wouldn't change for anything, dear; but there are times you want to take a frying pan and slam it over your husband's head. It's not all love. Sometimes there's, well, I think, something close to despising him for paying so little attention to me. But then something will happen, and when he makes love to me, or rubs my back or kisses me when he comes home, or I'm listening to the yelling and laughter of the children, I know it's all worth it. But it's confining being held so close to your home. You have your profession. We have always envied you for that."

Watching the changing expressions on her sister's face, and looking at Marie who nodded agreement, Brigit smiled slightly, wiped at her eyes thinking of Gregory. "You know, I still love him. I want to hate him, and I can't. I don't know if I'll ever be free. For that I despise him. So I love and despise." She stopped, catching her breath, feeling her heart beat faster, "Oh I don't know. But please, please don't ever tell mom and dad what I just said."

"Mom called us and told us about when you walked into the house with that look of pleasure on your face, how she followed you to your room and what happened when dad came home."

"She would," was all that Brigit answered. Her sisters faded, and she was just coming home and she and her mother were standing together, both crying from happiness at seeing each other and at the horrible unjustness Brigit had experienced.

Brigit remembered thinking and wanting to tell her mother, *Oh, mom. I gave myself to him. I slept with him, lived with him, and I know that hurt you, my living with a man in sin. Forgive me.* Yet, immediately she realized she could not say that, for she did not regret that love between them and the joy of their lovemaking, how they had learned to accept what was good and imperfect in each of them.

Then her father had come home, and rather than go to wash up, shower, as he always did, he came to Brigit's bedroom where she was resting, her head turned to the window, seeing what? Thinking what? The door was open enough so her father saw her and did not want to disturb her. However, she heard his step, turned from her dreaming, looking at him, while wiping at her eyes.

"May I come in, Brigit?"

"Yes." She sat up. "I guess I was just resting and thinking. You know, I wondered whether I should even go to Hotel Santé and find out if they have an opening in my field. But then, I don't know, dad. I don't know anything right now."

He sat on her bed and pulled her to him. "It's so good to see you, to have you home." He faltered, unsure of what to say. "You look good."

"Dad, don't be afraid to talk. Just don't tell me what to do. I have to work through this myself."

"I, well, I wasn't going to tell you . . ."

"Oh, forget it. You don't have to apologize and worry whether you're saying something wrong. What is there to say? I have to work through this myself," she repeated.

Inadvertently he raised her left hand. She looked at the bare ring finger, as did he, and could not stop the tears. Luke dropped the hand, his face reddened by anger and mindlessness. "What a stupid man." He couldn't help himself. "To have a woman like you."

She blurted unintentionally. "Dad, I love him. He's always going to be in my heart. I may despise him right now, but all you men," and she smiled weakly at her father. "Oh, I don't mean you, but admit it. You see a pretty woman in town and you look and wonder. Women do it too. It's all human, only this particular woman turned him from the one who would support him come the worst, if he lost his standing or . . . oh I don't know."

"I guess you're right."

"I am right, but . . ."

"You'll never forgive him."

"You mean you'll never forgive him, that if he were here you'd batter him for hurting your daughter. What good is revenge? Don't forget your Bible, dad," she finished sarcastically.

Bible. Who created those stories? But who can turn her back on Jesus' words. He raised Mary Magdalene. Will He do the same for me? How do I know? Damn you, Gregory. You took all of me, feasted on me, and here I am asking Jesus to raise me like he did the Magdalene. Hah, I'll go back to my Celtic ancestors before there was the Saint Brigit, when there was only the healer Brigit. Is she that good,

Gregory? Is she that good in bed, better than I? Is she . . . . Oh I don't know. I just don't. But I know. I know. Something is going to happen. She's that kind of woman. You can't see it, your eyes glazed over by that delusory woman, given a body no better than mine. The difference? She has that deceptive mind. Enjoy yourself, Gregory. It's funny. I remember the first time we hugged. I turned my body to be certain you could feel the softness of my breast against your body. I wonder what you thought. Stop it, Brigit. You're driving yourself mad.

Luke left the bed. She felt the mattress's light upward movement. "When you're rested, dear, come down. Your mother and I will be there. Do you mind if we invite Ellen and Marie and their families to dinner? I wish Anne, well Sister Angelina, could be here too. By the way, you are going to see her?"

"Yes and no. Let's have the whole family here."

And so Brigit managed to become an actress, but she did enjoy the prattling children and the family warmth.

Later in the week she went to Sister Angelina. As she approached the convent, there were memories of school, of the sisters lecturing them about being good girls, protected by God and honored by their future husbands, unless they decided to enter Orders and become a servant of God, a truly blessed life. But purity is most important whether in Orders or as a wife.

They went to the chapel, knelt and said their prayers. Sister Angelina seemed so different to Brigit, her calmness and certainty. Brigit realized she felt a twinge of envy at what seemed to be the peace that enfolded her. But would she ever know life? There was so much beyond the convent that perhaps Sister Angelina would never even feel. Yet, she was jealous of the peace and listened as her sister quietly told her to believe in herself and her ability and her willingness to help people that would bring her peace, the peace, perhaps, that Sister Angelina experiences. *Yet, you are a woman with woman's feelings and desires. I know it. You're just as human as I, but you have learned to discipline yourself. I can listen to you and be soothed, but I am a Woman and need the love not only of my profession but of a man.*

They sat on a cement bench against the wall of the cloister, so quiet, green with flora, trees, prickly pear cacti tended by the Sisters. Brigit started to speak in a whisper, caught herself, laughing. "Anne," "Call me Angelina, Brigit. It's my name now. I could have kept Anne." "I'll try to get used to it. It reminds me of Galileo and his daughter. They always used her religious name."

Angelina perhaps thought her sister a grave sinner. Maureen had told her that Brigit, unmarried, was living with a man she met during the war. Sister Angelina told Maureen she would pray for her soul and that God forgive and protect her. Maureen blanched, thinking of her daughter's soul and cohabitation with a Jew of all things. How many times multiplied was her sin? Nothing the family could have said would have been well received. Moreover, Maureen did not believe she should interfere in any of her children's lives. She loved them too deeply. It was often a wonder to her that they rarely quarreled, that they could often talk rather intimately as women do with one another. Growing up may have been different when there was friction; but, for the most part, it seemed to have disappeared, except when it came to Brigit who, though she deeply loved her mother, would never allow her to direct her life, nor her father either. Luke and Maureen had learned to accept Brigit for who she was and how she lived, and her independence. That was the meaning of love to Maureen. Acceptance, sheltering.

After a time, Brigit told them she was going to Taos. She would stop in Santa Fe to look through the galleries, but she wanted to be in Taos, still remembering that Indian woman in the doorway, posing perhaps, communing but so peaceful. Brigit would find her own peace in that town.

~

In the small hotel overlooking the square, she rose early to watch the men wrapped in their blankets, feeling the familiarity, soothed by the apparent tranquility as they sat, the silent communication with the coolness of morning, oblivious to all around them but Nature's morning sky.

She had also been reading D.H. Lawrence lately and knew that Ravagli and Frieda Lawrence were in Taos. When she went downstairs for a small lunch, she saw Ravalgi enter the bar and wanted to follow him, to ask what he did to take Frieda from Lawrence. She wouldn't because of the imposition on a personal life. She did wonder how Lawrence had come between Frieda and her husband and children whom she abandoned for her lower-class lover. What was the effect on her conscience? What was it like sleeping with a man with whom she had fled to Italy and then come with him to Taos? What was her sense of desertion when she slept with Ravalgi? Or was she perhaps like Deirdre? She wanted to visit Frieda, perhaps help herself, if Frieda would answer her questions. She lay there imagining a conversation.

"Why did you leave your children and the security of a home, Mrs. Lawrence?"

"My life was not too terribly exciting before I met Lawrence. He was handsome, intelligent. Before too much time, he persuaded me to go with him to Taormina. I was happy. I did think of the children but knew they would be taken care of. But Lawrence was the man I wanted. And, yes, I did have an affair with Ravalgi, and as you know, he and I are now married."

"I saw him going into the bar at the hotel. Truthfully, he looked at me the way men usually do."

"Men and women wonder about one another. It's natural. And sometimes it turns out the way my life has. And you. You are not married. A woman like you should attract many lovers or those who

would be. I know what it's like."

"Doesn't every woman? And if not, even if they are homely, they hope."

"Well, Lawrence and I had a rocky time. One time up at the ranch – have you seen it?"

Brigit interrupted. "I am going there. I wanted to meet you first."

"Love is, well, you ought to know. One time I got so angry, I threw a coffee mug at him that, I suppose if it hit him, would have killed him. Anyhow, tell me about you, so lovely, so enticing. I was not as thin as you, but, oh, the men looked at me."

"I wanted to meet you because I had become fascinated by Lawrence and you. I wanted to meet you because of your experiences. You see," Brigit hesitated, "I was deserted. I lived with the man I thought was going to be my husband, but he left me for another woman. I couldn't compete with her." Brigit felt quite free with Frieda and could talk to her as she never could with her family. Oh, perhaps Mary. But they hadn't talked much to one another since Gregory left.

"Perhaps."

"No. I couldn't. Certainly I can flirt, but I can't flaunt myself."

"You're angry."

"Yes. I'm angry at him, at her, at myself. I feel desolate." There were tears in Brigit's eyes. "Oh, I'm sorry. I never meant for the visit to be like this. I was so pleased that you would see and talk to me, that you're so approachable."

"Perhaps because at times I felt guilt at what I had done with Lawrence and Ravalgi. I also missed my children and fought against Lawrence's jealousy when I wanted to and did go to see my children. I know jealousy also, hurt, especially when he spent so much time with Mrs. Sterne on a book. And I was sometimes jealous of Lady Brett being with us. But would I change anything? No. I have liked it here. We both did, Lawrence felt such freedom at Kiowa, the mountain ranch. You must go there. It's overwhelming being on Mt. Lobo. The family taking care of the ranch now is very friendly.

"Would you change anything?"

"I do not regret giving myself to him although it makes me angry when I think of what he and she have done to me – left me lonely and longing, wondering what is wrong with me when I know I'm so attractive."

"Brigit." She felt Frieda placing her hand on her knee. "You are experiencing what men and women have done to one another forever. You go to the ranch. Up there in the mountains you will find answers. Do you have another man?"

"Oh, there is someone who has been after me," and Brigit smiled. "Now I'll wonder if he's sincere, that is, if I allow myself to be with him, to see him. I have to be sure of myself again."

"Go to the ranch. It will soothe you, give you something good to think about and how strong you can be."

They sat for a while longer. "I will," and they parted, Brigit feeling lighter, more like herself.

Brigit laughed, at herself and her imagination. She rose, setting her mind on a drive to the Kiowa ranch. She felt inexplicably more secure and at peace than she had since leaving Boston. Adding to her satisfaction was the rutted drive up the mountainside to Kiowa ranch where she met a young woman caring for what was now Frieda's possession. They sat before the chapel looking out at the mountains, the sun coming through the trees, the distant multi-painted peaks, and spoke of the Lawrences, of the tranquilizing beauty surrounding them. Brigit felt close to the woman, for the identical emotions they appeared to experience. The soothing freshness of the air, of the slight breeze that blew against Brigit's face, informing her she had rediscovered herself. All found in a mythical Utopia created by an author whom she now understood and who reawakened in her the spirit to which she had been born and grown in. The hurt would perhaps remain, straining her mind, her body, but she still had known love, knew love, what it was.

On the ride back, she went to the pueblo again, wishing impossibly she would see the young Indian woman in relief against the entrance to her pueblo. The image would remain with her. Here on this trip she believed she had rediscovered herself. As she drove along the two-lane road away from Taos, she decided she would go all the way to Albuquerque. She smiled, visualizing living in that imagined world that could give its strength to a receptive spirit.

Arriving in the dark, tired, she thought she would skip dinner but decided against it. In the dining room, she saw a man who looked similar to Thomas. Her heart skipped. Thomas. She may have thought of him when she came to her family. She couldn't remember. She didn't want to think of men. Perhaps her sister had found the answer in a life of service and devotion in the convent. *That isn't for me, not who I am. Thomas. He certainly doesn't make my heart beat any faster, doesn't arouse me. Foolish. You're thinking of sex. You had that. Oh. Don't knock it. You enjoyed, loved it. I just don't want to think about it now. Or do I? My lower belly. That feeling. Stop. All because you thought you saw Thomas. Don't you dare waste this trip on Gregory and what might have been. It's not worth it. Thomas. He's a nice guy. Stop. Now.*

Back in her room, she turned on the radio, lay on the bed, listening, "One alone, to be my own/ I alone to know her caresses" rose, turned the station, thinking of Taos, her eyes starting to close. She woke during the night, perspiring, her heart rapidly beating *It was a car going off the road and down a steep decline. It turned over and over. I screamed. Gregory pitched toward the windshield. We lay outside, breathlessly and slowly trying to reach one another. He was bleeding from his leg and I from my chest. I couldn't move. He crept toward me but could go no further. I passed out. Was I dead? I think so. Then she came toward me, bending over me, making a cross. She drifted toward Gregory, rose, leaving him to care for himself.*

She sat, still fully clothed, listening to her heart, feeling wet from the perspiration. When she calmed, she slowly undressed, crying. Looking at her tear-blurred figure in the mirror she spoke loudly, "You Fool," wiped at her eyes. "Fool." She lightly slapped her face, as she wiped at her eyes, still shaking, and raised her leg to climb into the tub shower, staying a long while, allowing the warm water to comfort her.

When she arrived home. She talked little about Boston or what had happened. Taos kept coming back to her, and she made passing reference to it, keeping its spiritual influence to herself.

"We missed you, dear, but I'm pleased you went and had such a good time," Maureen told her.

Brigit never mentioned the nightmare, but for some reason it made her think about Thomas, perhaps that by accepting an invitation from him would further ease the wound. She laughed. The Ob/Gyn man would cure her heart of this particular cancer that she now knew was still and forever a love she would have for Gregory.

Chapter X

Buffeted

The wedding between Deirdre and Gregory took place between Christmas and New Years, 1952. She would give him the gift of herself for the New Year. Edward and Christine were quite excited. Not only had their daughter begun to make her way in Boston with the well-known Frenchman with whom she sometimes traveled - they wondered about a woman traveling with a man - but now, "Look at her," Christine pulling at Edward's shirt sleeve. "She's such a beauty, and she's marrying into that well-known family in Cape Astraea. Even though we've met, I still get nervous thinking about it. They've accepted her. But they're above us."

"Stop that. No one is above us. And stop thinking about social standing. We are who we are. If they want to talk to us after this wedding, they will. I won't go out of my way. I've spent what I could to give her a good wedding, one anyone could be proud of."

"I agree. Yes. I agree. He's lucky to get her."

The Hurwitzes arrived the day before the wedding. It was the first time Mary met Deirdre. The two talked to one another, embraced, Mary comparing her to Brigit, having already decided she would not like her, thinking of her as a tidal wave that swept over her brother. Deirdre's dark brown eyes and raven hair, the straight, small nose, and cheek bones that showed slightly, the trim and pleasingly well-proportioned body could attract most men. Was she better than Brigit? Mary thought Brigit more attractive, less showy. Perhaps it was because her voice was softer and she dressed more plainly. Deirdre wore a lavender dress, a rolled small collar open to the breasts, her left shoulder showing a bit as the dress folded into her right side, the skirt coming just below her knees, and surely worn to exhibit herself as an attractive addition to the Hurwitz family. The women smiled while judging one another. They knew they were dueling and why.

Mary could not help herself. *She did it with sex. That body is well suited for it, the way she shows it off even when she tries not to. That's my brother. He fell for the looks, not what's inside. Maybe I'm being unfair. I'm also thinking back to Lynne. I liked her – was it because she was from Astraea? There's something about her that bothers me. She's too sophisticated. And she walks and sways her rear end more than just from walking. Everything has a purpose. Why couldn't that fool see that?*

Deirdre looked closely at her future sister-in-law's eyes, watched the way her mouth moved, how she smiled, whether Mary showed acceptance in those blue-gray eyes, while Mary asked herself, *What would that veil be hiding?*

Just then Jocelyn came in, gave her obligatory hug, then told Deirdre, "I ordered camellias for your bouquet. I thought you'd like that. They're my favorite flower, and this is their time of year – just right for this joyous celebration – the new year wedding and families coming together." Jocelyn hid her concern for the quickness of this conjoining. She then walked toward another room but heard.

"She picked my flowers," Deirdre's voice rising indignantly. "What right? That's up to me!" her voice rising more. "I'm not the great singer's . . . ." and she stopped, trying to catch herself.

Gregory stood impassively.

"Greg, you stop her." Mary sharply ordered. "She's insulting mother. If you don't, I'm leaving, getting out, going home." She started to leave.

"Mary," Deirdre pleaded. "I didn't," and she stopped. "Mary. You're my Maid of Honor." Deirdre didn't want to apologize, wouldn't. Mary turned toward them, grimacing, and with muted sarcasm, "I know, sister-in-law. I'm honored." She couldn't help herself and glared at Gregory, thinking, *I hope she was a fantastic lay. Ass. Yeah, a piece of ass. Maybe all yours, you damn, fucking fool.* She smiled. "I'm honored, Deirdre." And both women now knew they would never be friends.

Muted adversarial conflict was now a tacit actuality. Neither Jocelyn nor Mary would ever submit. They also knew that Deirdre was formidable. Where was Aaron? Although he rarely spoke of the marriage, actor that he was, he forced his apparent affection. Calm was a necessity. He loved his youngest son too dearly. Occasionally he would laugh to himself, comparing his family's disgruntlement with country and world affairs. The Korean War still being waged began to weary the public, and the newly elected President Eisenhower had decided he would go there. Intelligent Stevenson could not compete with the national hero. At home also, people and politicians grew tired of Joe McCarthy's defamation of writers, actors, politicians, State Department personnel. Worn from political confrontation, he apparently was ill, having lost twenty pounds and shown in *Life Magazine* slumped in a chair with bottles of medicine sitting on a table beside him. What comfort could there be?

Deirdre was apparently happy with her young, handsome, and well-known doctor who loved her. He could offer her more openings to influential people who could help Étienne and her projects. So Deirdre and Gregory bound themselves by self-created exhilarating sexual experimentation and the usual hugs and kisses and the obligatory "I love you." Suddenly, however, one spring day in 1953, Deirdre knew she was pregnant. She realized it occurred during a night or nights without protection. Gregory was ecstatic. Deirdre grimaced when the doctor confirmed it, thinking about the disappearance of her alluring figure and clothes. Now men would only see her growing womb. Somehow she would find eye-pleasing maternity clothes and be sure to show her face as fascinating as always. *Will it fatten like the rest of my body? I won't allow it. I'll eat as little as possible, won't fall for that pregnancy need for a special dish or food or awaken Greg, like women do all those fawning husbands, to get me something in the middle of the night. And I won't have this baby in Maine. I'll get Greg to stay in Boston. I must for the museum possessions and the money. Museum possessions? What a prize. No one has caught on, never will, and I'll still travel occasionally with Étienne, and we'll have our good times. Loyalty to Greg? Here I am. PREGNANT. How the hell did I let that happen? You and your urges and Gregory's. Anyhow, I've got my young lover and the old, just as I suspected and planned. Something out of the ancient world told me this would happen, two lovers – at least. I read a story out of the past like that. Now I'm scared. What if this baby kills me?* She saw herself lying on a blood soaked sheet, hemorrhaging, dead.

When Gregory came home that night, she had dinner ready, wine out. She had thought she would stop liquor, but after tonight. They would celebrate, although there was to be, more importantly, her request, or was it a demand?

"Hi darling." She kissed him, hugged him tightly. "Everything's almost ready. We'll have some wine and talk. I have to ask you something."

"What?"

"Just wait," alluringly, as though she had to tell him something unexpected, perhaps to do with the baby. "Nothing now, except I went shopping and bought some maternity clothes. I think you'll just love them."

When she showed them, before he sat, "You like?"

"They're beautiful. You'll be as becoming as you always are. What a lovely mother you'll be. A mother the children will, child, I mean, will always want to show off. Well, we will have more, won't we?"

She hid a grimace, answering without enthusiasm, "Yes."

After the wine and dinner, she took his hand, "Leave the dishes. The new maid, her name's Andrea. I got her from the agency. Anyhow, she'll be here tomorrow. I want to talk to you, something important for both of us.

"I want to give up the apartment. You have money now. I want to get a house in Belmont. Ask them to wait in Maine. They'll always want you. Please," drawn out plaintively. "Think of it as a gift for the baby and what a good environment for it to grow up in and the others we have." She pictured herself matronly, promising herself that would never happen. *I'll think about that later. This is more important for now.*

They talked about Belmont and a house quietly for a bit, Deirdre beginning to feel certain she had won. Only she wondered about his sudden silence. Without looking up, his face reddening, for the first time since their wedding, he shouted. "No. We've got to go. They're expecting me in Maine."

Startled, she sat stunned. "Why?" trying to control her rising temper. "They want you badly. They'll wait." She tried to control herself but couldn't. She screamed, "You want children. What a laugh. This is where to raise them," knowing Cape Astraea was better. But she mustn't give in.

Startled, Gregory hollered, "NO!"

"Goddamn it, Gregory, think of me, the child for once, not yourself. You're so damn self-centered."

Surprised by her uncontrollable anger, he watched her face more closely, the distorted features, a drop of saliva at the corner of her mouth, her eyes wide, flashing at him. Suddenly, however, she caught herself, almost whining, "Gregory, I don't mean to fight. I don't want to," forcing tears that she knew would stream down her cheeks. "I'm sorry. It's just that I know you'll be happy in that town. There's a house for sale now. I saw it the other day when I drove there." What she didn't mention was that Étienne had a house there, aside from the apartment close to Beacon Hill. These for when he would come to Boston where he entertained politicians and Boston Society, primarily in Belmont. She would be part of that, she had determined before they married, more so than she now was.

Seeing her tears, he calmed himself. "I'm sorry Deirdre. I didn't mean to hurt you, make you so angry. Please stop crying. I'm sorry I yelled. Let's just talk quietly. You do have a point."

She wiped her cheeks, forced a smile. *I've won.*

"But you know how I feel. And I'd be the head of the projects up there. I guess they'd wait, but I can't put them off too long, maybe a year, two at the most or that will be lost, and I don't want to lose the opportunity to work and live there. I know you'll enjoy being back in Maine. But," he hesitated, disliking giving in, "we'll stay here. Promise me, though," and he stopped. He'd wait, but . . . *Brigit would never have acted this way. Why am I thinking about her? They're so different. But Deirdre had a point. I have to think of her too. We'll look at the house, and if we like it, done. I can't stand arguments like we just had. They'll wait for me. But there's got to be a limit.*

Later that night, while Gregory was at his desk working at a paper he was writing, Deirdre went to the bedroom. She undressed before her mirror, stood naked, looking at herself, the slight bulge in her stomach. She had become pregnant in March. Here it was a warm July night. She gazed at herself, her firm, straight, full breasts, fondled her nipples so they would harden and present a more alluring picture of herself. *I won't breast feed. I just won't ruin these, have them start to droop. They're too beautiful, tantalizing. What they do to the drooling men. Don't they wish they could see them and me now? Except for my belly. Accept it, girl. You're pregnant. That won't last.*

As she was looking at the bulging, she began to feel sorry for herself. *But people will fawn over me for this, the women. Crap. No. I won't ruin this body. I'll do whatever it takes to get it back.*

She looked at her dark pubic hair. Ran her fingers lightly through it, rubbed lower to feel the pleasing sensation, moved them lower, thinking of the pain and blood to come, grimacing. She shook her head, spoke aloud, "You can have all this, Greg, when I let you or surrender to it myself. Mutual satisfaction. He is a good lover. But . . . ." She didn't finish. She was thinking of Étienne. *How he showed me to enjoy myself and how a man should please. We could enjoy ourselves without worry. Do I want him to see me this way? Oh hell. Accept it. You're pregnant. The way Gregory runs his hand over my stomach. He's so pleased. Why aren't I? He's a good husband. I made the right choice, the moneyed family, the prestige to go with E's and my ventures. How I found out about him the first time I saw him at the Ritz. He intrigued me. That Brigit he was with. So dull. She must have been a good lay. But I never counted on pregnancy, though I worried about it if I was never careful. And here I am.* She looked at herself again, studying her body. *I'll be that way again, like I was before.* She laughed. *Seductive Deirdre. That doctor. Yeah. He appeals to me. He gets to see us women; spreads us. Does he think of us only as specimens? I could show him. Any man. I'll always do the choosing. What made me this way? Forget it. I am what I am come hell or heaven.*

Just then Gregory came in. "You're up sort of late. Let's get in bed. I'm tired. You know, Deirdre, I not only love you but that you're giving us a child. I know we'll love it and be happy. Forgive me, dear, for fighting."

She turned to him, somewhat embarrassed that he found her still undressed. "I know. I'm sorry too. It will all work out. I promise you, dearest." She walked slowly toward him, took him by the arm. "Hug me, and get undressed. Like what you see? Let's do it. You see I'm ready and want no more fights like tonight."

In the morning, after he had gone to his hospital office, she drove to Belmont, saw the For Sale sign, went home and called the agent. She made the appointment for early evening, called Gregory. "Dear, I went and saw the house from the outside? I made an appointment. We could see it and then go out to dinner. O.K.?"

Resignedly, "Sure, dear. I'll pick you up about 5. O.K.? How about eating at that French restaurant on Newberry Street?"

"Great. See you." She felt as though she could prance throughout the day. She took her afternoon nap. She was in France. There were explosions. She screamed. Blood was running down her face and between her legs. Étienne appeared, wiped away the blood, kissing and calming her, leading her to a ragged sofa where he lay down on her. Another explosion. It blew them off the sofa. Gregory was in the doorway. Deirdre woke.

She was perspiring, wiped her neck, her face. She got up and went to the bathroom, pulled a towel from the rack, held it, while she had to sit on the toilet. She decided to take another shower. She would take her time, choose a dress and jewelry, make up her face. The dream would disappear. But would the idea of it ever? The war had done something to her, she convinced herself for now. That's why she was the way she was. She trembled, peed some more. She spoke to herself. "We'll go see the house, I know he'll like it, especially when he sees me and how happy he's making me. That horrible dream. It's as if I drowned in blood."

~

In August, 1953, they settled in the Belmont house. Deirdre was now six months pregnant, felt the baby move, watched the joy on Gregory's face when he felt the child. Now Deirdre was happy. She had her house and would have a beautiful child, despite her misgivings. She shopped for the latest fashions in maternity clothes, dresses and skirts with blouses, color being important to match her skin tone. She was pleased with herself, her address, honestly proud of her husband about whom people, particularly the women she met in the neighborhood, talked, asked about his work. It was now important for Deirdre to learn as much as possible about his research that would eventually take him near the top of his field.

As the months passed, she thought of the increasing acceptance by the neighbors, her correspondence with Étienne, the coming child, what it might be like, still annoyed by her distending.

December seemed to approach quite fast. Deirdre watched herself swell, taking greetings from neighboring women with graciousness, accepting their apparent excitement. "Oh, it must be so soon. How exciting." "Greg and I can't wait." But when she was home, she would look at her swollen body, often angrily. "I can't stand looking at you. Whoever said pregnancy was joyful? When the hell are you coming out," looking at her stomach and trying to avoid the mirror. "Greg says I'm beautiful and hopes it will look like me. Bull. Who cares?" she caught her breath. "What am I thinking? I'm cursing myself and whatever's coming out. Oh, hell. Who cares? The wonder of being a woman." She lay on her chaise, tears starting to appear from her self-pity. "I'll never again be the siren I was." She laughed loudly, almost hysterically. "Siren. My desirable, enticing body. Étienne. No."

A short time later she felt a twinge. Pain. She pushed herself up. She was alone but for the maid. She'd call Greg. "Damn it. I asked him not to go to work today. I was right." Another pain. Now they were less than ten minutes apart. She called Andrea. "Get the car. Hurry. Call Dr. Hurwitz too."

The hospital was in Boston, close to Gregory's lab. In agony, she cried out. A nurse tried to comfort her. In a small room, she lay waiting for the doctor. The pain became more excruciating. She yelled more loudly. The head nurse softly talked to her. “You’ll be in the delivery room soon. Try to relax. Take deep breaths. It will help some.” After a bit, when she was about to lose her patience, and remembering Deirdre was a doctor's wife, she left, shaking her head, looking up, her eyes wide with question. This woman, constantly screaming her pain, may have been more interested in herself than in her coming child. Deirdre would listen to no one, refused the nurse's relaxation advice. The doctor was now there, ordered Deirdre to the delivery room. He gave her a sedative. Gently, “Now Mrs. Hurwitz, push. It's coming. You're fine. Push.” The head appeared, the body, the first cries of Melinda, a baby who would only physically resemble her mother.

They cleaned and wrapped the baby, showed her to Deirdre, later laid her next to Deirdre’s breast. Deirdre looked at her, smiled snidely, whispered weakly, “You gave me so much pain and trouble. But you belong to me. Oh, you curled a finger on mine. But you’re not going to suckle my breast for long, girl.”

Gregory, smiling, finally saw them both. He kissed Deirdre. “I love you, dear. You’ve given us this beautiful girl.”

Deirdre watched Gregory’s face. “Perhaps you’d like to go through all the pain.”

“Stop that,” he told her softly. “We’re going to love her and give her everything we can - but not spoil her, mind you. I thought of a name. Melinda. Do you like it?”

“Yes. It’s fine.” She managed a smile, thought, smiled more sincerely, “It’s fine, Greg. And she’s all ours. We made her. Perhaps we ought to get another maid, someone who can look after her when I’m busy.”

“Well, it’ll be expensive, but if that’s what you want, we’ll manage.

“I wanted to wait, but I have to tell you. I bought you a

present."

"Ooh. What?"

He took from his pocket a small velvet box. "Just look." It was a jade ring in a platinum setting. "For our first child. Maybe the next one we'll call Jade."

"Our next one," she answered loudly. "This was terrible. Men should feel it. You got all the joy. I got all the agony."

He stared at her. "You don't mean that. You'll love watching her grow. Knowing you, you'll spoil her." Yet, the way she answered. *She's been through a lot. She's weary. I'll get someone else in the house to help her. She deserves it.* When he left, he could not stop thinking of what she said.

The war in Korea continued off and on despite the peace talks. Neither side would achieve its goal. But in Belmont there was an apparent peace. Melinda was almost standing, wanted to walk. Gregory enjoyed watching and playing with her. Deirdre bottle fed her at first, then sat and fed her baby food but often having Andrea feed the child.

Also about this time, having recovered from illness, Joseph McCarthy began to stumble politically as Democrats on the Committee refused to participate, leaving the Republican hearings with vacant chairs. Then there was Joseph Welch who famously stated, "Have you no sense of decency . . . ?" bringing applause and the beginning of the downfall of the alcoholic, diabolic, calamitous McCarthy who had even tried to destroy one of Gregory's colleagues. Eventually, in December, the Senate censured McCarthy.

They celebrated Melinda's first birthday, obviously a bright child, walking, mouthing words.

Yet, Joseph McCarthy caused a rift in the family that at first Gregory ignored but which Deirdre knew was there, telling herself she would never let this man go despite whatever else she might do.

Gregory, like many, had followed the hearings on television, when he could, especially because of a colleague McCarthy accused of being a communist. It hit the Boston newspapers front pages. There was a belated apology but marked the researcher a communist for some. One woman in the Senate stood out, the only one in that body, Margaret Chase Smith whom even Democrats like the Hurwitzes admired. The damage McCarthy wrought was destructive of reputations and justifiably his own, though later some people would after his death remake him an American hero.

This was a battle that occurred in Gregory's house. Deirdre thought McCarthy a self-sacrificing American attacked by ignorant people. He was protecting the United States.

Gregory would lose his temper listening to her praise, and she would accuse him of disloyalty. Two veterans, a man and a wife, a family fighting over a man Gregory loudly told her was a charlatan.

Then, along with the political wrangling, she announced to Gregory several months later, "I'm going away. I have to help take care of some museum business."

"Where?"

"Probably Greece. I'll let you know."

"What do you mean, you'll let me know?"

"Because I don't know yet exactly what country."

"That Frenchman."

"He's not 'that Frenchman.' His name's Étienne. You've met him."

"I don't trust him."

She smiled, pleased. "You're jealous."

"Jealous, shit. I don't like the bastard understand? And you're leaving Melinda to a maid."

"Oh shut up. You act like I'm deserting my child. It's necessary. I support you. You support me, or else . . ."

"Or else what?"

"Or else, oh I don't know." She forced tears. "I don't want to argue. I won't." She cried now, loudly. "You don't want me to get us money too. And I'm helping you in your work as I get to know the right people."

"WHAT? What right people?" I advance through my brain and the people who benefit from what I do. Don't you ever talk to me again like that."

Still crying loudly, she ran from the room, wiped at her face, smiled, then erased it, realizing she would have to be more tender. Tonight, bed. She went to the bedroom, hesitated, went to Melinda and kissed her, hurried back to their room, brushed her hair, lightly perfumed herself, changed into a lace sheer black negligee. *Maybe I'll take this one with me on the trip.*

~

Brigit had moved to an apartment nearer the hospital where there were trees and large grassy areas, where people even had gardens in which they could plant vegetables. There were pools of water that flowed from underground. The open space reminded her of the skies she would see at home, the brightness of the night sky, where she could view stars and watch the phases of the moon. Nor did she have to fear walking along the paths in early evening or during the day. It was her escape and hope that she wouldn't see Gregory. Her apartment was in a smaller building, cozier with a living room, dining room, kitchen and two bedrooms. She wanted to erase any trace of Gregory except that she kept some of the jewelry he gave her. Most of the time she would avoid wearing it, yet occasionally she could not help herself. Putting it on, a ring, earrings, a necklace, at first brought tears but later memory alone that came from the touch or feel or remembering when he had given a piece to her. She just could not bring herself to send it to one of her sisters.

Too, from the apartment she could walk up a broad avenue for about half a mile to be at work. There were two schools nearby from which she could hear the joyfulness of the children and wonder when she might someday have one of her own. Yes, she missed the thought of a man beside her at night, lying spooned together. The thought of somehow getting even with Gregory occurred to her, and she would accuse herself of wicked thoughts and not getting on with her life. She had heard people talk of his marriage and the new house. She had also heard that Deirdre took trips abroad with a man to purchase museum pieces. Did Gregory mind? Apparently not. When she heard this, she hoped he was married to an adulteress, that he would suffer as he had made her. Then she would again become angry with herself for her thoughts.

One day they did meet as he was walking from the lab to the hospital. Both attempted cordiality, but she saw his face redden while she felt nothing but anger when they said hello. He tried to stop her for a bit to find out how she was, where she was living, if she were still on the birthing floor. She answered, then walked away trembling, her heart beating faster. But looking in his eyes, she knew that he could never forget her, that there was something bright in them that told her he still loved her. She tried to hide her feelings, but he must have known. Perhaps there would always be aside from remembrance, love that would linger and occasionally come to the surface with sadness.

She did not wish to go out with anyone else. She couldn't. Not for sometime. Yet, there was the ob/gyn doctor, Thomas Erickson, with whom she often worked and who was always attracted to her, rather in love with her though he hid it, had been since he first met her. Often he would think about her, watch her as she worked with him, for him even in gloves, her lovely hands, her face when she took off her mask. He would wonder what she looked like dressed for an evening out. As others in the hospital had heard about Gregory and Deirdre, so had he. Eventually, there was a day - she had changed to the 7-3 shift - when one of the patients was having a placenta previa birth. The placenta was covering the cervix. Erickson wasn't sure he could save the patient and baby by C-Section because she had had one before. They worked quickly together, she anticipating what he would want or need. The mother was hemorrhaging.

"I'm not going to lose her, Brigit. Give her blood."

"I already ordered more, in case."

The woman loudly moaned, despite the sedative. Slowly her moans faded. "I'm not going to let her die." Erickson was desperate. "Terrible. This placenta previa. Goddamn. I can't operate," he repeated in despair. "She's already had one by Caesarean."

Brigit interrupted, forcing herself to hide her turmoil of emotion. "I've read the chart. This is a bad one. She's been bleeding before. What are you going to do?"

"Well, I've been treating her all along. Had her on bed rest. She began in the second trimester. Now look. I told her everything. My God, Brigit, she could die."

Before saying more, he noticed Brigit's face, wondering what she was thinking.

How I wanted a child with Gregory. Still want one. What if it were I? Would I want to die to have a child? But we could both die. This poor woman. The Caesarean. How's he going to stop the hemorrhaging? I have the blood ready. How I love being a woman, and this is what we have to endure. And betrayal. Thank goodness I didn't get pregnant. Oh, this poor woman. The BABY! Stop thinking. Only saving them now. Concentrate on assisting Erickson.

Brigit watched him, the perspiration that she wiped away. The blood arrived, and she started the IV. The baby moved out more. He was able to grasp and turn it. The blood was slippery and getting in his way. Brigit leaned over him, touching his shoulder. She asked if she could do something and reached to help him, her hands and his coming away with blood, holding the baby with difficulty until another nurse took and cleaned it. The blood still flowed from the mother. "Give her another transfusion."

Brigit's face was wan, her voice sorrowful. "Dr. Erickson, her heart is slowing."

"Give her the blood. I'm going to save her. The boy needs his mother."

Brigit wondered what it would be like to go through life saying, "My mother died in childbirth." Yet, she stood there, admiring Erickson, realizing at the same time her hands were shaking. She wrapped them in her gown so others would not see while they stood watching the woman, keeping her warm, color beginning to return to her face.

Brigit and Erickson smiled at one another. "You did a fine job, Doctor."

Intently he looked at her, then at her gown with large bloodstains. He wanted to hug her, to feel her close to him. She watched his reaction, knowingly, and placed her hand on his arm. He felt a thrill, relaxation, put his hand on her arm, "Thank you for your help," turning to avoid her notice of his pleasure.

Sometime later he came to her station after seeing a patient. "Hi. Brigit, I wonder if you'd go to dinner with me Friday or Saturday night. I'm off this weekend. We could go to one of those nice restaurants on Newbury Street or downtown."

She hesitated, telling herself she did not want to get mixed up with another man, especially one with whom she worked. Yet she wanted to be with one, to smell, to feel him, hear his restful voice. She wanted love, but she would not allow herself to fall into another Gregory situation.

"Yes. That would be wonderful, Doct . . ."

"Hold on. Call me Thomas. Tom, whichever you use. Outside work we're friends. O.K.?"

She smiled. "O.K." Brigit was happy.

"Where do you live?" She told him, gave him her phone number if anything changed.

"Seven-thirty all right?"

"Fine. See you then. Thank you."

When he left, pleased, she thought, *I haven't bought anything new for a while. I'll buy a new dress, have my hair done this week instead of my usual time, get a manicure. Why not? He's a nice guy. Maybe a little flirting.*

The next day she went to her hairdresser. Her hair no longer fell to her shoulders but was in the cut of the time, shorter in back, gathered so it swept from her forehead and bunched by a gold band she bought before her hair appointment. Manicured and confident she went to the stores, looked through dresses, picked at one, another, finally found a light blue off-the-shoulder that had a red cape attached to show her bare arms and her bust, and had a broad skirt that came to her calves and which would swirl as she walked. She also bought a new pair of shoes. Telling herself she was being extravagant, she also said she didn't care. She was going to enjoy and show herself to this man and the public.

He brought the usual corsage, and when he saw and heard her, he was certain he would keep after and marry her.

It was a usual courtship in ways. They danced, went to cocktail lounges, and though she did not usually drink, she did with him, but only one each time. There were also the usual goodnight kisses. For one date, eventually, he asked if she would like to see his home in Belmont and eat there.

"You never told me you had a house. Were you married?"

"No. I inherited it from my folks and live alone. I think you'll like it and the neighborhood."

"How come you inherited the house?".

"Well, my dad was a M.D."

She interrupted. "Good heavens. Everybody's dad is a doctor. Mine is just a mere farmer." She did not mention, 'a wealthy rancher-farmer.' "Anyhow, what then?"

He laughed. "Well, I'm an only child. He wanted me to stay in Boston, so I did. I wanted to practice in New Mexico where I was in the Air Corps until shipped over to Europe."

"New Mexico! That's my home," she about shouted. Well they had something almost in common. "Belmont. It must be something."

He laughed. "No. It's on one of the streets below the hill, but, yes, it's nice."

"Well, I'll cook. How about it?"

"Great." He hesitated," If you want to stay over," but before he could say more, she interrupted.

"How can I stay at your house?" He surprised her, both pleasingly and a bit sadly that he would confront her so soon with what she considered a sexual invitation.

"Brigit. I didn't mean it that way. I have so much space. I just thought you could bring some clothes, and we wouldn't have to rush." His smile and slight movement of his head were, as she suspected, an invitation to bed. He wanted to sleep with her, to see her. In fact, were she honest just now, she wanted to make love other than in the car as they had begun to do. The bump disappeared.

"Thomas, take that smirk off your face."

"I'm not smirking."

"I'll cook and stay. I want to see the house." Brigit was beginning to feel love for him, but she was not in love, hadn't that exhilarating feeling. She knew she would never care as she did with Gregory.

They drove up a quiet street, tree-lined, brick houses with

gardens set in back. Inside, left was a stairway up, a living room off to the right, a dining room off of it and beyond, a sunroom. There were bookcases, a TV and stereo, a collection of classical music. Beyond the sunroom was a bedroom, his, with its own bath.

She did like it. "It's lovely, Tom."

He had thought he would wait until after dinner but couldn't help himself.

"It could be yours too, Brigit."

He did not surprise her. She turned to him as though he had. "What do . . . ."

"I was going to wait to see how you cook," he laughed but was suddenly serious. "Come here." He led her to the sofa, took her hand, and seated her. Beside her, he leaned a bit toward her. "Brigit. I do love you. I want you to be my wife."

Though she expected this when he invited her, she still caught her breath and felt a pleasing sensation course through her. She was not in love. Did she love him enough to marry, feel warmth and comfort, certainty? "Tom, I must be honest. You know . . . ."

"You don't have to say anything about before."

"Well. I care for you very much. I think we could be happy, but do you want me that way?"

"Go get ready in whatever you wear for cooking and we'll talk more. *Is she saying yes or no? It is yes if I push just a bit, not push, gently persuade. I have to have her.*

After dinner through which he played some romantic Tchaikovsky, they went back to the living room. Standing just a few inches above her, he looked down, at her bust shown more advantageously by her bra, her bare shoulders for which he reached. She felt warm when he touched her, liked the feel of his hands. "I love, you, Brigit. I'll be a good husband for you."

"I know," she answered quietly. She softly, still thinking of her lack of intense emotion, told him, "I'd love to be your wife."

He took from his pocket a diamond ring, raised her hand, and placed it on her finger.

This has happened to me before. But he's so kind, loving. The ring, It's beautiful, and he does love me. I feel enough toward him to wear this.

She put her arms about him, pulled him to her, kissed him long, hard. "We'll have a wonderful home. My goodness. You're giving me everything at once."

"You're worth everything here and more." They kissed again, long. His hand wandered to her breasts, and they kissed more. She pulled away. "The dishes," she laughed.

"'Nuts.' Isn't that what General McCauliffe said?"

Later in the night, after an evening of foreplay, as she started upstairs for her room, she stopped. She had already decided she would be in his bed as she knew he wished. "Why am I going up here?" she turned. He watched.

"Come on, dear. My room's nicer."

She undressed before him, so he could admire her body. She watched him and liked his nakedness. They fell on the bed together; and once inside her, she felt him ejaculate, she having an orgasm soon after. Satisfying one another, she sighed, "Simultaneous equation." It would be a good marriage Brigit assured herself. The sex was good, but it was his kindness and warmth that would protect them.

In the morning, she put on her nurse's uniform, embarrassed that neighbors might see them, then trying to tell herself she didn't care, as they drove to the hospital. They went in separately, as though that would prevent people from noticing. After rounds he would go to his office.

~

The wedding took place in August in Las Cruces among her

pleased and happy family. As she had with Gregory, she took him to Cloudcroft, to Albuquerque, to El Paso, but she could not bring herself to take him to Taos.

In Cloudcroft, as they made love, she looked at him. "Tom. I'd like to have a baby. Would you mind if we had one soon?"

He hesitated. "We're . . . ." and he stopped. He could not deny her. "If you wish," but there was a sadness in his assent. He thought quickly. "Could we wait a few months?"

"Yes, dear. But not too long. O.K.? I so want a child, and I know you would love it."

They had decided after the wedding and seeing New Mexico they would go to the Virgin Islands for a week. It was there she became pregnant, in early September. It would be a May baby. They would at least have that much time to themselves. He was happy, and she looked forward to watching her belly grow and feeling the baby inside her. Perhaps life would, after all, be happy, good, satisfying. Yet, she could not entirely forget Gregory as much as she tried. By the sixth month she left work, had bought an entire wardrobe of maternity clothes, chatted with neighbor women and became friendly with some to whom she could talk more freely about the baby and how she felt.

Her pregnancy was uneventful except for the usual discomforts, the excitement of the first movements, and the anticipation of early May, 1955. She knew what to expect, hoping but not believing that would make it easier for her. It ought to be an uneventful birth to which she looked forward. She did ask Thomas that the doctor not be a close friend, not wanting to expose herself to someone they knew. He promised her the head of the department with whom he was friendly but no one to whom he was particularly close.

Late in the afternoon she called Tom and asked him to take her to the hospital. The contractions were becoming more frequent. In the hospital, the labor continued longer than expected. She thought of patients who had been almost uncontrollable in their misery and promised herself she would be calm and quiet as possible. She wanted the labor to end, to see the baby, hold it. She had decided to breast feed at least for a few months, to feel the child close to her, to love it. She was about to give herself and Thomas a new life. In the delivery room she did moan, at one point yell out, "Push. Push, Brigit. It's almost here." Then she heard the first cries and wearily smiled. "Here's your son," a nurse with whom she had worked presenting him to her. "Oh, Doris, a boy. Look at him. Let me hold him. Tom will be so happy." She hadn't wanted him in the delivery room, fearful of embarrassing him. *A son. Mine. The baby I've wanted for so long. We'll give you a good life, young man. How about if we call you Robert Thomas Erickson, my handsome one?*

The months went by. Within a year, 1956, Robert was walking. On her way back from a visit to the pediatrician, she decided to stop at the delicatessen in the town. She drove under the railroad bridge that was now for trolleys. Beyond was a large stone bearing the date of the town's founding and beyond that rows of stores on either side of the street. When she went into the store, she stopped suddenly. She was aware the Hurwitzes lived in Belmont. The town newspaper had announced a gathering at their home for new museum pieces donated by Deirdre and her partner. Brigit stopped, thought of walking out and returning later, but Deirdre had already seen her.

Without hesitation, Deirdre confronted her with a large, forced smile. "What a handsome little fellow. What's his name?" pretending they were strangers. Brigit felt herself shaking slightly, her anger appearing from desire to protect her son from this viper. Frostily she answered, "Robert." She quickly picked up the package she bought and Robert, abruptly turned away. *You fucking fake bitch. I hope you both suffer. That fool, trusting her. You obviously have kept him from Maine.*

Deirdre called after her, as though they were friends. "Take care, dear. He's a handsome boy. Oh, by the way, Brigit," drawing out the name distastefully and hopefully to hurt her, "I'm having another one."

Outside, having ignored 'another one,' it occurred to Brigit that perhaps Deirdre truly was a fake, that hopefully there was something terribly unusual about all these museum pieces she was donating. Anyhow, somehow she would avoid both of them. Still shaking somewhat and very angry now, she wanted to go back and confront her with, "Do you want me present in the delivery room for the next one?" She didn't though and quickly walked to the car, sitting in the driver's seat, catching her breath. "Your day's coming, bitch. I just know it." Brigit apologizing to something or someone for her evil thoughts, drove home, looked at Robert with love, leaned over, kissed him, took his hand, and walked into the comfort and safety of her home.

When Deirdre returned to her house, annoyed by Melinda bothering her, and helpless in another pregnancy, her mind was in a slight turmoil; she remembered an article she had read a month or two earlier. That was the problem.

The newspaper had a story just come to light about an OSS lieutenant being accused of killing an OSS major in Italy while behind German lines. Eventually, on a technicality, he was acquitted. This took her back in time. She was thinking of Juliette and her rape by Germans, not one but two. Did she tell the truth? Was it possible it could have been OSS agents on a mission for which they wore German uniforms? She told herself this thinking was an absurdity. But why not, if the article she read was true? She had discovered that woman traitor, Diane, among them when she was in France, and the men just killed her.

That night, asleep, she dreamed again of blood. Waking

suddenly, she thought of the next baby. But then her mind returned to Juliette. The blood of the rape, the pain Juliette had described. She felt herself kissing Juliette on the mouth, the searing sensations that coursed to her nipples, to her sex. She acknowledged what she blocked in her mind. Juliette and she had slept together, arms about one another for comfort. Without thought but knowing what to do to satisfy one another as women, they had made intense, satisfying love.

Would they have been shot had the men known? The bed had squeaked, and both quietly laughed about it, though fearful.

Deirdre tried to calm her anxiety. Always blood? The war? Well surely. Fear of another child? Gregory would not help her when she told him she wanted an abortion. She avoided the word. How had she told him? He was terribly upset. *I did use abortion. I asked him to take me to that doctor who rides around in that beautiful convertible. Greg told me he does abortions, that all the doctors knew it. But he was adamant, so angry he scared me. It was against the law. I was supposed to know better. His face. 'It was so unnatural.' He yelled that I would think of that when I knew he wanted more children. He kept screaming, 'It's illegal' Well, hell, wars are illegal even when we say they aren't. He scared Melinda. As far as I'm concerned, the hell with what he wants. Things shouldn't be like that. It shouldn't be. Why can't I have a baby or not? It's what I want. Gregory. So honest. I killed during the war. Blood. Lyon. That traitor Diane. She hated the sight of Diane's falling, bloody body, the thought. No blood and placentas from her. That simpleton Brigit I met in the store. Loves being a mother. Obvious. Plus all the blood she has seen. Ha. But not in war. Why am I always dreaming of blood?*

In January, 1956, Deirdre gave birth to Pamela. In March, 1958, there would be another daughter, Kaitlin. A month later in that same year, Brigit would also have a daughter they named Kathryn.

As for Deirdre, she was her usual unruly patient,

demanding, crying out, damning Gregory and her body, that sexually attractive body that she had used to trap him, that could be used to entice others. She would not breast feed Pamela either. At home she constantly watched herself in the mirror, ate little, exercised so she would be admirable. Her hips were larger, her stomach softer, but she could still display that body and attract desire.

For Brigit the birth of a daughter, Kathryn, was joyful. However, she did tell Thomas it would be their last one. He laughed. "Oh, I believe you'll change your mind when I think of the family you come from." Smiling, she pushed him while he sat by her bed. "Only if it's a mistake. You don't mind, do you dear?" He leaned over, hugged and lightly kissed her. "You and our children are enough for me."

She loved Thomas more but still had never been in love. Sometimes it seemed to her he was so much warmer than she. There was Gregory still in her mind, especially as she read about him and his work or heard of something else about Deirdre. Then she heard that Gregory was leaving the hospital research staff to become head of research in Maine, as he had always wanted. Somehow they waited. The man who had been there apparently had done something wrong. Gregory's friend wrote, pleading with him to come home to this position. Brigit imagined the turmoil in his house, knew his wife reveled in the upper society associated with Belmont. While watching the children one day, she did think of Gregory with his children, knowing he enjoyed them and wondering what happened when he told his wife they were moving. She wanted to stop thinking about him and give all of herself to Thomas, but the effect of Gregory would never leave her. She would, however, always be loyal to Thomas and be thankful for the comfort and the children and husband who would sacrifice anything for her.

~

"Deirdre, we have to talk. We're moving to Maine. I was offered the job again and I'm taking it. It's almost three years since they first asked and they won't again."

"That's ridiculous. We're settled here. And you're just making it harder for me to help the museum."

"The museum can get along without you, or you can travel down when you have to."

"You don't need that job. And I don't want to be stuck in Maine."

"Stuck in Maine? What the hell do you mean? You think it's Siberia or Alaska?"

"Don't you swear at me. I just don't want to live there. And I know where it is. I come from there, remember?"

"Deirdre, this is the chance I've been waiting for. It's a better position than they first offered me. I'd be the head of the whole thing. It's a good position. And think of raising the girls there. It'd be great for them. I know they'll like Cape Astraea."

"You don't know anything about girls. You're being selfish and stupid. I grew up in isolation on that farm."

"Like you never had any friends? You're being selfish now. You know damn well this is a good move for me. You're just thinking of yourself. Well, you go ahead. Be stubborn. Think only about what you want. This move is for the whole family."

She was frustrated and getting very angry. "Fuck you."

"What?"

"You heard me. Fuck. Fuck. Fuck you."

"His face red, his heart beating faster, he left the room, yelling behind him, "We're moving. Get used to it."

She started to answer, "*Shit . . .*" and stopped. *I married that ass, and after everything I've been through, back to Maine. What for? Security, Deirdre. I had security through Étienne. Social standing. I fell for him. Admit it. Yeah. And you wanted to show your power over the simpleton he was going with. Well, give in. Let him have his way, for now. The kids will just have to grow up there. I did. So what if it was a farm? Look what I have now. I always manage to get my way. He'll think he's won.*

They would move in the summer. Gregory told his folks, she hers. Jocelyn looked at houses but knew she could not choose for them, although she did see one she thought they'd both like.

Both families were happy about the move but were ignorant of how Deirdre felt, even Gregory who was happy to be going but stunned by her objections. For the morning after he told her he was accepting the position, they hardly spoke. She took the breakfast from Andrea, slamming the dishes on the table. The banging scared Melinda and Pamela. Kaitlin cried. Deirdre stared at the children. "Why don't you feed the children? It's your responsibility too."

Deirdre left the kitchen, did not return, and let Andrea finish clearing the table.

Her behavior reminded Gregory of the earthquake that had struck the Aleutians and the tidal wave it caused that swept into Hawaii, flooding roads, sweeping a submarine along the ocean bottom. The wave had changed course and was sweeping through the house. "Where are you? Come back here. I'm already late."

"I don't give a damn," she shouted, coming to the door. "You surprise me, don't even ask me, and we're off on a flight. What am I? Some fucking Negro maid in this house? Well, like them, I want my freedom. So you take care of everything. That's what you're doing."

"Don't you dare use that word again in front of the children. And stop talking about race in this house. I won't have it. They deserve every right we have."

"So says the great Dr. Gregory Hurwitz."

Kaitlin and Pamela were now crying loudly. Melinda stood behind her chair, staring.

"Look what you've done." Gregory rose and went to the girls, soothing them. "Mommy just didn't sleep well last night."

"You're goddamn right she didn't." Although upset, she wanted the children to stop crying, was sad she had scared them. She went to Kaitlin, picked her up, then moved to Pamela, rubbed her hand through Melinda's hair. "It's all right, dears. Mommy's just upset." She glared at Gregory. "Why don't you just get the hell out of here and go play with your bugs."

He scowled, didn't answer, went to the children, kissed them, and left, slamming the front door.

He calmed driving to work. *The whole world's a mess. The Arabs and Israelis are fussing. Golda Meir was right to give back to Egypt Aquaba and Gaza.* He thought of the plane blown up in 1955 by John Graham so he could kill his mother, except that he also killed 144 other people. *Well, I guess my house isn't that bad yet. Why's she always talking about the black people? She hates them so. What did they ever do to her? Chicago. They told the bus drivers if they allowed Negroes to mix with whites, the drivers would be arrested. Some country, President Eisenhower. Nice guy though. He's got his hands full with the Near East. The Arabs don't know what they want. Maybe Deirdre's an Arab.* He laughed, then was talking to himself, "I like that John Kennedy. Smart. The Democrats need new ideas, new policies, new faces. He's right. They say he'll run in '60. His brother is something too, being the counselor for that Select Committee investigating the Teamsters in Oregon. Kennedy getting them to admit they have been involved in illegal activities like bringing that madam to set up a house of prostitution, and the D.A. from Portland, Oregon being indicted. Nice world. And that bastard McCarthy is on the committee, still in the Senate. Oh well. My house." He hesitated. "MY house. She'll come around. Is it my house? My home?"

When he did come home late, though she was still angry, she had Andrea hold his meal for him. She met him at the door, sweetly telling him she loved him, kissed and hugged him. "It'll be all right, dear. Let's not fight about going. You have to."

However, during the day she had made her own plans.

The next day she told Andrea she might not be home until late. "If my husband gets home before me, tell him I had to meet one of our State Reps."

In the meantime, Deirdre had insisted that Étienne return from Athens, for, without telling him, she had already decided she would, perhaps must, agree to Maine.

Before leaving, she had been supervising the selling and packing of the house when she pressed Étienne for his company. He took the first flight from Athens and was with Deirdre within a day of landing. They commiserated, made plans for meeting, while fondling one another.

"Now tell me why you married him. I told you not to, that I was enough for you."

"And your wife? I was supposed to be the faithful mistress forever? I needed some security. I found it. I have a husband who loves me."

He interrupted. "Love?" He started to laugh. The only love is what's between you and me."

Angrily, she retorted, "I have a loving husband, my children, a new home in Maine."

"Where you don't even want to go. Face it, Deirdre, you're mine, and you best stay that way."

"You're threatening me?" She shouted at him.

"No threat. Just the truth. You'll never have a better lover." He grabbed her by the arm, pressing tightly.

"Stop that. You'll make me black and blue. How will I explain that?"

"Explain. You love roughness." He put his hand on her throat, "Love it," as he pulled her toward him, kissed her hard, ran his hand to her vagina, placing his fingers inside.

She softened, leaned into him, sliding her hand along his

hard penis.

"You love it and me, Deirdre. No matter what happens, you belong to me."

"Oh, shut up." She taunted him. "I have a young husband who can please me better than you." She laughed. "Try me."

"Bitch." He undressed her, pulled at her clothing while she did the same to him.

They pleased themselves in their nakedness, spent the afternoon making love, promising faithfulness while using their hands and mouths, warming to her sitting atop him, tightening to please him, feeling his pulsating into her, then she rubbing until she screamed, clenched his chest to the rhythm of the flowing heat and the spasms of her orgasm that traveled throughout her body, as she moaned and fell upon him, whispering, "I'll never let you down, will always be yours."

Chapter XI

The Maine Coast and Home

Deirdre took her car, the maid, and children. She drove to Warrington first, though the trip was longer, purposely bypassing Cape Astraea. She wanted to avoid as long as possible what she thought of as the isolation of that place. She did want to stop and see her parents who hadn't seen the children since Kaitlin's birth. The farm and chicks would please the children. Christine and Edward, naturally, were quite happy seeing the children and their daughter. At first, Christine thought little about Deirdre having come to Warrington first. Yet it bothered her that she did not go with her husband or start, at least, to settle her new home.

"It's so wonderful having you and the children. But I'm wondering. Shouldn't you be in your new home helping settling it? There must be a lot that has to be done."

"Yes, mother. There is. But right now, I feel like I'll get it done when I get there. If Gregory can't get along for a little while and perhaps do some of it himself, then that's that."

"But he has to work. He's got a new job, and he may need you."

"Mother, I go away at various times because of my work. I have a maid. I have everything. I was even in the army. Remember? I think I can make my own decisions."

"You may have been a lot of places and done a lot, but you're married."

"Why does everyone think marriage is supposed to tie you

down? I won't live that way." She thought about the children. "Yeah. I have three children. I love them. They know it. But they're learning that sometimes I'm away. Do I always have to prove myself?"

Christine was sorry she said anything. "I don't want us to argue, dear. I just thought . . . ." and she decided she would say no more as much as she disapproved.

"O.K, mom, have we got that settled? I'm here to be with you and dad and so you can see the children for a while."

Deirdre felt she had put her mother in her place, that there would be no grandmotherly advice or interference. Her father wouldn't even think about it. Or maybe he would. He was one of those men who felt a woman's place was in her home, taking care of her children and her husband. And if she were lucky enough to have a maid, then she would have to tell the maid what to do.

Andrea overheard Deirdre and her mother and laughed to herself. She knew Deirdre had to tolerate having a black woman in the house, knew about her prejudice. Aside from that, she did not really like Deirdre, thought her selfish, had seen her preening before a mirror. It was a nice figure. But Andrea loved the children, enjoyed playing with them. Melinda and she were becoming great friends. And she liked Gregory who was always so kind to her. Sometimes it was almost as if the children were hers. Melinda and Pamela came to her with their troubles, and Kaitlin was always pulling at her skirt. Yet, there were times when she and Deirdre would quarrel, and Deirdre would remind Andrea the children were not hers, to stop trying to take her place. Because Andrea came from a poor family, it pleased her to work and have a place to live in a rich home. She had no idea how much money there was in the family, but all doctors were rich her parents had taught her. A job with a doctor would be security. Yes, there were times she wished she had a man and her own family. For now, however, she would have to be content and make the best of it with Deirdre. She also decided that perhaps things weren't too good between Gregory and Deirdre, the way Deirdre disappeared, had her call her at that number, only if absolutely necessary, where that man with a foreign accent answered when they lived in Belmont. This bothered Andrea. She had called once when they still lived in Belmont.

"Why are you bothering me? I'm very busy." Her voice was husky and sounded as though she were breathing harder.

"Kaitlin fell down and has hurt her leg. She doesn't seem to be able to stand the way she usually does. I'm sorry, ma'm, but I touched her ankle and she cried."

"Is it twisted or anything like that?"

"I don't think so, but she's still crying."

"Well. It sounds like she's all right, just scared."

"I think, Mrs. Hurwitz, you should come home and see if she's all right."

Andrea heard a soft "Damn."

"Mrs. Hurwitz, did you say something?"

Resentfully, she answered, "I'll be there in a little bit."

Deirdre slammed down the phone, glared at Étienne. "That damned maid can't take care of anything. I ought to fire her. The damn Negroes are hopeless. I better go." She dressed quickly, brushed her hair with her hands, put on some lipstick. "I'm sorry, dearest." He lay in the bed watching her, angrily admiring her body. "You married him, dearest," he sarcastically told her. "You had his babies."

"Oh, shut up."

He laughed while thinking, *You may not quite regret it now, but you will. Screw around with me? Non. Non. I begged you not to do it.* "Come over here." He reached for her breasts, rubbed them, pulled her to him and kissed her hard. "Just remember, we're in this together, and you're mine. Despite that ring on your finger."

For just an instant, Deirdre wondered about her uncertain life.

"Mother, let's just enjoy ourselves. Tell you what. Let me take you to Rockland for dinner. O.K.? It will be a nice break for you and dad."

"I like that."

"You know, I was thinking about the war, how uncertain everything was and is."

"Now why should you be thinking that way."

"I guess what you said about my new home and Gregory. I won't stay too long and get there. You're right. Gregory's going to need me."

~

In Cape Astraea there were also questions. Jocelyn and Aaron had never been happy about Gregory's marriage to Deirdre. Mary, who was now an intern, loved Brigit and wanted to push her brother into a rolling surf for what he did. The marriage to Deirdre was as though a stormy sea had crashed against them. She and Brigit had remained friends, corresponded with one another, talked on the phone. She never told Gregory. She had decided she would try to come home to see the family and her nieces. In Boston she had seen the children, enjoying when Melinda began to talk, then Pamela, and she had seen Kaitlin crawl and try to stand. She forced herself to befriend Deirdre, although she would never forgive her for the scene that had made Mary so angry.

Aaron found Jocelyn in her music room. "What the hell is it with that woman?"

"What?" Jocelyn looked up surprised.

"That Deirdre. Why the hell isn't she here?"

"She wanted to see her parents, show them the children."

"Bull shit. She could have done that later. There's so much to be done here."

"Aaron, would you please after all these years try to stop swearing. Don't forget, when you meet your Lord . . ."

He interrupted. "What Lord?"

Jocelyn started laughing. "I know you'll never change. Let's not argue about her. She'll get here in her time. Gregory loves her and that's what matters."

"And she?"

Jocelyn didn't answer, thought, and changed the subject. "Mary's going to try and get home for a day. I hope she can."

~

The ocean was calm, stars filled the sky; the moon shed its shimmering light across the water. In the distance was one lighthouse among others that protected the harbor entrance. Mary enjoyed this view as she drove closer to home, wishing Evelyn could be beside her seeing this enchanting scene. She was also anxious to see Greg's new house and wished the children were with him. Perhaps Deirdre would come before she had to leave the next evening. When she walked into the house, there were the usual cries of joy.

"Greg will be here for dinner, knowing you'd be coming home, as short a time as it is," Jocelyn told her. "He's anxious to see you. You'll love his house. I have a key and we can go in the morning after he's at work. He loves the job. Then we can look about and decide where Deirdre should put everything. I'm certain she'll listen," she said sarcastically. "Oh well, let's be nice. It will be fun with the children, except that she probably won't get here before you leave."

"Mother, I saw Brigit at the hospital before I left. She had the children and was waiting for Tom who was seeing some patients, I suppose wondering whether he'd be called during the night for a delivery. That woman gets more beautiful with age and her two beauties. Her son, Robert is so handsome and Kathryn is almost a copy of her mother. Wait 'til she grows up. Wow. I'm sorry. But I still think Greg was a fool. Secretly, I think he still loves her. Brigit asked about him and seemed a little down when I told her he was now in Maine and what he's doing. They were meant for each other, and if either would admit it, they're still in love."

"Stop it, Mary. Things are as they are. He loves his wife. I admit, sometimes she seems a little distant, especially toward me. She does like your father. Who wouldn't, that charmer? Oh, Mary, it's so good to have you both here." The women looked at each other, the love between them obvious not only to both but to anyone who would have observed them. Hugs and a kiss on the cheek were enough. Mary felt the warmth of her home, smelled her mother's perfume that she had always loved, the feel of her smooth hands.

"Mary." Aaron came toward them. "I thought I heard the rustle of women and their voices. I'm glad you were able to come." He hugged her and asked them to come to the living room.

Not long after, Gregory came. "Hi everyone. I had a call from Deirdre. She'll be here tomorrow. She wants Mary to see the children and you, too, dad and mom." "No doubt," Aaron told himself.

Deirdre decided to surprise everyone and drive to Cape Astraea that night. In fact, she surprised herself, enjoying the relatively rougher ocean, the same deeper dark star-filled sky, the full moon casting its light across windblown increasing waves, the white foam barely seen against the shore. *It is so peaceful and beautiful. Perhaps I will like it here. Besides, I can always count on my trips.* She started to laugh aloud, thought of Andrea or waking the children. *My ventures in antiquities. What the public never realizes is what we go through, must do. Thank God for Étienne – and not just the sex. But what ecstasy he gives my body. And then with Gregory as the climax.* She did laugh. *You are clever. How I have learned to satisfy my desires. The children are becoming more delightful as they get older. Maybe I can be a good mother. Well, put your mind to it when you think about it.*

As she drove to their house, she thought about the mess it would be. *The tiresome and tiring unpacking and putting everything in its place, telling Andrea what to do before she in her – what's that expression? – "uppity" that's it – nice word, not too denigrating – decides she'll just do what she wants. I'll put her in her place, and when I need her, then I'll use her. I've got to admit she's not a lazy black like all those southern ones I've been reading about. Anyhow, she's got a useless family, so we're all she's got. Oh, my God, she does. No matter.*

When she came to the house, before going to the Hurwitz's, there were some lights that Gregory had left on. The moon was higher in the sky. A street light near the driveway guided her. She looked at the house, before entering the driveway, admiring its structure, not a Victorian like her in-laws' but just as spacious, the same number of floors, three. There was a bedroom for each of the girls, though she thought she'd have Kaitlin sleep with Pamela for a year perhaps. Andrea would be on the third.

When she went in, she was surprised to see some order. Gregory must have gotten someone to put out some of the furniture. The rooms surprised her. All were in place. She let out a joyful scream, "He did it. It's lovely. I can get used to this house. And we'll have company. I'll get to know the people as soon as possible." She quickly went through the entire house. It was perfectly laid out, the living room across from the large dining room, the center stairway curving upward. It did remind her of the Hurwitz house. It was just as good. That was important. They would have to impress Gregory's staff and lab help. Perhaps she shouldn't have caused such a fuss. The children could go to the beach, wade in the water, search for shells. She'd help them. Yes, that would be fun.

When she showed the children their rooms, they squealed with delight. "But our dolls aren't here, mommy," Melinda cried. "Where are our toys?"

"Well, dear, we have to unpack them. Don't worry. We'll get them out tomorrow. O.K.?" She told Andrea, "Why don't you get them ready for bed?"

Oh, I've got to call their father and his folks. I may run over there.

Mary answered. She paused, recognizing Deirdre's voice but asked, "Deirdre?"

"Yes. Mary? I got here a little while ago. I wanted to surprise Greg."

Mary forced brightness to her voice. "Oh, that's wonderful. I wish I could see the children, but I thought I'd best get going. I'm on duty tomorrow afternoon. Mother hates it when I drive at night, but you know how it is. Perhaps you all could come over before I leave."

"Wait a minute." Deirdre called upstairs. "Andrea, don't put the children in bed. I'm going to take them to my in-laws'."

"They're already in bed," she shouted back.

"Well, get them up and dressed. Mary has to get back to Boston."

"Mary. It's all set. Let me just say hello to Greg, please."

"Yup. Here he is. I'll wait."

And so the family settled, all the Hurwitzes together with their progeny, Deirdre thinking of her parents missing all this excitement, the children sleepily rubbing their eyes but happy, Kaitlin whining for her bed. Aaron continually calling the children 'the girls,' never using their names. He wanted a grandson and that child was Brigit's. Later Melinda would tell him, "Grandpa, my name's Melinda. You call me that, not 'the girls.'" Aaron laughed, held her tightly, "You win, dear. It's now Melinda, Pamela, and Kaitlin." Occasionally he did slip. Once he annoyed Deirdre. "You know, wouldn't it be nice to have a boy?"

"Father, them's all yer gettin.'"

She thought of her one mistake. Why had she a third? Perhaps to make it up to Gregory for the abortion request; perhaps because she wanted a boy; perhaps because she wanted to love a child as soon as it came from her womb, like other mothers. Was there actually something wrong with her? She knew she was strong, that she could dominate almost anyone she pleased. Or perhaps the war had really done something to her, perhaps because she had fallen in with Étienne and really did feel she had to make it up to Gregory somehow. Whatever it was, Kaitlin was the last child they would ever have.

As time passed, she did come to know the people of the town well. She joined all the right groups like the Art Museum, the Historical Society, the Preservation Society. She invited all the right people to cocktail parties, especially any politicians who might help with some antique acquisitions. She gathered any of Gregory's important colleagues. By the early 1960s, Deirdre was well known throughout the state, in cities such as Portland, Augusta, Bangor, Farmington. In Cape Astraea they asked her to run for the City Council but she refused. Aside from her work with museums, she hinted at her wartime exploits, assuring she did not tell what the government did not want revealed as yet, but also measuring the little she told for its social effect.

It was the 1960s, the time of President John F. Kennedy and soon the Berlin Wall and "Ich bin ein Berliner," and his national challenge for a mission to the moon after being stunned by Russia's Sputnik. It was a time of advancing grief and a country deadened by the assassinations of the President, later his brother, Robert, and then Martin Luther King. In Boston, in the latter part of the decade, there was Louise Day Hicks whom Deirdre glorified for her stand against integration and school busing but who saddened Deirdre by Hicks' losses that decade when she ran for mayor. "The blacks will never learn their place. I don't care if we are in the north." Earlier, someone black Gregory knew was not admitted to a movie theater in Maine because of his race. So, before King's death, the country was to wait for Lyndon Johnson and King. It seemed it was a decade of dying. However, people still had their lives, families, and work to consider.

Recently Gregory became interested in genetics, because of some of the work being done at the Research Institute. More papers were being published under his direction with a number by him as first author. His work spread so that it influenced other parts of the body beside the liver, such as diagnosis of thyroid cancer. He believed that eventually nuclear medicine would be extremely important, that DNA research would advance. He wanted the laboratories involved in such research.

Gregory's and Deirdre's accomplishments pleased Jocelyn and Aaron, though regarding Deirdre, there was some skepticism. That included Mary who felt as they did. Her relationship with Deirdre would always be cool, and further, in Mary's mind, the marriage was a mistake; and the discord would never thaw, even after she returned home at the end of her fellowship in gastroenterology and began her own good reputation.

And so the family settled. Melinda and Pamela were now in school, and that was not too far off for Kaitlin. Andrea was still with them and beloved by the children who began telling her their secrets even as Melinda and Pamela giggled, gossiped, and played or listened to the adults, slowly taking Kaitlin in with them as she grew more talkative and could somewhat run with them. Andrea often took them to the ocean.

It was early summer. The night before there had been a bad storm, wind, thunder, lightning. The agitated ocean was a turmoil of giant waves, huge, deceptively attractive sprays of white against the rocks.

The following day, the ocean was still unsettled. Deirdre decided to take the children to the beach to see the water. "Mommy, let's take Andrea with us," Pamela insisted. Although Deirdre didn't want her, thinking she should have a day with the girls by herself, she gave in when the children insisted.

Andrea was hesitant. "Mrs. Hurwitz, are you sure you want to go? The water is probably still rough. You know the wind's still pretty strong."

"Yes, we're going. I told them we would. Besides, if we don't go now there'll be crying, screaming."

The beach they chose was at a cove lying between Ice Age rocks. Melinda and Pamela ran to the rocks, carefully walking on them, their hands to their mouths, watching and laughing at the waves as they hit and sprayed them. No one noticed that Kaitlin had followed, except Melinda who yelled for her to go back. Andrea started to chase after her, but Kaitlin had already reached her sisters. "Kaitlin. Kaitlin. Come back."

It was then Deirdre who had been talking to another woman, pointing to her children, that she heard Andrea and started after her.

Kaitlin looked back, laughed. As she did, she slipped, rolling down the wet rock as a huge wave hit where she was and dragged her back. The last Andrea heard was, "Mommy," as the water grasped her and carried her seaward. "Mom . . ." All, stunned, horrified, watched as she sank. Deirdre, Andrea, Melinda, and Pamela shrieked. Melinda started to go after Kaitlin but stopped, hearing her mother, "Melinda, NO!"

She noticed a Forest Service agent who had just put his boat in the water, called to him, but he had seen and was trying already to get to Kaitlin. He reached where she had gone under, circled. Kaitlin was gone.

The grief was unendurable. No one could speak. The only sounds were shrieks, Deirdre and Andrea crying loudly, other women in tears, some soundless in horror.

"Oh. My God. My five-year-old baby. My baby." And as she thought how frightened Kaitlin must have been, she began to shake. Andrea, also terrified and shaking, placed her arms about Deirdre, as Melinda and Pamela grasped and pulled at her skirt. In the background the ocean crashed again, again, unrelenting.

The agent called the police. It was a woman who gently led them toward the patrol car. The questioning would come later.

Deirdre could barely drive. She called Gregory, her voice trembling, asking him in her crying to come home as soon as possible. All Deirdre could say was that Kaitlin was dead.

"How did it happen? Wasn't anyone watching her? Deirdre, where were you?" Realizing he too was in shock and that he had raised his voice, he placed his arms about her, tried to hold the girls at the same time. "I thought Andrea was with them." If there was to be blame, it would have to be Andrea. She did not mention she had been talking to women and ignored the children. Perhaps she told him the truth. Everyone was in shock. "Andrea," Gregory asked, "did you see what happened. How? Why?"

Defensively, still crying, and in a trembling voice, "I was watching, but she slipped away from me. Oh, God. Was it my fault?"

"Stop that, now. You were doing what you should," Gregory told her, trying to comfort her.

Angrily, Deirdre woke momentarily from her grief, and shouted, "She let her go. It's her fault. She killed our child. I want that woman out of my sight, out of my house."

Gregory softly told her, "Deirdre. Stop. Please, dear. It wasn't Andrea's fault, no one's. It happened. My God, it happened." He, too, was crying. "Please," drawing it out. "Let's not fight, turn on one another. It . . . ." and he could not go on. Melinda and Pamela were going from their father to their mother, clinging to Andrea, everyone now sitting in a circle, silent, crying, sobbing.

Gregory thought to call his parents and his in-laws. It was an entire family in grief. Beautiful Maine for now was terror. There would be a time that Deirdre would, aside from Andrea, even blame Gregory, because of his selfishness, for moving the family to Maine.

Days later, Kaitlin's body was found on a shore farther south.

As in the United States, after the shocks of President Kennedy, Martin Luther King, and Robert Kennedy, nothing could ever be the same again.

Chapter XII

The Sea's Nether Region

By 1969 the United States was, it appeared, inextricably involved in Viet Nam despite President Richard Nixon's promise later, in 1970, to extricate us by promising withdrawal of 150,000 troops. The country was in a depressed state. Yet, instead of this becoming encouraging news, Nixon announced we would invade Cambodia. Well it bore out earlier words from Mr. Nixon. During the Eisenhower administration, Vice-President Nixon said the United States might have to go to war in Viet Nam. Now here he was talking of withdrawal while invading and bombing Cambodia. The United States was deluged by protests of college students and many Viet Nam veterans who were trying to stop the senseless war in which they had been deployed and despite people treating other homecoming veterans like criminals. Deirdre despised the protesters, while Gregory supported them and had no respect for Nixon. In this atmosphere, whether in the American society or in the Hurwitz home, in May of this year was Kent State, the National Guard inflicting a national wound that could never actually heal.

Perhaps it is similar to Brigit's heart. She tried to cure the festering wound despite caring deeply for Thomas and being immersed in happiness with her children. She sadly admitted that only Gregory could truly hold her heart. She often thought about him and imagined what it might be living in Maine that had so appealed to her. She was a World War II displaced person, except that Thomas, Robert, and Kathryn had rescued her. Within her was a continual conflict, even a desire to revenge herself on Deirdre, knowing the woman was causing him unhappiness. At times, reverting to the night Deirdre in that alluring dress captivated Gregory, she had seen through the superficiality of the flirtation, the approaching danger, and had done nothing. She had even thought of asking Thomas to move to Maine, even if it meant seeing Gregory and Deirdre together with their children. But could she be seen as following Gregory? At these times, quarreling with herself, she forced remembrance of Thomas's devotion and that she could do nothing that might hurt her children.

What she did not know was that Thomas had been in contact with Gregory. They had been friendly in Boston. Gregory was glad when he knew Brigit and he would marry. There may have been some conscience involved. He was quite aware of the pain he caused. He never recovered from how he left Brigit, though he told himself he loved Deirdre, yet finally admitted never having been in love with his wife. There were times also when he questioned her love for him. It often seemed they were drawing apart. The loss of Kaitlin affected them greatly. At times, after a dispute, silently he would blame her for the death. They were quarreling more. He was also correct that she was withdrawing. When they prepared for bed at night and he felt the twinge of movement in his testicles and penis and the desire it aroused, she would sense this or he would tell her. She would show herself sensually but then just get in bed and ignore him or rather than allow him to penetrate her would use her hand, occasionally her mouth. Then there were nights she would feel a need and turn to him, drawing him inside her but after, just turn away, sometimes partially satisfied, rarely fulfilled. She tried to imagine she was with someone else. She wanted someone else. It was always the same. Gregory was growing tiresome. He was immersed in his research and hospital politics, had become president of an association and traveled more. It was then she decided she would travel more frequently to Europe with Étienne, but before that she would have a "sweet sixteen" party for Melinda. Thus 1969 became a crucial year with 1970 hovering with not only Cambodia but a drifting ice floe.

She invited politicians who could help her, the wealthier people in the community. Melinda complained. She did not want what she knew her mother considered a 'coming out party.' Most of her friends never had one or had to endure its distastefulness.

"Dad, I don't want to be a show piece." He smiled, though he took her seriously. She was becoming as much a beauty as her mother. In fact, both girls were tall, attractive, and becoming aware of their sexuality and how to use it, how to flirt. If only, he would think, neither Melinda nor Pamela would become a twin to Deirdre. Yet, and he knew it, they were unlike Deirdre, for they were more like him, wanting to accomplish something satisfying, like him or their Aunt Mary.

"Mom just wants this party for herself, glorifying herself. She's using me. I hate it. I'm telling you, dad, I won't be here."

"Now don't overreact. Your mother loves you and wants people to see and get to know you. C'mon my beauty, settle down and just have a good time."

Melinda sneered. "Dad, if I thought this was your idea and wanted it, I might feel differently. You know very well, she's up to her usual tricks. I sometimes wonder if she cares what Pamela or I think." She looked at her father, seeing the love in his face, her charming and loveable dad. "Dad, don't you think Pamela and I know what's happening at home, that we feel it?"

Gregory turned away and mumbled, but she heard, "Yes. I know you both are aware."

In the meantime, Gregory and Thomas continued their correspondence. In one letter Thomas wrote, "Brigit liked Maine so much when she visited." It hurt Thomas to write that, but he had to say it even as he feared losing Brigit to Gregory. "So I've been thinking about it. What are the chances of someone new in my specialty, perhaps in Portland?" Would he be throwing Brigit at her former love? Would he lose her? He started to throw away the letter, but he wanted Brigit happy as she always seemed to be. Besides, he had spent time in Maine as a boy, and he did enjoy it. His family had a camp at Embden, not far from the Hurwitz camp. The families were friendly. One time as a teen-ager, sitting by a stream, he told himself he would live in this state.

He thought a while about his youth, of his marriage and his children, how good it had all been. Brigit had made her commitment to him and the children. That would last, because that is the woman she was. He rewrote the letter and sent it.

He did surprise Gregory who wondered why he would give up a good practice in Boston and suddenly move. Gregory thought back to their boyhood and the wandering through the woods together on the opposite side of the lake where there were no cottages, of fishing and the excitement when he caught his first salmon while he and Thomas were with Aaron. Brigit? *Oh, God, how I never should have left her, married her and my daughters would be hers, someone they would always love and respect. They are growing apart from Deirdre, just as she seems to be leaving me behind in search of something more than I can give or want to. To hell with it. That fellow who just retired. Perhaps the practice would want Thomas.* They'd *be fools not to. I'll write him.*

"Tom," he wrote, "I was just thinking of Embden and the fun we had there. There's a man who just retired. I'm certain they would take someone like you. But you're certainly giving up a lot. Yes. I know Brigit liked it here. I think your children will too. Truthfully, there are times I miss Boston, but I love it here. My family thrives where we are" - but not Deirdre he might have added. "It's funny, we never got together when we lived in Belmont. Are you sure you want to give up the family home? I do know Deirdre and Brigit met in town at least once. Deirdre was pregnant with, I believe it was, our third daughter. Think about it. Our oldest, Melinda is having a party for her sixteenth birthday that has passed already, but her mother wanted to wait 'til spring. Why don't you all try to come up for that? It's the 20th of this month. Perhaps you could see the people here. If you want, I'll tell them you're interested."

Thomas told him he had made up his mind and Brigit agreed, "was very pleased when she heard we might move. She's also a little sad about giving up the house, if they want me up there. The children are excited. They would be. Robert is now fifteen and Kathryn twelve, a little younger than yours. But you had a head start. Thanks for the address and the phone number. I'll get in touch right away and let you know what happens. I appreciate it, Greg."

Why Thomas would have wanted to move is a question. For some reason he was being naïve about placing Brigit and Gregory so close. However, when he thought more about it, he felt they had lived in Belmont at the same time. She never talked much about them except for the time she met Deirdre in the delicatessen.

Brigit answered Deirdre about the party, telling her they would attend. Deirdre, when she received the note, was peeved that Gregory invited them without asking her.

There was another argument, those more and more occurring annoyances that made Deirdre feel she had made a terrible error marrying Greg. Why did she do it? She was going to settle with him once and for all. She called to Melinda. There was no answer. She called Pamela. No answer. She wanted to try out the dress she bought for Melinda as a surprise. "Where the hell are they?"

Pamela came home without her sister.

"Where's Melinda?"

"She said she was going to a friend's house."

"Why didn't she tell me? I've told both of you I want to know where you are or where you're going."

"Yes, ma," she answered wearily.

"You listen to me without the faces and disgust. I'm your mother."

Pamela whispered to herself, "Don't I know it. Doesn't Melinda know it. You'll be lucky if she puts on that dress."

About this time, Gregory came home. "Those girls. I guess I drove my parents crazy too. I want to talk to you - alone."

She took him into his office and closed the door.

"What the hell is going on? You invited your old girlfriend and her husband to my party, to my daughter's party? What the fuck are you thinking? You want her back? Shit, I'll give her back to you. I can do it." She stopped. What was she saying, what message conveying?

"I told you I'm sick of hearing you swearing at me. I live here. It's my house, my children too. I can invite. Besides" and this was the first time Deirdre heard it from him, "Tom will probably be practicing in Portland. I've been helping him get a position here."

"Here?" She was now furious. "WHY?" For the first time in their marriage she felt insecure, that she had lost her dominance. "F . . .," she caught herself. "Crap. Go invite all your friends from Boston, the whole fucking staff from the hospital here. I'm trying to have a, well, coming-out party of sorts for our older daughter, and you screw it up."

"You shut your mouth, Deirdre." He began to shake. "I'm not listening to crap like that." He started toward her, grabbed her arm, staring directly in her eyes, those dark eyes he thought he loved so much, had seduced him with their brightness, depth, intelligence. He wanted to squeeze her arm but resisted. He glared. "You decided on the party. Did you ever think of asking Melinda if she wanted one? Do you have any idea how she feels about it?"

Deirdre shoved his hand away, backed several feet from him, staring. "I'm doing this for her. She's my beautiful daughter that I want the world to see," her voice trembling.

"You or Melinda, Deirdre?" his voice somewhat quieter but still angry.

"Damn you. I'm sick of being the evil one here."

He stared at her, struck by 'evil.' He felt suddenly sad. "You know, Deirdre, you are beginning to tell all of us how to live. You come and go. Do I ever question? You go overseas every so often. I don't object. But this is it. You have left me feeling like I don't belong any longer. I have to beg for sex."

"Beg?" Again she shouted. "Like hell. I'm supposed to spread my legs any time you want it. Well, we've been married some time now, no? Well, there are times. Goddamn it. You're a doctor. You know there are times a woman doesn't feel like it. Even you don't."

"I'm not going to beg. I don't even want to talk about this. But when you back away, and you have, I begin to think there's a chasm between us, a dangerous one."

Melinda returned home in time to stand with Pamela at the door listening to their parents, both horrified. "I've heard enough," Melinda told Pamela. "I'm home for spring vacation and come for this. This terrible party should have been last year, but she had to be away. She's always away, always doing something. Don't you ever wonder why she goes away so much?"

"Sure I do. Well, anyhow, you'll be in college next year, and I'll be away at the Bennett School. Neither of us will have to listen."

"Pam. Have you noticed some of the art stuff she's brought home, like the Chinese vase we aren't supposed to touch, and that little Greek statuette? Even the living room is becoming a museum. It's a wonder she lets us go in there. And that jewelry. She sure does make money with that foreign joker. And she's always buying clothes for us, and bought the new car. "

"Well, sure I've noticed. So have my friends. The clothes, with all the comments the kids make, make me feel like a freak."

Just then the door opened and Deirdre came rushing out, slapping Melinda.

"Where have you been?" she loudly demanded. "Who do you think you are just disappearing?"

Pamela looked in the room at her father, watching him with his head lowered. When he heard Deirdre, he started for them. Pamela kicked Melinda in the heel, letting her know their father was coming and not to argue with their mother. However, Melinda ignored the slight pain of her sister's warning. "I'm old enough to go see friends. How do you know, anyhow, what I do when I'm away at school? How will you know what Pamela is doing? In fact, do you even care? You're hardly ever around. You shoved us off to school so we could be proper ladies. Well I'm grown up now, and I'll do what I want."

Without warning, Deirdre slapped her again. Gregory saw and hurried toward them. "Who do you think you are? You're talking to your mother, young lady," Deirdre's yelled. She grabbed her and started to pull her toward the sitting room. "You will never talk to me like that again. And you will never stay away from this house or visit anyone without my knowing where you are. You hear me?" Deirdre, her face red, raised her hand again. She felt a strong hand stop her. "Don't you ever, EVER hit one of those girls again, NEVER."

"And don't you ever raise your voice at me like that again,

Gregory Hurwitz, my great doctor. Why don't you help me discipline these girls? I send them away to a good school and this is what they learn and come home with. Disobedience."

Gregory, startled by the "I", hesitated, deciding what to answer. "Fine, Deirdre. Maybe we'll just let her finish the year and keep Pamela home next year. Since you're the one who sends them, pays for them."

By now, Andrea had come into the room. Everyone stopped, looked at her. "What the hell do you want?" Deirdre demanded.

Because she had been with the family so long, she didn't answer, took Melinda and Pamela by the hand and walked out of the room, in effect, daring Deirdre to fire her.

"I hate her," Melinda told Andrea, sobbing now, barely able through her tears to see her sister also crying, both trembling, wondering about their home, their mother and father. "I hate her, I tell you." Andrea stroked her hair, Pamela's, held them to her. They were her girls too, even if she never had them. Why hadn't she married that Steve guy she had met in Boston? She just didn't trust him. Now older, all left to her were these two young girls, growing toward womanhood and its sadnesses and joys. They would be good women coming from a fine home. She stayed with the Hurwitzes because of the doctor, such a fine man with such good manners, always kind and sympathetic. There were no airs about him. But his wife. Everyone knew where she went to school and all the things she did or does. Dr. Hurwitz never said anything about who or what he was. He didn't have to. He came from a grand family and had done grand things for people. This is why she stayed on. She hugged the children to her. "C'mon, my dearies, it was only an argument. You've heard and had them before."

"Not like this," Pamela sobbed. "You didn't see her slap Melinda. She'll have a mark on her face." Pamela looked at her sister's cheek. "See how red it is, how hard she hit her. She's not my mother anymore."

"Stop that silly talk. She is your mother. You just be who you are and everything'll be all right."

They sat about the kitchen table, the three in tears, then smiling some for the love among them. Melinda laughed. "Andrea, if we were the same color, maybe you could be our mother. Ooo. Excuse me."

Andrea laughed. "There you go again." They had conversations about color and different ethnic peoples. Andrea had taught both of them about slavery, about Abraham Lincoln, about going to Washington and hearing the great Dr. Martin Luther King. Deirdre did not want to give her the time off, but Gregory gave her airfare and hotel expenses and some extra spending money, telling her he wished he could go.

Listening to Andrea laughing, suddenly Melinda thought of her father. There had been another woman. Why didn't he marry her? Aunt Mary had mentioned her once, maybe more. They were friends.

"Pam, do you remember Aunt Mary telling us about that woman, oh, what's her name - Brigit."

"Aw, yes."

"Aunt Mary said dad loved her. But she never told us what happened. She lived in Belmont when we did. I wonder what she's like."

"What for? We never met her."

"I saw her once, Pam, when we were little. She and mom met in a store. I wonder."

"About what?"

"Just wonder. I think she and dad had something going."

"So what?"

"Nothing."

Andrea, knowing who Brigit was and having also met her, smiled. "She's just some nice lady who has a boy and a girl, a little younger than you two."

But the letter Thomas sent to Gregory was unknown to them nor the fact that Thomas had been urged to come to Portland after the interview. A calm came over the kitchen, as the sisters and Andrea stroked one another's arms with love, unaware they would meet that Brigit.

~

The night of the party, Melinda refused to dress. She took the gown and threw it in a corner. "I won't go down. They're all her friends. Everyone has to make an impression."

Deirdre knocked, came in. "Why aren't you dressed?" She looked at the bed, expecting to see it there, then in the corner where it had been thrown.

"What's going on? Guests are arriving."

Pouting, "Your guests."

"Now, dear, let's not get into an argument. Some of your friends are here too. This is your evening."

"Yeah. Thanks, mother."

Although the sarcasm annoyed Deirdre who began to get angry, she held back. She picked up the dress, shook it to see if there were wrinkles. She saw some creases in the skirt that annoyed her. "C'mon. We'll get this ironed out in no time," which she did without saying anything but the anger visible in her face. "Here you are, sweetie."

The sarcasm did not escape Melinda. "O.K., mommy, dear," she mimicked.

"You keep quiet and mind your manners. I didn't have to go through all this for you to be so resentful. You want another mother, another home?"

"Yes, I DO," she yelled. Tears came to her eyes. "Why are you so mean sometimes, mother? And the way you treat dad.

What did he ever do to you?"

Trying to withhold her temper, not answering, she said, "Look, this is no time for us to fight. Please just get on the gown. You'll be beautiful."

Crying now, Melinda stepped into the dress, pulled up just above her bosom while Deirdre automatically zipped the back. "Let me see you. Oh, Magnificent. Melinda. Please look at yourself in the long mirror. Isn't it lovely? The gown comes just to your bare shoulders. See how beautiful you are. Perfect. Everyone will admire you. Oh. Here." Deirdre gave her a handkerchief. "Dry your eyes. I'll put a little liner on them, and no one will ever know." She put her arms about Melinda, pulled her close. "I love you, darling. Don't ever doubt it."

Hesitantly, Melinds answered, "Yes, I know, mother," but she didn't believe her words.

"I'll go down. You come alone, so all eyes will be on you. O.K.?" Deirdre smiled sweetly. "And, dear. You don't need to tell dad that we had an argument. All right? Let him enjoy the evening too."

"Yes, m'am"

Deirdre turned to her, her face red, but she fought to control herself, whispering to herself, "I raised a bitch." She laughed aloud, placed her hand on her mouth. *Like her mother.*

Or was it that she left the girls no other choice but to react to her as she did to them and to Gregory? She thought of their births, the discomfort of the pregnancies she endured. But she did give birth to lovely, attractive, and one day, alluring daughters. Yes, she did love them. *But how do I measure or weigh my love? By what I'm doing tonight, for one? Be honest Deirdre.*

What her parents did not know was that she had called her closest friend who lived near the private school, asking if she could stay with her for a few days but not to tell her parents why she was there except that her folks were going away for a few days, so she was returning before spring break was over. She pleaded over the phone, "I'm just so mad about this party. My mother wanted it. I didn't. I don't want to be here. Do you think you could drive here and your folks will let me stay? And if you think so, promise me you won't tell any one."

"Oh, with that excuse, I think they will. I'll tell them you just wanted to be with me after the party so we could talk about school, whatever, that you told your parents and they didn't mind."

Deirdre had already gone down to announce the young lady would soon appear. As Melinda walked the stairs, she stared at all the people, smiled at the applause and the greetings, thinking perhaps she could enjoy herself. Most of the time she looked toward her father, watching his pride, aware of the love in his eyes. That was enough for her, helping her to endure her mother's guests.

Melinda greeted the people, pleasantly received their compliments, answered when asked her college choices. Meanwhile, Deirdre saw a politician eyeing her and went to him, "She's too young for you, Barry. I'm more your age, no?"

His face reddened. He forced a smile. "I can't argue that. How about a jaunt tonight?"

"Jaunt?" she smiled coyly. "What's in it for me?" her voice soft, seductive. She was now forty-six, had gained some weight about her waist. Her breasts fell some, not as attractive to her as they had been, yet still full enough to excite a man. Her face had no creases though it was somewhat more full, erasing a bit of the angularity that was so much a part of her beauty. Her hands kept their softness with the creams and oils she used; and her fingers could still direct with a subtlety of movement or silken soothingly arouse emotion or settle imagined or real pains.

Later she beckoned to Barry when she believed her absence would not be noticed but not before she was certain Gregory wasn't about. Still she wondered where he was while Melinda stood alone at the door saying goodnight to several of her guests.

In that interval, Deirdre and Barry left, Deirdre knowing Gregory had to appear and, if necessary, make an excuse for her.

She would be absent just long enough to satisfy this lascivious politician and get what she wanted, more political help from a conservative who believed about Viet Nam as she did. They both hated the protests. He would get her money in return for a tryst. They walked to his large car, looked quickly about, went to the back seat. He raised her skirts, her slip, grabbed at her panties.

"Just a minute, Barry. Promise me I get the money."

He was impatient, pulling down his pants. "Damn. You'll get it. Now give me what I want."

She laughed. "Give me your handkerchief." She spread it, and rubbed slowly, gently, harder on the shaft and head until she felt the release into the cloth. "Feel good?" He nodded, yet dissatisfied. "Barry, give me what I want, and then I'll give you more."

"O.K. Promise me."

"When you come through," placing her lips on his. "Look forward to it. I guarantee you'll be satisfied."

When she returned and the guests were gone, she and Gregory could not find Melinda.

Gregory was frantic, having looked throughout their large home. Deirdre upset, forgot her short sexual rendezvous with Barry, being concerned but angry, thinking of Melinda's ingratitude.

"Did you let her go somewhere with one of the boys she knows?" Deirdre demanded. "What are you talking about? I don' t know where she is." He started to raise his voice. "Don't you shout at me. I'm getting damn sick and tired of your temper."

"Look, damn it. This is no time for an argument. We have to find our daughter. Think of someone else for a change?" For an instant he envisioned an image of Kaitlin reaching tearfully to him. He shook his head.

"Pamela," he called. Deirdre started to call also. He wanted to tell her to keep quiet. He felt suddenly weary, the fighting, her advancing frigidness with him, his wish she would just disappear like Melinda. But did he truly want this?

"Pam," he called again. "What, dad?"

Deirdre reached out and started to shake her. Pamela, scared, pulled away.

"Leave her alone, Deirdre. Pam, have you seen your sister?"

"No. Why?"

"She's not here."

Pamela already knew. She hated to lie to her father, wasn't even convinced her mother cared. In fact, Deirdre was in tears, feeling, knowing, blaming herself. She did care for the girls, but some flaw, *Is that the word I should use?*, kept her from being the mother they needed. Gregory interrupted Deirdre's guilt conversation with herself, the self only she could understand, that she wanted to expunge but knew she wouldn't for the desires that satisfied her. This life was hers to fulfill as she molded it.

Gregory, interrupting her self-satisfaction, promised to locate Melinda. He thought of her close friends, called until it occurred to him that perhaps she had gone with her friend from school.

He took Pamela aside. "Now tell me truthfully, Pam. You know where she is and who she's with. I know it."

Pamela did not want her father to suffer, felt the fear in him, his desire to protect her and her sister.

"Yes. Dad. She's with Anita. They went in Anita's car. She's mad, daddy. She thinks mom took advantage of her and invited people who could help mom. She'll listen to you. I know it." Pamela was now crying as she spoke. "I'm sorry, daddy. I promised her."

"It's O.K. Stop crying, dear. I know how Melinda feels. But your mother is your mother, and she deserves your respect," hesitantly speaking the last words.

He did call Anita's home and spoke to Melinda. He said he'd come to her. He'd take clean clothes, and they'd talk.

Deirdre immediately wanted to know where she was.

"She's with a friend."

"What friend?" she harshly demanded. "She doesn't care a damn about what she's doing to me. And you too," she managed to add.

"I know she does."

"Oh, yes. You know."

Rather than answer and argue, he started to leave for Melinda's room.

"Where are you going?"

"To her room to get her more clothes. I'm going to go get her and bring her home for the last few days."

"You're taking me!"

"NO." He could not help himself. "She feels hurt enough. I'll go alone."

"She's my daughter. And Pamela has Andrea to look after her."

He turned to her, his voice cold and difficult to control. "I said I'm going, and that's that."

Deirdre wanted to go after him and pull him back into the room. "What for?" she asked herself. *Sometimes I think the whole bunch of them should just go to hell. He's a weakling. Face it. Deirdre. You married a weakling. They have him wound around their fingers. Oh, you're funny. Just like I did. I just don't care anymore. Like when he wants to watch TV and something about the World War or that flag of his he wants to hang. Not on your life, Greg. Why don't you let him watch about the war? Because of your own hurt and Étienne?*

She decided there was no sense in fighting more about Melinda. He could drive by himself and get her. *Sure. Then they can talk about me. The mean mother, the wicked witch. Snow White and the one dwarf. So why don't you divorce him if you feel this way? Prestige, dear. Prestige. I never had that in Warrington. The chicken farm. My poor dad and what my mother had to put up with. I wasn't about to live like that. Well, I wouldn't have had to. Fuck. Forget it. I have what I want, and I'll get Étienne too in my way.*

~

Gregory drove to Anita's home in New Hampshire and got Melinda. When Melinda came to the door, she leaped at her father, hugged him tightly. Her eyes tearful, "Daddy. I'm sorry. I didn't mean to scare or hurt you. But mom makes me so mad."

He took her arms, moved her away. "Let me look at you. But dry your eyes first. The tears don't belong with those eyes." Her eyes, hazel, reminded him of Brigit at times when they were bright. "There." He took out his handkerchief and gently wiped at her tears. "Let's thank Anita and her parents and get on our way."

At first there was silence. He had put on the radio to music she would like. "Why did you do it, Melinda?"

"I couldn't help it. I was so mad. Did she tell you what I did with my dress before I got ready."

"Nope. It looked great and was just right for you."

"I threw it in a corner I was so mad."

Gently he led her. "Why? What for?"

"Because, as I said before, everything's for her. She's probably also mad because I want to go to med school too, like grandpa, you, Aunt Mary."

He laughed. "You mean you don't want to be a singer like my mother?"

"Oh, stop," she smiled and pushed him in the arm.

"Careful. I'll go off the road." At that he stopped. They were by a lake, fields and trees surrounding it. Ducks floated near the shore. He thought he heard a loon. "Did you hear that, Melinda?"

"Hmmm."

"Isn't it as though all heaven were laid out before us? Or perhaps we drove through a black hole and came upon a mysterious world where if we look, we can find out all the answers to our problems." He looked at her, smiled.

"What do you do when you have problems? You must at work and with all those people you have to work with and boss."

"I don't boss, dear, and yes, I do have problems. But I don't run away."

She squeezed her eyes as she wrinkled her brow, thinking he was criticizing her.

"Take that look off your face. I wasn't criticizing you," starting the car again. "Just talk. I'll listen. Promise."

"Dad. She wanted that party for herself. You know it as well as Pamela and I do. Sure, she wanted to show me off, because I'm some sleeping beauty just awakened for all the people to ogle at. I'm not a thing in a glass cabinet, or one of her Chinese vases. I'm me.

"And," she hesitated. "And, we know how she treats you. And we heard at the door that day. Why do you put up with it? You know I know all about sex. She talked to me, before I had my first period. I know what married people do. I guess they do because they love each other. Well, it didn't sound that way to us."

His face turned red, he swallowed. "People didn't come to

ogle, Melinda. Sure, you're a good-looking girl. That's something to like. But those people there know us. Your friends from around Cape Astraea were there."

"Oh, dad, stop making excuses for her. I know. She's my mother and I, oh, I'll say it my way, I should love her, but . . . ." and she stopped.

"But what?"

"Well, sometime I just hate her, the way she bosses. Everyone knows it. Who cares what school she went to, what she did in the war? You were in that too, and no one hears you bragging or putting on the dog. Sure, I'm proud of both of you for that. And sure. I want to go to her college. But pushing. Pushing. I can't stand it, dad. I don't even want to be home anymore - well, except for you. I mean that. We love you."

"You make me sound like a weak man."

"I didn't mean that. It's just that you're so nice. You treat us like we're people. I don't mean your equals. We know we're family, but there's a wrenching. I feel it. Pam feels it."

He waited. She was crying again.

"Melinda, dear, don't cry." He stopped the car. "Look at me." She did. "You're the oldest, older," he slipped, again thinking of Kaitlin, "daughter. We want you to be everything you want, to enjoy yourself, especially now and when you go to college. You know, if you go to med school, it won't be easy. But you can have fun there too. And I want you to have fun, to be strong. You are." He laughed. "You sure did show you own your own mind, didn't you?"

She sniffled, smiled. "I did. I'm sorry I scared you." She wiped at her eyes, took a tissue from her handbag. "I love you, daddy." She put her arms about him. "I do love you," sniffled some more, forced a smile. "I won't ever do this again to you, well, to either of you. I know I upset her too." Another interval. "But I wanted to. Oh shoot, I've said all I want to. You understand, don't you?"

"I understand," and he kissed her cheek.

Deirdre also understood and summoned her love for her fortune at having given birth to two future enchanting daughters. Tortuous Peace. Korean style.

~

Nixon kept the troops in Cambodia for two months, while at home women's hemlines became shorter, almost to the thighs. That was the pleasant war of spring and summer. That became the men's ogle. But the real problem Nixon tried to avoid. Instead of finding an enemy, he bombed Cambodia, left the country in ruins, weakened that government. Nixon was close to declaring the war unwinnable and called for more Paris peace talks.

On campuses about the country there were protests. Then, in May, were the criminal, repugnant Kent State killings of four students, two coeds and two males, the embedded photograph of disbelieving grief in the country's mind and conscience. Thousands gathered at Yale and Harvard and other campuses, cities, and towns.

President Nixon spoke to the nation of the 'bums' who were destroying the country while his wretched Vice-President Agnew descried the 'elites' who were undermining American confidence and aiding the enemy.

It would take a while longer, but those undermining the country were the Vice-President who had to depart his office for fraud before the President announced his resignation for criminal acts. The attorney general, Mitchell, whose wife spoke out about the evil in the administration - unlike Deirdre who agreed with Nixon and Agnew - and was sent to an institution for mental problems and to keep her quiet. Deirdre, unlike Mrs.

Mitchell, went out in public gatherings to speak in defense of the war and the government, embarrassing herself, her children, especially her husband who was being criticized, aloud and in whispers, for 'permitting' his wife to become a political figure in favor of the war. Melinda and Pamela begged her to stop being a stage spectacle; and had they known of vaudeville, they would have found what they needed, a long hook to drag her from the stage of her embarrassing antics. They were ashamed.

While there appeared to be a wrenching in the younger Hurwitz family, the country was in contortions. However, Deirdre wasn't hooked away and would go about the house blaming the students and the traitorous protesting military men returned from Viet Nam, who were angry at the loss of life and wounds they suffered, begging to save the country from itself and its folly.

Chapter XIII

Sea's Angry and Soothing Tides

There was joy in Gregory's home, a young woman's screech when the letter came accepting Melinda at Radcliffe; Pamela was now away at the private school, Bennett, attended by her older sister; Brigit and Gregory had met several times for lunch or coffee, innocently they felt, both telling their spouses; Brigit talked of Robert and Kathryn, he now a senior in high school, she a sophomore, having skipped a grade. Two parents talked proudly of their children, wife or husband occasionally mentioned out of necessity, their heads tilted a bit downward, raised, gazing longingly in one another's eyes, hands reaching toward one anther below the table, the troubled smiling, the thrill when they felt a hand on thighs, the desire never lost.

By now, too, Jocelyn had sung her last performance; Aaron was considering retiring, finally weary of the constant battles he had won over time for his eventual recognized work, for his award of a Medal of Freedom because he foresaw the health needs for the country's less fortunate.

Mary, living with her partner Evelyn, was now the successful gastroenterologist also practicing nearby, still a visitor to Brigit's home, loving her children as she did her nieces, the tender, loving hugs and cheek kisses when they met, the sadness at times Mary felt and wished away when she thought of Gregory and Deirdre. Brigit and hers was a friendship nothing could end.

Oh, so peaceful, so wonderful this happy, sad life. For on a day in 1964, that tumultuous year, as Gregory examined specimens, he unconsciously placed a finger on a lymph node. There was no pain. He ignored it. Yet, he had been feeling fatigue, did now. He had been working longer hours. There were some nights he had been called in when something seemed amiss at a laboratory. About a month or two later he began to feel sweaty at night. Deciding to weigh himself, he noticed a troubling loss.

~

By the next year, I thought I knew what was happening but tried to ignore it. Perhaps I shouldn't have. They used to tell me I'd make such a good diagnostician. However, I ignored what I believed, until that day at the lab, and I just could not do more and went home to bed. I had a bad cold and was coughing. I placed my fingers on lymph nodes, thought of the weight loss. That night too I perspired more, coughed a lot. Deirdre, awakened, wanted to know what was wrong, but she had not forgotten and was obviously annoyed. She had wanted me to have sex with her, surprising me, but I was too weary. That was the beginning of another angry encounter. "I'm going to one of the girls' rooms and sleep. I've got a long day tomorrow. I have to go to Boston."

I was about to ask her to put it off for a day so she could accompany me to the doctor. I decided, though, I'd see my doctor alone, thinking she'd probably go to Boston anyway. What I didn't know was that she was meeting Étienne while I was being initially diagnosed with the possibility of Chronic Lymphocytic Leukemia. There followed blood tests, talking and confirmation. I had cancer that could last for years and would need family support. How to tell the girls bothered me. Deirdre would take it in, think of what she could do for help. But how much, she'd be asking herself. I knew her mind, admitted the truth of her feelings toward me that I never revealed to anyone. That left my folks who would be exceedingly upset but who could not be kept in ignorance. My dad and I could talk. My mother would be terribly distressed. Mary. Mary would pretend, dress herself in her professional demeanor, then truthfully show her emotion in tears like mother's. Oh. She would tell Brigit. If I asked her not to? She would promise, but would it come out? I believed so. And it did, later when I was in treatment and getting all those necessary blood tests. Mary kept Brigit informed.

Her children now older, Brigit had returned to nursing. We did meet one day for coffee at a shop in our town, perhaps not the best idea. We sat as she cheerily told me about Robert and Kathryn, but suddenly her face changed when she glanced at me, her eyes watery.

"Tell me how you're holding up, Greg. I think so much about you."

Cheerfully, at least trying to be, I told her, "Well, dear concerned one, I still work. My brain still functions in the lab. I probably will be around for years yet. If it comes to that, and I get too weary, I'll give up my position and just, well, you know, get into some research. I imagine some of the women or the men will let me help. Say, I'd make a great assistant."

"Oh, keep quiet." She looked directly at me, with those eyes that always mesmerized me. "Greg, if you ever need me. Oh, damn, I wish I could be your nurse, be with you." She looked away, forcing herself to take a sip of coffee.

"Brigit, if I ever need you, would Thomas get upset?"

"Perhaps. Maybe he would. He considers you a friend, though. Perhaps. I wouldn't care, if you needed me. Promise that you'd let me know."

There was that ocean again, roughly separating us, the

waves washing us in separate directions. “Brigit, I . . . I love you, always will.”

“Greg, you shouldn’t say that. Don’t.” Her face reddened, I thought with pleasure, although her words were a gentle reprimand.

“We should go. The children will wonder where I am. You know, I almost wish I could go back to the night shift. But I enjoy seeing the children when I come home. Then I’m awake too when Thomas comes, unless . . . . You doctors.”

I placed my hand on her knee. She moved it hard against the touch and rose. “You tell me. I mean it. If you need me. But you have your family too, we both do, don’t we?” she spoke wistfully.

The loneliness I felt was of loss when I paid the check and we left the shop and I watched her walk away. I could not stop, watching the slight sway of her hips, her lovely legs, the red hair blown by the breeze. At that moment, the memories hurt more than the cancer, were the cancer.

~

Deirdre met Étienne who surprised her at the museum. He had persuaded the Board that they needed another member and to vote for her. Delighted, she also knew what it meant for Étienne and her, the pieces they could more easily prod the museum to take, having some control of the funds with her voice and vote. She would be the enchantress who she believed could influence votes. She did, with her soft voice, smile, and use of her practiced striking expressions at the appropriate time.

After her election to the Board, Étienne and she went to his apartment in Boston.

She called home to assure herself there was no suspicion.

“Gregory, dear. I'm so happy. I know you'll be too.”

"What happened?"

"I was elected to the museum board. Isn't that wonderful? What an honor."

He forced his enthusiasm. "That's marvelous. The girls will be so proud of you." *Maybe.*

She quickly changed tone. "Gregory, enough about me. What happened at the doctor's?"

"Oh, we just discussed the results of the blood tests."

"And everything's O.K.?"

"Oh sure," and he added bitingly, "What we expected. We'll talk when you get home. By the way, when are you coming?"

"Well with what's happened, it may be the day after tomorrow. But I'll try to make it late tomorrow night. You do understand, darling."

He felt like telling her to go to hell. "Oh fine." Then forcing a pleasant voice, yet with the meaning quite clear, "Andrea's taking great care of everything as usual. Bye now. Got some work to review." He barely gave her time to say, "Bye, darling."

She ignored his anger, and turned cheerfully, expectantly, to Étienne.

He pulled her to the sofa, and she lay slowly back, unhooking her bra and letting him remove her panties. He played his hands about her body, kissed, bit, sucked where he knew it gave enjoyment: her neck, ears, breasts and nipples, between her thighs. Several times that night and the following afternoon they made love until she left him, each of them weary from the enjoyment and exertion. She must catch the last bus home with her new dresses and still feeling his hands over her body, his mouth, his slipping in and out and the ultimate sensation of her tightening around his throbbing release inside, while hearing her sounds of fulfillment.

~

She changed quickly into a sheer nightgown, crept into the bed, made certain Gregory was asleep, and reluctantly placed her arm about him, rubbing his chest lightly and his nipples. He stirred. She felt her husband move closer to her as she thought of the pleasure of Étienne, her new position, and the money they could accumulate. She closed her eyes and fell quickly asleep. Deep sleep. Ignorance. Neither she nor her companion from wartime were aware a new person had been employed for provenance of art or that soon a friend of Mary would also become a member. Nor did Deirdre know that later she would take the office of Treasurer.

As the year passed, the country began to wonder about women who wanted their freedom. There had been a story of a woman who left her children and husband to return to college and fulfill her dream of professional work. A sociologist claimed the problems with the United States' social problems all went back to 1960 and the changes among women, civil rights, the assassinations, women using contraceptives, achieving higher positions in the professions, and in government. They were destroying the home. Woodstock, 1969, that repellant gathering of peace and love and sex. Deirdre hated it all, except when it came to her own sexual freedom. She didn't have to worry about birth control, for she had had her tubes tied after Kaitlin's birth. It never occurred to her, however, that perhaps Étienne, having sex with other women, which he did, may have contacted a disease he could pass to her as a bonus. Her only thought with him or any other man she should choose was that she could do what she wanted and when. Yes, she was, in her mind, the new woman who had been there years ahead of the likes of Gloria Steinem. Her exception was like many or some of the other liberated females, that she would keep her family.

The following morning, she, being the empathetic wifely companion, delayed Greg to ask questions about his illness and how he felt. He coughed some at breakfast, did not have his usual appetite, but knew this was part of what his life, perhaps for many years, would be. Deirdre showed a face of worry. "Are you all right?"

"It's just the way it is. This will probably get worse, though, and I'll need your help."

"But I'm not a nurse."

"Oh, it doesn't require a nurse, at least not now."

"What do you mean 'at least not now'?"

"Well, with this illness it could go on for some years. So don't worry about it." He wondered whether or how much she would worry.

I'll especially worry if it interferes with my travels. But if necessary, I can get Pamela home to look after him and have her go to school nearby.

"I'll be here when you come home. Just take it easy at work. All right. Bye, dear," she tenderly told him, kissing him on his mouth, hugging him tightly.

Suddenly, without reason, he returned as he opened the door, reached for her, hugged and softly kissed her, running his hand along her cheek. "Sometimes," he thought, "I do wish it was as before, when there was, or seemed to be, deep, honest feeling." Sadly, he went to the car, started driving off, looking back to the house, the front door closed.

He did at times think back to that day in 1973, and the feeling of sadness when he saw the front door closed, wishing she had at least lovingly watched after him through an open door until the car disappeared. As he drove he also wondered whether he had been such a fool as to forsake Brigit for an image that floated to him as though that then unknown seductive woman's feet never touched the ground, wearing that gown which showed her bosom and her bare lovely shoulders so well. As she drifted toward him, he thought of his face mirrored in those bright, smiling brown eyes.

Now, here, here he was in 1977, still able to work but feeling at times so rotten. It was post Watergate. If the country could recover from that, then, hell, he could get along. Melinda was about to start her medical internship, and Pam was in her senior year and home on vacation. "Now that was something."

That year Deirdre wanted Pamela to come home to finish college when Gregory began to feel more weary. His physician had him go to the hospital, because his cough was suddenly worse and he had a fever. It was summer, and the girls were home. While he was undergoing tests and treatment, Deirdre decided she'd talk to Pamela about college.

"Pam, love, I think you should forget Wellesley because of dad. He's going to need help. And you know sometimes I'll have to be away."

"Well, why can't you give up your trips? You know how much it means to me." Naturally, Pamela also wanted her freedom. "No. I'm going back to Wellesley. Dad wants me to. You're always away. For what? For that museum you got some politician to get money for?"

Unknowingly, Pamela had thrown a dart.

~

Barry had had his way with Deirdre on an afternoon that she did meet him. He had made sure the funds went through committee and that it went to her to be funneled to the museum, at least so he thought and everyone else.

"O. K. Deirdre, pay up." Those words angrily burned her, making her feel like a prostitute. She regained her composure, made him wait, then seriously but with a teasing look, opening and closing her eyes and then focusing straight at him, she asked, "You do have a condom, Barry?" Annoyed, he told her he did. Teasing further, delaying, to arouse him, "You must keep a huge supply. Cautious man, Barry, but you're the one I'm worried about, what gals you've been with. You know. Girl's got to be careful." He, restraining himself from answering, forced a smile, took her hand. "So soft."

"For playing, Barry."

He took her to a room off his office. They moved from floor to a sofa that he quickly opened to a bed as she delayed, telling him, "Slow down, Barry. It's more enjoyable." Eventually she listened to Barry in ecstasy, grimaced, though she had some enjoyment.

Her attention quickly shifted back to Pamela. Now her anger flared, remembering . . . .

~

"Don't you EVER talk to me like that, you selfish imp." Deirdre stepped toward her, her hand raised to slap her face, stopped. "Don't you EVER, or you'll never forget it. I won't have it, you hear?"

Pamela stepped back, her eyes widened, her mouth contorted. Whether she was to scream or cry, was hard to tell. She ran from the kitchen, but before losing sight of her mother, she shouted, "You're not a mother. Mothers love their children." She hesitated. "You're the selfish, self-centered one. You don't care what happens to any of us. You and your precious antiques. I hate you," and she ran toward her room crying.

"You, little bitch. Tell me I don't love you. I gave birth to you, raised you. Gave you everything. You *will* apologize." At that, Deirdre ran after her, grabbed Pamela's blouse collar, turned her, and slapped her hard, Pamela's face reddening. Deirdre momentarily worried about a bruise. "Now get out of my sight until you apologize."

Pamela lay on her bed, loudly crying, sobbing, simultaneously beating her pillow and raising her legs and then banging them down on the bed. "I won't let her say those things to me, treat me like a slave. She's always done everything she wanted. Why do I have to suffer? I'm going to see dad. Damn her," she shouted, hoping her mother would hear.

Later Pamela, calming some, purposely took Deirdre's car, who, when she heard the motor, promised herself Pamela would feel the punishment. After coming home, Pamela went to her father's room. He was half asleep but looked up in happy surprise, the smile fading, seeing her drawn face

"Pam." A pause, "Pam, what's wrong?" He coughed a bit.

"Oh, dad, I have to talk to you. I was going to wait and come with Melinda, but she's shopping. I didn't want to bother you. Are you all right?"

"I'm O.K., considering."

"Really?"

"I wouldn't lie to you, dear. Now tell me what's wrong. I can see it in your face."

"It's mom," and her tears started again

"Come here. Sit." He moved over, put his arm about her. "Come on. Tell me. You obviously had a fight."

"I said terrible things. Well, it was her fault. She doesn't want me to go back to Wellesley but to stay here. It's not fair." She hesitated. "She wants me to go to school near here so I can be with you and take care of you."

"To . . . ." he stopped. "I don't need you to take care of me. If the time comes and I need help, I'll get the nurse to stay here. You're going back to Wellesley. I won't have it any other way. It's what you want and what you'll have."

She smiled, wiping at her eyes. "Why are you so good and she's so mean?"

"Pam, you have to have patience with your mother. She's

busy and smart. Well you know." He hid his anger.

"You'll have a fight with her."

"That's not your worry. I'll talk to her. You're going to Wellesley."

"Oh, daddy, I love you," and she hugged him. "I'm causing you another argument though."

"That's my problem. Not yours. Now calm down. Tell you what. Why don't you tell the nurse or Andrea I'd like to have a cup of tea, and, if you want, you have a cup with me. Now go ahead."

When she was gone, he felt the sadness return.

Sickness and sadness, a marvelous combination.

There isn't any love between us now. Everything is habit, Deirdre occasionally allowing me to fuck her while she just lies there, hardly a breath, a sigh, oh occasionally a moan, faking an orgasm. Once in a while she'll drive and we'll go to the cove to watch the ocean. Yet. There's hardly ever any conversation. I put up with it. Then there's the music. If I want to listen, I have to go in the music room, even had to tell Mary that one day when she was home and we listened to Die Fledermaus aria, Heimat, Brigit's favorite, and I shut the door, kept the hi-fi low. Well, once in a while we do see a play. There's nothing very admirable about that. No. I've had it. She's damn well not going to ruin my daughter's life.

Before Pamela returned, Gregory called to Deirdre. Without waiting, he yelled up to her, "Pamela's going back to Wellesley. And you damn well keep out of it." He started coughing. Deirdre had come downstairs by now, and he could hear her breathing hard. He thought, *How ironic, both of us breathless.*

"Listen to yourself. Don't you yell at me. Don't yell. It's bad for you. Now settle down. I only thought . . . ."

"Well, forget thinking. If I need care, we'll get it." Suddenly Brigit was in his mind again, but he knew she was an impossibility.

"Do you know how fresh she was, what she said to me? I

won't have it, Greg. I won't. I won't have a fresh child in my house. The things she accused me of. I won't have it," her voice rising.

"She told me she was fresh and that she misbehaved, but you upset her. She's not my nurse, isn't going to be. She's going to have her schooling, becoming a young woman and the joy that comes with it, dating, studying."

"But it makes no difference she upset me?"

"Certainly it does, but she's a right to her life. Remember that, Deirdre. C'mon, let's not have another fight. I can't put up with it right now."

"I am certainly aware you can't. That's why you may need her nearby."

"NO. You won't do that to her. You WON'T." He slammed his hand on a the bed table, trembling. Just then, too, Pamela came in. She had heard part of the argument. "Thanks, dad," looking to her mother and then to her father, "but you shouldn't get so upset. I'm sorry I did this to you."

At that, Deirdre rushed from the room, banging the door.

Good, sweet, loveable wife, get the hell out of here.

He looked at Pamela who's face was red, her eyes again tearing. "You didn't do anything except be my loving daughter. Remember that."

"Boy," a quiver in her voice but forcing a smile, "Melinda and I'll both get it tonight. Poor Melinda. She won't know what hit her."

That night at home was terrible for the two. Deirdre criticized everything they did. They kept kicking gently or hitting one another to keep quiet and let their mother rant. After Andrea served dinner, they both went to watch TV.

"Pam. Let's go see grandma and grandpa. And Aunt Mary's there. You know, I never give it much thought, she being lesbian. She has a right to her life. Why did I bring that up? Oh, because look at dad and mom. I'm sure Aunt Mary and Evelyn argue. But I doubt it's that bitter. Well how would we know? Anyhow, let's go see them."

Melinda, whom Deirdre began to respect more now that she was a M.D. and, in fact, with whom she didn't dare interfere, told their mother where they were going.

The following day, Pamela kept away from her mother. Being warm, she went to her favorite place to read, the gardens so well kept both by her mother and a gardener.

"Pamela," Deirdre called. "Where is she?" She saw her in the garden, reading.

"Pamela. Can you put down a book for a minute? All you do at home is read or go to your room and write those stories of yours, unless you have one of the boys from around town running after you for a date. Want to be a writer," this last mocking. "I need to talk to you."

"Mom, I'll just finish this page."

"Well, finish it." Deirdre closed the back door and waited in the kitchen.

Rather than wait, Pamela closed the book and went inside.

"That was fast."

"I'm a fast reader," she answered sarcastically.

"I don't like your tone of voice."

"Mom, when are you going to decide that Melinda and I are women? C'mon. Admit it. We have the same bodies like yours, all filled out."

"Don't say another word." She actually smiled. "I don't want to know."

"What? Whether we've done *it*."

"Stop. Now." She imagined them in bed, their lost virginity.

"Mom. I'm still a virgin. You can still love me. *In your way, whatever that is.* Anyhow, would it make any difference as long as we don't get pregnant? I know about birth control, whenever it comes to that. So don't worry. I won't embarrass you and dad. Nor Melinda either. She's a doctor. Hey, mom, maybe she screws every night."

That remark unknowingly pierced Deirdre, embarrassing and angering her. "Shut up, you bitch. I don't want to hear anymore. Stop."

Pamela smiled. "C'mon. I'm teasing you, mom."

"Then don't tease. Don't you ever." She calmed some. "Look, I called you in, because I've talked to your father. We've agreed that you'll finish at Wellesley. Perhaps, though, and we haven't talked about this, you'd put off your Master's for a while. If it were necessary, we'll get a permanent nurse. Hopefully, that won't happen. It's just that I worry about him and my traveling."

Oh, God. You and you're traveling again. When will you stop and realize you're a wife whose husband may need you?

There were times when Melinda, after she started her internship, had some hours off to be home when Pamela and she talked about their mother's travels and wondered what she did, where she and that *man* found everything, more and more about the appearance in the house of rare pieces and, did she sleep with him? Then they'd look at each other. In the silence their faces changed to concern. "I'd be so furious with her," Melinda told her. "But we'll never know. Dad wouldn't. You know, Pam, if Brigit . . . . Oh, forget it."

"Yeah, you wouldn't care if he did it with Brigit, because we love her. It's all so mixed up. Aunt Mary is such good friends with Brigit, and she seems to hate mom. Something happened between them, but Aunt Mary never talks about it."

"It's something I can't help thinking about."

"Me too, but what good does it do?" She was looking at the floor, somewhat unhappily.

"What's wrong?"

"Being home and seeing and hearing everything. At least you're away from it most of the time. We need a good shopping trip. How about the next time you're off, if you can get that much, we meet in Portland? I want some new dresses and some blouses, a pair of slacks. What about you?" She paused. "I go to your room sometimes and look in your closet, and I feel empty as if you had taken everything with you to the hospital."

"Don't do that to yourself, Pam. Listen, if you want to get away to school, go in the fall or even this summer. Dad doesn't need you to pamper him. He's tough, and don't forget that. It means a lot."

"It's not that so much, although I want to write and learn more at school. It's depressing sometimes living with her. She hugs me, kisses me, well you know. But, shit, she thinks I'm a kid. She keeps talking to me about sex, and I thought one night she was going to throw me on the bed, lift my legs and examine me. I sound crazy."

"She did the same thing to me, only I never told you. I was furious. Like I hadn't learned anything or read. As med students, I guess I never told you, the guys examined us and we did them. It was embarrassing, and weird, but we got used to it. But there she is, lecturing. I wonder how hard grandma Cunningham was with her. I'll bet mom gave it to grandma. Oh. This is nonsense. Spending our time talking about it. Let's go to the beach."

The wind was picking up. The water and sky were grey, the waves larger with white caps leaping and falling on the shore and against rocks. Seagulls seemed caught in the wind, gliding with it, allowing it to carry them where it would. The sisters laughed as they brushed their hair out of their eyes, then placed their arms about one another, laughing into the breeze, daring it to part them. They let their hair go, walked, skipped over a bump of tufted grass, hollered at the gods. "Nothing can part us."

~

1980 and I'm getting worse. I thought by now I'd be getting along better, fooling myself, I guess. Physician, heal thyself of thy wishes and desperation.

Catastrophe is part of human nature, whether we create it for ourselves or the gods of destruction hurl their venom at or entomb us in it. Mount St. Helens, fifty-one people killed, forests destroyed, including all that animal life. Why think of the billions of dollars from that eruption? Or why, later in the year, in December would someone kill John Lennon who harmed no one and gave pleasure. And why would we elect an actor Ronald Reagan President who on death would be installed as the first American god? He was on Olympus while Washington and Lincoln were on a ledge below.

Ah, all this is my life, and I either walk or lie and cough, am feverish, and my beautiful daughters must endure my weakness while my wife. My wife. Is she my wife? She did have a nurse come to the house, and I told Pamela to get herself to her Masters in Creative Writing. Often it is hard being alone, scary, wondering whether I'll cough too hard and cause a blood vessel rupture, and Deirdre will come home and find nothing, Nothing. Only blood. Medical man that I am, my thoughts are like that. After all, physicians have problems too. They fall ill, they injure themselves, they die. Ah. Pam will be home within a few days on vacation. Melinda is on her fellowship but manages to sneak off. And Deirdre sneaks off to where?

I was in the hospital again for about a week. I don't remember. But I do remember Brigit coming to see me, bending over me, kissing me on the mouth, oh so softly, and I reached up and brought her closer to me so I could feel her mouth more warmly and the touch of her pliant, soft breast. We stayed together like that for some time until she rose, placed her hand on my forehead and then slid it down along my cheek, the way she would when she wanted to calm me when I was angry about something at the lab in Boston.

Something peculiar happened. The nurse Deirdre hired appeared less often. Somehow, Brigit managed that and took care of me. She told me Thomas didn't mind. Her children are now fifteen and twelve. I've seen them occasionally. Kathryn resembles her in many ways, probably will be as fetching as her mother. Oh well.

Pamela came home. When she saw Brigit, she halted, looked at that stunning woman, the two of them staring, then moving toward one another. Pamela spoke first. "Brigit. Oh, Brigit. What are you doing here?" and then hugged her, kissed her cheek. They stood there for a bit hugging one another. I wonder what was in their minds. Love between them was obvious.

Pamela then looked at me, my smile. She hurried to me. "Dad," and she hugged, kissed me. Looking back at Brigit then again at me, "Are you.O.K.?"

"Sure. Don't you see my nurse making sure I don't do anything bad?" Bad, that was the wrong word. I did want to be in bed with Brigit, to make love to her as though it were for the first time. I wanted her warm, lithe body naked lying against me. I wonder if she thought about it. She must have. Anyhow, after a few days, Brigit had become used to the house and occasionally went looking about from curiosity, perhaps wanting to know how we lived. I never said anything. Once I called to her. "What are you doing?"

"Oh, nothing, Looking at this museum you have in the house."

It was sometime about then when Pamela was upstairs.

Neither of us could help ourselves.

After, we heard Pamela coming down the stairs and Brigit slipped quickly from the bed and straightened her clothes and brushed back her hair. I think Pamela knew when she came to the door. There was her somewhat surprised look, her quick gaze going from Brigit's hair, reddened face, to her skirt. But if she suspected, she ignored it.

Pamela looked at me, hesitated, and came in when I motioned. Pamela walked to Brigit, looking intently in her eyes. Of course Pamela knew. "I hope you're making him happy. He needs that," she stopped a moment, "and you." Her face flushed. She was uncertain about continuing. "Brigit, there's something I've wanted to say."

Blushing again, she blurted, "You all belong together." Her voice dropped. "But you're both married to others. Oh, God and damn."

Brigit had cheated on Thomas, I on her, more so than I thought on Deirdre. I know she was screwing that Frenchman and God knows whom else. What did it matter anymore? Except for Brigit's pain.

I knew Pamela would talk to Melinda. "If only," perhaps Pamela was thinking. "But onlys don't count." She paused, stammering, "I love you both. I'm going back to my room. O.K.? probably write a little." She hurried off.

After she left, and despite the love and hugs exchanged, we all felt awkwardness. Watching after Pam, Brigit turned to me. "Well, that was close." She smiled. "Love, you're - I'm - stuck now. Listen, though, we're not giving up ever again. I won't let you go." I told her, "Never." She sat beside me, holding my hand. Looking at the open door and to the darkened space beyond - it seemed her shoulders shivered - whatever was beyond there, she didn't say, just held my hand more tightly.

She looked back at me. "I do love your daughters, Greg, and

I intend to take care of you all, regardless of cost - except for my daughter - and son."

She sat silently for several minutes and then told me what she saw, an art piece with doors that aroused her curiosity, thinking she had seen it in a magazine. The shiver in her shoulders must have been an image in her mind that made her wonder, frightened her. In the dark she saw something painful.

For now, though, her expression serious, her eyes intent on me, her voice low, she muttered, "Greg, I'm going to get Pam."

"What's wrong?"

"If I'm right, you'll soon find out."

Brigit went upstairs, "Pamela, I need you."

Startled, her eyes widened in fright. "Is dad all right?"

"It's not your dad. I want you with me to look at something downstairs. I don't feel comfortable about looking through your dad's or mother's possessions."

"Well," Pamela answered somewhat irritated. "I wouldn't think you would." She paused. "Now I am curious."

They went to the darkened den where there was a wardrobe, with drawers behind closed doors. Brigit opened them. "Pamela, let's look in a drawer, it's such an unusual piece, but I wouldn't do it without you here. I just stumbled on this when I was looking around the house at the antiques. I can't deny I'm curious. You know the saying," she smiled, "a woman's curiosity." She was suspicious regarding such obviously expensive antiques and did want to see inside.

"I just don't want to do anything that may bother or hurt you, your sister, or your father."

Pamela did catch the omission of her mother. *Was Brigit just a jealous woman after all? Was my love misplaced?* "Well," her voice somewhat cold, "open it," although now Pamela was not only curious but frightened.

Brigit realized what was going through Pamela and placed

her hand gently on her arm. She opened a drawer in which there was a key, perhaps inadvertently left, and brought out some papers with numbers and also references to museum pieces.

Pamela stopped her. "You have no right. I don't."

"Pamela. Listen to me. I'm asking you to trust me. You must. This is important. You're a grown woman and have to learn to take it." Brigit's impulse was to hug her. There were tears in her eyes that Pamela noticed. "I trust you, Brigit," she said uncertainly, still frightened looking at the papers Brigit held.

"Come here. Let's sit. I didn't want to ask your father just now. He, he's, oh damn." And she started crying.

Pamela moved quite close to her, their thighs touching, and placed her arm about her shoulders. "Brigit. You love him. I know it. Melinda knows," she told her tenderly.

Brigit brushed at her eyes. "Oh damn, Pamela. I've been clumsy. I didn't intend it this way."

"Here wipe your eyes." Pamela's hand shaking, she took a tissue from her jean pocket. Brigit sniffled, wiped. "I need another," wiped, shook her head. "We've got things to do here. You don't need a weeping woman on top of it all."

"O.K., Brigit. Go ahead and let's see what's in there."

Brigit opened another drawer and unthinkingly pulled out additional sheets with a series of numbers with dollar signs, places of deposit, and dates.

"What is that?"

"Pamela. You're mother is very methodical. Let's see." Brigit hesitated. *I have no right.*

Pamela looked at the bottom of the paper, seeing Total: $14 million in her mother's handwriting. There were also references to offshore and Swiss accounts, all in her name. They looked further and found certificates of deposit, a number of large-figure withdrawals.

On another list were references to some museum pieces, sold by her, with the notation, "Étienne took these from sites (unnamed)."

"Brigit. My mother's a thief. Oh, God. She can't be. She's all kinds of things sometimes. I admit it. I've even hated her. This will kill dad, blow up the whole family, all of us."

"Pam," and Brigit held her closely. Now Pamela was crying and shaking. "Shh. Shh. It's something we'll deal with." Brigit kissed her cheek, pulling her tightly to her. "You're going to be a brave woman, dear. Shh."

"Oh, Oh, my God. We'll be in the papers. Dad will be ruined, the family so shamed."

"Stop, Pam. We both have to calm down. We have to tell your dad."

"Oh, my God, Why the hell is she my mother? That Fucking Bitch."

"It'll be all right. Nothing can hurt your dad. He's too well thought of. And I promise, I'll protect you and Melinda." *However I can, I'll do it. They're my children too.* She paused. "However I can. Damn. Why did I ever look?"

She waited for Pamela to calm some. "Come, dear. We'll go see your father."

~

When Pam and Brigit came back to my room, they both looked as though they had had an argument or had emerged from a confessional booth, damned, to be saved only by countless Hail Marys that perhaps would erase their tear-blurred eyes.

"Dad," Pamela started.

Brigit interrupted. It was then I saw Brigit holding a sheaf of papers. "Let me, Pamela. O.K.?"

Pamela nodded a "yes."

"Greg," Brigit began. "I was looking at the art works, wondering how there could be so many and some seeming so unusual. I called Pam, because the wardrobe fascinated me, having, I think, seen it in a magazine. I wanted to look inside. I guess I shouldn't have, I know."

I was struck that she would have done that, as though she were possessing my home. However, I wasn't that annoyed, because I wouldn't stop her from doing anything here. It was as though it were her house, that my children were hers. That we had lost all those years was what truly bothered me. I waited for her to continue.

She appeared as though she expected disapproval, but continued. "Pamela and I agreed that I'd talk.

"I think there could be something funny going on with Deirdre."

I thought she was going to tell me about love letters full of innuendo and explicit sex talk.

"She could be holding back objects from the museum. It's possible she's not only been misleading the museum but her partner. Maybe I'm all wrong and want to believe this."

"Is that what those papers are you're holding?"

Her eyes were now filled with tears, and she had a difficult time answering me. Pamela, too, looked terrible, her face white, her hands shaking, even though she tried to hold them close to her sides.

"Dad." Pamela never hesitated. "She's a thief. My mother's a thief," she shouted and sobbed loudly. "She's probably cheated on you too." She inadvertently looked at Brigit, perhaps thinking about finding us. I don't know. It made no difference. "She's no good, dad. I can't stand it. My mother, your wife, our mother, Oh. What about Melinda?"

I sat stunned. What bothered me at the moment was Pamela

and thinking of Melinda, then my disbelief. "Brigit, I don't believe this. I admit I've had some bad thoughts about her," as I glanced at Pamela. I began to cough and couldn't stop. Brigit came to me, rubbed my back and forehead, "I knew I should have approached this differently," as she lightly continued rubbing my back, hearing her whispering to herself, "How differently? Impossible." I coughed more.

"Here, lie back on the pillows." She raised them so I would be able to cough without choking. My arm pits were wet, my head and face hot. I could feel perspiration in other parts of my body.

"Pamela, go get a warm, wet towel and a dry one, please," Brigit asked her.

"I hate this, Greg. I just Hate it. I didn't want to . . . ." She stopped. Then she put the papers in my hand. "Here. When you feel calmer, please, dear, look at them. You'll agree with me, I'm sure. I'm so sorry." She did feel terrible. There was no doubt. But she would tell me later that she didn't care a bit for Deirdre but for me. And for the girls and what we all would have to endure.

As I read through the papers, Pam came with the towels. Brigit gently wiped me. She looked at Pamela as if to say it was O.K. what she might see Brigit do. She helped me off with my shirt and wiped more and dried with the towel. I wondered what she thought of my body now. I had lost some weight. What difference did that make? She started to reach for my pajama bottoms, stopped, turned to Pamela again, "Let's let your dad do this."

"No. Don't leave. This can wait." I watched my daughter and waved my hand for her to come sit beside me, likewise with Brigit. With both women beside me, I slowly and with some stammer told them, "We've got to report this. Oh, Jesus. What the f . . .," I started to say; "whatever possessed her?" But I knew. She needed money and recognition, more than I could give her. "Perhaps," I thought, "it was the war." But it wasn't the war. It was in her character, buried in that effervescent, extroverted facade of hers. The one that enraptured me and cheated me of Brigit. Brigit knew what she was then and what she is now. Is she pleased?

As though knowing what I was thinking, Brigit interrupted my thoughts. Neglecting Pamela, she said, "Dearest, I'm so awfully sorry. I feel hurt and hated to tell either of you. I even thought of trying to forget it, but that was impossible." She turned my head toward her. "Gregory, if you think I've had my revenge, forget that. I just feel so horribly rotten inside. She reached across me to Pamela's hand, limp at first, but then pressing into Brigit's. "For you too, Pamela. You have no idea."

"I do," Pamela murmured. She started shaking, crying loudly. "My mother. My mother. How will I ever get over this?" She shook. Brigit rose and sat beside her, pulling Pam to her, holding her very tightly, and allowing her to cry into her shoulder.

~

The following day, giving herself time, as well as Gregory, Brigit pondered over Mary's knowing a museum Board member and whether to draw her into this. She also knew that Deirdre had been elected Treasurer perhaps two or three years ago. That explained her opportunity. It was self-explanatory. She hesitated, still concerned for Gregory and his daughters.

Another day passed. Uncomfortably, she decided to confront Gregory with her idea. She also wanted Pamela to listen, wishing Melinda could be with them. However, while she thought and asked herself what right she had in Gregory's family affairs, the enormity of Deirdre's activities swayed her.

She drove to the house, waited, trembling some but determined. When Pamela let her in, Brigit told her, "Pamela, I know what we . . ."

The word struck Pamela. *We. Is she now part of our family? Is she the one suffering? Perhaps she is for us. She loves dad. It's obvious. Always has. But she's got her own children and husband. I should feel hateful after finding them pretending they hadn't, call it what it was, been fucking. But why didn't I care then? Why now? Because of my thieving mother who doesn't give a damn for us. She's going to end up in jail and embarrass us all. Just stop. You love Brigit, told her so. She loves dad. She does care what happens.*

Without thinking Pamela quickly put her arms about Brigit, kissing her. Surprised, Brigit thought she knew what Pamela was thinking, kissed her back, moved her away. "Come, let's go to your father. I believe I know how to settle this." But, then, there could be unknown consequences for them. What though? "Like hating me." She shook her head to clear her mind, her heart beating faster; she wished to ignore it, but she was now determined.

Gregory was in the music room, the door open, because Deirdre was away again.

"Dad. Brigit is here." Hearing her name, he smiled, shut off the high fi, looked brightly at Brigit and Pamela. "Oh. I've been waiting for my nurse. Here. Take my pulse." He put out his wrist. "It's fast, doctor. Have you got a fever?" The innuendo though obvious, she placed her hand on his forehead. It was warm. "Pamela, please get the thermometer. He's not smart enough to take care of himself." He did have a fever. Brigit decided that would not stop her.

"First, why don't you get in bed and rest?"

"What do you think my music is?"

"I know." She felt the embrace of love in her heart, aware they had just exchanged their feelings for one another. "Are you sure, though, you wouldn't want to lie down."

"I'm sure. I'm no different than yesterday." He knew she had something she wanted to say. "Tell us, Brigit."

She laughed. "I'm too transparent. Some woman." *Maybe that's how she got him so easily.* "Gregory, Pamela, I've got an idea. Mary knows someone on the museum Board. If so, perhaps we can get her to talk to the person, ask him to call a meeting or something like that, to check the finances." By now she was nervous, troubled she was interfering.

"Well," Gregory answered, "that's keeping it in the family. It's the family that's going to suffer from the whole rotten thing anyhow."

Brigit quickly took to Mary. "Try her, Greg." *Mary will be hesitant. Or maybe she'll be glad. We both love that woman.*

That evening, Gregory called Mary, asked her to come over alone after her dinner. She and Evelyn had now bought a house. Brigit had also called her home, lied, something that bothered her terribly, and said that Gregory wasn't feeling too well. She'd explain later. She turned red-faced from the phone. Pamela pretended not to notice. To ease the awkwardness, Brigit told them, "Well, we've got a guest nurse for the rest of the day. Tell Andrea to take time off so we'll have privacy." Her voice caught, "I'll make dinner for us."

Thus, in effect, Brigit moved in that day and took over the home. Still somewhat nervous, she wanted to shower, wished she had brought a change of clothes. Later she asked Pamela if she could use Melinda's vacant room and bathroom. She wanted to rest, if she could. She would run a bath, rather than shower, and then rest, perhaps sleep for a while.

Hearing the bath running, Pamela knocked. "Brigit, may I come in?"

"Why yes. I decided to lie in the bathtub, relax."

"That's what I wanted to see you about. Brigit, I'm scared, really scared. I think of what's going to happen and it makes me so nervous. I feel as though there's always going to be a black mark against us. And here we are conspiring against my mother. My conscience, maybe. I know Melinda is feeling it. We talk when she has time. She said she'd get time off and come home. I told her you're here a lot. She was glad but worried about your family."

"Pamela, my family is fine. I know the children are O.K. The maid will get dinner. If he needs me, Thomas will call." She wanted to tell Pamela she felt comfortable here but said nothing. "I'm nervous too, Pam."

"I was thinking, what if my mother suddenly appeared. What would happen?"

"If that happens, we'll take care of it then. Now don't worry about that. You know what happens when women face off against one another. Besides, your dad is here. He's no weakling. He can handle her himself." Suddenly Brigit stopped, looked straight at Pamela, realizing she had revealed so much of herself.

"You hate my mother, don't you? You hope she'll go to jail, and she will."

"Well," Brigit stammered. "Well, one time I did hate her." She decided to be honest. Why avoid the truth? Pamela was a very intelligent woman. "Maybe I still do, but there's no reason. I have my own family. I'm aware you know your father and I love one another. There's no sense in denying that. You probably think I'm a terrible woman, deceitful. But I despise what's going to happen with your mother and what's she's done."

Ignoring the last of her words, Pamela answered, "I did once think you were trying to destroy our family when you first appeared. But I knew better. I trusted you almost from the beginning. And I meant what I told you. I do love you, Brigit, and I still wish . . . ."

"Shhh. I know." And they kissed again, hugged, held each other tightly, crying for themselves, one another, and the horror of Deirdre.

"Pamela," softly, "You wet me, Brigit. Is it O.K. if I get in the tub too?"

"I'll leave, if you prefer, but it won't embarrass me if we're in here together."

"No. You can stay. It doesn't faze me either. We can relax and talk." She undressed. "The water's so nice and warm."

~

Mary did come alone and promised not to tell Evelyn.

After the greetings and cheek kisses, Mary told them she did know a doctor on the Board. They did want to protect the papers they found. So, the next day, Mary put them through a Xerox. Returning them, she tried to stay calm but couldn't prevent her outburst.

"Fuck your Deirdre, Greg. I knew all along she was poison. Godamn you, Greg. I tried to tell you."

"Shut the hell up, Mary." His voice was raspy.

Mary stepped back, startled both by what she said and her brother's temper. Worried about the effect on him and Brigit whose presence her temper had neglected, she started to apologize, to Pamela, Brigit, and him. She choked back her tears but then placed her hand to her mouth, crying, her face wretched. She looked at Brigit whose face had become pallid. Mary reached out her arms for her. "Oh, dear. I didn't mean to hurt you, not for anything. I love you so."

Brigit tried to smile. There was no need for apology, for Mary was thinking of her and how Greg had abandoned her for a temptress. "There's no need, Mary," she weakly replied. "I love you too, and I understand what you meant. It just . . . ."

and she stopped, trying to hold back tears for the past. Both women were hugging, Pamela gazing, relaxed some. This was her family. Here was love, something Melinda and she had missed from a fiendish mother who had borne them.

Gregory pushed himself from the sofa, and went to them, pleading softly, "Don't. It's all right. I realize what I did. Please, Mary." She released Brigit, and leaned into him. "Forgive me," through her sobs. "Oh, God, forgive me, both of you." She tried to fake a laugh. "But I won't take back a word about that bitch." She sniffled some, wiped lightly at her eyes. "I've got to call Evelyn. I promised. She feared there was something wrong with Greg when I wouldn't tell her why I was coming."

The thought of Evelyn cheered and softened her. One day they would marry, if that were ever allowed. She wanted to get back to her, to feel Evelyn's arms about her, the tenderness, the softness of her body, her scent. But this wreckage Deirdre had created. That must be taken care of. She called the doctor in Boston, told him she'd come down for a day and would tell him then why it was urgent to see him. *You're a dead woman, Deirdre. That fake cosmopolitanism, that desire for fortune and social upper crust. What are you going to do when you fall into the sewer you created for yourself?*

~

Deirdre appeared at home suddenly about two days later to find Pamela out and Brigit alone with Gregory. She walked into the bedroom, surprising them, having seen Brigit tending Gregory, taking his temperature, wiping his forehead, helping him get ready for a doctor's appointment. He stood partially undressed.

"What's going on here?" She startled them.

"You're home," Gregory calmly told her. "You were gone long enough. Did you see your Frenchman?"

She ignored him. "What is she doing here?" She glared at Brigit.

Brigit, quite calm, answered her, "I'm taking care of your husband. I'm a nurse, remember? And," her voice hardening, "you're never here when he needs attention."

"And nurses fuck like the rest of us." Suddenly Deirdre stopped, knowing she had condemned herself, then staring at Brigit, her face hardened, her eyes bright with hatred, "Well, you go and finish, nurse dear. You don't need me." She thought of Pamela. "Where's Pam?"

Brigit answered calmly, sarcastically, "I told her to go out and enjoy herself, that I'd take care of everything."

"Well, I hope it was a good fuck, dear," and Deirdre abruptly left, decided to look at mail. Then she saw it. The letter was from the Board requesting her appearance for a hearing. Her heart raced. She forgot Gregory and Brigit immediately, thinking that she must get to Étienne. She also told herself she would never enter this house again. She walked quickly to the bedroom. "Gregory Hurwitz. I'm leaving this house. I'll get a lawyer if and when." She had no idea of how ironically she had spoken.

Gregory looked at the crumpled letter she held tightly in her hand.

"What's that letter, Deirdre?"

She glanced at the letter. "I have a Board meeting in a couple of days. That can't be of any interest to you. Nothing I do apparently is. The two of you, get out of my bedroom. Get a sleazy motel room for yourselves. I have to pack." She hesitated but could not hold back. "I'll be leaving this house. You can fuck here, although who knows if it comes to a divorce."

"Well, Deirdre, before we enjoy ourselves, why don't you explain these." Gregory then went to a drawer where he had hidden the papers. "Brigit," he knew he shouldn't have used her name, "found these and thought they might explain some of the museum pieces in the house. Oh, and that money I've never seen."

"What are you talking about? And that bitch has already taken over my house. Look at her like she's the protecting Virgin Mary. You fuck her in our bed, don't you?"

"Or MY bed. And don't you insult her.

"Now explain these." He held out the papers.

Her face paled, her hands shook, and she felt a shock through her body as though she had placed her finger in a socket. She felt unsteady, as her eyes seemed to fail her. She did manage to move to him more slowly than she intended. Her body it seemed was failing her. Her heart pounding, she reached, managed loudly, "Give me those. They're . . . ."

"They're proof that you're a liar and a thief. Now get the hell out of my house. Call your lawyer."

She steadied herself, her voice low and menacing, "I'll get you, Gregory. You watch your back. And while you're at it, protect that bitch, hiding in the corner there, your . . . ."

"Whore? Is that what you were about to say, Mother?" as Pamela walked in.

"Mother. Mother?" Pamela's eyes filled with tears. "Mother. Shit. You hate all of us. When I needed a hug, even advice, where were you? Robbing? With that Frenchman? Did you ever love us, Melinda, Kaitlin. Oh, Kaitlin," and she sobbed. "Get out of our lives, whoever you are. I heard it all. Any love I thought I had," she continued sobbing. "Oh. damn," and she ran to Gregory, who himself weak from the confrontation, held her as tightly as he could and led her to the bedroom chaise to comfort them both, while Brigit, scared for Gregory, glared at Deirdre as she went to make certain he was all right. "Why don't you just get your things and leave? This man is sick. Sick, you hear me, and somehow I'll take care of him for as long. . . ." And she stopped, her face colorless, thinking of Gregory dead.

~

In Belmont, she went to Étienne's house that felt more like home to her. She was weary of all those years of Gregory's illness. Here she felt secure from that eventual fatality, increasing her enjoyment of her sexual encounters with her lover-business partner. Here in Boston and Belmont, she was Étienne's wife. He was attentive and kept no photos of the Frenchwoman to remind Deirdre of her temporariness. Although occasionally she recognized she was a paid mistress, more like a prostitute, she also knew the apparent admiration of Belmont's and Boston's social whirl. Here she was rid of Gregory and the concerns of motherhood. Melinda and Pamela were grown women who also were no longer her problem. If necessary, they could rely on their father until that CLL killed him, soon she hoped. No more unwanted sexual humoring. The visions of their encounters disgusted her, his more difficult breathing when she handed or mouthed him, or as he entered and moved to her pretended willingness. No more. Now she was alone until Étienne came. Only it wouldn't be until after her meeting with the Board. Until then she was alone. *I'm alone. Jesus, oh Jesus, God, I'm scared. What are they confronting me with? I'd almost just as soon have Gregory with me. I'd welcome his fingers and hands, his penis pulsating in me. I don't want to be alone. Where the hell are you, Étienne?*

She hardly ate anything, walked continuously about the house, put on the TV. Nothing satisfied her. She undressed late, lay naked on the bed, and in an attempt to quiet herself, she placed her fingers below, moved them inside, sucked the wetness, rubbed, trying to arouse herself by imagining Étienne, as she did so many times lying on her back allowing Gregory inside her. But she stopped, turned on her stomach. Wetting her pillow with tears, she was a woman moaning a family death. Perhaps she should return to Gregory, even though it would mean begging. That is what she would do. She'd be a helping wife, even though she no longer cared. *I never loved him. You knew it from the beginning. It was a game. But somehow I'll make it up to him and the girls. Do you really want that? You took him away from that weak bitch just to show your power to tantalize. And what did you get for it? Why the hell didn't you stay with Étienne, marry him? Crap. I don't know what I want. Tomorrow. I'll take care of that too. Charm them as I always have.*

~

Her first activity of the morning when she woke from a restless sleep was to place a call to Étienne who was in Philadelphia where he said he had to see an art dealer who could help them. She asked him to come to Boston that day because of the meeting. She wanted to talk to him afterwards. She had already called and told him about the meeting, of her concern regarding the tone of the person who contacted her.

"Well, what did you do to cause any unease, if there is any?"

"I don't know," she lied.

"Don't play games with me, Deirdre. What's it about?"

They want to ask about some money and contributions to the museum." She hesitated. "They may ask about provenance. I don't know," she desperately replied.

" Calm yourself. Are you telling me everything? I can take care of provenance. What about the contributions?"

"Nothing. Nothing. I can't think of anything," she answered plaintively.

Étienne caught her tone, the dread. He never told her he had talked to an ally on the Board who told him there were questions about her, that he was uncertain whether it involved Étienne; but the ally would be in touch after, or even during, the meeting.

Finishing the conversation, she went angrily through her wardrobe. *He's questioning me. Should I worry? I can handle him. Forget it. I have a date with my hairdresser. But what to wear?* She decided on a rose-colored dress adorned with small sequined flowers from the bust to the waist, print on the skirt. At the hairdresser early, the woman shaped her hair to show its wave that curved just above her neck. The manicurist did her fingernails in light red. Her lipstick matched. She wore Indian turquoise earrings that hung below her hairline. Satisfied, after lunch, which she barely ate, she took a taxi to the museum.

The meeting began as usual. Deirdre looked directly at each member, holding her back erect, forcing herself to smile when necessary, pretended to take notes, until the chairman addressed her. "Mrs. Hurwitz."

Though she felt her heart quicken, she answered calmly, smiling flirtingly at him, looking away, then back; for she knew he had always wanted to approach her privately but was too afraid.

The chairman cleared his throat, saddened. "Mrs. Hurwitz. You've met the auditor."

"Yes."

"He seems to have found some discrepancies. We need your answers."

"Why, of course." Now her voice shook slightly, her poise disappearing some.

"Mrs. Hurwitz," the auditor continued. "There are over $14 million dollars that appear unaccounted for."

She managed. "I don't know why." She felt herself failing, wondering how long she could maintain the costume in which she psychologically tried to clothe herself.

Now he was direct. "We've called in an investigator. Bluntly. The money's missing, and we believe you know where it is."

"You what?" she managed unbelievingly. "You're accusing me of theft? Do you understand what you're saying?"

"Very well. You can make it easier if you just tell us . . . . And, naturally, there's some question about the provenance of several pieces."

"This is absurd. I resent what you are accusing me of." The self-assured, tantalizing woman was disappearing, the costume falling, leaving her naked, unprotected. She interlaced her fingers. "I resent this," she said more quietly. Recovering some, she told them, "I'll gather everything I have, all my records, and report to you tomorrow at which time I'll expect an apology."

The man's voice hard, "We will give you until tomorrow not only to tell us about the funds but also the pieces we suspect were stolen that you and your partner, or one or the other, sold to the museum. And please, Mrs. Hurwitz, all exits from the city will be watched. In the meantime, if you don't mind, we have a policewoman who will be with you tonight and with whom you'll return tomorrow. We will also be calling in the FBI. If we are wrong, you will receive our deepest apologies," this last sounding rather sarcastic.

Deirdre stood her full length, showing herself an assured, desirable woman. "You bring on your guard, gentlemen," she coldly told them. "I'll see you tomorrow and expect that apology and legal compensation when I sue you for defamation."

~

Although the plain-clothed policewoman accompanied her to Étienne's Boston apartment, Deirdre slammed the study door to close her out, and desperately called Étienne; but he was already on his way to Boston. She sighed. He'd know what to do.

"There's food in the refrigerator," she told the policewoman. "Go and make yourself something. I'm eating later. And, oh, you'll have to sleep on the sofa, but it is comfortable."

"Don't worry about me, ma'm."

With that, Deirdre, for now, self-satisfied, waited for her lover and protector from the war in which they fought together. She smiled remembering yet still troubled by the horror they had endured.

Later, the front door opened. The policewoman waiting, surprised him, but not overwhelmingly. "And who and what are you doing here?" he asked pleasantly.

"I'm here to guard Mrs. Hurwitz."

"Oh. She does need that. She's been threatened," he smiled. "I'm Mr. Moreau, owner of this flat. Mrs. Hurwitz, I presume, is in the study."

"Yes."

"Good." He started for Deirdre. "Oh, don't follow. I'll protect her. You just amuse yourself with the television. Perhaps we can all have a coffee in a little bit."

"What happened, Deirdre? Be honest with me. No screwing around."

"Étienne, love." She hugged and kissed him, felt the coldness of his lips. She moved back. "They've accused me of taking money. They also questioned where we got some of the pieces and where some are."

"What money, Deirdre?"

"The money they paid us."

"Is that all? Where is it? How much?"

"Your questions. They're confusing me."

"Where's the money?" He grabbed her shoulders. "Where? Come. We're leaving here."

"How? We can't get out."

"Deirdre, love, you've forgotten the war. Diane? And by the

way, how's your husband?" The question was intentionally mocking and threatening. Obviously, there was no way he would have been aware of the encounter in Cape Astraea. Deirdre grimaced while feeling the sting of a slap. Recovering, she not only feared him but the policewoman. "She's," Deirdre emphasized, "out there."

"Don't worry, I said," he gruffly answered, smiling grotesquely. "It will be easier than Diane."

" But there'll be a replacement soon."

" It's no matter, and then it's off to my private plane."

"What?"

"How did you think I got here so fast? We're getting out."

"Where?"

"It's my hideaway. Be patient, lover." The sarcasm scared her more.

"I don't think . . . ."

"Stop thinking. Just do. Follow me. I've never let you down, love."

He had never frightened her before but did now. She felt a jolt throughout her body, shuddered, felt the rising pimplings along her skin. *Why? Be careful. He's hiding anger. He's never behaved like this with me. I wish he'd kiss me. Hug me, or feel my breasts, show some feeling toward me. What? Oh shit. What have I done? I can handle him. You sure? I can. I know I can whenever I want to turn it on. And I will as never before.*

He interrupted. "Deirdre, get behind me. We're going out there. She's probably getting restless. We've been in here too long. Remember, behind me."

They went to the living room. Smiling, as though there had been something conspiratorial happening, the policewoman rose and said she was just about to get them. The smile changed as she stood. She raised her arm bent at the elbow either to strike or protect herself as Étienne pushed her arm aside, held it with one hand and with the other turned her quickly before she could strike at him with her leg, tightened a grasp on her throat cutting air and blood, cracking a vertebrae in her neck, as she slowly sank to the ground.

"C'mon. Let's go."

"You killed her. Now they'll really be after us, you goddamn fool. You think we're fighting Nazis?"

"Oui, mon amoureuse prostituée"

"You fucking bastard."

"Come," and he grabbed her arm, pulling her down the hallway as she stumbled repeatedly, struggling uselessly against his strength.

She started to scream. Before she could finish, he slapped her hard across her face, knocking her head sideways. "Shut up, or you'll end up like that woman we left lying on the floor. A third Diane," as he grimly feigned a laugh.

"All right, now just get on your feet, and let's get out of here."

Shaking, terrified, her voice unsteady, "Why are you treating me like this? What did I do to you?" Forcing some composure, "I love you, and you call me a whore, drag me like you didn't get enough for your money. Is that the way you treat the loyal woman who loves you, a love you have always returned? " She forced herself to cry. "I resent your cruelty. You probably left marks all over me."

He smiled, spoke endearingly. "Shut up and stop your whimpering. That policewoman upset me. They'll find her soon, if they haven't already. She'll recover eventually. I suppose I should have outright killed her, not just shut off the breathing and - oh you heard it - that little crack - I'm sorry, dear one. Just shut up or else. Hurry. We have to get to my plane."

He drove toward the West End, turned into a narrow street, while asking about the money. "Now where is it, Deirdre?"

Frightened again, she told him, "It's in a Swiss account and one of the islands."

"Which? Where? The numbers. You *were* planning to tell me."

"I was. I was. I swear it. I love you, Étienne, and would never hurt or betray you."

"And you weren't going to cheat me, or," and he laughed, "share it with your cuckold husband?"

"I resent that." She reached in her purse, pulled out the crumpled papers, moved still closer to him, placing her hand on his thigh, "Here. Here's all of it just as. . . ."

He interrupted. "Just what?" taking her hand and moving it to his zipper. "A little fun first," he growled. "Thanks, Deirdre."

He sped a bit faster, reached across, brushing her breasts. "One last feel. Oh some more." "Then stop. It's dark here." She tried keeping her voice soft, seductive.

He sped a little more.

"What are you doing?" She cried out.

"Making out with you, dearest Deirdre."And he thrust open the door, shoved, "No more deceit." He shoved harder against her fearful crying out and resistance, forced strongly between her thigh and ribs, "And no jail time," he loudly laughed, as her head hit the edge of the sidewalk and she rolled onto the street. To be certain, he ran over her, pressed hard on the gas pedal as he turned again in the direction of the airport tunnel, looking about to determine whether anyone had seen or heard. He knew there was blood on the car. He decided to leave it at the outer edge of the car rental, not caring when it was found. He had given a false name and license, something he was accustomed to with the friends he had made during the war.

He took a cab, his face covered by a pulled-down hat and coat collar upward. He told the driver in a muffled voice to take him to the private area, waited for the cab to leave, filed his papers, giving a false flight plan, ran, waited impatiently for the control tower to give him permission to take off. By the time he was in the air, both the policewoman's and Deirdre's body had been found. In the ambulance, they were able to rouse the policewoman.

Étienne's escape was wearying yet well planned. After island hopping, he eventually landed in Morocco, took a flight to Rhodes and went to an inconspicuous house in a narrow, ancient alleyway. He would figure later how to get the money, believing he would never be caught. Yet, he did not need her filchings, for he, too, had kept funds from her. But he had Deirdre's signature, if he so decided. His actual need was to kill a betrayer. Diane, Deirdre, intermingled in life and death.

By morning, in Boston and in Maine, the newspapers told of the two women, one injured badly, the other, Deirdre Hurwitz dead, whether hit and run or deliberate, the police would have to determine, though they already knew. They issued a description of Étienne, although it was quite unlikely they would find him. Eventually they would contact the FBI and Interpol.

A day later the headline read, "Prominent Art Connoisseur Apparently Murdered."

~

When the police arrived at Gregory's home, both Pamela and Brigit were there. Everyone overwhelmed, no one knew what to say. Brigit recovered sufficiently to call Thomas and tell him what happened and that she would stay with Gregory to make certain he was all right. By now Thomas was beginning to weary of her lengthy visits with Gregory, although she was always present for Robert and Kathryn who knew she was there when they needed her, whether before or after school, or if they had problems. She could never neglect being a mother for anyone or anything.

With this horror enveloping the house, she did feel guilty. She had dug into places in the house she shouldn't have. She had revealed the withheld secrets. She had hurt Gregory and his daughters. Would they blame her?

For now, everyone was crying, gasping, and breathless. Gregory, when he recovered some, immediately called Melinda. "Dearest."

"Hi, dad."

"You have some time?"

"Right now I do. One of the interns is seeing a patient of mine. What's up?" Obviously she hadn't seen any papers or no one had said anything to her.

"Melinda. It's your mother."

"Is she away again? Are you O.K.?"

"Melinda, hon," he choked some, "Melinda, she's dead."

"What? How?" She shivered.

"The police in Boston say she's been murdered."

"Daaad," she screamed. "How? When?"

"No one knows. Can you come home? I'm making arrangements to have the body shipped here."

Melinda was crying now. "Oh, dad, are Pam and you going to be all right 'til I get there?"

"Yes, dear. What about you?"

"I'll manage, dad. I'll be home in the morning. O.K.?"

"Yes. Just be careful. O.K.?"

"I will," she sobbed. Off the phone, she ran from the emergency room to her room, lay on the bed shaking the length of her body. She could not control herself. Her roommate came in.

"Melinda. They said you ran out. Are you all right?" She watched Melinda's shaking body, sat beside her, rubbing her back.

"It's my mother. It's unbelievable. Someone murdered her."

Her roommate stopped rubbing, stunned, recovered. "Can I get you a sedative?"

"I guess," as she continued shaking. "Yes."

By the next morning, having recovered some, one of the doctors asked if she could drive. He would get someone to take her, and she agreed.

Étienne – Angry Seas

The police gave them time for the funeral and family gathering and several acquaintances, including Deirdre's. She was buried with an honor guard for her wartime duty, a flag given to her parents at Gregory's request. He rejected a burial at Arlington, believing she did not belong there after what the family discovered. He kept wondering when the truth would emerge either through police or investigation or a curious reporter. The museum Board had already decided to do nothing more for now but to write off the money, until, if ever, the police found Étienne. They would, however, look for the owners of the questioned pieces.

The FBI followed leads after examining the car. Unfortunately for Étienne, a woman who checked out the car remembered his accent and was able to describe him. They surmised he left in a private plane. They contacted Interpol. A bulletin described him and that he was wanted for theft, assault on a policewoman, and a possible murder. The search included all countries from which he and Deirdre had either stolen or bought antiquities.

A year passed. Étienne vaguely felt he had succeeded in hiding his identity, neglected his wife left in France. Within that year she contacted the police about her missing husband. However they were of no help, although they had received notice he was an unapprehended murder suspect.

~

Aware that possibly Interpol could be searching for him, he

had hidden in an old narrow street where he felt no one would think to look. For further cover, he had also taken up with a Greek woman who lived with him. He began to learn the language with her help. She reveled in her fortune at having become the mistress of a wealthy man. Occasionally, she wondered why he wanted to live in the ancient city.

"Why do we not move out into the countryside? There are houses, or you could build one. We could overlook the sea, enjoy the weather more, the beauty."

"No. Just pay attention to what we're doing now. You make me feel inadequate asking such questions."

She laughed, annoying him. "Inadequate with what you have down there. I love it," as she moved from under him and bent to put him in her mouth. "Don't be angry. I'll soothe you. See. I'm unselfish; get you back in the mood."

He moved away, slapped her, shouting, "Don't ask me to build you a palace. Is that supposed to be payment for sex? I like it here. This is Rhodes for me. No more questions. We live here. If you don't like it, then get out."

She started crying. "That was cruel. Your temper seems to be getting worse." She was right. He was beginning to worry there was no other place to which he could flee and increasingly felt cornered, not only by his crime and the possibility of being found but also by this woman who was already irritating him.

Unaware, of course, how he felt, she continued, "And if you keep it up, to hell with you and your money. I'll leave. Find yourself another screw." She jumped from the bed.

"And where do you think you're going?" He grabbed at her, caught her by the waist, scratching her.

She pulled further from him. "You go to hell." She went to the closet and started to get her clothes, knowing he would stop her.

"You think I care, Irene? But get away from those clothes. I bought them."

"You want me walking out of here naked?"

"Why not? The police would have a fine time. Perhaps you could pleasure them."

"You bastard." She picked up a shoe and threw it. It hit above the eye.

"No one does that to me." He jumped from the bed, grabbed her breasts and pulled. She screamed at the pain. He struck her. She screamed more loudly, tears flowing down her cheeks. "I'll kill you." She twisted away from him, ran to the kitchen, grabbed a knife, ran back at him. As he quickly reached her hand, the knife struck and cut his lower arm.

"Bitch. I'll kill you."

Frightened, she backed away. She saw a dress on the floor. Reached for it before he could catch her and ran to the door somehow managing to slip into the dress as she got to the street, screaming she was being attacked. People looked from windows. One person only, gently stopped her. "Your face, woman. Go to the police."

Irene, shivering, was fearful of reporting him. "I can't do that. He'll kill me."

"You must go. Come. I'll take you." She unconsciously followed the man, trembling. At the police station she told of the fight, describing unknowingly the man they had heard about from Interpol.

The police did not wait, went to the narrow street, banged on the door and arrested him. It was then they looked through their bulletins again. Soon newspaper headlines appeared in Rhodes, in France, in the United States and elsewhere, SUSPECTED MURDERER, FORMER HERO OF THE FRENCH RESISTANCE, IN CUSTODY.

A dead woman and a live, beaten lover, and deserted wife testified about and against a past Maquis leader now wanted in the United States. After extradition proceedings that he naturally fought, Interpol sent him to Boston where the FBI met and took him to maximum security Suffolk Bay. Eventually, after evidence and trial, Étienne Moreau received a life sentence and imprisoned in Leavenworth where the past, rage, and time eventually ended his luxurious post-war days.

Tide Pool

Despite the pall of public animosity and gossip, the community of Cape Astraea, for the most part, sympathized with Gregory and his daughters. Some grumbled at the military burial, refusing to honor a thief's engagement in life-threatening situations for the country. Deirdre had sewn her own death gown. Black would clothe her for many years.

Worse was the embarrassment for her parents, who now old, would never understand how their outstanding daughter who had such a proud war record could have become so greedy that she engaged in activities so shameful and dishonest. The photos of their beautiful, brilliant daughter haunted them. Their present pain overshadowed their past pleasure in the woman they produced. They could only think that their daughter's entire life had been enclosed in a shadow. They also, at times, rationalized and blamed Gregory and his family for exposing Deirdre, aware condemnation of Gregory was unreasonable. They needed some string to bind them to the love they had for Deirdre, to prevent them from hating her for what she had done to them and her entire family. The confusion overwhelmed Edward and Christine. The gossip in Warrington hurt and devastated them. Edward sold the farm. They then moved to western Massachusetts where they would be unknown, made arrangements for home help, grieved until Edward died of a heart attack, leaving Christine a lonely, sad widow to end her days trying to finish the puzzle that was their daughter. Nevertheless, she rationalized and never lost her love for Deirdre.

In Cape Astraea, Gregory, who had now been ill all these

years, knew that the disease was going to be the victor, despite medical advancements. Mary, Melinda, Pamela, and Brigit also knew.

Pamela having finished her master's degree, called Gregory. "Dad. I'd like to come home and live with you. I know you have good people to look after the house for you, and I would love to be home by the sea. I can write there, as you know. Why, I might even write about the sailor in our family."

She faltered some. "You know I'm living with Larry. Oh, Dad, before I decide, are you well enough for me to stay here?"

"Why do you ask? I'm getting along."

"Well, if you feel comfortable enough without me."

"Sweetheart, you know I have all the help I need." He was thinking of Brigit, as well as of the night nurse. Andrea was getting old but wouldn't quit and was part of the family. She still fixed meals for him.

"You're not pulling my leg?"

"C'mon, Pam. What's on your mind?"

"Truthfully? I don't want to leave my boy friend. I'm not sure I can take a long distance relationship."

"Then don't."

"You're sure?"

"Pam, I'm O.K. Now cut it out."

"Is Brigit there?"

"Yes."

"Is she there a lot?"

"Well, yes. Why are you giving me this grilling? Cut it out. I'm all right," he emphasized. "Look, you live your life. You be happy. But, Pam, make sure you love him, that you're not giving in to 'I think so.'"

Pamela smiled, silently interpreting, "In other words don't make the mistake you made." She smiled more and asked, "May I talk to Brigit?"

"I'll get her. She left so we could talk privately, I think. Well, before I call her, I want to know. Pam, if this is what you truly want, Larry, and you're staying because you love him."

"I'm not a kid, dad."

He laughed. "How well I know." Both daughters were so attractive, desirable. Like their mother, but thank goodness absent her character.

"Now let me talk to Brigit."

She thought of Brigit. Whatever those two did now was their choice and no one had a right to interfere. *Oh. Her husband. Her children have finished college. They're working out of state. What would happen if? If what, Pamela? If Thomas divorced Brigit? What about their family? Well, would Brigit be with dad? Aunt Mary's there to help him too. Hmm. Melinda married. Now that's interesting. Here are two doctors and then the complication of Brigit.*

"Pam, are you still on the line?"

"Oh, yes, dad. I was just thinking."

"Of what?"

"Truthfully?"

"Truthfully."

"Brigit, dad. You and Brigit, her family."

"Well," startled, though he shouldn't have been, he continued, "She does come to the house. I'd be . . . ." He stopped.

"You'd be lost without her, right? You love her. She loves you. We're all grown-ups now. Oh I guess it's like Larry and me only we don't want to marry, at least not now."

He was actually pleased Pamela would stay where she was, because he wanted his freedom to be with Brigit. They had been sleeping together for some time now. He wanted his life to end with her. She wished she could just stay and live with him until . . . . But there was Thomas and her own home.

He thought he owed Pamela an escape clause. "Pamela. If you ever, well, if you ever decide what you're doing isn't for you, you can always come live here, if that's what you want, dear. But remember, my life . . . ."

"Don't finish. Although I worry about Brigit and her family, if it ever comes to that, I'd keep out of your way. I still love her, you know. And I do wish she had been my mother. Damn it, dad, I know what happened. Fuck that dead mother of ours, Melinda's and mine. Fuck her for what she was, what she did, what an embarrassment she is and always will be. She made a hell of a mark on all of us. Fuck her." She was very angry now. "That woman could have ruined your reputation, ruined Melinda's chances. Then I think of grandma. What she must have suffered. Grandpa."

"Pamela. Stop. Stop now. Please. You're," he was going to tell her she was hurting him but didn't. "Pam, it's the way things are. We can't change them, can we? So we live with what we have and are. You don't need that teen-age lecture."

"No, dad."

She laughed slightly. "You still think if I asked to come home you'd want me? I use that f word."

They both laughed. "I'd manage to stand it. But I better warn you. Brigit hates it." They laughed again.

"Just let me say something to Brigit."

He called to her, and she appeared from close to the door.

"You sneak. You listened. Pamela wants to talk to you."

"Pam. I'm here as usual. How are you dear?"

"Like my dad was a damn fool for not making you our mother." Brigit's face turned red as she felt a sting in her stomach, instantly thinking of Thomas.

"Oh, forgive me, Brigit. I shouldn't have said that."

"It's O.K. I love you as if you were my daughter. You know that."

"Well, I love you for everything, for taking care of dad, for making Melinda and me feel like we have someone to turn to, for helping us make it through the hell. Oh, forget it. I love you for allowing us to depend on you. So, before I start crying, I'm hanging up. My eyes are wet."

"So are mine. So long, sweet."

When she hung up, her eyes were filled. Gregory noticed but said nothing. It was between Brigit and Pamela. Watching her tears fall along her cheeks, he did think of Thomas. His conscience began to bother him more than it had. Thomas had been his friend all these years, but the relationship had grown colder.

Brigit, who had been standing while talking to Pamela, sat on the bed, brushing his hair with her hand, kissing his cheek. "You're concerned about something, Greg, and it's not your illness right now. What is it?"

"I thought about Thomas. I don't want to. But I also don't want you in pain because of me. I know my children care so much for you. In fact, even though Melinda's now married and Pamela has a guy. I know they turn to you. But is it fair?"

"Yes. Definitely, yes. I'd give them my all, if I had to, just like I would for my own children. I'm not saying they take Robert's and Kathryn's places, but . . . . Crap, Gregory. They could have been ours, all four." She hesitated. "All five."

She barely heard him. "I know. I just can't bear losing you again. I'd rather this damn CLL would kill me."

She ignored 'kill me.' "I would live here, but I hurt for Thomas, and even for myself when I think of what we are doing. Yet, I would never give up taking care of you. Remember my Celtic past. I'm the healer." She weakly smiled, wiping at the tears. "No one can make me. Not Thomas, not God." She was crying harder now.

"Well, perhaps I should come less often, dearest. We can't continue like we have. Admit it, Greg. You are concerned. We can't keep away from," she paused, "the sex, the fondling. I don't want to. You don't. But we're wrong. Oh, damn, I can't stop crying. Why do we have to suffer because of love?"

She went to the bathroom, washed her face, put on some eye shadow, smoothed her dress, brushed her hair, put some perfume behind her ears and on her wrists, renewed her lipstick. Satisfied with her looks, she decided there was not much more either of them could say. When she came from the bathroom, she told Greg the night nurse would come soon.

"You don't want to wait?"

"I don't want to leave," as she sat, took his hand, placed it in her lap, wanting the closeness.

"I must."

She pressed him harder against herself, desiring the comfort and need. "Greg, I have to settle things with Thomas."

"He's really upset, isn't he?"

"Yes. I know he is. He hasn't said anything yet, but I know it's coming. He's getting cross, and rightfully he doesn't trust me any longer, even though I think he may be trying to convince himself I'm faithful. Oh. What's the sense?" Tears formed again, filling her eyes. She could barely see, sniffed, wiped at her nose and eyes. "Give me one of your tissues." She wiped trying to calm herself. "Damn, I just did my eyes. I'll have to again. Oh well. But Greg. I just," she did not want to say it. "I just don't seem to care. In fact I believe I don't. It's the children I love so, what I may be doing to them. Oh God, why did you and I ever meet?"

She stood, again went to the bathroom to make certain her eyes looked all right, returned, "I'm leaving," and she kissed him, hard, placing her tongue in his mouth, kissing his neck, then pulling sharply from him to prevent herself from becoming aroused. "Good night."

"Brigit. Be kind to yourself. You're good. You always have been. Brigit, I don't want to lose you."

She resisted going back to him. "I'm leaving. See you." She had decided this was the night she and Thomas would talk frankly about what he was thinking.

When she arrived home, she quickly changed clothes, showered, put on another dress, cotton, with a straight skirt that came to just below her knees but was tight at the bosom. It would show her legs when she sat. She brushed her hair again, because of the wind that caught it coming from the car, again made certain of her perfume and lips. She then made dinner, chose a bottle of red Thomas liked and decided to have a chocolate desert she made the previous day. She walked about the house, waiting for him. Hearing the car, she went to the door, opened it and waited. He smiled seeing her, came to her, kissed her. She placed her arms about his neck, pulling him closer so he could feel her body.

"Hm. What a greeting. Ooh. You smell good. He put his nose in her hair and about her ears and neck. I need more greetings like this." He didn't ask what she was thinking because of this sudden show of affection.

"C'mon, Thomas. Loosen your tie. And sit before we eat. Want a drink?"

"I'll get it, a scotch. Want one?"

"Yes."

They sat in the living room, sipping.

"I've got some swordfish. It ought to be ready soon. How's that?"

"Why so cheerful. Did you buy a new dress?"

"I think I should have. O.K. I'll go shopping tomorrow. I need a new evening dress, maybe a few other things, my underwear." She wished she hadn't mentioned the underwear. She didn't want him thinking about her in clothes or undressed and wanted to wait until after dinner to talk to him. But he started.

"Incidentally, did you hear the news? I was listening when coming home. All the trouble with Iran isn't bad enough. Carter decided to do something about the hostages. It's about time. Why fool around with those people? Khomeini. A religious dictator. Anyhow, he sent in helicopters to rescue the people held at the embassy. It was a disaster. The helicopters crashed. The Iranians were gleeful, chanting against the United States. You'd think we could conduct a military operation properly by now. It's bad, Brigit. Bad. It's going to mean a lot of trouble for us. And those poor hostages. The sanctions didn't free them. Well, he tried, but he failed. It reminds me of the gas situation when we got the new car."

"Oh, that's terrible. Those poor men killed and their families."

"Let's not make the evening too sad, Brigit. Yes, those poor families. You're so right. Incidentally, how's Gregory? What that poor fellow has had to endure." He thought of his wife and Greg together so much, watched as her face visually saddened, his becoming taut.

"I think he's going to go to the hospital soon. It's been coming on. I can see it." She also noticed her husband's face that softened some, as he told her, "I should go see him. I haven't been a good friend. I will. Maybe," and he thought of Brigit alone with Gregory so many months now, since Deirdre's death and before. "Maybe, I ought to go in the next couple of days."

"That would be nice." To end the conversation she told him she could smell the oven and would see if the fish were done.

"Thomas, c'mon. It's ready. Pour the wine."

"Brigit, the helicopter and Carter. It made me think of something, how fighting affects people. How secret missions can go wrong." He watched her closely. She felt the shock of innuendo, suddenly stopped as she opened the oven. "Oooh. That hurts."

"What?" He thought she was answering him.

"I burned my hand on the oven." Still stung from his remark, as well as the burn, she ran cold water over her hand. She shook some, and tried to talk while the cold washed over her hand, but she wanted the offense tonight. She had made up her mind, but apparently he had also been thinking about it since she greeted him. Perhaps she had overdone it. She felt a pressure in her chest, breathed deeply, turned her head so Thomas would not see her. She forced, "That's better. Now let's get on with dinner."

After a quiet meal with little talk and clearing the table, she told him, "Let the dishes stand. I'll put them in the dishwasher later. I want," she hesitated. "Let's go in the living room and talk."

"Fine," he was smiling. *This has been a long time coming. You won't wiggle out of this, my loving wife.*

"Want some music?" he asked.

"If you do." She felt herself tremble, her skin rise. "Tom." She stopped.

"What is it?"

"I guess we have to talk."

He burst, could not contain his anger. "Talk," he shouted. "How about a good, honest tête-à-tête. The kids aren't here to hear about their parents," he paused, "their mother."

Her face colored with the tenseness of her body. He had already made up his mind. She had lost the advantage. *I won't let him do this to me. I won't. Oh. You knew it was coming. So take it and give it.*

"I know you married me and wasn't in love with me, Brigit. But I . . . ."

"Stop now, Thomas. We married because you were in love with me, and I was honest with you about my feelings. You took me on that."

"But I never took you on being unfaithful."

"How many women have you had, Thomas?"

"That's not the point. The point is now. You and Gregory. I . . ." He didn't want to say they'd been sleeping together. He had no proof, just the often lateness of her homecoming. "I believe you've been sleeping with him. Oh, I don't mind your taking care of him. I knew, know you love him. You were honest about that from the beginning. But . . . ."

"But what? Now I'm unfaithful. Well, fuck it, Thomas."

His face reddened. He grit his teeth, as his face then turned pale from the expectation of her next words.

"Yes. I hate the word, but Fuck," she shouted. She began crying, crying quite hard and loudly. "O damn. Yes, I've slept with him. Divorce me. Tell the children their mother's a whore. I can't help it, Thomas. I felt so sorry for him, and then. I'd be more dishonest if I told you I slept with him because he's ill. I do love you, Thomas, but . . . ."

"Please don't say it. I took you at your word when we married. We've been happy. Damn." He placed his head between his white knuckled hands. "I wanted to get even with you, Brigit, for everything I was imagining and knew in my heart was true, that you couldn't help yourself."

"What do you mean I couldn't help myself? Do you think I'm sort of a weak, dumb female? Oh, you goddamn men wanting us in our place, our legs spread in bed when you want, whatever. I didn't know what I was doing?"

"Don't say that. I didn't mean it that way. You didn't let me finish. Well, yeah, I'll say it. I wanted to tell you. I wanted to get even on an assumption. But damn you, you had to go and prove it true. I got one of the nurses at the hospital that's been after me. I told you about her. She's always telling people what a love I am, how good I am with everyone. I went home with her, Brigit. I was going to get even imagining you two. There's no sense in going through all the details, is there? I left her there, lying ashamed, naked in bed, crying. She and I did do a few things. But I couldn't go all the way. That was terrible. I humiliated her. And I thought of you, and went back to her, but she threw me out, screamed at me. I had to tell you. But. But. Oh. I want to forgive you. But . . . . I'm hurt, angry at you, at myself."

"So we both failed. Do you hate me for what I'm doing?"

"Hate you? I wish. But. . . ." and he grew angry again. "You let me down, and the children. What would they think?"

"They don't have to know."

"No. They don't have to know."

"Do you want me to leave?"

He thought, wanted to say, "yes," but knew he couldn't. "No, Brigit. I want to live with you. Just let's see how it goes. You go back to your lover. Maybe I'll apologize to that nurse and take her. Maybe I'll feel better about you."

"Fuck you, Thomas." She was very angry. "You're playing games with me and with another woman. Fuck you. I'm leaving. I'm going to go live with Gregory until . . . ." and she began to cry again.

He started toward her. "No, don't come near me. Don't touch me. If you need something, call me at Gregory's or see if your nurse will relent and give you comfort. You can even have her come and stay here with you." She rushed up the stairs, thinking of her anger at Gregory over Deirdre, packed as much as she could carry, called Gregory and told him she was coming to stay.

~

Driving to his house, she rode past the water, stopped, felt both hurt and humiliated from the argument but soothed as though her body were covered in silk as she looked up at the three-quarter moon, the light as it spread in a ray across the ripples in the windless night, the stars, spangles to the unseen worlds. She imagined the horizon in the blackness, curving within and under itself as though in an ancient time when the world was flat, picturing herself falling over into the nether regions where she would find her love and peace. She sat, silently weeping, for the losses and joys of the past, for the present, the eventual loss of Gregory, her argument with Thomas, her children who she wished now were with her. "What's the use?" she whispered. "Dream, think whatever you do, but we have made our lives in our image. Greg, I want you inside me, all about me, to calm this whirlpool inside."

She started the car, looked at the sea once more and drove along the shore until she reached his house. The light was on in the den. *He must be listening to his music with the door open, no Deirdre to tell him to shut it off or lower it until she would no longer hear, and she doesn't. Poor Deirdre, so foolish, so destructive. You are like the Celtic myth, falling from the moving chariot and killed. I feel for you right now, only right now. I feel for all women, for myself. We exhibit ourselves to empower us; we capture; we surrender; we open ourselves to swallow like a black hole, and that is when we what? Win? Lose? Find momentary rapture and loss?*

She went to the door and rather than use her key, she rang to avoid startling the nurse. When the nurse answered, she could not hide her surprise.

"Hello. I've come to stay with Dr. Hurwitz. We've been friends for so long, I thought it would be nice if he had someone close to him." Brigit noticed the nurse's smirk, as she looked at the suit cases Brigit held. The nurse would have enjoyed asking what Brigit's husband thought, how she cared for Dr. Hurwitz.

"In other words, you're telling me you don't need me anymore. Isn't that for the doctor to say?"

"I didn't come to dismiss you. I haven't that right, but the two of us." Brigit hesitated. "Look. What's the sense in the two of us being here?"

The nurse openly sneered. Looking at her, Brigit thought, "Here goes my reputation. And Rob and Kathryn will hear. What have I done?" Brigit forced a smile. "Let's go talk to the doctor."

Gregory quickly sat up, smiling, happy. "Brigit."

"I thought I'd come and stay. You won't need Nurse Willis. I mean, unless you would rather we both be here."

The question in his face was obvious. She had to have left Thomas. Flustered, he forced himself to ask Willis, "How about if you came, say every third or fourth day for several hours to give Brigit some time to rest, to go shopping, whatever?"

"I'll do whatever you think, Dr. Hurwitz. I can be here and will arrange other times and appointments. Just tell me when you want me, not now, but by tomorrow, please."

"That's fine," he answered, looking at Brigit and then at Willis.

"Well, I'll just get my things and leave now. An early night will be nice," she lied, laughing to herself thinking of them hurrying off to bed.

When they heard the door close, Brigit told him what had happened. "I brought most of what I wanted. I'll go back for the rest tomorrow maybe."

"Come here." He reached for her. She wanted to leap at him. "I love you. Oh how I love you and need you," he spoke into her ear, feeling her hair and face against his.

"I love you too." The past, the future, nothing mattered. "Oh how I love you and have. And I'm going to take care of you and keep you with me for as long as I can."

The days passed. Mary came and disappeared with Brigit. They shopped for clothing together. One night she brought Evelyn for dinner. Melinda came with her husband. Pamela called often and did come home for several days. They all managed a surprise for Brigit. Robert and Kathryn arranged a time they both could come from New York. Hard as it was for them, accusing their mother of desertion and adultery, they still wanted her but stayed with their father who told them little but that Gregory needed their mother, that time was short.

The company always roused Gregory. But he was also happy when he and Brigit were alone. They slept together, made love happily, unencumbered, thoughtful of only one another, fulfilling themselves perhaps for the lost years.

Then one day, Gregory called to Brigit. "Dearest. I'd like to go to the cove. The sun's warm and it would be so nice. Or better, let's go toward evening. We'll watch the sunset, see the quarter moon, listen to the waves."

"I like that. I'll take something along in case we get hungry."

"Brigit. Do you ever regret being with me, doing what you have?"

The suddenness of his question sent a pang of distress through her. "Greg, stop. Stop now. I regret nothing but the," she stopped, not wanting to hurt him but decided to finish. "I regret nothing but the years lost to both of us." She watched his face, the anguish. "Oh, Greg, I didn't mean to hurt you. Whatever has happened, we can't undo, obviously. So let's not ask questions, just enjoy being together."

They drove to the cove close to twilight.

"It's lovely, Greg. Look. The tide's coming in. Look. Over there. The white caps against the rocks. But they're gentle. And the horizon. Doesn't it seem as though we could just walk out there and fall off together?" She relaxed against his chest, his arm about her. "Put your hand here." She took it and placed it on her breast.

The sky changed its appearance, yellows, blues, reds, purple drifting clouds, the crescent moon now visible and Venus seemingly not so far off.

"Look, Brigit, Love. It will always be there."

"It will." But she felt a shudder in his shoulder. She raised her head. "Are you all right?"

"Well, I feel a bit weary."

"Then let's go home, and I'll make dinner."

In the morning, he woke her. "Brigit, I think you better take me to the hospital."

She tried to hide her fright. "O.K." speaking as evenly as she could. "Let me get your clothes. You want me to dress sexy?" She forced a laugh.

"Sexy's great."

She went to another room and phoned the hospital and his doctor, fed him, noticing he hardly ate, not even drinking his coffee.

"Are you ready? I packed your things and put a book in there."

He was in the hospital for several days, growing weaker, holding Brigit's hand as much as possible, squeezing it. "Remember, dearest. I'll always and forever love you." He laughed a bit. "I just thought of our first kiss. Kiss me, please." His voice was weak.

Melinda and Pamela came; Mary would stop by when she was not in the office, and especially if she were on hospital duty. The women would gather, hold tightly to one another, crying softly.

Another day, the doctor as he often did, talked seriously to him. "Gregory, you must know this is all I can do."

"Yes." He looked straight at the doctor. "You're telling me I won't get to see the leaves change color. Perhaps that's best, not looking at those bare branches stabbing at the sky, begging for their dress. Always thinking of the females. I'll never change." *I've been surrounded by women. Deirdre, oh the stupidity; Melinda, Pamela, Kaitlin. Oh my Kaitlin. What might you have been?*

The doctor placed his hand on Gregory's. "You're quite a guy. And don't ever forget what your research accomplished and all the people you helped."

"Thanks, Dave."

While Melinda and Pamela were in a waiting room, Brigit stood in the doorway, tears filling her eyes. She suddenly felt a hand on her shoulder. "Brigit." She looked. It was Thomas. "I heard and want to see him."

"You're sweet. Always have been."

"Brigit, perhaps this isn't the time, but I've missed you so. Would you consider coming home?"

Surprised, sad, pleased, "If you truly want me, Thomas."

"I do."

"Give me time, please, to settle myself? I need it. Oh, God, how I need."

"You take your time. I'm going in to see Greg."

Brigit composed herself. "Greg, look who's here to see you."

"Tom," weakly. "You're fine for. . . ."

Thomas would not let him finish. "You think I'm going to allow a friend to turn his back on me."

The three women faintly smiled.

Several days later, during the night, Gregory died.

Brigit gave way to Melinda and Pamela who had their father cremated. On a sunny day, when the sea was calm, they rented a sailing yacht, hoping their father could feel the sway and the wind in the sails. They sat on either side of Brigit, arms wrapped about one another. They asked Brigit to spread the ashes. She started, then slowly handed them to Melinda and Pamela. The three stood, watching as the sea gently as in a tide pool took their father and lover.

~

A meteor
seared the sky
lost below
the horizon,
emblazoning the pillars
of
Hecate
beckoning
to the seas of fear and love.

RSC

The End

ABOUT THE AUTHOR

Richard Shain Cohen of Cape Elizabeth, Maine, is originally from Boston. He retired from the University of Maine at Presque Isle after serving as Vice President of Academic Affairs and Professor of English. He holds B.S., M.A., and Ph.D. degrees.

He served as editor of the journal *Husson Review* and was principal participant in a National Endowment for the Arts Grant for "Images of Aroostook" that was exhibited throughout the State of Maine.

His own publications include: *Healing After Dark: Pioneering Compassionate Medicine at the Boston Evening Clinic* (2011), *The Forgotten Longfellow: Man in the Shadows* (2010), *Only God Can Make a Tree*, poetry from himself and his brother, Alfred Robert Cohen; and the novels *Our Seas of Fear and Love*, *Monday: End of the Week*, *Be Still, My Soul*, and *Petal on a Black Bough*. He also wrote chapters for *Aroostook: Land of Promise*, academic reviews, other articles, and - with the help of a Shell Grant - a monograph on Samuel Richardson that can be found in major library holdings.

www.ingramcontent.com/pod-product-compliance
Lightning Source LLC
Chambersburg PA
CBHW022146010726
47493CB00002B/364

* 9 7 8 1 7 7 1 4 3 0 7 9 1 *